Advance Praise for *The Midnight Club*

"A strange, riveting, brilliant fable about smart people seduced by the darkest, most forbidden fantasy. Like a fever-dream of Donna Tartt's *The Secret History*."

—Lev Grossman, *New York Times* bestselling author of *The Magicians*

"I devoured *The Midnight Club*. It's a smart, surprising, and gripping mystery about the reality that we can't change who we were, but we'd all be a lot better off if we could."

—Chris Bohjalian, #1 *New York Times* bestselling author of *The Flight Attendant*

"Savvy, suspenseful, and surprisingly tender, Margot Harrison's *The Midnight Club* takes the classic murder-reunion trope and transforms it into a reflection on friendship and surviving our youth. With each twist, this marvelously inventive novel will keep you guessing whodunnit—but also who couldn't stop it, and why."

—Maria Hummel, author of *Still Lives*

"*The Secret History* meets *Black Mirror* in Margot Harrison's richly imagined, time-traveling debut. A nostalgia-soaked campus novel about second and even third chances, *The Midnight Club* asks the question: what price is too high to undo your greatest mistake?"

—Alison B. Hart, author of *The Work Wife*

Praise for Margot Harrison's Young Adult Novels

"Intense, thrilling, and addictive—you won't be able to put this book down until all the parts slide beautifully into place. A masterful blend of character study, social critique, and mystery."

—Kathleen Glasgow, *New York Times* bestselling author of *Girl in Pieces*, on *Only She Came Back*

"Readers will devour this tale of twisted obsessions and blurred lines."

—April Henry, *New York Times* bestselling author of *Girl, Stolen* and *Girl Forgotten*, on *Only She Came Back*

Also by Margot Harrison

Young Adult Novels

Only She Came Back
The Glare
The Killer in Me
We Made It All Up

THE
MIDNIGHT
CLUB

A NOVEL

MARGOT HARRISON

GRAYDON
HOUSE

For Emily Greenley and Matthew Drummy,
two fine writers who left us too soon.

MAY 22, 2014

1

SONIA

> *You are hereby formally invited to a reunion of the Midnight Brunch Club. October 27th through 31st, 2014, 12 Railroad Street in Dunstan, Vermont.*
>
> *Come to celebrate the life of Jennifer (Jennet) Sherilyn Stark (1967–89) and revisit our shared past through the elixir of the pines. There are still secrets to be discovered; the past is not even past (Faulkner); we are boats against the current (Fitzgerald). Leave all doubts and inhibitions at home. RSVP to Auraleigh Lydgate.*

The first time Sonia ever received an invitation from Auraleigh Lydgate was in the *Dove-Cat* room freshman year, on the first warm spring day in Vermont, forsythia bursting forth on the quad.

Sonia was bent over a Mac Classic when Auraleigh swept in, wearing a leather jacket and drop-waist minidress, and noisily slid out a chair. "Oh my God, I'm dealing with a roommate nightmare! Marina got this brilliant idea to backpack in Europe, so now Paul and I are short a person for the townhouse."

"Paul Bretton?" Sonia couldn't hide her surprise. He was the newly elected editor of their lit magazine—quiet, earnest, and formidably intellectual. Auraleigh was rich and from LA and had a husky laugh that made boys' eyes glaze over. They seemed like a complete mismatch.

"Yeah." Auraleigh grinned. "No, we're not dating. I like his espresso machine, and he likes my cooking. Hey, wait—do you have housing for next year?"

"I was just going to do the lottery." This was only their second or third conversation, and Sonia, the daughter of an itinerant hippie who could only afford the college because of her mom's job in the admin office, could barely understand why Auraleigh would talk to her to begin with.

When Auraleigh spoke again, Sonia almost thought she was hearing wrong: would she like to share the townhouse with them instead?

It cost more than the dorm, but Sonia barely hesitated in saying yes. She was tired of studying alone in the library and coming back to a silent room. She was tired of feeling like she didn't belong.

Never mind that Auraleigh later admitted the invitation had been spur-of-the-moment, based more on what Sonia wasn't than what she was. (*You seemed quiet. I figured it would balance out my loud.*) In that instant, whether Sonia realized it or not, she became part of a circle she would never quite be able to leave.

⋆ ◆ ⋆

Crossing the campus of the New Mexico college where she had taught for the past decade, Sonia no longer felt the desert heat. Here was another invitation from Auraleigh, twenty-seven years later, but Sonia wasn't the same person she'd been back then.

She climbed the library steps in a daze. At the entrance to the stacks, she pressed her ID card to the sensor. The light blinked red. She tried it again, then handed her card to the circulation assistant, a hungover-looking student who put down a copy of *Teaching to Transgress* to examine it.

"Semester ended yesterday." The student had bangs in her face, too many barrettes doing too little work. She typed a number into her computer and peered at the screen. "This is invalid. Did you just graduate?"

"No, I'm faculty." Were those bangs keeping the kid from seeing the fine lines and sags of middle age? But then Sonia understood. "I... My contract wasn't renewed for next semester."

The student handed her back the ID. "That'd be it."

Sonia took the meaningless laminated rectangle that had given her access to every campus facility. She'd hoped to use the job databases that were only accessible from terminals in the chilly bowels of the library. To reach them, she would have traversed the concrete gallery hung with mementos of faculty achievements—including a one-sheet for the 1998 semi-cult film *Retrophiliac*, with her own name right after the director's.

Instead she felt like a criminal. "I didn't realize it would be invalid this soon."

"You could apply for a temporary pass," the girl said.

But Sonia was already headed back outside, through two sets of hissing doors and down the stucco steps into the furnace heat. She just needed to rest for a moment before cleaning out her office.

She found a shady table on the quad, sat down, and pulled out the mail she'd stuffed in her bag earlier.

The invitation.

Sonia turned over the heavy, cream-colored card and really read it this time.

You are hereby formally invited to a reunion of the Midnight Brunch Club. October 27th through 31st, 2014, 12 Railroad Street in Dunstan, Vermont.

Come to celebrate the life of Jennifer (Jennet) Sherilyn Stark (1967–89) and revisit our shared past through the elixir of the pines.

Of course—today, May 22, was the twenty-fifth anniversary of Jennet's death.

The "reunion" was five days in October in Dunstan. Auraleigh had moved back to their college town to watch over her daughter, who was now a freshman there, and had gotten busy transforming a rundown Victorian into a cozy home. The reno must have gone well, or Auraleigh wouldn't have invited all of them to stay there in high-foliage season.

Still, the invitation came as a surprise, because Auraleigh hadn't called Sonia since December. During their last phone conversation, she'd grown borderline huffy when Sonia failed to show interest in the intricacies of spray-foam insulation. Since then, there'd been pictures on Facebook of the evolving home/ B and B—gables, bathroom fixtures. Sonia had commented on a few of them, then gotten bored and stopped.

October was midterm season, packed with grading and tearful emails from students begging for conferences. Where would Sonia be next October? In a month, she would have no campus mailbox, no email address, no health insurance.

Take it as a sign from the universe! Auraleigh would probably say, flinging her arms out. *Go back to LA! Follow your dreams!*

Sonia tried but failed to tear the card in half. When you followed your dreams, you ended up like her mother—moving seven times in ten years, from the shabby-chic environs of Morningside Heights to the Vermont wilderness, always chasing a great love or transcendence in a commune's soybean field. When you reached a certain age, you realized that the real dream, the only one that mattered, was safety.

As she shoved the card back into the envelope, her eyes again ran over the lines: *There are still secrets to be discovered; the past is not even past (Faulkner); we are boats against the current (Fitzgerald).*

Auraleigh had used only half the quote from *The Great Gatsby;* the next part was *borne back ceaselessly into the past.* Borne back into the past, against the inexorable current of time, by an elixir of the pines...

Sonia rose, her heart racing. In December, Auraleigh had asked if she remembered the boy with the time travel drug. Sonia had laughed and said, "Don't be silly. That was a campus myth. There was no time travel drug."

But she knew exactly who—and what—Auraleigh was talking about.

There was a way to go back, if you really wanted to—an *elixir of the pines*. People just weren't supposed to know about it.

Sonia, who did know, had spent the past twenty-five years trying to forget.

Voluntary Memory
March 1988 (sophomore year)

SONIA

A time travel drug. That was what Auraleigh called it as she tried to persuade Sonia to leave campus for a townie party in a place called Belle Venere, which was a hole in the landscape, not even a town. She'd heard they would find a boy there who sold a drug that showed you your "bright, bright future."

"Remember that weirdo story about time travel that someone submitted anonymously to the lit mag last fall?" she asked, sprawling on the battered couch in the townhouse they shared with Paul Bretton. "Well, I asked around, and someone told me the guy who wrote it will sell you the stuff."

Sonia remembered the story; it was fiction. "Why do you want to see your future, anyway?" she asked. "Don't you want to be surprised?"

"I don't believe I'll actually see the future, dummy. It's probably just your garden-variety psychedelic. But Toddy Kuller's going—he's the one who told me about it—and he's being *so* elusive."

"I'm not taking any psychedelics," Sonia said, wiping down the kitchenette counter. More than a semester into being roommates, they'd turned out to be surprisingly complementary: Paul made espressos for anyone at any hour, Auraleigh cooked, and Sonia cleaned obsessively. Her fear of insect infestation, learned in New York apartments, was something she didn't discuss with the other two, who'd both grown up in nice suburban homes.

Auraleigh rolled her eyes dramatically. "You're so pure. Fine. Come for moral support."

Sonia had no interest in townie parties. Thanks to their inopportune move to Vermont a decade ago, she was practically a townie herself. In those days, though, she would follow wherever Auraleigh led, because Auraleigh still seemed like a miraculous vision that one breath might dispel. Was she *allowed* to have friends like these?

That night, with Sonia in the passenger seat charting their course using the state atlas and a flashlight, they drove five miles up and down a washboard road through gnarled thickets of bare buckthorn and maple. Belle Venere contributed only a trickle of students to the county high school Sonia had attended, but she'd heard kids talking about beer bashes at someone's farm up there, far from parental eyes.

"It's dangerous to see the future," she yelled over the roar of Auraleigh's Jeep, hoping it was clear she was being ironic. "There are paradoxes."

Auraleigh passed Sonia her flask. She wore a tiny camo mini, a safety-pinned jean jacket, and ripped tights, but her baby-fat cheeks and corn-silk hair softened the effect. She said, "I think it'd be a trip."

Sonia took a careful drink. Auraleigh had started plying her with Stoli back in the apartment, telling her to loosen up; it was working. "Why's Toddy at a party in this dump?"

"Beats me."

Dump was not a word Sonia would have used when sober—too crude. She'd learned to choose her words carefully as a child who had trouble pronouncing certain sounds (*R*s, mainly) and was often mocked into silence. Even now, with speech therapy far behind her, she always ran a sentence in her head before saying it.

But *dump* felt like the right word for their destination: a rambling complex of slumped roofs and peeling paint that could have been the residence of Leatherface's slightly more presentable cousins. There were no streetlights or other signs of a town, only a steeple poking the sky.

The music flooding the cold March air was stupidly jubilant hair metal. Inside, the house was lit by cockeyed floor lamps and stank of stale beer and smoke and mildew. It was packed with current students and recent alumni of Sonia's high school: bellowing boys in soccer jerseys and stout girls in chamois shirts and patterned turtlenecks. The floor was crusted with mud from their hiking boots, the Lamoille County footgear of choice.

Sonia stuck close to Auraleigh. When a couple of people from high school yelled, "Hey, Sonia!" she smiled at the floor, a flicker of panic running through her. These people had not been her friends; a few had even called her names. What if they told Auraleigh who she really was—the awkward girl who never made eye contact and wore corduroy pants with ankle zippers to school? Maybe it was an irrational fear, since Auraleigh was a city girl herself. But the old feeling of not belonging bubbled back up.

She asked Auraleigh for the flask and paused beside a leaning china hutch, drinking so deeply that everything quivered and liquefied. When the room straightened out again, Auraleigh was already over on the far side of the room. Sonia watched her step out a side door onto a deck where a row of girls perched on a railing. Their thick parkas made them hard to tell apart, but one sneer was unmistakable: it belonged to Kim Gardner, aka Red Nikes, the most dangerous Kim in the class of '86.

Those girls had hated Sonia. No, not even hated, because you didn't bother to hate someone like her—a flatlander, an outsider.

The vodka made time slippery along with everything else. Sonia darted away from the Kims, through a door that brought her to the foot of a staircase. From above came a thumping rhythm that clashed with the hair metal, and she made out the discordant licks of the Pixies.

She didn't stop to wonder who was playing college rock here. She fled up two flights of stairs into an attic jammed with boxes and stinking of mothballs, the walls bleeding cotton-candy insulation.

Eight or nine people her age were smoking under a bare bulb. They looked like students. One tall boy even had a blazer and moussed hair. Toddy! She made her way to him, relieved. Once he and Auraleigh connected, maybe they could get out of here.

The boy beside Toddy turned toward her, and she stopped short. He was a tow-headed townie with raw pink eyelids—Scott Lemorne, known for dealing drugs and whispering obscenities to any girl who got within earshot. Like the Kims, he knew her true identity as an outcast.

Toddy noticed her presence, proffering a joint and a gleaming smile. "Hey, Sonia."

"Hey." Sonia took the joint, barely inhaled, and handed it back. She kept her distance from Scott Lemorne. "I came with Auraleigh. She's downstairs."

Toddy said something, showing his dimples, but Sonia was too close to the speakers to hear. She nodded and smiled. When a girl in knock-off Calvins grabbed Toddy's elbow and murmured in his ear, Sonia edged back toward the stairs. If Auraleigh wanted Toddy, she could come and get him.

"I know you."

The deep voice came from a tall boy who leaned against the window frame, squinting through the smoke. Another student: Sonia recognized him from campus, his lank black hair and long, angular face like an actor on *Masterpiece Theatre*. He wasn't smooth or pretty like Toddy. He was beautiful.

She swiveled a hip toward him, letting the wave of vodka carry her, and said in what she hoped was an Auraleigh tone of voice, "Oh, do you? Because I don't know you. Are you on the *Dove-Cat?*" she added a second later, embarrassment catching up to her. "I'm Paul and Auraleigh's roommate." Everybody at Dunstan knew one or both of them.

"No," the boy said. "I'm from the future." He didn't sound like he was joking. "Toddy, got a smoke?"

Toddy tossed him a pack and lighter.

"People still smoke in the future?" she asked him.

"They're not any smarter, that's for sure." The future boy lit the cigarette and let it burn between his fingers. "I know you," he repeated. "I'm Hayworth." A grin, as if to acknowledge his name was a mouthful.

"Hayworth's on something stronger than us, man," Toddy said and strolled off toward the turntable with the girl. Scott disappeared downstairs, and Sonia relaxed a little.

She and Hayworth stood alone now, at the fly-specked window. His shoulders were broad and loose at once, his elbows bony. She imagined cupping those elbows in her palms—couldn't help it, he was just so *tall.*

You're out of your depth, warned a voice inside her.

But Sonia didn't feel out of her depth. She felt in control. She'd just put two and two together. "You're the one. You wrote that story, 'The Warning.' You sell the drug."

Hayworth's face closed. "I don't sell anything."

"But you said you're from the future." Sonia took another swig from the flask. "Does the drug show it to you? Or are you an actual time traveler?"

She meant this to be arch and witty, but Hayworth didn't smile. He stubbed out the cigarette, and his sleeve rode up, exposing a striped oxford cuff and a Movado museum watch like the ones she'd seen advertised in her dad's *New Yorkers.* He didn't seem like the Scott Lemorne kind of dealer, if he was a dealer.

"Nobody can time travel," he said. "My body is stuck here, just like yours. I have memories of the future, that's all." And then, before she could ask questions: "At the PFA, that's where I saw you. They were showing *Tokyo Drifter*."

"What?" Sonia could feel the static off his tweed jacket, though they weren't touching—a delicious shiver that traveled over her from head to toe.

"Pacific Film Archive."

"I didn't—I don't know what that is."

"That's because it hasn't happened yet."

"Oh, right. The future." Sonia gulped some vodka and managed not to choke. She was acutely conscious of him there, close enough to reach out and brush her hair out of her eyes. "What else do you see in the future? How to get rich off stocks?"

"It doesn't work that way," Hayworth said. "It comes in bits and pieces, not enough for you ever to get the whole picture. It doesn't allow you to see enough to *know* to change things, or how they should change. And you don't choose what you see, so you can't even really *try* to put the pieces together, either."

"You can't change the future? What's the point, then?" She probably sounded like an idiot.

A teasing hint played around his lips. "You don't want just a peek?"

She couldn't tell him that when she tried to think about the future, she found only a quivering, abject mass of fears. *Please don't let me die tomorrow. Please let me get out of Vermont. Please don't let me be a sad little mousy hanger-on to Auraleigh forever. Please let me be a real person someday.*

She said, "My mom raised us to think we wouldn't live to see the year 2000. You know, the nuclear-doomsday clock."

"Your mom's wrong," Hayworth said. "I've been to the twenty-first century."

The room wobbled and telescoped. Warm light bouncing off the black window, distant thump of music. "I thought you weren't a time traveler."

"I'm not." His tone was casual. His eyes focused far off. "Everything we've ever experienced or will experience is locked up inside us somewhere, and sog unlocks it. When you're young, it shows you your future. When you're older, it shows you your past."

"So I would see my future?"

Hayworth laughed, a hoarse sound that made Sonia tingle lightly all over. Black stubble stood out on the pale skin of his neck. "You have to be thirty or forty before you sog backward. My memories got mixed up with some of the memories of the older me, and you're in those memories. You're different in the future."

"Different how?" He was talking nonsense, but she still wanted to know.

"Pretty—no, wait, I don't mean that." He held up a hand. "I don't mean you're not pretty now. I just mean that in the future, you're more...finished. Right now you're only half here, same as me."

A shudder gripped her shoulders. He was putting into words what she'd always known, what Scott Lemorne and the Kims knew: all those moves during her childhood, having to continually adjust to a new place and new school and new culture, had left her raw, unfinished, a collection of fragments. "I don't belong anywhere," she said. "Do you feel that way?"

He nodded. "I feel like a ghost—maybe that's because I have these pieces of the future in my head, or maybe I've always felt that way."

The words sank into Sonia's skin. *Like a ghost*, someone people looked through. A latchkey kid with ragged bangs, high-water pants, dirty nails. A girl whose hippie mom dated a million freaks. A college sophomore who still got nervous talking to boys.

Paul and Auraleigh had taken her in, and these days, when she was drunk or feeling unusually confident, she liked to think of herself as the elegant one in their group—not the prettiest, no, but attractive in her own serene way, as long as she didn't smile too much. She was the only one of them who knew anything about film; even Paul listened attentively when she talked about *Ugetsu* or *My Beautiful Laundrette*.

But none of that was enough to make her belong with them, not really. She wanted to be stunning, brilliant, unmissable. What she wanted from the future was a bolt of electricity to galvanize her into motion, to give her the trajectory of a shooting star.

The record ended. She heard it revolving, then the click of the needle withdrawing, the turntable stopping.

"Can I try it?" she asked.

Hayworth's gaze came unfixed again. "You sure? Gas prices keep going up, and there are a bunch of wars coming. It's messy. Worse. Always worse. Or that's what people say."

A future where people bought gas and saw movies still seemed manageable. "Please," she said, the word slipping out.

Hayworth gave her another glance, then pulled a jam jar from his jacket and unscrewed it. Inside was a half-inch of what looked like low-grade maple syrup or bacon grease about to congeal.

He held it up to the light. Black flecks floated in the golden-brown liquid. Sonia's stomach clenched.

"Don't worry, it can't physically hurt you." He stuck a finger in the jar. It came out glossy brown, and he popped it in his mouth as if he couldn't resist a taste.

The liquid stank like a pine forest rubbed on the inside of your sinuses, like the essence of this soggy, rotting county. When Hayworth leaned toward her, the jar seemed to vibrate between them. But he didn't pass it to her, only said, "Cup your hand."

Right then, Sonia believed it all: that he was from the future. That he was half seeing her now and half seeing her as she'd be someday—brave and glowing, finally belonging in some indefinable way.

"I'll go with you," he said, dribbling dark liquid into her palm. "We won't actually go to the same place, though. We won't see the same things."

Sonia raised her hand to her mouth and licked off the sticky stuff. She tasted Pine-Sol, only sweeter, and gagged before finally getting it down.

"We need to lie down," Hayworth said, leading her into a dim space between high stacks of boxes. "Don't worry. Just like a nap."

Sonia stretched out and closed her eyes. Were the others all gone? It was so quiet; no one had put on another record.

Tension drained out of her, leaving only a heavy sense of well-being. She forgot about Auraleigh, about Scott and Toddy and the most dangerous Kim, even about Hayworth. Her head buzzed. The air weighed on her, moving rhythmically like a great bird beating its wings.

In the darkness, she saw and felt...

Herself in a car. On a highway. A yellow desert landscape flickering past, impossibly bright.

Cool rush of air on her bare legs. Afternoon sun on her bare arms. A hammer-shaped cloud on the horizon. Beside her, a voice speaking— tinny, as if from the radio.

Throat tight. Eyes blurred with tears. The sense of something roaring up all at once, life sharpening to a point. Things becoming clear.

In the rearview, blue lights flashing. A black car, tall as a military tank, stopped on the shoulder.

In the back seat, cardboard boxes and a vase with a Navajo pattern.

Foot on the pedal, easing. Her own voice replying to the tinny voice. Her voice saying Yes. *Her eyes following the curve of the road between enormous banks of brightness, taking it in without being blinded. Brightness without end.*

Later, she would remember the vision as a slideshow—each image sharp-edged, saturated with color, indelible. As quickly as the pictures came, they vanished, leaving only the relentless buzzing in her head.

Eventually, she floated upward, through liquid blackness into wan electric light. She sat up with a jerk. Where was she? Who was she?

For an instant, no answers. There was only a thudding beat, rattling old walls, and a tightness in her throat. Beside her, stretched out on his side with one cheek against the boards, lay a tall, black-haired boy.

Then, all at once, her memories snapped back. The party. Dunstan College. Sophomore year. Auraleigh, downstairs. Hayworth.

Sonia was afraid to know what would happen when he woke up. Maybe he'd only wanted to get her hooked on the drug; maybe he didn't like her at all. She scrambled to her feet, dead sober again, grabbed her backpack, and took the stairs.

The party was winding down. She hurried from group to group until she located Auraleigh—not with Toddy, but with a bearded, twinkly-eyed townie who was funneling a Jell-O shot into her mouth.

Sonia watched them as if from a great distance. She had seen the future. She would live in the desert someday, out west, in brightness. Maybe in Hollywood. Maybe she could start writing screenplays—maybe, maybe.

After consuming two more Jell-O shots, Auraleigh gave the guy her number, and he wandered off. "You drive," Auraleigh said to Sonia.

On the way home, they talked about Auraleigh's new friend, who was apparently a bow hunter. Sonia said, "I told Toddy you were downstairs," and Auraleigh screwed up her face and said, "Toddy's such a tool."

Back in the three-bedroom townhouse, Auraleigh went upstairs to watch TV. In the downstairs bathroom, Sonia pulled off her tights and everything else and put on a bathrobe and washed off the eyeliner and drank three glasses of lukewarm water.

She found Jennet in her bed, curled in a nest of blankets, reading an English translation of Roland Barthes's *Mythologies*. She had the spare key to the townhouse, so you never knew when to expect her. "My hallway was having another kegger," she said by way of explanation.

Sonia was always on her guard with most of her friends, but Jennet's presence was like another layer of her own skin. "Auraleigh and I went to a townie party," she said. "I didn't think you'd want to come."

"I can't believe *you* went."

Sonia turned her back to Jennet and slipped on pajamas under her bathrobe. Jennet never mocked her modesty; they were both that way.

"Barthes says we're all inoculating ourselves against the urge to rebel," Jennet said, adjusting her oversize round glasses. "We get a smidgen of freedom and bolt back to our cozy conventionality. Is that why I hate parties?"

"No. Parties are terrible." Sonia sat opposite Jennet and propped a pillow behind her head. Sometimes they slept this way, head to toe in the single bed, each with a book under her cheek or balanced on her chest. It reminded Sonia of childhood sleepovers—the giggling, the ghost stories, the aimless talk with no expectations.

The heater ticked. Sonia was no longer staggering around a party in itchy tights. In the warm yellow puddle of light from her gooseneck lamp, everything that had happened with Hayworth seemed far away.

On the ride home, she'd tried to memorize each image she'd seen in the sog. They shone inside her like stained-glass windows or illuminated posters outside a movie theater. She didn't really know if they were prophecies, yet she was afraid of losing them all the same.

Sonia burrowed her bare feet into the comforter. "I met a boy from the future at the townie party. At least, that's what he said. I think he wrote that story, 'The Warning.'"

After she explained everything, Jennet asked, "Are you going to do the drug again?"

Sonia told herself she would probably never see Hayworth again. But if she did, and he asked... "I don't know. Maybe. Promise not to tell Auraleigh? She might start thinking I'm trying to be 'cool' and offer me coke or something." She hadn't mentioned anything to Auraleigh because Auraleigh would call it a "trip," and it had seemed so solid, nothing like Sonia imagined an acid trip might feel. But more than that, Auraleigh didn't seem to share her anxiety about the future, her fear of personal and global disasters. She wouldn't understand how much it meant to see a vision of the world still intact.

Jennet laughed. Her knee nudged Sonia's. "When have I ever told her anything?"

Their eyes met, complicit. And for a moment, Sonia thought, she belonged here more than she would ever belong anywhere else.

2

BYRON

Two months and nine days had passed since Byron Orloff moved out of the home where he and his wife had raised their children, but he still had a key.

He took the back way in through the gate to the patio and stopped to examine the surface of the pool, turquoise shading to violet. It didn't need cleaning yet—and anyway, that was Christa's responsibility now.

So many times, he'd sat on this deck at dusk, listening to the drone of a mower over the fence and the distant yakking of the evening news, falling asleep in the lounge chair after a week of sixteen-hour workdays, like some retiree in Florida, like the normal dad he'd never had.

Sometimes, in the hazy state between sleep and waking, he imagined he heard Jennet Stark's voice. *Well, Byron*, she always said, wry and grave at once, and then she was gone.

It was just a sound bite from his memory, but he always felt as if she were judging him. She'd teased him about his wanderlust, how he would never settle down, so she probably wouldn't be surprised to see him here, watching his family from the outside as if he'd never been part of it at all.

They were all three assembled around the kitchen island, their voices audible from several paces. The slider door framed the bright interior like a movie screen. Eliza was waving her arms, Rohan chiding her. Their mother was about to intervene, the tip of her chef's knife poised over a Napa cabbage.

Byron opened the slider, and they fell silent like living-history actors who'd been caught chattering about their latest binge watch when they were supposed to be churning butter. Eliza contemplated her phone, one high-arched foot itching at her other calf under the bar. Rohan just stared at Byron, wide eyes, sneaky smile.

Christa broke the silence: "Hey."

"Hey." Byron cleared his throat. "Smells good."

"We're grilling tonight," Rohan said.

"Right." Byron met his wife's eyes—she *was* still his wife, for now. "I'm gonna grab those files, okay?"

"I put the boxes in the hall for you." Christa smiled at him in a way he recognized as calculated to soothe unruly tenth graders. She still taught in the Oakland Public Schools system—as Byron had, until he'd glanced at the sticker prices on real estate and college tuition and realized one of them would need to earn a real salary to stay in the Bay Area.

"Thanks." He appealed to his daughter. "You're gonna eat, right?" When the kids stayed with him last weekend, he'd bought some delectable ribs at Whole Foods, hoping to tempt Eliza, but she'd made a face and picked at the salad.

"I don't eat meat anymore."

"No kidding. When did that happen?" He glanced at Christa, who shrugged.

Eliza continued to ogle her screen—what was so fascinating there? "I've been phasing it out."

"Well, that's good! Good for the planet!" My God, Byron sounded like a sitcom dad. You'd never guess he'd been raised by a single mother who marched against nukes with him on her shoulders. "I hope you're getting lots of protein, though. Hey, Rohan, how'd the trig test go?"

"Eighty-six out of a hundred." Rohan's phone was out now, too.

"Awesome." Byron considered going in for a fist bump. Thought better of it. He'd accidentally misgendered Rohan last week, the way he still sometimes did, and they hadn't talked about it. He wanted to apologize, but he kept reading about apologies that made things worse. He settled for saying, "Told you you'd ace it."

Rohan was absorbed in the phone.

Christa said, "Hon, there's snail mail for you." She darted to the far end of the island where the cookbooks and recipe binders were. "Guess there's a friend you haven't shared your new address with."

She looked him in the eye as she handed Byron the heavy envelope. She always looked people in the eye; it was the first thing he'd noticed when they met. It had taken him years to learn that sometimes her warmth wasn't real.

Just five months ago, when Byron had completed the sale of his company, an app that helped financial managers fiddle with their spreadsheets wherever they were, even on the beach, the plan was to use his new state of gainful unemployment to spend time with the kids before they went to college. He'd given his all to his startup, working day and night for fifteen years and seldom surfacing to take a breath. He'd bought them a house in the hills with a bay view and sent the kids to the best schools that were private and progressive both.

He'd been lost in fantasies of biking in Marin with Eliza and teaching Rohan to play guitar when Christa invited him to a special dinner, just the two of them, and told him *I think we should amicably separate.*

Byron asked her to explain. And explain again. By the end

of the dinner, all he really knew was that she'd been wanting out for a while. The specter of unlimited quality time with him made it a pressing matter.

He told himself he could still do everything with the kids that he wanted to do—biking, guitar, pickup basketball, hiking Mount Tamalpais. All the things he hadn't been there to do when they were younger. But right now, as he stood in what had once been his kitchen, the twitch of Eliza's bare feet and the tap of Rohan's fingers said they were counting the seconds till he retreated and they could be a family again.

I'm not the enemy, Byron wanted to protest.

"Okay," he said instead, slinging his backpack over a shoulder, letter in the other hand. "Guess I'll grab the boxes."

The envelope was hefty and creamy, engraved in a swoony-script font—wedding invitation? Then he saw the return address, the name Auraleigh Lydgate, and a jolt went through his whole body.

Halfway up the stairs, around the bend where his family couldn't see him, Byron tore open the letter, nearly slashing the envelope in two. There was no good reason for Auraleigh to send him anything after all these years.

Back in college, they'd been inseparable for a while—he and Jennet and Sonia and Paul and Auraleigh, working on the *Dove-Cat*, the campus literary magazine, its name a whimsical joke (in the forties, it had been the *Dove-Cote*) and its logo a whiskered avian-feline hybrid. Auraleigh would make brunch at any hour in the townhouse's second-floor kitchenette, so their sophomore spring and junior fall had been full of long, tequila-sodden nights eating her omelet concoctions and editing the magazine on a Mac SE while Elvis Costello sang about how accidents would happen and his aim was true. Auraleigh called them the Midnight Brunch Club, a name Byron hadn't thought of in years. Though he occasionally emailed with Sonia, and he read Paul's pieces in the *Times*, he hadn't kept in touch with Auraleigh and hadn't regretted it.

Even before his eyes ran over the invitation and found Jennet's name glowing like a hologram, he knew exactly what this was about.

She wanted to rehash the night Jennet died. To make sense of a senseless tragedy that had seeped into Byron's youth and filled it with a choking stench that reminded him of his grandmother's asbestos-ridden attic: a foretaste of death.

He read the invitation a second time. A third.

This was about her self-dramatization. Auraleigh and Jennet hadn't been nearly as close as he and Jennet had. She couldn't possibly understand how it felt to wonder all your life why you hadn't been there when the person you loved needed you the most.

It pissed him off so much that he wanted to go and tell Auraleigh so to her face. Maybe he wouldn't still feel that way in five months, but he wouldn't have much to distract him, either. His schedule was wide open.

Autumn in Vermont: the hard nip in the air, the scent of trodden and fermented apples. He could tell Christa and the kids he was flying across the country to visit friends, reminding them he'd once had a life that had nothing to do with them.

He could. If he dared. Christa was the one who'd woken him up all those years ago, eased him out of his grief over Jennet, but she wouldn't be around to do it a second time.

He was at the top of the stairs when Jennet said, *Well, Byron,* soft and clear. He sat down on the maple wood and watched as dark specks blurred and swam in his vision.

I'm sorry, he thought. *Tell me,* he thought. *Tell me my next step.*

No answer.

3

SONIA

In her office, Sonia filled boxes and Albertsons bags with unclaimed student papers and grading grids, unreadable floppy and Zip discs, professional journals—all the debris of fourteen years spent in a frigidly air-conditioned basement room the size of a walk-in closet. She peeled her posters off the wall: *Retrophiliac* at SXSW, at a midnight screening in Greenwich Village. She had always meant to get them framed, and now they were ragged around the edges.

When she had arrived at the college, straight from LA and trailing the glamour of Slamdance and Telluride behind her, she'd still hoped to do something more than teach three-act screenplay structure to undergrads. Now she knew *Retrophiliac* had been a stroke of luck, a matter of knowing the right people at the right time. The movie had since become a trivia question, a forgotten relic of the grunge era. It was too late to go back to LA; that was a young person's game.

At the last minute, she remembered to grab the large Navajo vase on the bookshelf. Inside were Faustus's ashes in a plastic bag, transferred out of the box the crematorium had given her. Faustus had died four months ago at the age of seventeen. He'd had a wonderful life and a reasonably peaceful death, but she would never forget how he had snarled as the vet pricked his scruff with the sedative-bearing needle.

She carried everything into the hall outside the office, fished out her unwieldy key ring, a rectangle of gummy plastic with a keepsake folded inside, and locked the door for the last time.

Walking to the car, she kept her gaze on the horizon. She couldn't let this setback throw her, yet here she was. As she gunned it to Albuquerque on I-25 with the packing boxes and her dead cat's ashes in the back seat, tears streamed down her cheeks. The landscape was a familiar blur of sage and juniper and late-afternoon sunlight. Every single time she crossed it, she wondered if this was the desert where she'd seen herself with Hayworth in sog visions that hadn't come true.

Falling in love with him had been the first mistake of many. She should have left him on the attic floor that first time and never looked back.

The speed stopped her from wailing, stopped her from scream-ing, so she leadfooted to pass a semitruck and didn't let up. Sev-enty. Seventy-five. Eighty. She passed a minivan, another semi.

She never cried, so what was this? Were the tears for Jennet, gone twenty-five years now? Or for Faustus? Or for herself, the up-and-coming screenwriter who'd filled two albums with her new kitten's "baby" pictures, every photo a blinding splash of cobalt blue and Pacific sun? The girl who wanted to believe that, if she could keep a cat alive, she could also take care of herself?

Eighty-five. Ninety.

Beside her on the seat, the phone buzzed, and she saw the name Byron Orloff.

She'd forgotten his number was in her contacts. They'd had coffee ten years ago when he came to town for a conference, but conversation had been awkward, too many things unspoken between them. After that, they'd emailed occasionally and she'd followed his news on Facebook—the sale of his company, the end of his marriage. Any day now, she expected to see photos of him with a woman at least a decade his junior.

Normally she wouldn't have answered the phone in the car, but it was Byron, and the tears made her reckless. She hit the accept and speaker buttons. "Hi."

"Hey." Byron's deep, scratchy voice was so familiar and oddly intimate that Sonia felt a tugging sensation in her chest. "Been a while," he said.

"Right?"

"I'm sorry we haven't kept up. You finishing the semester?"

"That's right." Sonia didn't want to get into the issue of her job—and anyway, there was an edge on his voice that told her he hadn't called just to reconnect. "I heard about you and Christa. I'm sorry."

"Yeah. Well. I'm doing okay." He cleared his throat, sounding uncomfortable. "I've been thinking a lot about the old Midnight Brunch Club today because, well... Did you get the invitation, too? What's Auraleigh even doing in Dunstan?"

Her eyes on the road, Sonia explained how Auraleigh had moved from LA to the tiny college town when her daughter enrolled, right after her divorce papers were processed. "She's opened a B and B," she added, imagining what Byron was thinking, that Auraleigh was a helicopter parent, a case of midlife crisis.

Which was true but not the whole story: Auraleigh's girl twin, Frances, had struggled with disordered eating and serious depression in her first two years of high school, and Auraleigh wanted to stay close. Whatever else you might say about her, she was a devoted mom.

"She must've invited Paul, too," Byron said.

"Probably so." It occurred to Sonia that in her current position, Paul Bretton might be a valuable friend—he'd written for a few TV shows. She just had to get over the embarrassment of approaching him. "What do you think? Are you going?"

She expected an immediate no. Instead Byron said, "I think a lot about college. I think a lot about Dunstan. Auraleigh, though—I don't get it." His voice faltered. "So you keep in touch?"

"We talk on the phone—or we did." Those calls had stopped in December, right after Auraleigh asked her about Hayworth, Sonia realized. She hadn't used Hayworth's name, but she had to have been referring to him.

"Do you think Auraleigh's maybe a little...unhinged?" Byron asked now.

Her voice thickened by alcohol, Auraleigh would begin each call by asking about Sonia's "fabulous life" and then get around to her own latest drama: a fight with her husband, an embarrassing rant at book club, something disturbing Frances had posted on Tumblr. But the conversations always circled back to Jennet Stark. "I dreamed she was standing outside my house in the middle of the street," Auraleigh might say, "and the traffic went right through her." Or "I wonder what Jennet would post on Tumblr if she were Frances's age. If they would be friends." And those reminiscences would spiral into a tearful discussion of *that* night.

"Her heart's in the right place," Sonia told Byron.

"Are *you* going?" he asked. "I'd like to see you."

Something rose in Sonia's throat too quickly, closing her airway and flooding her eyes with tears again. "I'd like to see all of you, too." *I'd like to go back, boats against the current. The past is not past.*

She pressed hard on the accelerator and plunged toward the burning horizon. A cloud formation had appeared there, tall and solid-looking, blocking the sun.

Byron was still talking. "We could fly into Logan. Get a

rental and carpool, so if the reunion gets boring, we could go do some sightseeing."

A siren chirped, and Sonia eased up on the pedal. "Yes," she said to no one in particular. She checked the mirrors, preparing to pull over and put on the flashers and a meek smile. She'd never gotten a speeding ticket, but there was a first time for everything.

The cloud still hovered to the southwest, its end hammerlike and its shaft blinding. She could swear she'd seen it before.

"Then, it's a plan," Byron said.

He sounded so positive that Sonia's shakiness receded. She glanced again in the rearview and saw that the trooper had pulled to the shoulder, flashers strobing, behind a black SUV.

And then she realized she *had* seen this scene before. All of it.

The cloud, the desert, the trooper, the SUV, the Navajo vase, the blurring of tears. She'd seen it all on the floor of a stinking attic in Belle Venere in 1988.

So many years she had waited for her sog visions to come true. Sometimes she'd experience déjà vu and hope that, finally, it was happening, but the sensation always melted away.

Now, though, she was sure of it. But she felt no excitement, no satisfaction, nothing she had expected. There was nothing special about the desert road and the cloud after all. Just another day in a life that had turned out way too ordinary.

When she'd had that vision, she still believed in a bright future. Now she had little to look forward to, and all that swarmed inside her was the past, the past, the past. Her head was so full of memories it hurt. Jennet's too-bright lipstick. Byron's battered leather jacket and teasing sidelong glance. Paul's notebooks jammed with his tiny, precise writing. Auraleigh's omelet with avocado and sour cream and salsa and crispy bacon. Hayworth's shack by the river where the woodstove glowed and the whole world smelled of disintegrating leaves and she willed him desperately to touch her.

She wanted with all her being to see Dunstan again. She

wished she could go back to the beginning of her adult life, do it over, make it *work*.

But since she couldn't do that, perhaps she could at least figure out where it had all gone wrong.

Voluntary Memory
May 26, 1989 (junior year)

SONIA

They came together, parking in the pullout and walking across the railroad tracks, up the brambled trail. Around them, the leaves were unfurling, neon puce against the gray sky. Spring had come late, as it often did in Vermont in those days. Paul carried grocery-store daffodils, and Sonia held cut bruise-dark lilacs. Byron had a binder of Jennet's poems in his backpack. Auraleigh had the booze.

Until that moment, Sonia had never consciously thought of them as a circle of friends, the kind of friends everybody wants to have in college. But Jennet's absence made her realize that was exactly what they were—or had been.

When they reached the river, with its natural limestone bridge and narrow stream of white water, Auraleigh began to cry silently. Her tears were such a familiar sight by then, four days afterward, that Sonia pretended not to notice.

They walked out on the apron of rock as far as they felt safe. Paul and Sonia placed their flowers on the edge, wedging them into cracks. Byron peered down at the falls and said, "It looks so...puny."

Sonia had often thought the same thing. When her family first moved to Vermont, everyone had warned her and her sister not to explore Dogssnout Falls alone. One body had been discovered in the fifties and another in the early seventies, the first probably an accidental drowning and the second stabbed by a romantic rival before going in the water.

Now Jennet. Her body had been found downstream, wedged under a fallen tree, by fishermen the morning after.

It didn't feel real yet. Sonia had been so busy with her junior essay this semester that she had neglected both the *Dove-Cat* and Jennet. The nights when she came home to find her friend tucked in her bed were over, and the conversations they did have were more awkward. When had they even seen each other last? She remembered eating outdoors on the quad, a shadow of blooming forsythia on Jennet's forehead, feeling Jennet's hand brush the back of hers. And then, the night it happened—but no, she wouldn't think about that. She hoped Byron wasn't, either.

◆ ◆ ◆

Sonia tried not to look at Byron. Instead, she dropped a sprig of lilacs and watched the white water trap it in a compact, deadly spiral and suck it under. She had smelled lilacs the night Jennet drowned, as she walked down to her mom's apartment from the *Dove-Cat* room.

This wasn't supposed to happen. Jennet was a year older than the rest of them. She'd had a plan. She would stick around after her graduation, working at Café Polaire and renting in town.

Beside Sonia, Auraleigh wiped her eyes. She seemed very small standing there with the woods behind her. "I can't believe I don't even remember it happening," she said, a sob warping her voice. "I need to remember."

Auraleigh had been with Jennet that night—so drunk she had blacked out what happened.

Paul said, "Shh. You were probably passed out by that time."

"I don't believe she jumped."

You could speculate forever. The sheriff had told the newspaper it was a "tragic accident" that was under investigation. People in the dining commons whispered about suicide. The real question was, with all the time Sonia had spent sogging to her future over the past year, why hadn't she glimpsed even a hint of this?

Hayworth warned her nothing she saw in the sog would be useful, every time she asked him for another dose and every time he gave her one. But she wanted to believe that if she *had* known, she could have done something—stopped Jennet from coming here that night. Spent more time with her, paid more attention to her this semester. *Anything.*

Paper floated through the air. Cheap blue-lined sheets caught the breeze and soared briefly before hitting the water and turning to rags. Sonia recognized Jennet's tight, cryptic handwriting.

Byron wasn't going to read one of her poems. He was getting rid of them.

Without thinking, Sonia grabbed for one of the pages. Her foot slipped, her balance lurching—*this is it, this is how she fell*—until strong fingers closed on her arm, pulling her back to solid ground.

Realizing it was Byron, she stiffened in his grip, and he released her. "She wanted her poems destroyed, the unrevised ones. If she died. She told me."

"Like Kafka." Jennet had told Sonia the same thing, but she'd forgotten. Byron had remembered.

"Those are *poems*? You can't destroy her poems!" Auraleigh cried with the outrage of someone who knows poetry mainly by reputation.

Across the way, something stirred, and Sonia froze, scanning the limestone cliffs and leafing trees. The shack where she and Hayworth sogged was up there. But Hayworth was never there during the day, and even if he were, he wouldn't want to see her.

"Shh," Paul said again. "If Jennet wanted this, she wanted it."

That was just like Paul: to end the scene with calm, conclusive words. As if, by casting Jennet's oblique bits of free verse into the waves, they could put her to rest and acknowledge they were only college friends, thrown together by musty dorm rooms and convenience. And once they'd done that, they could ride on into their real lives—their bright, bright futures.

Maybe Paul would ride on. Maybe Auraleigh, too. But not Sonia—she knew it even then—and not Byron. Jennet was with them for life.

DAY 1

October 27, 2014

4

BYRON

Sonia was wearing jeans and a red sweater, which startled Byron as they met in the arrivals lounge. She'd worn mostly black in college, like one of their hip young English professors, and rarely smiled, even for photos.

Now Sonia was smiling, but she still had some of the severity he remembered—her tall, angular body posed with deliberation. He'd always tried to respect her personal space, reading the signals before approaching her. This time, he decided it was safe to hug.

"You look great," he said as they pulled apart. "Just the same." It wasn't quite true, of course, but it was close enough.

"You, too. Oh my God, is that your old jacket?"

Byron had chosen his leather bomber jacket from college, the one with the patched shoulder, which he was proud to say still fit, though it was a tight squeeze. He laughed, a deep-down belly laugh. "First time I've worn it since the nineties. Thought I'd get into the reunion spirit. You got more bags?"

They went to the carousel, where Byron handled Sonia's bigger suitcase despite her protests. "I rented a Forester. We'll do this Vermont-style."

The sky was a forbidding pewter over Boston, but patches cleared as they reached the suburbs. The trip across New Hampshire into Vermont took nearly three hours, spruce and brilliant maples filling more and more of the horizon.

Byron drove with the smooth speed of a Californian, making easy conversation on safe subjects—Santa Fe subcultures, Whole Foods' prices, his kids' college prospects. He told her what his mom was doing (repartnered, making pottery in Tucson) and asked about her mother and sister, who were running a farm stand together in Maine.

Small talk was fine, but Byron wasn't a huge fan of secrets. The longer you kept something hidden, the more it festered inside you. As they merged onto a highway that had been blasted through granite, rising high and grooved on both sides, he said, "It's been tough since Christa and I separated. I don't love living on my own."

"Oh." She looked straight ahead, not at him, and he could tell she was embarrassed. "I'm sorry... Should I be sorry? I never met Christa, but you seemed great together."

He laughed again, feeling tickled by her candor. "We were great, and then I guess we were less great. We're still friendly." Then it was his turn to feel awkward, because that was a slight exaggeration, and he asked, "How about you? Any husbands you didn't bother to tell me about? Torrid affairs? Close calls?"

Oh no—she wasn't smiling. Maybe his tone had been too flirtatious. One of Christa's perennial grievances was that he "enjoyed talking to women a little too much," as she put it. Especially prickly women, ones whose boundaries posed a bit of a challenge—he liked earning their trust and finding out what made them tick.

He and Sonia had never talked about the fact that their moms had raised them alone, but he knew it made a difference. While some of their classmates floundered through the new tasks of adulthood, neither of them could remember a time when they *didn't* know how to do laundry or boil an egg. Once, at a *Dove-Cat* meeting, Auraleigh had quoted some stat connecting children's "broken homes" to low achievement, and Byron's eyes had met Sonia's across the table. *People can underestimate us all they want*, they said silently to each other. *They'll see.*

"Sorry," he said. "I swear I didn't mean that to be a probing question."

"No, it's okay." She looked at him, finally. "There've been... things, but nothing serious. Sometimes I think I just can't feel as intensely now as I did back in college."

Whom had she felt things for back then? Byron was curious but said only, "I know what you mean."

Exit after exit, cars with out-of-state plates peeled off—leaf peepers headed for Quechee, Woodstock, Brandon, Middlebury. When Byron fiddled with the GPS as they left the interstate, Sonia reassured him: "I remember the way."

"I keep forgetting you grew up here." She'd never seemed remotely like a Vermonter to him.

"Not really. I was eleven when we moved." She cleared her throat. "I haven't been back since my mom moved away in the late nineties, but even by that time, it had changed. More flatlanders, fewer old-timers. It used to be sort of impenetrable to outsiders."

He followed Sonia's directions through Stowe, a blur of resort traffic on a narrow street dotted with steeples and ice cream shops. "Auraleigh still thinks a lot about Jennet," she said as they emerged into the countryside again. "About what happened that night."

It was the first time today either of them had spoken Jennet's name. "I figured from the invitation." Byron took a deep breath and sighed. "I have to tell you, I never liked how Auraleigh would carry on, saying it was her fault. Making it all about her, when it was an accident."

Or suicide. But he didn't like to mention that possibility, even after all these years. Back in 1989, people were only starting to understand that depression was an illness rather than a character flaw, and Jennet had discussed her struggle mainly in hints and riddles.

"Accidents can be hard to accept," Sonia said.

Trees were closing in again on both sides of the two-lane highway. Byron kept his gaze on the road. There was a time when he'd found it hard to accept accidents, too—when he raged and grieved and struggled with the facts of Jennet's death—but you couldn't spend your whole life fighting reality. He had buried those turbulent emotions, and he wasn't used to having them dug up.

"It's true what you said before," he said after a moment, "about our feelings back then. I mean, nothing can compare to how I feel about my kids, so I'm leaving that out of the equation. But how I felt about Jennet was intense, all right."

Voluntary Memory
August 1986 (freshman year)

BYRON

Byron's second day on campus, Dunstan held an assembly for incoming freshmen in the "Chapel," a redbrick church with a towering white steeple. Inside, all was gloom and echoes, slanting roofs and stained-glass windows that corralled the summer sun into scenes of Jesus doing solemn things Byron couldn't identify. He'd been in a church maybe four times in his life.

People poured past him and seated themselves in the pews—boys in white T-shirts speaking in lazy rumbles; girls with demure little voices and Princess Di hair. For all the carefully curated diversity promised by the brochures, this place was White Prepland.

The sixth-top-rated small liberal arts college in the country, Dunstan was known as the school where fabled outsider prose poet Typhon Pith spent three years before dropping out, and to which he returned, in the seventies, for a victory lap of guest lectures. When Byron had typed up the Dunstan application at his mom's kitchen table, he'd imagined a school full of rugged oddball geniuses. So far the closest to someone like that he'd met was a fellow freshman named Paul Bretton who claimed to be a Pith fan but dressed like a middle manager.

He prayed he hadn't made a big mistake as he stood in the aisle, the pews filling around him. Violins tuned up; a flute gave a wild bray. Christ floated above the waves, hands spread.

A small, clear voice spoke behind him. "You know, they won't throw you out if you don't believe in any of that."

It was a girl in a full blue skirt, with a pale oval face and pink lips. Over her shoulder she hauled a cello case that was nearly her size.

Byron said, "I'm not going to have to recite the Lord's Prayer or be expelled?"

"These days, heathenism isn't worth expulsion." She pushed her glasses up her nose. "We have been known to stone people in Vermont, though. There's that."

Someone on the podium fiddled with the mics. The musicians had stopped tuning, and the students began to quiet by degrees.

"Yeah?" Byron asked, trying to sound flippant. He couldn't let her know this place and its rituals spooked him.

"Haven't you read 'The Lottery'?" At last, the ghost of a smile. "I have to go." A head tilt toward the orchestra. "They're waiting. Don't worry, a couple speeches and it'll be over."

She lugged her cello down the aisle, leaving Byron to scramble for a seat.

He found her again four days later, at breakfast in the dining commons. She was lifting the steel bell to pour milk on her cornflakes, light glinting on her round glasses. Byron's tray was embarrassingly laden with omelet, bacon, hash browns.

"I *have* read 'The Lottery,'" Byron said without preamble. He'd looked up the story in the library the day they met, immediately remembered that he'd read it in eighth grade, and read it again.

"So you know about small towns," the girl said, picking up

her cup of Lipton tea. And then, grandly, "Shall we breakfast on the terrace?"

To reach the terrace, they had to barge through doors posted with warnings about taking trays outdoors. His new friend exchanged a glance with a worker who was rinsing down plates, and they exited without incident.

"I work here," she explained as they sat at a picnic table, facing a sweep of oaks and yellow-pocked maples that stretched uphill to the horizon.

Now, at last, came the dreaded small talk. At home, Byron could always talk to girls, but Dunstan had made him timid.

His new friend wasn't much for small talk, either. Asked her name, she said, "I'm Jennifer, technically, but there's a surplus of those, so I go by Jennet. It's an archaic nickname for Jane, but it'll do."

"There's no surplus of my name," Byron said. He revealed his name, and they both laughed, and the gold-turning maples shivered, and he thought, *Maybe this is it, how it feels to meet the person you're going to spend your whole adult life with.*

5

SONIA

The road narrowed and twisted, the land rising and falling with dizzying speed. Long ago, Sonia had ridden this route twice daily on the school bus. Though she hated Lamoille County, its chaotic topography suited her—a burrow, a warren, a network of hiding places under the dense cover of maple and spruce and white pine.

Byron steered them through the county seat, along the river. Some of the houses were well-kept Colonials with decks and rock gardens and neat signs declaring them the residence of "The Welch's" or "The Dodges." Others were mossy teardowns with front yards full of vehicles on blocks.

"I just wish I knew what Auraleigh was planning," Byron said. "A reunion is a nice idea, but there's always another reason with her."

Sonia recalled how his voice got deeper and grittier when he was uncomfortable. She gazed out at the houses. Nice families and getting-by families, newcomers and fifth- or sixth-generation Vermonters—subtle distinctions that mattered to a degree you couldn't imagine if you hadn't lived here. "It is her past, too," she said.

"I know, I just don't want her to own it. Or try to rewrite it."

Sonia stiffened at the use of that word—*rewrite*. Hayworth had once told her it was dangerous to try to *rewrite* the past. But Byron hadn't given any indication he knew about sog, hadn't questioned the phrase "elixir of the pines" in the invitation.

She looked him in the eye and tried to smile, to set him at ease. He still had the wide stride, the subtle cowboy elegance that made people step out of his way. His hair was thick and scruffy, the gray staging a slow takeover. She'd had a crush on him freshman year, but as soon as she saw him with Jennet, all that changed. They so clearly belonged together that she'd stopped looking at him that way. Well, mostly.

Outside the car window, the world was green, mud brown, green, gray, green again. Impossible quantities of green. All of it draped in soggy foliage—scarlet maples and grapevines, lemony oaks—that made even the cinder-blocked cars appear to have been placed there by design.

As the road slid them down into Dunstan, a slot in a steep ravine, wooded hills rose on both sides, enclosing the town and enfolding the sidewalks in shadow. There were hardly any pedestrians, but one drew her eye—a tall, rangy man in a buffalo plaid, something jagged and middle-aged in his gait. When they passed him, she caught a glimpse of dark hair.

What if that were Hayworth—still here? He was a native Vermonter, after all, though from a high-tax-bracket suburb of Burlington.

She craned to look, but the man was already a block away, and if she didn't pay attention, she would miss the town flashing by.

When Sonia moved to Dunstan with her mother and sister in 1979, the corner pharmacy still sold ice cream cones for a dime. People picked up their letters at the post office. The winters were long, brutal, and exquisite, with snowbanks arching over the sidewalks and holding pedestrians in a motherly embrace.

Today, the town looked a little ragged. Someone had stenciled an anarchy symbol on the cold spring in its venerable concrete enclosure. The Victorians along Main Street had weedy yards and makeshift curtains—student rentals. Neon signs touted scratch tickets in the windows of the convenience store at the turnoff to Route 60-C.

From the town line, it took ten seconds to reach the single crosswalk at the intersection of Main and Railroad. Ahead was the supermarket, now a Price Chopper. To the right—was that Café Polaire, after all these years?

"It's Café Something, anyway," Sonia said as Byron turned left onto Railroad Street, where maples shaded what had once been gracious single-family homes. "There's a sign."

"Can't have a college town without a café."

Railroad Street stretched three blocks from Main to the Lamoille River, where a bridge took you to the dingy apartment complex where Sonia had lived for most of her adolescence. She'd walked that route the night Jennet died, smelling lilacs in the dark, fleeing home to review for her last final because Auraleigh had threatened to turn the townhouse into Party Central.

And now Auraleigh lived on this street, in a three-story gingerbread Victorian she claimed to have bought for a song, with a turret and a recent paint job of peach, saffron, and violet.

The B and B's wide driveway held a shabby whitish van, a shiny black Legacy, and a nondescript Civic. They unloaded their bags from the Forester and crossed the front lawn—bumpy, as if cropped with a push mower, though the flower beds looked tended. *Come in, ring bell*, read a hand-lettered sign at the top of the porch steps.

Inside, the wallpaper was vintage seventies, purple vortexes in the mudroom and giant sunflowers in the foyer. To the right, an archway opened into a parlor with a marble fireplace and woodstove; to the left, an oak staircase with a majestic newel post rose into shadow. It was a fine-boned house, but the furniture had a Goodwill drabness and the scuffed floorboards creaked.

Byron rang the bell on the front desk. "Hope she's around, because—"

Whatever he was about to say was drowned out by the thudding of small, determined feet as Auraleigh shot into the parlor. She covered the distance like a cat and caught Byron in a hug—a tight one, to judge by the flexed sinews of her arms.

Then she released him and stared into his face and said, "Fuck, fuck, fuck."

"Back atcha," Byron said, smiling goofily.

Auraleigh darted to Sonia next and cinched her in that same embrace. Sonia's lids fluttered at the grainy stench of tobacco, and she remembered how that smell—awful, yet so grown-up—used to permeate their townhouse.

"Oh, fuck." Auraleigh pulled back and looked at Sonia. She seemed to be silently asking a question, but said only, "You actually came."

Auraleigh wore a giant fleece with a faux-Navajo pattern and a bleached pixie cut. If you looked hard, you could still see the outlines of her twenty-year-old self: the downy-haired madcap ingenue, soft and golden as a fresh-hatched chick. But everything had shrunk and hardened, skin tightening over bones.

"Please don't smother the guests, Auraleigh," a man's dry voice said from the parlor. "I've already set the table for four."

Sonia turned to see Paul Bretton perched on the edge of a loveseat. Slim frame, tiny glasses, crisp black hair with a hint of curl and now a hint of gray. It worked on him. Youth had never suited the calm, compact presence who had guided them through so many contentious lit-mag meetings, always finding the right phrase to smooth over their public and private feuds.

"I'm so glad you're here," Sonia said. She hadn't realized how much she missed him. Face-to-face, her plan to draw on his professional contacts struck her as cold.

"I told you he'd come." Auraleigh shook her head as if someone had doubted it, though it wasn't clear whether she meant Paul or Byron.

"I *am* the closest," Paul said, standing up to offer Byron and then Sonia his hand.

As they performed the ritual greeting, the present moment seemed to waver and dissolve, the town reshaping itself effortlessly into the place it had been a quarter-century ago. Bitter espresso at Polaire, new wave on staticky New York stations, mist rising from the mountain ridge that loomed over the hilltop campus.

"Shit." Byron sounded dazed. "The gang's all here."

Auraleigh said, "Wait till you see what I have planned."

6

SONIA

After a little small talk about the quirky decor of the foyer and parlor, Byron tried to carry their bags upstairs. "Not yet!" Auraleigh cried. "Just dump everything here for now. Let's take a field trip to campus before it gets dark."

"Field trip? For what?" Byron asked.

"To remember! Isn't that what you're here for?"

Elixir of the pines. Sooner or later, Sonia hoped, they would learn what exactly Auraleigh had meant by that phrase.

They went out again and piled into the rental Forester, with Byron driving. In the back seat, Auraleigh tapped Sonia's knee. "We're going to explore the past," she said to all three of them. "We're going to *soak* ourselves in it. For the next few days, it's 1987 and 1988 and 1989 all over again."

"Reliving the eighties is my nightmare," Paul said from the front as Byron turned off Main Street.

"You hated rooming with me so much?" Auraleigh asked, pulling a face.

"You cranking the Butthole Surfers at three in the morning was the least bad part of it."

The town vanished into the valley. Sonia saw that Byron was taking the long way up the campus hill. "Oh, good," she said. "This way we can see the townhouse."

"That's the idea! So," Byron said to Auraleigh, "I hear one of your twins is here? How's she liking it?"

His tone was neutral, but Sonia felt Auraleigh tense up. "I know it looks hover-y, me moving out here. But finding the house was serendipity."

"You don't have to justify yourself," Paul said. "You and Frances are both thriving."

"I explained it all on Facebook," Auraleigh said, visibly relaxing again. Mentioning Frances was the way to get on her good side. "My baby's doing so much better than she was in high school. She's milking goats and rolling around in the dirt."

"I keep telling my daughter to look at more liberal arts colleges. She thinks…" Byron broke off as they approached the townhouses, clumped on a hill to their left. "Were they always this crappy-looking?"

"They've seen better days," Auraleigh said.

Sonia was gazing in the opposite direction, where a small wooded knoll fell to a glitter of water. "Remember that one time we had a snowball fight? And how Jennet dared us to walk out on that frozen pond?"

"Sure," Paul said. "We were always up late editing the magazine, and we'd get so antsy we'd have stupid arguments until Auraleigh made us all go outside."

Sonia remembered the arguments—it was the boys having them, mostly, not serious disagreements but silly debates about politics or philosophy or whether Pynchon or Nabokov was superior. Eventually, Auraleigh would say something like "You're making my head hurt. Fresh air time!"

Sonia could almost hear the round yellow lamps of the townhouse complex making tiny *tings* as snowflakes hit them, as they floundered through the drifts, the only people outdoors under a soupy sky.

Now, in the Forester, Auraleigh said, "*I* was the one who dared you all to walk out on the ice that one time."

"No, I think Sonia's right," Byron said. "It was Jennet."

"I don't remember walking on the pond," Paul said. "Just you bombarding me with snowballs, Byron. Your aim was way too good."

Imagination fills in the details that memory leaves blank. How they sank in the untouched snow to their thighs. How they passed the knoll, furred and formless under the snow.

"Come to the dark side!" Byron had bellowed, hurling snowballs at them. "Resistance is futile!"

Sonia was sure Jennet had been the first to walk out onto the untracked whiteness of the pond, not pausing to test the ice, slipping and sliding with each step. The air must have been a scythe in Sonia's lungs, painful and purifying, as she squinted through the flakes at Jennet. Maybe Auraleigh shouted, "It's fine!"—showing off—and slipped and fell on her ass. Maybe Paul lit a cigarette and asked Sonia, "Which one of us is going to rescue them?" Maybe Byron skidded down the bank and stamped to test the surface.

Definitely, Jennet flopped on her back and made a snow angel.

Sonia remembered approaching Jennet with careful steps, while Auraleigh cackled wildly at Byron: "It's not gonna break. Big, strong man. Oh my God, your face!"

When she was a kid, Sonia told them, the winters here were even worse. And Jennet said something like this: "Sonia and I are basically Wordsworth poems. Little lost girl haunting the snow-swept woods, apple of my eye. It's amazing we didn't die young like Lucy Black."

Lucy Gray, actually. They'd both taken Romanticism last semester. *A slumber did my spirit seal...*

Under the snow, the ice was gritty and offered good traction.

Jennet pulled Sonia into the pond's center where they spun together, playing ring-around-the-rosy on the wind-swept ice, laughing madly.

Then Jennet lay down again and said, "Look up," and they looked up into the whirling gray. The solar wind, the blackness of space. Sonia felt the ice steady under her back, and beyond it the earth. She felt her blood pumping ruthlessly through her veins.

Lucy died, of course.

No motion has she now, no force;
She neither hears nor sees;
Rolled round in earth's diurnal course,
With rocks, and stones, and trees.

The snow kept falling as if another muddy spring might never come.

But spring after spring had come, and now here they were in the visitor parking lot, still debating the details of that snowy night as they left the Forester.

"Was Jennet that much of a daredevil?" Auraleigh asked. "I didn't think she was."

"She had a reckless streak," Byron said.

"Flights of fancy," Paul offered.

The sky was enormous up here, framed by the maternal mountain ridge that dominated the horizon. As they strolled onto campus via the science complex, Byron and Auraleigh returned to comparing notes on college admissions and the ups and downs of teenagers. Paul, who was married to an older man, a Columbia professor, with no children, offered an occasional comment.

Sonia said nothing. This was her first glimpse in decades of the central quad: a mix of classic brick and brutalist concrete with lecture halls, library, dorms, dining commons, green playing fields in the background. A boulder marked the center, spray-painted eye-searing pink with a mauve slogan about "ending identity erasure." Painting it was an annual ritual, she recalled, and sometimes an act of spontaneous protest or vandalism.

Byron was telling Auraleigh about the demise of his marriage: "I see the kids every week, and we'll have joint custody. While I'm here, I'm going to plan a spring break for the three of us."

"You sold your company for oodles of money, didn't you? Cash out, baby, while you can." Auraleigh glanced at a couple of students who were engrossed in their phones, patting Byron's arm. "Treasure every moment, Byron. When they leave the nest, there's nothing left."

Then somehow they were both making guilty faces in Sonia's direction. She swallowed. Why her? Why not Paul? But no, people always found a childless woman a sadder spectacle than a childless man.

"My students give me enough to deal with, year after year," she said, skirting a lie. "Believe me."

It wasn't that she'd never thought about or wanted kids. She'd simply chosen not to repeat her mother's mistakes. Without a father who would always be there—who *wanted* to be there, the way Byron clearly was for his kids—what was the point?

Auraleigh was back to observing the Dunstan students surrounding them. She frowned at girls in microskirts and black leggings and glared at a boy who sat on a concrete parapet shoving a Pop-Tart in his mouth. "Do they ever look up from those phones? I can't help it, they seem so entitled."

"It does rankle," Paul said. "Here they are where we were, doing what we did, feeling as if they invented it all. As if it were made for them."

They headed toward the dining commons. "I hope they don't think they're too cool for Halloween," Auraleigh said. "Remember the year we got dressed up in costumes and then just sat and drank in the townhouse instead of going to a party?"

"You were a sexy punk nun," Byron said. "I was Ernest Hemingway."

"Jennet was the 'Where's the beef?' lady. Sonia and Paul were nothing, because they're no fun."

"I was Death!" Sonia protested as they passed the sunken dining hall and descended concrete stairs into the basement rathskeller. "I had white makeup and black clothes."

"Some costume—you *always* wore black!"

The stale tang of fried food and beer had sunk into the walls of the rathskeller. The ashtrays were long gone, and the eight-bit arcade games had been swapped out for nostalgic imitations of eight-bit arcade games.

Auraleigh ordered giant lattes for everyone. "On me."

"Nonsense." Paul flashed his Amex artlessly, like someone's visiting dad.

"Fine—feel free to treat me, Mr. Big Spender."

Their whole time as roommates, Auraleigh had never let Sonia pay for anything, making sure the townhouse was stocked with groceries on her own dime. She bought fresh avocadoes, kept flowers on the table, gave Sonia thoughtful trinkets and gift certificates to Benetton for her birthday.

When Sonia pointed out that she wasn't actually *poor*, Auraleigh would insist "Your money's no good here." She was loud and bossy, but she also liked to shower people with gifts, to be responsible for their happiness.

"I fought with Frances, you know," Auraleigh said now, steering them out onto the terrace where she could smoke. "I told her anywhere *but* Dunstan. She applied on the sly."

"Why not here?" Paul asked.

"Are you kidding? The vibes, Paul? I kept imagining Jennet's parents and how they must have thought she'd be safer here because it was close to home."

"I don't think Jennet's parents were that protective," Sonia said. "They didn't even expect her to go to college. She filled out the application for an in-state scholarship herself."

"A parent is a parent."

Sonia rested her elbows on the parapet and watched a sea of golden maples shift in the breeze. More students passed below—hundred-dollar backpacks, straightened teeth. Neither she nor Jennet was "poor," exactly, but they hadn't fit in here, either.

"Haven't you moved on to vaping?" Byron asked Auraleigh. "All the cool kids are doing it."

"You may have noticed, I'm not cool. Until recently, I was a desperate housewife of Orange County."

"Don't be silly," Paul said. "You were sneaking into the Viper Room at what, age ten?"

"Oh, I *was* cool. In 1979, I was the coolest jailbait in the tightest jeans and the flattest Capezios in the Valley." Auraleigh paused to exhale smoke at two girls in peasant tops. They shot her steely glances.

Paul said, "Auraleigh, I'm starting to suspect this is a non-smoking campus."

"They can take it, these little princesses. They can take it." But she stubbed out her cigarette. "I'm bored. Let's go somewhere else. Let's go to the *Dove-Cat* room."

Sonia glanced at Byron—couldn't help it. But if the thought of seeing that particular place bothered him, he gave no sign.

As they crossed to the far northern corner of the quad, Auraleigh jabbed her phone. "Walking on Sunshine" by Katrina and the Waves burst into the open air like a prisoner released from a cell.

"*What* is that?" Paul asked.

"It's the eighties, remember?" Auraleigh swung her hips.

"If there's one song I'd keep *off* the soundtrack of an eighties-nostalgia piece…"

"Don't listen to him." Auraleigh grabbed Sonia's hand and pulled her along, bopping like a zany apprentice fashion designer in a rom-com. "Dance, you buzzkills! Amuse me! It's your turn to embarrass yourselves."

Sonia was mortified. But the beat was infectious, and it wasn't fair to let Auraleigh make a fool of herself alone, so she did start to—well, not dance but stride to the song's rhythm.

Paul was comically aghast. Byron hummed, then sang softly along in a good baritone. They proceeded across the quad, students dodging out of their way. Sonia imagined her younger self among them, disgusted by the antics of her elders: *you don't do that*.

Katrina was just launching into the final chorus, and they were climbing the steps of Byers Hall, when Auraleigh stopped the music, the noise replaced by echoing murmurs from inside the building.

"Thank you," Paul said.

But Auraleigh hadn't done it for him. She was standing stock-still. Sonia followed her gaze and saw a young woman coming down the steps, not making eye contact with them. She wore an oversize shawl that looked hand knitted, her hair a golden nimbus.

Auraleigh stared at her, eyes almost pleading. The girl didn't return her silent appeal, vanishing into a knot of other students.

"Wasn't that Frances?" Paul asked.

Auraleigh came alive again. "Oh, look, it's open!" She darted inside and across the foyer to the door of the *Dove-Cat* room. "It's exactly the same!"

Sonia paused on the threshold, bracing herself, then slowly entered the room.

Sure enough, it still had the built-in bookshelves and a massive oak board table with a throne-like chair at one end. Paul ran his hand possessively over the wooden laurel wreaths that crowned it. "I've missed this."

They'd interrupted two students who sat camped at the other

end of the table, surrounded by laptops and printouts. "Don't mind us," Auraleigh said. "We're just revisiting our pasts."

The students drew wordlessly into themselves with the ungainliness of youth. Behind them was the red leather couch—faded to dull rose, scored and scuffed. Still there.

Sonia's cheeks stung. The couch made her think of May: finishing finals, being hopped-up on all-nighters and the closeness of vacation, doing things you shouldn't.

She saw that Byron was poking through the shelves of hardbound issues. If he noticed the couch, he gave no sign.

"Jennet had an interesting theory," Paul said to Auraleigh, running a fingertip over a picture frame. "She told me you only joined the *Dove-Cat* because you were in love with me."

"Nah, I was never dumb enough to crush on you. That was every *other* girl at the magazine. I could just tell you'd have cultural capital someday, so I held on tight."

Paul feigned offense. "I feel used." He examined the plaques on the wall. "They've hung these—good on them. We just stacked them in the cabinets to gather dust with the old manuscripts and half-empty vodka bottles."

As Sonia stepped toward him, a red flash blinded her—sunlight streaming through the stained-glass window. For an instant she was disoriented, the smell and feel of the room taking her back. Looking at the table, she half expected to see them and the rest of the editorial board.

Byron drew one of the bound volumes from the bookshelf and splayed it open. "Look. This is her."

They gathered around him. It was the December 1987 issue, an elegant woodprint of a fat little nuclear missile with the headline Do You Still Love the Bomb? on the cover.

"Jennet was good," Sonia said, memory rising like a taste in her mouth. She knew the story the image accompanied all too well. "We used to talk about her going to CalArts for grad school."

Or she had, anyway, pushing Jennet to apply, but Jennet wanted to stick around, work at Polaire, save money. Only later did it occur to Sonia that she might have been afraid to start a new life across the country by herself. Unlike Sonia, she had never lived outside Vermont.

"Isn't that the issue with the weird story that wasn't a story?" Auraleigh asked. "The anonymous one?"

Sonia bit her lip, waiting for Auraleigh to repeat what she'd discovered back in 1988—that the author of the story was a boy who claimed to have a time travel drug. Surely she hadn't forgotten telling Sonia that.

They were standing almost shoulder to shoulder, gazing down at the issue as Byron flipped pages. "I had some issues with that story," he said. "I thought the author was trolling us. Made for a great cover image, though."

"You and Paul practically fought about it—he was its biggest fan." Auraleigh gave Paul a nudge. "You wrote it yourself, right?"

Had Auraleigh forgotten?

Paul smiled cryptically. "As you said, the author was anonymous."

Voluntary Memory
November 1987 (sophomore year)

SONIA

Sun flooded through the red Dunstan crest in the window and landed on Paul's shoulder. He sat at the head of the table, carved laurel wreaths above him, telling them there was one last story they needed to consider, a story that had gotten lost at the bottom of the submission box.

He flattened a page on the table and said, "It's so short, I might as well read it to you. It's called 'The Warning.'"

Twelve or fifteen of them sat around the table, Sonia opposite Jennet, whose braid poked over her shoulder like a small, snouted familiar. They'd laid out the October issue in the townhouse together, but Sonia was still shy with Jennet, because their first meeting had embarrassed her.

Last spring, Sonia and Byron had shared a literary theory seminar that often spilled out into lively one-on-one discussions in the dining commons. One evening, he invited Sonia back to his room, where she pretended to listen to his explanation of Baudrillard's society of the spectacle while imagining how it would feel to kiss him. Then, all of a sudden, a pair of hands gripped the window frame. A girl with a long flaxen braid straddled the sill, her skinny legs in black tights, and hopped down onto the floor. She looked up at Sonia like a solemn child in a Victorian painting. "Hello. I'm the girlfriend."

She didn't say this in a pointed or accusatory way, more amused, as if Sonia's friendship with Byron didn't concern her at all. Maybe she assumed Sonia was a bore—the worst thing you could be around the *Dove-Cat* table.

Paul began reading the story: "'Something is rotten in the state of Dunstan. Let this cliché be my warning to anyone who tries to talk the problem out of existence.'"

His voice was measured and even, with light ripples of tension in the right places. He would never be considered a bore, despite his conventional pressed oxford shirt and tiny, round glasses. "'I am part of that problem, but so are all of you. So drink up and listen.'"

Around this point, Auraleigh grabbed a bottle of Absolut from a cabinet and held it aloft. The rest of the editorial board cheered. Sonia blushed with pleasure, still hardly believing someone so well-liked was her housemate. And Paul—she had seen his dirty clothes in the hamper. They were like a celebrity couple, and she was their intimate.

"'Our generation's malady is retrophilia. We can't live our lives without remembering them as they happen. We're nostalgic before we've even done anything with our lives.'"

The Absolut was being passed around. Jennet didn't take a swig, but Sonia did—then wondered if Jennet might judge her for it.

Was this meeting something she would remember fondly someday? Was she already feeling nostalgic for it, the way the story said, rather than just enjoying it?

Paul waved the bottle away when it came to him. "'We nourish and coddle our memories till they fill crates and closets and attics. We cling to our albums of puffy stickers and our home movies and our childhood coin collections and our cassette tapes. We even feel nostalgic for times we never knew. We wear peplums and fedoras and crew cuts. We use cigarette holders. We quote sixties TV shows. We cannibalize other people's memories. We envy the baby boomers their stories of scooting under desks and scanning the skies from pine-paneled family dens. At least they had a life to protect. At least they had a world of their own.'"

Auraleigh rolled her eyes so far back she appeared demonically possessed. Byron frowned at her. But Jennet sat very still— too still, Sonia thought. As if she were curious to see how they all reacted.

"'I wanted to escape from all this suffocating nostalgia, this obsession with the past, so one day I found my way to the future. I know what you're thinking. But yes. In a tumbledown shack that smelled of rotting leaves, echoing with the sound of roaring waters, I crawled into my future and explored it, and it was just like the song says—so bright I had to wear shades.

"'It took a while getting used to. The future is different in a million mirror-shard ways. But after some time there, what did I learn? In the future, we'll still be retrophiliacs. We'll be obsessed with the past that is now our present, filling our homes with eighties memorabilia. The past keeps getting longer and deeper while the future gets shorter and shallower.'"

This was starting to sound like science fiction, which Sonia secretly loved but dared to discuss only with Byron. A fan of the mind-bending novels of Philip K. Dick, he was leaning forward, eyes narrow.

"'So here's my warning: STOP. Stick your heads up and look around. I know you're fretting about World War III and whether the Russians love their children, too. But you can forget all that. It's a distraction, and soon the global order will reshuffle itself, and we'll have new terrors to worry about.

"'Friends in spirit and fellow students of Dunstan: I warn

you. We have not stopped worrying, but we do love the bomb. We can make the bomb part of an ironic time capsule, but it is still armed.'"

Sonia looked up—and straight into Jennet's eyes. Jennet raised one pale brow as if to ask *Are you a retrophiliac?*

Sonia shook her head, though she didn't know what she was saying no to. Paul finished reading: "'What's going to kill us is that we can't stop looking backward. We can't even face a future that isn't a regurgitation of the past. We're too afraid of what we might find there.'"

◆

"Your dictionary could swallow five thousand copies of your book."

Sonia lifted her head from her tiny yellow Deutsche Verlag paperback and found Jennet standing at the café table in her green work apron.

"I brought you something." Jennet pushed a mug across the table. It was topped with a mound of pale brown fluff—café au lait with chocolate whipped cream, she explained. "Hervé mixes in melted Ghirardelli."

Chocolate whipped cream was nothing Sonia would have ordered. Her mom kept sweets out of the house, and she had taught herself to love the bitterness of plain espresso. But when she took a sip, the real cream melted on her tongue. She swallowed chocolate, dark and rich, and felt her neurons light up like a switchboard.

"Thank you," she said. Was it possible Jennet didn't think she was boring after all?

Jennet said, "You're reading Nietzsche? I had a fling with him in high school." She told a story about how she couldn't sleep after reading Nietzsche because he set her brain awhirl. She'd run out of the house and down the road in her pajamas, swinging her arms to keep warm in the frigid Vermont winter. "I wanted to be like *him*—strong. Not weak."

Sonia felt herself blush with the strange pleasure of hearing Jennet open up and talk about herself for the first time. At *Dove-Cat* meetings, she spoke without stammers or false starts, like a midcentury film ingenue, but now Sonia realized that might be an act.

Jennet had a fifteen-minute break, so they went for a walk, trudging down Main Street under a red-brown sky. It was the Tuesday before Thanksgiving, and many of their classmates had already left. "This town is a sad shred of nothing without the students," Jennet said, then asked if Sonia was going home tomorrow.

"I am home."

"Me too. Unfortunately." Sonia must have looked surprised, because Jennet laughed. "Haven't you heard of the Stark brothers?"

They were associates of Scott Lemorne, often in trouble with the county sheriff. People said they smuggled drugs from Canada. "I didn't think..." Sonia said, trying not to stare. Jennet didn't belong with people like Scott; it made no sense.

"That's right, I'm one of *those* Starks." The special in-state scholarship, Jennet explained, had made Dunstan her only college option. Before Sonia could ask any more about her brothers, she said, "I thought you were from New York City, though."

"I used to be." Then, because Jennet had already been so honest, Sonia took a risk she'd never taken with anyone else at Dunstan. She told Jennet why her family had come here from the city—because her mother had fallen in love with a would-be prophet of the apocalypse who raised goats and pigs. For eight months, they lived in his house: pervasive smell of shit, no central heat.

Some people would have judged her for that. Around here, most people. But Jennet only listened and sometimes smiled in a way that was both sympathetic and ironic, as if to say *I get it*.

Sonia filled Jennet in on some of her mother's other great loves: the married professor, the peace activist who convinced her not to pay taxes, the former mental patient who wanted to close all the institutions.

"She sounds like a romantic," Jennet said. "They always like lost causes."

Later in their friendship, Jennet would share stories about her notorious older brothers in fragments, hair-raising anecdotes relayed with a devil-may-care smile. The time they dragged half a buck into the house and covered the kitchen table with blood. The time they taught her to skin a squirrel. The time one brother spilled boiling sap on her arm and it left a scar.

In this conversation, however, Jennet volunteered nothing more than she already had, so Sonia said, "I should stop dwelling on the past. I'm a retrophiliac, just like in 'The Warning.'"

Jennet only nodded, but Sonia was feeling flush with their new intimacy. "I was just wondering... You didn't by any chance write that story, did you?" It had been a week since the meeting where Paul had read it to them, and Sonia hadn't forgotten how carefully Jennet had watched them all.

After a moment, Jennet shook her head. "I hope we never find out who wrote it. I think colleges should have dark, gnarled mysteries. I always dreamed of going to one of those colleges where people talk like Dorothy Parker and wear long black opera gloves and eat chocolates in bed."

"Couldn't we do that here?"

After a discussion of where one might buy long black opera gloves, Jennet said, "I don't know why I even said Dorothy Parker. My fantasy sounds so precious, ugh. Except for the chocolate."

"I don't think it's precious." Sonia already knew she would never forget the first chocolate-whipped-cream café au lait that Jennet had brought her—a gift of concentrated energy, of friendship, of trust.

7

SONIA

"Time for a house tour," Auraleigh said when they returned to the B and B. "Dinner's in a half hour. Then we'll rest up for tonight."

"Tonight?" Byron asked.

"It's a surprise. You'll see." Her face lit up with a childlike eagerness.

There were seven guest rooms, counting the finished part of the attic: the Rose Room, the Mint Room, the Lavender Room, the Yellow Room, the Zebra Room, the Rumpus Room, and the Crow's Nest. The whole house was silent, but perhaps the other guests were out leaf peeping.

As Sonia peered from a window of the Crow's Nest, Byron leaned over her shoulder and said, "What I said in the *Dove-Cat* room about how the author of 'The Warning' was trolling us— that's just something I thought back then. But the story grew on me. I never forgot it."

Sonia turned to see him looking almost apologetically at her. "Same with me." Surely he couldn't know that Hayworth had written "The Warning," or that she knew Hayworth? Then she caught on. "You think *I* wrote it?"

Byron looked embarrassed. "It's about retrophilia, retrophiliacs, and that's the name of your movie."

"The story is probably where she got the idea for her amazing movie," Auraleigh said, behind them.

"You really didn't write it?" Byron asked. "Because the line in the movie about the boomers and their pine-paneled family dens—that's the same."

Sonia shook her head. "I stole that line from 'The Warning'—the concept, too, I guess." Wondering if Hayworth had ever heard of her movie, she said to Auraleigh, "I thought you found out who the author was, and it wasn't any of us. I swear I remember you telling me that, maybe junior year."

"God, that was so long ago. C'mon, Byron, let's go to your room."

Byron and Sonia had rooms on the second floor. After they left Byron to unpack, Auraleigh ushered Sonia into hers with a flourish. "For you, the Mint Room."

The only thing mint was the bedspread. Fir-green carpet covered a stretch of scuffed oak boards. The yellowed wallpaper offered a repeating scene of shepherds on rolling hills. Sonia dropped her suitcase and laptop bag and went to the window, which faced the front yard and street. "It's even better than your pictures. Very rustic."

"Isn't it?" Auraleigh sounded absurdly proud of the place. Sonia wondered how much you'd have to bribe her to stay in an equivalent B and B in LA.

But here she was, bustling around and pointing out finds rescued from local antique stores: twin china owls, an armchair with a pillow on the sprung seat, a brass towel rack. There was even a shelf of books about Dunstan history—"For families on college visits."

All so innocent.

All so orchestrated.

Auraleigh had tried to bring up sog back in December, and her invite had referred to "the elixir of the pines." She had to know about it. But if Auraleigh had sog, where was she getting it? Sonia couldn't imagine Hayworth had stuck around for all these years. If she asked outright, though, she might have to reveal she'd sogged with him, and it still hurt to remember the sudden, unexplained way he'd turned a cold shoulder to her.

Hayworth hadn't been the one who cooked up the sog, anyway. Scott Lemorne and Jennet's brothers were involved in that. "Do you see other alums here?" she asked. "Is there anyone still around from our year?"

"God, no. Everybody I knew got out as fast as they could."

"No one stuck around? Or came back?"

Auraleigh giggled. "When *I* came back here, you called me crazy."

"I didn't!" Sonia flopped down on the bed. "Okay, maybe I had doubts. But now I'm kind of bowled over by everything you've done. Starting a business from scratch, renovating, all that carpentry and laying tiles."

"I found this local kid who's an amazing handyman. And it's okay. I'm used to being underestimated."

"I don't underestimate you." Sonia cleared her throat. Remembering Auraleigh passing around the bottle of Absolut at the *Dove-Cat* meeting—always the organizer, the life of the party—she said, "I'm glad we went to campus. Seeing that room after all these years, so much the same...it was good."

"Right? I guess we're all retrophiles, just like the story said. Now, bathroom's down the hall. Continental breakfast downstairs in the kitchen, six to ten," Auraleigh announced from the doorway. "Whatever you do, don't go down the street for a latte. The coffee there's shite and it's teeming with students. I've got an espresso machine here, imported from Rome."

And with that, she was gone.

BYRON

Stuffy and windowless, the dining room had a bare, paint-spattered table and peeling yellow paper on the walls. No pictures, only a corkboard draped with stained cheesecloth.

"How are the rooms working?" Auraleigh asked, ladling turmeric-scented stew into four bowls.

They were drinking wine at the table, a sauvignon blanc that Byron could tell hadn't been purchased locally.

"Great. It's so quiet." He traded a glance with Sonia; like him, she probably hadn't seen or heard another guest since their arrival.

"There are only two guests other than you this week," Auraleigh said, answering the implied question. "Anyway, I only take quiet people, no screaming kids if I can help it. Right, Paul?"

"Last night was quiet as a tomb," Paul said as he portioned out the silverware. "Granted, I didn't get in till after midnight. Took the train to Albany, then the Northway."

"Stop working!" Auraleigh shooed him into a chair. "You're a guest. In the winter, I have a bunch of regulars, people I know from LA on ski vacay. It's been a bitch getting this place off the ground, but I love every minute." She swept out an arm to encompass the room, which seemed untouched by renovation. "All DIY, baby." She tugged out an unmatched chair for herself. "Dig in! Don't be polite. Also, start thinking about your costumes. I don't have my decorations up yet, but this house is *the* place to celebrate spooky season."

"I almost forgot it was Halloween," Byron said.

Paul looked comically horrified. "There will be no costumes. We're adults."

"Shut up!" Auraleigh flicked her napkin at him. "You thought I chose the dates randomly? No one's too old for Halloween."

They dug into a stew full of tender fish and sweet corn, proof that Auraleigh could still whip up a fine meal with minimal fuss. Byron hadn't eaten since 5:00 a.m. in California, and he was so focused on the food that he couldn't help being a little annoyed when Paul got up to give a toast.

With his glass aloft, Paul said, "Some people are indelible. I still think of Jennet when I'm at parties in the city, meeting people who are renowned for sharing their thoughts in books or films or, yes, even tweets. So many people try desperately to be interesting, but Jennet didn't strive to be anything. She simply was."

"Amen to that," Auraleigh said, and they clinked glasses.

It was a good tribute, Byron thought, but there were sides of Jennet that Paul must not have seen. He remembered watching her carefully reapply her coral lipstick before leaving his dorm room, examining her face from different angles, ignoring him when he said she looked perfect. It had felt good to see the *Dove-Cat* room and campus, to get the Midnight Brunch Club back together, but he had plenty of memories of Jennet that he preferred to keep private.

As he returned his attention to the stew, Auraleigh said, "Do you think Jennet could've been famous, Paul?"

"Celebrity is overrated."

"That's easy for you to say." That came from Sonia. Byron looked up in surprise—she wasn't normally so tart.

"Good lord, I'm nowhere near famous. Not like you with your Hollywood connections."

Sonia was blushing, so Byron came to her rescue. He supposed she wasn't comfortable being seen as a shallow Hollywood type. "Don't be coy, Paul. Your byline's everywhere."

"I'm a glorified freelancer. You're the one who gets written *about*."

"It was one little article." Now it was his turn to be embarrassed. "I'm no Bill Gates. I don't innovate or disrupt or even create anything."

"But you make a lot of money doing whatever it is you actually do," Paul said, his tone sharper.

Was he implying that Byron was some insufferable tech bro? Byron opened his mouth to ask just that, but then he recalled how Paul used to troll him at their midnight brunches, luring him into debates he couldn't win.

Jennet said once that Paul's second-greatest vice was his fondness for provoking people with hotter tempers than his. When Byron had asked what she thought Paul's greatest vice was, then, she'd said, "Secrecy. He hides things, and you hate that, which is why you don't always get along."

Refusing to take the bait, Byron shifted gears. "Back when I met Jennet, freshman year, I was a poet. Remember? That's why I joined the *Dove-Cat*."

"You were a good poet," Sonia said.

"Jennet and I used to talk about being professors together at some little college. We'd live in a big Victorian full of books and cats and mediocre art created by our friends, and she'd illustrate my books and show her work at galleries. I assumed we'd be married, but she said no, we'd both want our freedom. We might have a kid or two, though—Felix and Lucretia." He hadn't thought of their future fantasies in years—it was strange how easily they came back. He blinked hard as heat rose behind his eyes. "Her choices. It was all planned out."

"I can see it," Paul said, earnest now. "I can see it happening exactly like that."

They ate for a few minutes in silence, and then Auraleigh put down her spoon and said, "I'm sure you're all still thinking I'm a little nuts, calling you here for a trip down memory lane."

"Nuts?" Paul said. "You?"

"You're on notice, sweetheart." Auraleigh stood, clutching her glass. "I know it's kind of a damper on the evening, but we aren't here just to reminisce randomly. We have a goal."

She stepped over to the corkboard and whipped off the cloth, revealing an assemblage of photos, brittle newspaper clippings, and scraps of paper printed with strident block letters. Byron squinted to read a few: *I call Byron, approx. 11 p.m. I call Paul, approx. 11:15 p.m. We leave Polaire, 12 a.m.*

"What the hell?" he asked.

Paul seemed less concerned. "Edgar makes me watch crime dramas. That's an evidence board."

Auraleigh said, "I've spent a lot of time trying to reconstruct what happened on the night of May twenty-second, 1989."

Byron was still staring at the board, zeroing in on a murky, greenish photo. He'd snapped that in his dorm room—Jennet with her long hair pinned back by a crooked barrette, looking away from the camera, not quite smiling.

Halfway out of his seat, he jabbed a finger at it. "That's my only photo of her! She hated having her picture taken. How'd you even get it?"

Auraleigh recoiled—was he yelling? "From the memorial page you put up in the nineties."

"Shit." Byron slumped down and leaned forward on his elbows, rubbing his eyes. "Forgot all about that."

He kept the original of that picture in a safe place, because when he tried to remember Jennet, he couldn't always see her clearly. A smudge of blond hair, light reflecting off her glasses, and her voice—oh yes, he remembered her voice, the one that occasionally said *Well, Byron* inside his head like a broken record. But the rest of her was harder to reconstruct. A reproachful tilt of the head, a soft trill of laughter, the warm press of a hand. Was she locked inside his brain on a memory card he couldn't access, he sometimes wondered? And if he could forget her so easily, had he really loved her?

He needed that photo. He didn't like sharing it. He said in a low voice, "I wish you hadn't used that for…whatever-this-is."

Paul sipped his wine. "That's a good point—what's going on, Auraleigh? Detective cosplay?"

She tapped the edge of the corkboard, and in a stiff, theatrical voice said, "This could be our last chance to find out what really happened on May twenty-second, 1989. Or May twenty-third, if you prefer—it was after midnight. The more we remember, the closer we get."

Closer to what? Byron glanced at Sonia, who looked as troubled as he felt. Paul, by contrast, was gazing at Auraleigh like an eager pupil at his favorite teacher.

"At ten-thirty in the evening," Auraleigh continued, "I walked down from campus to Polaire, where Jennet and I decided to hike to the falls. I called Byron and Paul to see if either of you wanted to come, but neither of you answered. I left messages." Her head swiveled between them, intent as a vulture. "Correct?"

"I remember something half-coherent on our machine," Paul said. "I was in the library till after midnight, as I've told you a million times."

"I got mine, too." Byron felt a little dazed. "I half heard it through my sleep. I had three finals the next day."

Auraleigh turned to Sonia. "You had your own phone line in your room. I was going to call you, right before we left, but Jennet said she already had."

Sonia stared into her wineglass. "I went home that night to my mom's apartment, after Byron and I did some proofing in the *Dove-Cat* room. It was nine or ten. When I got back the next morning, I didn't have a message from Jennet. Maybe she never left one."

Proofing? Byron knew he hadn't been in the *Dove-Cat* room that night; she was probably confused on the date.

"Or maybe your answering machine was full or you accidentally erased the message," Paul said. "Or maybe you don't remember every detail because it was twenty-five years ago. Tell us where you're going with this, Auraleigh. Do you still think Jennet's death was suspicious? The sheriff and the medical examiner didn't, as I recall."

Auraleigh took a rapid swallow of wine. "I'm aware. Last year, I got hold of the police report. Her blood alcohol was high enough to make it an open-and-shut case of a college girl getting tanked and stupid in the eyes of what passes for the law here. Add in the fact that she'd seen a counselor for depression, and there you go."

There you go, indeed. Jennet would have hated this kind of talk—she was intensely private. Byron hadn't known for sure about the counselor until this second, because Jennet got vague and cryptic whenever she had to discuss something that made her uncomfortable.

It wasn't that he didn't want to know how she'd died. But every time he started wondering whether it was really an accident, he remembered something she'd said once about Sylvia Plath: *I hate how people are always going on about her suicide, like it matters why. That's her business and no one else's.*

"If they'd suspected foul play," Paul pointed out, "the prime suspect would have been you, Auraleigh. You were *there*."

"I get it." Auraleigh took another sip, looking embattled but determined. "You're thinking how tasteless I am to dredge this shit up and muddy the waters. But she was my friend, and yes, I was there, and I want to know why she died. Besides, I *saw* it."

That was the last straw. "You said you blacked out the whole—" Byron cried. But Paul spoke at the same time: "I don't see how you could—" Short-circuiting each other, they each broke off.

Auraleigh sat down, holding her glass protectively to her chest. "I got back some of the missing time when I was blacked out that night. Just a minute of it."

Byron's pulse was thudding, but he forced himself to speak evenly. "When you're blacked out, your brain doesn't make memories. So either you weren't blacked out, or you're remembering something different."

"Maybe you weren't blacked out the entire time," Paul suggested.

Auraleigh met Byron's gaze levelly. "Don't you want to know what I saw?"

Of course he did. He wanted desperately to fill in the blanks of Jennet's last moments. But Jennet would have said that death was private.

Sonia was the one who said, "Tell us."

Then there was only Auraleigh's voice: "It was just a flash, really. I'm sitting on a rock with a bottle in my hand, watching starlight in running water. There's a breeze like a Band-Aid being ripped off. Those spring frogs are singing. I hear Jennet's voice.

"It takes me a long time, or maybe just a second, but I look up. The whole sky's nothing but stars, and above the water, on the water, two pieces of the dark break free. I can't see their faces. One of them's down sort of clinging to the rock bridge, and one of them's standing—*looming*—and I hear a guy's voice say 'Watch yourself.' And that's all."

They were all silent, almost hearing the spring peepers, the rush of the falls.

"'Watch yourself' doesn't sound like what a murderer would say," Byron said. "Is that what you're suggesting, Auraleigh? That this person killed her?" If he let that ugly scenario get inside his head, he would never be free of it. "So you just suddenly recovered this memory? How do you know it's from *that* night? Forgive me for being skeptical, but I'm guessing there was no time stamp."

"Memories are powerful, but not always reliable," Paul agreed, but the way he looked at Byron was odd—borderline apologetic. "'Recovered' memories, in particular, are subject to confabulation—your brain filling in the empty spaces."

"I've read everything there is to read about memory, Paul." Auraleigh sighed, then placed both her hands flat on the table. "But there are things you can't learn in books—things no researcher has researched yet. Will you guys maybe just trust me on this? In the spirit of adventure? Just for a few hours, until I can show you?"

"Show us what?" Sonia asked. Her eyes were fixed on Auraleigh, intent.

Byron pushed his chair back and stood up. He needed to hear his children's voices before they went on to whatever surprise Auraleigh had planned. If she wanted to bring them to the riverbank to reenact Jennet's death, though, she could count him out.

"Can I help you clean up before I call my kids?" he asked.

Auraleigh had her hostess face back on. "No, be a guest. All of you. Yes, you too, Paul! But wait!"

Already at the door, Byron turned. The others had gone still, too.

"Tonight," Auraleigh said, sweeping her eyes over them. "Eleven. Meet out in the driveway, and don't bring your phones—I don't want anyone taking pictures. You don't know how to remember yet, not like I do. But you're going to learn."

· 8 ·

BYRON

Byron's shirt was damp with sweat. The dark room looked distended, full of muzzy, ominous shapes. The light in the hallway had gone out, and he heard a faint voice coming from out there, or above—humming, laughing.

He woke with a jolt and realized he'd been dreaming. His phone said five of eleven.

Maybe his first impulse on reading the invitation had been correct. On campus with the three of them, he'd been full of nostalgia-based goodwill. Now he felt uneasy about where things were going.

He rose and flicked the light switch, pulled on his jacket and wool beanie, and tucked his phone under his pillow. On second thought, he took the phone along. Auraleigh might be someone's controlling mother, but she wasn't his.

He tramped downstairs, where the parlor and foyer were lit only by bright oblongs from the porch and kitchen, and ran straight into Sonia, who was dressed up in her twilight-colored peacoat and combat boots.

"I worried you were going to sleep all night," she said.

"Nah, I wouldn't miss whatever-it-is." He tried to sound bluff and confident, game for anything. Auraleigh didn't need to know that her corkboard and recovered memory had shaken him. "Just as long as we don't end up at Dogssnout Falls in the dead of night."

Sonia looked appropriately horrified. "I hope not!"

Outside, the whitish van idled in the driveway, its headlights glaring on zinnias and late snapdragons. Auraleigh materialized from the shadows, arms crossed over her fleece against the evening chill. "If you have phones on you, give them to me now."

"We don't have phones, Auraleigh." Byron gave himself an ironic drawl. "Who gets to ride shotgun?"

Paul waved from the passenger seat.

For the first few miles into the countryside, the trip had a party atmosphere. Paul and Auraleigh bantered, arguing over whether to listen to public talk radio or fizzy Francophone pop. "Do *you* know where we're going?" Byron asked Paul. He was taking the mystery drive entirely too lightly.

Auraleigh said, "Of course he doesn't. If anyone did, it wouldn't be fun."

Byron tried in vain to think of something that might be a destination out here. They weren't headed for Jennet's death site, at least, and he was pretty sure this wasn't the way to her hometown, though he'd been there only once, for her funeral.

When the Montreal pop station spun away into static, Auraleigh switched the radio off, and a more somber mood took over. They drove godforsaken little roads that Byron didn't recognize—going north, he suspected. There were no more towns, just the occasional island of light holding a farmhouse anchored with its swing set or basketball hoop.

About twenty minutes into the drive—Byron couldn't see the dashboard clock and didn't dare check his phone—the van jogged onto rutted dirt. The bumps kept coming, and they held on. At one point, Auraleigh braked suddenly, and Byron released his breath as they watched a sharp-snouted opossum cross the road.

When the van finally jerked to a halt, he felt like he'd been through the spin cycle. By the squishy feel, they were parked on grass or mud. Auraleigh climbed out and slid the door open. "Byron, Sonia, would you pass me that stuff from the wayback?"

"That stuff" was three dingy sleeping bags. Byron gave one to Auraleigh and carried the other two himself.

Auraleigh handed hers to Paul, who said, "Campout? Will two of us have to share?" He still seemed delighted by the whole trip, though his expensive jeans and Williamsburg corduroy jacket weren't likely to survive a sit-down in the mud.

From what Byron could tell, they'd arrived in a wasteland. They stood in tall grass that had been tamped into hard humps by recent rains. Nearby loomed a three-story farmhouse with the traditional white siding, obviously abandoned, its additions and outbuildings sprawling in all directions. Byron gazed at the light reflected in the farmhouse's windows, and behind it he thought he spied a white face peering out. Someone watching them.

He blinked, and it was gone. A trick of the light.

Nonetheless he shivered under his leather jacket and sweater as they followed Auraleigh across the field, away from the farmhouse and toward a lit-up shed, smoke oozing from its chimney.

"Do *you* have any idea where the hell we are?" he asked Sonia, falling into step beside her.

"A ghost town, I think. I remember a party here in the eighties, when the main house was still inhabited." She sounded excited, or maybe just tense.

"I thought ghost towns were a southwestern thing," Byron said. His eyes were adjusting to the dark, aided by the spread of stars. There were other unlit buildings here and there, spruce and firs spiking the horizon. From the shed came a sweet, sharp scent that reminded Byron of walking in Muir Woods. It min-

gled with the smells of drying mud and rotting leaves, rich and
funereal at once.

He veered toward the shed, since it looked like the only in-
habitable building, but Auraleigh called, "We're going to the
church."

"What church?" Then he noticed a second island of light, inside
the hulk of another ruin. A steeple rose from the building. Its arched
windows were covered with cardboard and Tyvek, but twitching
radiance came through the cracks. *"That?"*

"There's a woodstove or something," Sonia said. "Auraleigh,
who else is here?"

"Is it usually deserted?" Byron turned to Paul. "Do you know
this place? Does everybody know about it but me?"

"I've never been here." Paul still didn't appear to be worried.

"Auraleigh!" Sonia hustled to catch up with her. "Who's in
the church?"

"Calm down. It's just us."

"Then, how…?"

"Auraleigh's bringing us to a pagan rite," Byron said too
loudly. "The other cult members will jump out any minute and
pull hoods over our faces."

The truth was, churches spooked him because he had so little
experience of them. There was the chapel where he'd first met
Jennet. The bland Unitarian boxes where he'd served soup and
collected signatures in his do-gooding twenties. Christa's folks'
church where they took the kids on occasional holidays. When
he entered a church, he still thought, as Jennet had trained him
to, of lotteries and stoning. And of her funeral.

But this church was deconsecrated, surely. The door hung off
its hinges. As they crossed the threshold into the pitch-dark vestibule, new smells rose to clog Byron's nostrils: weed and urine
and frozen rot. Something scuffled off to his left, and he stood
stock-still. Paul and Sonia hesitated, too.

"It's okay." Auraleigh was at the entrance to the nave, the

source of the firelight. It limned her as she turned to reassure them. "There's nobody here now but us. I asked my handyman to have the fire going when we came."

"Your handyman?" Byron walked toward her, each footstep setting off a chorus of creaks. "Do you own this shithole...uh, this place?"

The rude phrase had popped out because he didn't like feeling manipulated. Was it really so hard to explain what they were doing here?

"I own it, yeah." Auraleigh strode away from him, down the aisle. "It's a historic property, and they gave it up for a song—I guess you can see why. Don't worry, I got rid of the rats. Just watch your step. I promise you there's a reason for all of this."

If Byron had been more paranoid, he really might have thought Auraleigh had lured them there to be ritually murdered. The floorboards of the nave listed under their feet. The pews were still mostly intact, but some had tumbled through rotten patches in the floor. In a corner behind the altar, a woodstove crackled and glowed, its jerry-rigged pipe reaching into the half-light of the rafters.

Where on the property was this handyman lurking? He thought of the face he'd glimpsed in the window of the farmhouse.

"Take a pew!" Auraleigh's call echoed off the rafters. "Plenty of room! I recommend the front rows. More stable."

Byron dumped the sleeping bags on the foremost pew. Deconsecrated or not, being here felt wrong, if you believed in that sort of thing. "Do you just own the church? Or the whole godforsaken village?"

Auraleigh thudded up the steps to the platform at the far end of the nave—the altar, Byron supposed. "The whole acreage. It's not a village anymore. No minister's set foot here since the nineteen-fifties, so don't worry about sacrilege. Unroll your sleeping bags. You'll need to get inside them."

Across the aisle from him, Paul was already unrolling his bag and spreading it out. Maybe he thought he was engaging in some form of dark tourism that would make a good piece for *Rolling Stone*. "You always struck me as someone who would be an excellent proprietor of a postage stamp of countryside, Auraleigh," he said. "The Baroness of Brigadoon or the Earless of East Bumfuck."

"Shush." Auraleigh was laughing, fumbling with something below their sight line. The altar proper seemed to have been replaced by a folding table and a jumble of boxes, though the platform and wooden rail remained.

Behind Byron, Sonia asked, "Auraleigh, what are we doing?"

"Yeah. What *are* we doing?" Byron sat gingerly on the first pew. It was solid, the varnished wood sliding with surprising ease under his jeans.

What would Jennet say if she were here? *Where's your sense of adventure, Byron?* Or to Auraleigh, perhaps something cutting: *I didn't know you could be this interesting.*

As he'd told them earlier, Jennet had a reckless side. Once, she'd dropped acid just to see what the deal was, and she claimed she would try PCP if anyone offered. A moldy church wouldn't have fazed her—but then, she was so young. Byron saw it in his own kids now: every sketchy situation was weightless, an irresistible dare.

Again he tried to picture her. Firelight on pale hair. Mouth open in laughter—but no, Jennet rarely laughed. When she died, she was barely older than Eliza was now.

Auraleigh was pouring something from a mason jar into three shot glasses lined up on the altar rail. Firelight illuminated the liquid—deep dirt brown at the bottom, maple syrup–amber in the middle, gold near the surface.

"What is that?" he asked.

"It's the elixir of the pines," Sonia said. She stood motionless beside him, her eyes on Auraleigh and the shot glasses.

Auraleigh descended from the altar, solemn as a communion officiant, a shot glass in each hand. "Please keep open minds. This won't hurt you."

"You want us to *drink* that?" Byron's voice bounced off the lofty recesses of the ceiling. The stuff looked foul.

Sonia spoke softly: "It's okay."

"What do you mean? How do you know?"

"It's a local home brew. I had it once a long time ago. I was supposed to see the future."

"Wait, like in 'The Warning'?" He couldn't imagine Sonia experimenting with drugs—she was too skittish, too uptight, and he liked her that way. But she never lied, either. "You tripped? Hallucinated?"

"'The Warning' wasn't just some random piece of fantasy," Paul said, still in his casual way, as if the rotten church and the ghost town existed only to amuse his guests at some future dinner party. "I thought Jennet might have told you, Byron. Kids used to talk about a 'backwoods pine potion' that showed you visions of the future. It was our own campus legend."

"The bright, bright future," Sonia said in a singsong.

"Not the future," Auraleigh countered sharply. She held out a shot glass, and Paul took it. "Not anymore. When you're our age, it shows you the past."

Byron's breath caught, something jammed in his throat. As Auraleigh headed for him and Sonia, he could almost hear a small, self-possessed voice speak beside him: *Well, Byron.*

Always just that phrase, a dead memory repeating in his head.

The whole scene was starting to feel like a dream. Byron turned determinedly away from where he'd imagined he heard Jennet, watching as Auraleigh offered the second shot glass to Sonia.

Sonia plucked it from Auraleigh's hand. "It won't hurt you, Byron."

Her tone was so easy, so knowing. Dread inched down his spine.

But more than he feared what was in the shot glass, he wanted to access that memory card. To see Jennet in front of him, real and whole again. To have her solid, just for a few minutes. To hold her close and tell her everything she needed to know.

Auraleigh had looped back to the altar and nabbed the third glass. "The memory I told you at dinner? From that night? This is how I got it back."

She handed the last glass to Byron.

SONIA

Sonia brought the shot glass to her nose, and her head spun. The half-inch of liquid was viscous, grainy, like a suspension of soil in grease. The smell of pine pricked her nostrils.

Once you had sog, you never forgot.

"This thing has quite the nose to it." Paul already sounded a little tipsy. "Do I dare?"

Sonia had caught a whiff of the same scent outside, wafting from the shack. She could already taste it, feel her head buzzing.

Now that her suspicions about the reunion had been confirmed, did she *want* to take sog again? Asking herself that question was like running straight into a familiar dead end.

Sog was for young people who still thought they could have a bright future. In the sog, she had seen pictures that glowed with the cryptic glamour of a museum diorama arranged by godlike hands—pictures that might be a prophecy, if only you could decode them. But she had never seen her past. *Everything we've ever experienced or will experience is locked up inside us somewhere, and sog unlocks it,* Hayworth had told her.

Young people saw their future, or something that might be their future. Older ones looked backward. Back then, she'd asked him why, but now she thought it was probably just that older people had more past to see.

"I haven't done drugs since my kids were born," Byron was

saying. He sounded tentative, nervous—not like himself at all. "Not even weed. Christa and I made a pact."

"That's sweet." Auraleigh gave the word the slightest sarcastic edge. "You two have—*had*—the sweetest marriage. You look so cute in your pictures. But you don't have to answer to Christa anymore, and here's the thing—this isn't a drug. It's a one hundred percent natural substance sourced right here in the forests of northern Vermont. It won't get you high. All it does is put you to sleep for a few minutes and show you things. Exactly like your brain giving you a dream."

"A dream of the past," Paul said. "You're talking about involuntary memory."

"What?"

"In Search of Lost Time?" Paul's voice leveled off into lecturing mode. He was a beautiful speaker, the sort who could make audiences of courting hipster couples laugh softly over their negronis and sazeracs.

"Proust distinguished between voluntary memory," he said, "which is like a photograph creased and faded from handling, and involuntary memory, which is full sensory immersion in the past. Involuntary memory might be triggered by a smell or a taste—the famous madeleine cookie dunked in tea. For most people, it comes only in brief flashes, but it's a revelatory experience that can change your whole worldview."

"This is that," Auraleigh said. "The cookie-in-the-tea thing. Except it's not brief flashes—you'll see. It lasts for a while, and it's so real."

Hayworth had said the same thing about sogging backward—that it lasted longer and felt more solid than their fragmentary future visions. When Sonia asked how he knew, not being old enough to sog backward himself, he told her that was a long story.

Shadows danced on the pitched ceiling, the once-whitewashed walls, the cracked stained-glass windows. She raised her glass to the light. Faustus. Jennet. Hayworth. Any of them might be in there waiting for her. Or maybe she'd see parts of the past she didn't want to see, like the middle school nurse who'd lectured her on standing with her weight on both hips. Like her mother's boyfriends. Like long lines at the DMV.

"It sounds like a hallucinogen," Byron said. "Why aren't you doing it yourself, Auraleigh, if it's so safe and natural?"

"One of the rules is that one person has to stay awake to watch the others, like a designated driver."

"What are the other rules?" Paul's glass grazed his lips. "Don't tell anybody about Time Travel Club?"

"Time travel isn't possible." Auraleigh's voice wobbled, then strengthened as she went on: "This is sog. And these are the rules—never sog without a non-sogging person to watch you. Immediately after you drink, get in the sleeping bag and zip it. Stay that way until you float back up. Wait till someone asks you the question."

"The question?" Sonia asked. Hayworth had never mentioned any rules.

Auraleigh climbed back up the altar steps and perched on the rail, as if she felt more secure above them. "I'll abstain and watch tonight so you three can remember Jennet. Your regular memories are a copy of a copy of a copy of an out-of-focus photograph, like Paul said. This will be so much better."

"I understand *why* you want us to remember Jennet," Paul said. "But how? Can you just decide to see a particular memory?"

"No, but you can try. Focus on her. That's why I brought you to campus today—to help you target college memories."

"We could give it a shot," Paul said breezily. "For science, as it were."

Did he think this was a lark? Byron, by contrast, sounded almost frightened as he said, "We should research it first. I've never heard of a way to make your brain replay memories. We aren't...hard drives."

"You *want* to remember, don't you?" Auraleigh asked.

"That's not the point."

Sonia remembered those college nights in the townhouse, drinking margaritas and trying to playact what she hoped would be her adult life. She remembered the night Jennet died: reading proofs with Byron on the red leather couch in the *Dove-Cat* room and then turning to find him so close to her—a moment that felt wrong but exciting, too.

This is where it all begins. And the fear and guilt that came later, poisoned the life she'd hoped for.

She lifted the glass to her mouth and let the dark liquid slide down her throat.

Sog was chunkier and grainier than she recalled, sweet and pine-acrid at once. She gagged, blood rushing to her head.

"Sonia!" Byron sounded panicked, as if she'd stepped off something high.

"I'm fine, Byron, really." She tried to smile reassuringly. From the corner of her eye, she saw Paul drink down his own dose without hesitation.

Auraleigh said, "Go on. Hurry! Into the bags."

Sonia's chest burned as if she'd taken four shots of vodka. She'd forgotten how fast it came up on you. She had only enough time to lie down and zip the bag halfway before her head buzzed like a hive. Her body turned to lead, weariness dragging her down, down. The hard pew was only a distant annoyance.

"It's okay, Byron." She wanted to remind him of their intense discussions of those Philip K. Dick paperbacks, to say that a memory drug fit right in. But words weren't coming. "Really. Don't be…"

The darkness was warm and red and ceaselessly in motion—around her, inside her. Everything else fell away. She had time just to wonder what she would see before there were no thoughts.

There was only now.

Involuntary Memory
July 1988 (summer before junior year)

SONIA

At first, just the stifling blanket of heat. Then the hardness of sun-warmed stone. Then the chemical reek of bug spray and the rustle of leaves and the rushing of water.

The light is crimson through her eyelids. The water is somewhere to her right. Her limbs are bare, too heavy to move. A towel bunches under her shoulders; the rock beneath is giving her a crick in her back.

"It's cooler here, isn't it?"

A voice, grave and fine-grained. Jennet's.

Words press themselves up through Sonia's throat. She hears herself say, "But the bugs are worse."

"Worth it," Jennet says. "And we have it all to ourselves."

Sonia's eyelids are enormously heavy, but she forces them open. Sky: slate blue shading to green. Treetops. Dusk. The center of her vision has a painful clarity, a saturated vividness. Everything else is slightly out of focus, as if she's peering through a peephole in a sheet of frosted glass.

Though she doesn't dare turn her head, she knows they're at

Dogssnout Falls, the surrounding woods still locked in the eerie stillness of a Vermont early summer. No grasshoppers or crickets or katydids yet. The only noise comes from the river, and it must be running low, the falls almost soothing.

A whine in her ear. She slaps the mosquito, and the world lurches, the sky vibrating as the buzzing rises in her head again. She's being pulled away, out of her body. She can't draw air into her lungs.

Far away, Jennet says, "I dropped acid on a night like this."

The voice is a string tugging Sonia back. She gulps a breath, and the world settles again. The sky stops pulsing. Into the white noise of the falls, she asks, "With who? When?"

"Last year. Just a guy, the kind of guy who carries around tabs of LSD and gives them to girls." Jennet's shrug is a waft of air. "And no, he didn't do anything to me while we were tripping. This wasn't *Go Ask Alice*."

Buttery musk of Coppertone, acid of cheap wine. "How was it?" Sonia still has no sense of intending to speak; the words simply come.

"I thought the stars were telling me things. But when the trip was over, it just seemed like nothing, like randomness. How was yours?"

There are three stars out now. Sonia uses them to orient herself. If she moves too quickly toward Jennet, the buzzing will return, and she'll lose possession of this body again.

It's not her body anymore. She's in it, but it's not hers.

She laughs. It swells from deep in her throat. "I like this part of the summer best."

She wants to turn and look at Jennet, but that will start the buzzing again, too. Already the alcohol and the heat are turning everything hazy. She won't be able to stay much longer, and the knowledge is a blade against a fingertip, sharp as June.

In the distance, a tiny, contained boom. Thunder? No, there it goes again and again in a rippling cascade: fireworks.

"Happy Fourth. I wasn't sure we'd be able to hear them this far away." Another rush of air: Jennet sitting up. "You didn't answer my question."

"What question?" Sonia's own voice sounds distant.

Off on the horizon, more booms, echoing in the hills.

"I told you, he gets it from my brothers. If the bugs weren't so bad, we could stay here all night," Jennet says, a new tightness in her voice. "Are you wearing nail polish?"

Warm fingers pinch Sonia's big toe. "You think I shouldn't see him again," she says, lying absolutely still, eyes skyward, afraid to shatter the moment as Jennet's hand slips around the ball of her foot and rubs it.

"I guess I just don't trust rich-boy drug dealers." Again that tense note.

"He doesn't sell the drug!"

"No, but he gives it to impressionable girls—that's what my brothers say. You have calluses. We're two old hags, aren't we? No manicures and hairy calves. What if we end up living together in a witches' cottage? I wouldn't mind that, actually."

Sonia's vision clouds.

"Honestly, I'd rather just imagine our future," Jennet says. "More fun."

With you, it is. The words form in Sonia's brain, but she can't say them. The sky has come apart into whirling pixels, and the buzzing rises again, and her head floats loose from her body. She wants to stay, but there's nothing to grab hold of—no Jennet, no woods, no sky.

She tingles everywhere, without bones or boundaries. She tumbles through the keening air faster and faster until there is no her at all.

9

SONIA

"Month and year?"

Firelight quivered on ruined walls and beams. Dry rot clogged Sonia's nostrils. Where was she? A nightmare?

She closed her eyes, willing herself back to the humid dusk and the fireworks. She tried to recall Jennet's voice, cool as summer granite that holds the memory of snow. Jennet's hand, so close and now gone.

Hayworth was right. It had all been so real, and Jennet had seemed so young. So worried. Why hadn't Sonia remembered that part?

"What month and year are we in, Sonia?"

"I'm awake." She knew where she was now. In a church. She didn't know how long she'd lain here, her limbs heavy but no longer tingling.

"So answer the question."

Sonia knew who that voice belonged to. Rough from smoking. Nervous. She remembered the name just before she opened her eyes to find Auraleigh perched on the altar rail.

She almost remembered the year, too, but if she reached out to grab it, if she called it by name, Jennet would fully vanish. She peered over the top of the next pew and saw the pulsing hump of a man with closed eyes. He also had a name: Byron.

"October 2014," she answered at last. She felt as if she'd just stepped off a roller coaster, wobbly-legged and laughing.

"That's right." Auraleigh sounded relieved. "How was it?"

Sonia looked closer at Byron. He twitched in his sogged slumber, practically struggling against the bag. "I didn't think he'd do it," she said.

Auraleigh hopped down from the altar rail. She grimaced at the impact and rubbed the small of her back. "I wasn't sure any of you would. So, apparently you've done it before?" She didn't seem angry, just miffed. "Why didn't you ever tell me?"

"You didn't ask. Anyway, I thought I saw the future then— this was different." Sonia still felt weirdly dissociated, past and present slipping into superposition like slides jammed in a projector. Her body told her something more radical had happened than just remembering, something more akin to anesthesia.

As a kid, she'd been obsessed with "walk-ins," wandering spirits that took spiritual possession of depressed people, according to a paperback she found in a drugstore spinner. Possession by a walk-in manifested not as vomiting pea soup but as apparent amnesia. One minute, you knew who you were, and the next, you didn't because you were actually someone (or some*thing*) else.

That was how she felt—as if she had walked into her younger body and taken partial possession of it. She hadn't tried to control it, though, only observed.

"So, what did you see? Did you see Jennet?"

"Yes."

"Oh, wow. Isn't it fucking amazing?"

Oh, yes. It wasn't that Sonia had forgotten that Fourth of July in 1988. Until now, in fact, she'd thought she remembered it perfectly. But she hadn't remembered the precise sensations: the smells, the muted noise of the falls, Jennet touching her.

And she'd remembered so little of what they actually said. Jennet taking acid? The witches' cottage fantasy? Yes. But Jennet had said, *You didn't answer my question*—what was she referring to? And then, *He gets it from my brothers* and *I just don't trust rich-boy drug dealers.*

They must have been talking about Hayworth, with his fancy watch and his private school history—which was strange, because Sonia couldn't remember Jennet ever expressing an opinion on him. Other than the night Sonia met him, she hadn't thought they'd discussed him at all. Once, Hayworth had walked her home and they'd run into Jennet—but that was later, when she and Jennet were already drifting apart.

In the sog memory, Jennet had been probing for information about Hayworth, sounding almost concerned, and Sonia had said, *You think I shouldn't see him again.*

"When you get back, write down everything you saw," Auraleigh said. "Starting tomorrow, we'll tell each other every detail, too. We'll target our memories of Jennet, and then we'll share."

"Share what?" She didn't want to tell the others what she and Jennet had been talking about. Then she might have to discuss her future visions, the ones she knew now would never come true, and besides, none of that was relevant to Jennet's death.

"What we sog. All the clues."

Sonia watched Byron's fingers twitch on the rim of the sleeping bag. She hoped he was seeing something good in the sog and nothing nightmarish like the vision Auraleigh had described at dinner.

When he asked her to come with him to the reunion, she had imagined herself revisiting the past and discovering some precious knowledge—where she'd gone wrong, how to fix her life. Now she wondered how much else she had forgotten about Jennet, Hayworth, everything from those college years.

Involuntary Memory
February 1987 (freshman year)

BYRON

Darkness. Then light. The weary trundle of his legs, slipping and sliding. His thighs burn. Wet particles sting his eyes, and he blinks them away. He bangs into something hard, scratchy—a tree. Her laughter.

Jennet's laughter—ahead of him, somewhere. It's hard to tell because the whole world is in whirling pieces, glowing like a pearl. A wooded hill? A snowstorm? Under his arm, Byron holds two flat, hard things with raised edges—cafeteria trays. Shifting his gaze makes his vision blur, and his head starts to buzz again. He's falling behind.

"C'mon!" She sounds drunk or maybe just happy. "Slow-poke!"

Byron laughs, too. It bubbles up from inside him, and with it come words: "We're going to break our fucking necks."

"Don't wuss out!"

"Not a wuss. First time I saw snow was three months ago."

The body he's walking in is his body, with the recognizable thrum of his heart, yet its joints are different—springier. He doesn't have to pause for breath. He bounds up the hill, dodging trees, and catches up with Jennet just as she steps into the open.

Below is a near-vertical drop, a long run of virgin snow. Byron's thighs prickle. He lifts his head—slow, careful—and makes out the rounded outlines of mountains. The tiny lights of distant buildings. Snow trickles down his cuffs and collar, sending tingles of alarm through his nerves.

Jennet reaches out, and he hands her one of the plastic trays. "I should go first," he says.

But she's already planting herself on the tray, knees drawn up to her ears. Pushing off.

Snow parts around the tray with a *swoosh*, and she's off. His eyes follow her long trail to the bottom, where a spray of powder explodes, followed by a shriek.

Dread grips him—is she okay? Then he hears a burst of laughter, and he plunks down on his tray, digs his heels in, and sets off. The ground falls away. He turtles his limbs and clings to the tiny makeshift sled, wind singing in his ears, the world a fraying blur. The tray yanks itself from under him, and momentum keeps him tumbling down the slope, head over heels, bracing for a crushing impact that never comes because the world is pillowy soft and cold, the world is ice cream.

He lies very still. Arms encircle him; hot breath rushes in his ear. "Are you okay?" she says.

Nothing hurts, but Byron can't speak. He only laughs and laughs as he grabs Jennet and rolls her backward. Her coat is scratchy and her buttons are big toggles, and her lips are clammy as he kisses her, but the inside of her mouth is warm. She arches her body toward him, into him, bony and wiry and tight, her fingers tangling in his hair till it hurts.

Something's hidden from him. A part of her he desperately wants. Her tongue slithers against his teeth, *shepherd's pie with thyme*. There's a burn in his belly. And the flying snow, the buzzing in his chest, and his wet hair and wet everything, and the buzzing, buzzing, buzzing—

One moment she's real and hard and soft against him, and the next she's gone.

He comes apart, falling with the snow. He whirls for a long time at the wind's mercy, into darkness, before he opens his eyes into a body again.

A severe voice speaks. It sounds like a grade school teacher. "Month and year?"

· 10 ·

SONIA

No one spoke on the way home. Sonia kept rerunning the memory in her head, trying to preserve every detail.

For the first time in years, she felt the raw pain of losing her friend—the wrenching injustice of it. How could someone so real and alive simply disappear?

As they pulled into Auraleigh's driveway, Byron's phone rang. He didn't try to pretend it wasn't his. He yanked the side door open, jumped down with a single bound of his long legs, and answered the call with his back to them, speaking low.

"I said no phones," Auraleigh said as they passed him. "I don't want anyone snapping pictures of the church. If people found out about this…"

"I don't think Byron's going to slap the whole thing up on YouTube," Sonia said once they were inside.

But Auraleigh had a point. Hayworth had always been secretive about his sog supply, because, he said, the moment the public learned about a drug, the government made it illegal—if pharmaceutical companies didn't get their hooks in it first. The online era demanded a new level of precaution.

Paul headed past them for the stairs, his expression unreadable. "I'm wiped. 'Night, all."

Auraleigh dashed over and whispered something in his ear, then returned to Sonia. "They're boys," she said, indicating Paul's retreating form. "They don't talk about their feelings. But it *was* a fucking trip, wasn't it? Why didn't you tell me you'd done it before? Who gave it to you?"

Sonia could lie with a steady gaze when she wanted to, closing herself against Auraleigh's relentless probing. Her voluntary memories of Hayworth still felt raw and tender. "I did it *once*," she said, then turned and walked up the stairs.

BYRON

Byron sat bolt upright in bed. Someone had whistled—not a sharp whistle but a soft, mournful call like a loon's.

Jennet's whistle, the one she'd taught herself when she was fourteen. Whenever he heard that call outside his dorm window freshman year, he'd opened it for her to climb inside.

But he wasn't in his dorm at Dunstan. He was in Auraleigh's B and B, decades later.

He must have dreamed the whistle, but someone *was* outside the house. Faint voices drifted through the window, which he'd cracked open to get some air.

He went to the window and peered out. Auraleigh's pale hair caught the porch light as she swayed from foot to foot, smoke rising from one hand. Beside her stood Paul with his arms crossed, contemplating the ground.

"—won't even talk about him." Auraleigh gestured with the cigarette, her voice agitated. "At this rate, the week will end and we won't know anything. I'll have to dump it all when Sher-

iff Lachance comes back. He usually looks the other way, but
if he thinks I'm causing problems by bringing in guests from
outside, he might actually send his goons to raid the Belle Venere property."

"What about the stash you have downstairs?"

"Oh, you'd like me to keep that, wouldn't you? But here
might not be safe, either. I know the Stark brothers don't like
the outreach I'm doing, either. I know—"

Byron missed the rest, because Paul stepped in to reassure Auraleigh with inaudible murmurs. She kept complaining, but in
a lower voice, and Byron gave up and returned to bed.

So, Auraleigh was worried about the authorities—*it* and *the
stash* were probably sog. But he couldn't bring himself to focus
on the present. He was still shaken by that whistle piercing
through his sleep—too real, as if Jennet were alive.

And in a sense she was, wasn't she? If you believed in time as
a dimension in the multiverse, then all times were present si-
multaneously.

She had been *there*, inside his trip. She had been so real. But
what he hadn't expected was to find his past self there, too,
floundering in the snow, intoxicated by a romance that was
only just beginning.

He hadn't really remembered how it felt to be young: the
fizz of excitement at the back of your throat, the possibilities
spreading out in every direction, the power and confusion of a
firework primed to streak across the sky. Now he wanted it—
angrily, guiltily, the way you want that one last drink you can
already tell you can't handle. He wanted the past as much as he
feared what he'd discover there.

DAY 2

* ◆ *

October 28, 2014

11

SONIA

For an instant, Sonia had no idea where she was. Then she sat up in bed with the horrible realization that her friend had died.

The recent past snapped back quickly: it was nine, the house quiet, the sun a hazy radiance behind the maples. Still, as she showered and dressed, she kept hearing a small, plaintive voice inside her head that had been silent for decades: *Where's Jennet? What happened to her? Show me where and how or I won't believe it!*

It happened at the falls, she thought, trying to soothe that voice into dormancy again. But she couldn't picture the falls as a whole, only the specific perspective she'd had in her sog memory.

Downstairs in the kitchen, a stranger, a young woman in a camisole and hoodie, sat at the scuffed table. Maybe this was one of the elusive guests.

"Hey. Coffee's on the counter." Angling her sleek, dark head, the woman indicated the spread of bread, cheese, butter, and jam in front of her. "Help yourself. We're the only ones up."

Sun flooded the kitchen's southern window over a sill crowded with pots of basil and thyme. Sonia poured coffee into a chipped mug and sat down. "Thank you. I'm Sonia."

"Muriel Lu. You're here for the reunion, right? Auraleigh told me about you. Don't worry, I'm here for the memory spa, too."

Sonia had picked up the butter knife. It wobbled; she put it down. "That's what you call it?"

"I coined that." Muriel's tone was casual, urbane. Her hoodie hung open, exposing a tattoo of a tiny crocodile just above the scoop of her camisole. "Auraleigh says I'm being flippant, but it gets on my nerves when she treats the whole thing like a sacred mystery."

"That's what you're here for, though? For...*it*?" Hayworth had always been so secretive that Sonia had imagined sog as a microphenomenon, a piece of local lore that had never made it past the county's borders. "But how did you even find out? Do people know about it outside Vermont?"

"A few, I guess. A friend of a friend connected me to Auraleigh. I had to give her access to my bank account just to convince her I wouldn't take a sample to my employer—I work in biotech in the South Bay."

Muriel must have seen Sonia's mouth fall open, because she laughed. "It's really not as bad as it sounds. When Auraleigh started in with the top-secret business, I was pretty pissed off, but now I know she's not doing it for the money. If people ever find out about this stuff, it'll become a controlled substance, like ayahuasca. Psychiatry will get hold of it and prove that it has therapeutic benefits, but you'll have to pay a guru thousands of dollars and go on an exclusive retreat in Costa Rica to take advantage."

All these years, Sonia had seen sog as a secret between herself and Hayworth, a private ritual only they could perform. "Why refer to it as a spa?" she asked, carefully cutting a piece of soft cheese, trying to ignore the wrongness of discussing this with a stranger. "Is it...refreshing?"

"Most people who sog, I call them memory tourists," Muriel said. "Tina, for instance, the other guest who's here now. Her first husband died young, and she never got over it. It's all about the nostalgia. For me, though, it's more of a discipline."

"So you're training yourself to remember? But why? If it's not nostalgia?" Muriel looked no older than thirty-five—too young for that, surely.

"Detective work." Muriel's eyes sharpened on Sonia's, dark with flinty gray around the pupils. "What about you?"

Sonia stuffed a piece of baguette into her mouth, chewed, swallowed. Her one claim to fame, the *Retrophilia* screenplay, was about pathological nostalgia: a disturbed man in the nineties who imprisons his estranged parents in an exact replica of the house where they lived in 1965, trying to recapture his childhood. At the time, still excited about her future, she hadn't imagined herself ever falling prey to that same force.

But after last night, she could feel a crack of vulnerability starting to form, wistfulness about the past seeping through. "Auraleigh sees what we're doing as detective work, too," she said, evading the question.

Muriel reached for the jam. "Auraleigh told me what happened to your friend. I'm sorry. I'm trying to target something, too. I've been here sixty-two days, and at the end of this week— once I have what I'm looking for, I hope—I'll be off the sog for good."

She sounded so intrepid, like a time-traveling detective. "What do you mean, targeting?" Sonia asked, then remembered Auraleigh using that same word. "Can you trigger a specific memory?"

"It's not like cueing up a song, but sometimes. Journaling during the day helps. Remembering everything you can voluntarily— the physical setting, the before, the after, what was playing on the radio."

"I think I did that," Sonia said, recalling her voluntary memory of Jennet and the chocolate whipped cream at the café. It must have led her somehow to the Fourth of July. "Targeted a memory without realizing."

"Lucky." Muriel spread jam on a hunk of bread. "It doesn't always work. I'm searching for the guy who roofied and raped me when I was nineteen." She looked up, straight at Sonia. "I remember going to the bar with my friends, then only the tiniest flashes. I spent years blocking that night out, actively working to forget, but now I'm trying to reclaim as much of it as I can. I think I'm close to figuring out who the bastard is. I think I knew him. And even if the cops don't give a shit—" She shrugged, the gesture at once awkward and eloquent. "I do."

"What will you do if you find out?"

"Dunno yet."

They ate in silence, the dense, chewy bread giving them an excuse to drop the subject. For a guilty split second, Sonia envied Muriel. Imagine being able to pinpoint the one thing in your past that knocked you off course, one wrong you could avenge and purge and move on.

But she knew better than to envy what Muriel wanted to expunge, so she said, "You aren't worried about getting unstuck? Forgetting when you really are? I assume that's why Auraleigh makes us identify the month and year."

"Yup. I always snap back to the present, but sometimes it takes a while to really reorient. That's why it's good to have a watcher."

Hayworth used to say he had come unstuck in time. Then he would say in the next breath that sog wasn't time travel, that time travel was impossible, that his brain had only gotten "confused." But sogging did disorient you—Sonia had forgotten how much until last night.

She had inhabited her former self for a few minutes, and something of the past seemed to have returned with her, because Jennet's death felt like a fresh wound again, an absence, a wrongness. She didn't want to believe it could have happened at the falls, where they'd sat so peacefully nearly a year earlier on the Fourth of July.

If she could return to that same memory at the falls, maybe she could see more of their conversation, enough to understand why Jennet had seemed ill at ease with her, making those pointed little remarks.

She finished the coffee in one gulp, pushed her chair back, and stood up. "It was good to meet you, Muriel. If the others ask, you can tell them I'm on a walk."

· 12 ·

SONIA

Sonia walked alone toward Dogssnout Falls, taking a dirt road under yellow oaks, scarlet sugar maples, firs, and white pines. Leaves plastered the dirt, sodden with recent rain. The scent of the autumn air brought memories: stubble on Hayworth's cheek, woodsmoke mingled with tobacco smoke, the frustrating distance between them.

She pushed those thoughts away. It was her memory of Jennet she needed to target.

Here was the pullout, mainly used by fishermen, and the old railroad tracks just beyond. On May 22, 1989—or the twenty-third, actually, since it was after midnight—Jennet and Auraleigh would have crossed these tracks and taken the path that wound toward the river.

The thicket closed in quickly as she followed in her friends' footsteps. "Never go to Dogssnout alone," people always warned. But Jennet and Auraleigh had been together. She imagined Auraleigh keeping up a tipsy stream of chatter about her finals and summer plans while Jennet dropped an ironic remark here and there.

To her right, she spotted a couple of fixie bikes tucked behind a hemlock stand. In the Maxfield Parrish light, two students had set up easels and were sketching, their arms and legs bared to the mild air, on the same stretch of rock where Sonia and Jennet had spread out their towels on a long-ago Fourth of July. In the sog memory, Jennet had been happy they had this spot to themselves, but now, seeing how dense the underbrush grew, Sonia could easily imagine someone lurking in wait, unseen.

Here, where the river was narrow, a natural rock bridge stretched all the way across. The brittle limestone overhang looked like a beagle in profile, if you used your imagination.

According to the newspapers, the police thought Jennet had been on that bridge, close to the water's surface, when she fell.

Sonia couldn't remember getting a message that night, but maybe Paul was right—it had gotten lost. That spring, she had let the answering machine tape fill up with her mom and Jennet and her sister and her work-study supervisor and telemarketers, not bothering to erase any of it, because she had her junior essay due.

Today, rain-fed water funneled through the central chute in the rock and emerged below with seething force, creating a whirlpool. The bridge itself seemed dry, though. Sonia stepped onto it. If she was careful, it would be safe to walk to the opposite shore, where light bounced off the water and quivered on a cliff topped with dark cedars.

The shack where she and Hayworth sogged was up there, hidden from sight. The treacherous nostalgia rose within her again, and she thought it wouldn't hurt to see if it was still standing.

When Sonia went to meet Hayworth, she used a trail through the woods on that side of the river, rather than risk crossing the treacherous limestone bridge in the dark. How high had the water been on May 22, 1989?

Halfway across the bridge, a seductive, sinewy shoulder of ice-green river fed into the crashing white water. She stood and watched a bloodred leaf drift and rock, caught between countercurrents until the dominant one whisked it through the chute into the whirlpool.

This place, these rocks, had torn Jennet's body apart. Not for the first time, Sonia imagined falling. The instant of pure shock before the cold and the churn of water pressed the air from your lungs. The flailing. The dull, final impact of a rock against your skull.

A rock did it—quickly, they said. No wounds before she went in the water.

It hadn't felt real when she stood there in 1989 with the others, memorializing Jennet after the yellow police tape had been taken down, and it didn't now, either. It was one of the hypotheticals children bat back and forth on lazy days: *How would you rather die— freezing or burning? Drowning or thirst? A rock to the head or a dagger to the heart or a slow drip of poison?*

Real was drinking cheap wine here on the Fourth of July, their limbs slick with sweat. *Real* was Jennet's touch.

Across the river, behind the cedars, something moved. A flash of white. She twisted to get a better look, and then found herself crouched down and hugging the rock bridge. Her heart pounded, spray from the river wafting cold in her face. Stupid— she'd lost her balance.

She stayed there for a moment, appreciating how solid the rock felt, before rising and going on.

She breathed a sigh of relief when she reached the shore. A section of the cliff was crumbling, easy to climb. At the top, she pushed her way through prickly cedars and stepped out into a clearing.

The shack was still there—weathered and not much bigger than a bus shelter, its door hanging on one hinge. Beside it was an obviously man-made oval pond. Here you couldn't see the river, only hear its distant shushing.

She took a step toward the shack and another, and then she was inside. The floorboards groaned. Light seared through a rift in the roof. The woodstove was still there, but rusted out. The bench was rotting, with an unidentifiable nest underneath.

Sonia knelt beside the woodstove. Peering at the floor, she hoped to find some relic of her and Hayworth's presence, but all she saw were cigarette butts of every vintage. Had this really been their place?

Stepping outside again, she saw something shift in the woods— no, some*one*.

She stood stock-still, her pulse booming in her ears, and watched a young man emerge from the trees, a cigarette dangling from his lips. He looked like a townie in his buffalo plaid jacket and Carhartts, yet he was also familiar—the long, delicate head, the flaxen hair.

"Hey," he said quietly.

She forced herself to make eye contact, very conscious that they were alone. "Hey."

Instead of walking on down the trail, as she hoped, he remained where he was, plucking the cigarette from his mouth. "I'm Garrett. I do stuff for Auraleigh. She told me about you."

"Are you the one who made the fire in the church last night? The handyman?"

Garrett nodded, taking a drag on his cigarette. He kept his gaze down, and she found that reassuring. "Live up there. Sorry I followed you, but I couldn't talk to you by the house." He mashed his words into a monotone slurry. "She could've seen."

"Who? Auraleigh?"

"She told you not to go in the café, right?"

Sonia nodded—how had he known about Auraleigh telling her not to risk the coffee at the former Café Polaire?

"He's there. Wants to talk to you." Garrett raised his gaze at last. "Sent me here to tell you. Maybe you can talk some sense into him."

"Who?" Something jolted inside her.

Garrett tossed his cigarette to the sodden leaves and stamped on it. "Hayworth Darbisher," he said, turning back the way he had come. "Your old friend—that's what he says, anyway. Just don't tell Auraleigh I told you."

Voluntary Memory
Fall 1988 (junior year)

SONIA

"Are you with somebody in the future?" Sonia asked.

After a long moment, Hayworth's voice came from the dark. "You mean…romantically?"

A gale rattled the loose boards of the shack. They were snug in their separate sleeping bags, their warm jeans and sweaters. She would never have asked the question if she'd been able to see his face.

"I guess," she said.

"I try not to think about that stuff," Hayworth said. "Relationships. I've seen so much stuff in the future, it feels like I've already had my shot."

"But we only see flashes."

"It's different with me. I remember having a whole life in the future—it's hard to explain."

The note of warning in his voice sent prickles down Sonia's thighs. He had hinted before that he hadn't been kidding when he said he was from the future, and it frightened her a little. She understood feeling jaded beyond your years; watch-

ing her mother go through boyfriends had soured her on relationships. But to believe you were literally an older person in
a young body?

She tried to push the conversation onto a safer path: "I feel
the same way sometimes. Like I've used up all my chances."

Hayworth laughed gently. "I doubt that."

"You're just totally making assumptions about me." Did he
guess she was a virgin? "I'm not that innocent."

"I didn't mean that. It's just...you're so young. You'll have
chances, lots of them."

"I hope so." Sonia rarely told him what she saw in the sog.
She'd tried to describe her second vision: sitting on a restaurant terrace with a group of strangers, eating eggs and drinking
Bloody Marys and margaritas, surrounded by palm trees and
bougainvillea in the noonday sun. Hayworth had been polite,
but this piece of her possible future didn't seem to impress him.

So she didn't tell him about a subsequent vision: a service station in the glare of noon and a man in a white T-shirt pumping gas as she waited in the car. The man was Hayworth, older
and just as attractive. Under his arm was a rolled-up newspaper,
East Bay something.

She wanted to tell him every single thing she'd seen, heard,
and felt. Thighs sweating on a vinyl seat, his beside hers. Match-
ing Ray-Bans. A deep voice cursing as hands tried to fold a map.

But she couldn't be sure any of it was real. Maybe everything
the drug showed her was a fantasy. And she certainly didn't
want him to know she was fantasizing about him when he was
so frustratingly aloof.

She said, "I'm a *month* younger than you."

"You should be off doing all the wild things people our age
are supposed to do." The glowing woodstove reflected in his
eyes as they met hers.

"Wild things?" She had to laugh at that.

His hand fluttered, fingers inching across the gap between

them, and for an instant, just an instant, she thought he would reach for her. She held her breath.

But then he turned away with a sigh and said, "Let's drink now, okay?"

He drank his sog. Sonia drank hers, gagging only a little. She lay down beside him and spread the extra blanket over them both, so close together.

Coppery firelight wavered on the ceiling, and his body radiated heat that sent pleasant shivers over her. She closed her eyes. "You say you feel like you're from the future and everything's already happened. But that's only because you're mixed up, isn't it? Because sog mixed you up?"

"Sog fucked with my head, yeah." He sounded like he'd lived two or three lifetimes, a man speaking from the end of time.

She wanted to wrap her arms around him and force him to really see her. *Please don't let it be over. Please let us meet again and again and again.*

But the buzzing was already radiating outward from her spine to envelop her body. The cold of reality receded. She was going somewhere, taut with anticipation. Where? When?

From a great distance, she heard herself say, "You're young, too. Nothing's over for us yet. Everything's just starting."

13

SONIA

The former Café Polaire, reborn as the Buzz On Café, stood on Main Street between a bookstore (former bank) and a pizza gastropub (former pharmacy). It was a tall gingerbread Victorian that appeared to be slowly collapsing into a pile of pastel paint scabs. Unlike the vacant diner down the block, though, it had a plate-glass window that showcased tables and track lighting and a bustling clientele.

Sonia climbed the steep granite steps to the door. Her veins were still flooded with adrenaline, her cheeks warm.

If Hayworth was really here and wanted to see her, why hadn't he approached her himself? What could he possibly want her for? And what had Garrett meant by "talking some sense into him"?

Though the name had changed, the Buzz On was still very much Polaire, which had been opened by a grumpy Parisian expatriate who'd installed the first espresso machine in the county. The floorboards still had that farmhouse squeak. The dusty hallway still offered a bulletin board plastered with flyers: room for rent on Railroad Street; babysitting services; HUGE vinyl collection for sale.

Déjà vu gripped her as she entered the larger of the café's two rooms. The customers sported new fashions and technology, but the mismatched assortment of maple-, marble-, and Formica-topped tables hadn't changed. Nor had the framed posters of Mykonos and Saint-Tropez, or the nonfunctional grandfather clock, or the scuffed wainscoting, or the salt stains on the lino. Only the strident student art collages were new; the original owner, Hervé, would never have tolerated those.

The place was a retrophiliac's dream.

As she entered the second room, following the jet-engine howl of the milk frother, her throat clenched. Hervé's towering pewter espresso machine had been swapped out for a compact model, and there was a tall, aproned man behind the counter, holding a cup under the spout, his back to Sonia.

She walked up to the counter, not daring to breathe.

Beneath the apron, he wore jeans, an untucked flannel shirt, and Chucks. All his movements had the well-oiled quality of long-time service workers': knocking the grounds from the filter, packing it, screwing it back in.

As he moved into the light, turning to slide the finished drink across the counter, she caught a glimpse of the striking algae-green fleck in his right eye.

He was looking at someone across the room. Not at her. "Nonfat mocha?"

Heat massed behind her eyes, and she couldn't seem to make them focus. She saw him in strobing fragments: close to the same size and shape he'd been, only more rugged, with thick black hair and that mile-long face and the prominent cheekbones. Black brows smudged with gray.

He faced her. His eyes widened, and then he went still.

"A double latte, please." She almost wished he hadn't recognized her—what was she supposed to say?

The entire café vibrated to the same shuddering rhythm—the radiators, the hum of conversation, the dithery indie rock. Or maybe she was the one shuddering. Across the room, a girl's voice rose in a braying laugh—a sharp contrast to Hayworth's expression, which looked downright grim.

"You're not wearing black," he said at last. "You always used to."

Sonia tried to breathe. To smile. "I learned to like other colors."

Hayworth's frown faded. Still he stared at her with those fierce eyes, one brownish and the other with the startling green fleck. "Sorry," he said. "I wasn't quite ready for this."

Sonia had been prepared for false politeness. This was different. His gaze felt like a hand gripping hers too hard, nervously, as if he'd been waiting too long for her to return and wasn't sure what to do with her now she had.

"How did you know I was here?" she asked.

"It's a small town. And I know Auraleigh's handyman—he told me about the reunion."

"I wasn't sure if you knew Auraleigh," she said too quickly, while he began making her order. "She told me not to come here, but I wasn't sure why."

"She's not fond of me."

"She asked me about you nearly a year ago, when she first moved here. But she didn't use your name."

Hayworth poured foamed milk slowly, deliberately into her cup. "On the house," he said, handing her the drink. "Want to step outside?"

So much heaviness in his eyes, so much tension in his shoulders—had he been excited about her arrival? Or fearing it? "Okay," she said.

Hayworth called through a doorway behind him. A student-age woman with a green kerchief and a septum ring came out, wiping her hands on her apron, and took his place at the counter.

Sonia followed Hayworth down a short corridor and outside. Any other middle-aged man with that body would have strode or strutted, but he moved with a boy's unobtrusive glide, averting his eyes as he held the screen door open for her.

The cramped backyard had a line of arborvitae against a fence and a square of wet grass. The sky was an incongruous summer blue. Hayworth sat on the stoop and offered her a cigarette and lighter. Sonia shook her head but joined him on the stoop, keeping a few feet between them.

"People do still smoke in the future, I see," she said.

"I quit. Mostly." Hayworth's shoulders juddered, and she thought he was silently coughing until it occurred to her that he might be trembling.

The sight took her aback. "Sorry," she said before she could stop herself.

Hayworth covered his face, an artless gesture. "No, I'm sorry. Like I said, I'm not really ready."

"Same here," she said, groping for words. "I mean, I didn't think you'd still be around."

Hayworth looked straight across the yard. "Sometimes just… the past. It comes up quickly. You know?"

"I know." All too well, after last night. She struggled to put her thoughts in order. "When did you meet Auraleigh? In school?"

"Not then, no, but she came to me when she moved back here. Asked me about…things." A jagged motion with the cigarette.

"Let me guess. About sog."

The word silenced them both for a moment.

"She really wanted it," Hayworth said in a spent voice. "When people are grieving, when they have unfinished business, that's when they want it most."

"She's grieving our friend Jennet Stark. You didn't really know Jennet." But Hayworth had gone still, smoke unfurling from his outstretched hand, and Sonia remembered what she'd seen and heard in the sog last night. "Or maybe you did? Didn't her brothers supply you with sog?"

He flinched. "They used to, yeah. But the Stark brothers

haven't aged well—one dead, two busy drinking themselves into the grave. The only one still making sog is Ben Stark's kid, Jennet's nephew."

"Jennet had a nephew?" Has a nephew? Would have a nephew? It was hard to find the right tenses for someone who'd been out of the world so long.

"Yeah, Garrett—the kid who sent you here." He gestured toward the street as if Garrett were out there. "He used to go to Dunstan, but he dropped out, and now he makes the stuff for Auraleigh."

Sonia saw the boy in her mind's eye: the slender limbs, the long face, the furtive eyes. She heard the deep, arrestingly serious voice. The resemblance was eerie. *Of course.* "I can't believe Auraleigh didn't tell us about him."

Hayworth rubbed his knuckles through the dark stubble that crawled over his cheeks.

"Look," he said. "What happened is, Auraleigh came to me. That guy Toddy Kuller—he was at Dunstan with us—told her I could make the stuff. I said no freaking way—I played dumb, even—and she got angry. Thought I was holding out on her. Then she found Scott Lemorne, the one who taught Garrett which trees to tap, how to boil the stuff in the shed."

"Scott's still around?" she asked, surprised. A swallow streaked across the sky. Behind them, inside the house, someone laughed. All that seemed very distant; the world had shrunk to the two of them.

"Was. Before he retired to Florida, he sold the Belle Venere property to your friend and introduced her to Garrett. So now Garrett's your friend's hired hand. She likes to run the show, and she's got the money." Hayworth raised the cigarette slowly, as if he were holding himself in check. "Garrett says she's trying to find out how your friend died. I guess now you're part of her investigation?"

Under the surface of his question, Sonia heard the real one: *Are you sogging again?*

Had he stopped sogging himself? Something about the way he'd said the words *I said no freaking way* made her think so, but she didn't want to ask outright.

"You know," she said, "I live in the desert now, just like I always knew I would. I've been to the Pacific Film Archive a dozen times—even hosted a program of shorts there—but I never saw you when I was there."

Regret flickered over Hayworth's face. "I was in the Bay Area, but not for long. I guess we missed each other."

"What does that mean about the future we saw back then?" She lowered her voice, though no one else was within earshot. "It didn't come true."

Hayworth's exhalation sent smoke into her lungs. When she coughed, he gave a little start and stubbed out the cigarette. "I think it's always a possible future you see in the sog. It might be the one you end up living, or it might not."

Sonia remembered him saying something similar all those years ago. She had wanted so badly to believe in her future visions that she had dismissed it.

Now she had a more urgent concern, though. "What about when we sog into the past? Can we believe what we see?"

Hayworth's expression had gone hard. "I haven't sogged in ten years," he said. "It messes with my head. I told Auraleigh she shouldn't do it, and she did it anyway, and now she's got a bunch of other people doing it. Including you—am I right?"

Sonia wasn't going to let him shame her. "Yes," she said, rising and brushing off her jeans.

Hayworth rose, too, unfolding to his full height so quickly she winced. "You shouldn't. You should stop now."

His tone held an intimacy that wiped the soundscape clean of trucks rumbling on the state highway and stray voices and laughter. They might have been back in the river shack with only the stars for company.

"Why?" she asked.

"The past is harder to quit than the future." His mouth was set in a tight line. "Remember what I told you about that, back in college? Same as it ever was."

The phrase rang a bell. "When did you sog to the past? In that alternate lifetime you used to tell me about?"

"Never mind about that." He loomed over her. "Look at your friend Auraleigh—she thinks all she has to do is solve a mystery, and then she'll never sog again. But I think she won't stop sogging—or getting other people hooked—until someone makes her stop. She doesn't like me because a few weeks ago, after I heard she was planning this reunion, I gave her an ultimatum—stop making the stuff by the time Sheriff Lachance gets back from his vacation in Cabo, or I report her and shut her down. If she told you all not to come to the café, it's because she was afraid I'd warn you. You, though—you should've already known."

Sonia stared at him, trying to make sense of all this. "Known what?"

Behind them, a woman's voice called, "Hey, Aitch! Got a line ten deep!"

"Coming!" Hayworth opened the door for Sonia.

On the threshold of the café, he paused and turned to her again. "Auraleigh might tell you I can't be trusted. She's tight with Ben Stark, and he's got some weird ideas. But believe me, I don't have any secret agenda."

He stuck out a palm, and Sonia handed him her cup, a last smudge of foam at the bottom. "I'm just trying to understand," she said. "What do you think Auraleigh is doing wrong? She's a little obsessed, yeah, but I don't see how the memory spa is hurting anyone."

Hayworth's eyes, fixed on hers, were full of sorrow.

"Please just trust me," he said. "Grief, sog, middle age—put them together, you get poison."

Voluntary Memory
April 1989 (junior year)

SONIA

"Tell me again about the future," Sonia said to Hayworth on the stoop of the townhouse. "How you had a life there. I want to understand."

This was the first time in months she'd seen him—the shack was too cold in the winter for sogging, he'd said. After they ran into each other at a dance in the dining commons, he had walked her home.

Jennet had emerged from the townhouse just as they'd reached it. But she hadn't lingered to talk, and now they were alone, Hayworth sitting on the step below Sonia's, watching stray snowflakes whirl through the air. "I should stop talking about the future," he said. "People think I'm crazy."

"I won't think that."

He sighed as if he didn't quite believe her. "So, yeah. I have memories of a different version of my life where I still went to college here, only I didn't talk to you at that party, so we didn't know each other till later. I graduated and moved out to California and...lots of stuff happened."

Sonia thought of her own sog visions: the two of them sharing a car, a road trip, even an apartment. "Is that when we meet
at the Pacific Film Archive?"

"Yup." But he didn't elaborate. "I remember being older and
feeling discouraged, like my life had gone to shit. That's when I
came back home to Vermont and discovered sog. Sogging backward is different, you know—it's not just flashes. It feels real. It
gave me that old sense of possibility, and I spent as much time
in the past as I could."

"You were a retrophiliac, like in your story." Sonia wanted to
believe he was still just telling a story, unspooling a metaphor.

"I started sogging every day. I tried not to change anything
in the past, just experience it. But I think I did have an effect
on my past self, because he started sogging, too. He—I—wasn't
supposed to do that. It wasn't part of my memories, or it hadn't
been. My memories were getting muddled. And then one day,
instead of waking up from the past, I…stuck there. I stuck at
age sixteen, and I couldn't get back, and I just had to go on living from that point. And here I am."

Sonia kept imagining cheesy body-swap comedies. "But if
your older self got switched with your sixteen-year-old self,
where did the young self go?"

"I don't know! Maybe they didn't get switched. Maybe they
merged. All I know is that I woke up one day at sixteen with
memories of being decades older, and it confused the hell out
of me. You know that song 'Once in a Lifetime'? It was like
that. How did I end up here? Whose life is this? What am I supposed to do next?"

"I feel that way when I wake up from the sog." For Sonia, it
was a blissful feeling—like being pure possibility, no one and
everyone at once. "It's gone in a minute or so, though."

"That's normal," Hayworth said. "But when that feeling sticks
around, it can mess you up. I tried to send myself back to the
future by smashing my fist through a window, but that didn't

work. I kept mixing up my two lives. I didn't know what music I liked or how I wanted to dress or who I wanted to be friends with. I had to grow back my personality, stitching it together from pieces of new me and old me. I felt...alone."

Now, at last, he turned his shadowed face up to her. "That's why I changed things by walking up to you at that party. That's why I gave you sog. I was so excited to see somebody from my other life that I didn't care if I got you in the same trouble as me."

"I'm not in trouble!" The concern surprised and touched her. "I'm sorry that happened to you, but I'm glad we did it."

If that's what happened. Sonia kept her doubts to herself.

"Soon it'll be warm enough to go to the shack again. I'll be in touch, if you're sure you want to," he said, looking into her eyes.

Something was stuck in her throat. *That's not what I want, not really.* If sog was so dangerous, she didn't need to have it ever again. The future could take care of itself.

She just wanted to be with him in the present, "muddled" or not. But if she admitted the truth, she might frighten him away.

"Okay," she said.

14

BYRON

Byron volunteered to order the pizzas, toss the salad, and set the table. No one objected.

Auraleigh glued herself to Paul's side. "I can't believe you made me persuade you to come," she kept telling him, tousling his hair or popping a piece of locally cured sausage into his mouth. "I told you you'd have a blast here."

Paul looked embarrassed by the attention—who wouldn't be? Byron was glad he wasn't its focus, because even though he'd slept till nearly two in the afternoon, he was too exhausted to be good company.

Until he took sog, he hadn't believed his mind could preserve a perfect, crystalline record of the past. Intellectually, he was still skeptical. But he knew what he'd seen was nothing like his usual, well-worn memories of Jennet, or that sad loop of her voice saying *Well, Byron* in his head.

More importantly, the impact of the sog hadn't faded. It seemed to have unleashed something.

Last night in his room, drifting off to sleep after eavesdropping on Paul and Auraleigh, he'd felt Jennet beside him—breath shivering on his neck, fingertips resting just above the waistband of his briefs. And in the morning, there she was again, her legs tangled up with his, so *there* he couldn't open his eyes.

By the time he reminded himself he didn't believe in the supernatural, she was gone.

Not completely, though. She was a fleeting smile seen from the corner of his eye. A hauntingly familiar mix of scents, cheap lilac soap and Woolite and English Breakfast tea. A faint voice humming in the background as he sat on the sunporch with Paul earlier, discussing Tryce, the company he'd founded and recently sold, and privacy and behaviorist design principles and other tech-related issues that journalists like to belabor.

Byron set out plates in the dining room, avoiding the board that held Auraleigh's "evidence." He stiffened at a gale of laughter from the parlor, where the others were now making small talk over a cheese plate.

"Is it on my face?" Auraleigh was saying. "You know, this one time in college, Sonia and I had a whole convo over chips and guac, and when I went to the bathroom, I found a huge smear on my nose. She didn't bother to tell me! Remember, Sonia?"

Sonia mumbled something.

"We weren't civilized back then," Paul said. "Human communication was beyond us."

"Ha! *You* were born civilized."

"No. I put up a good front, but when it came to certain topics, like my sexuality—well, if anyone broached it, I became terminally elusive."

"Byron and Jennet didn't have any trouble expressing their sexuality," Auraleigh said wickedly.

As Byron arranged the silverware, using the salad forks, even though they were just having pizza, the doorbell echoed through the house.

"Pizza!" Auraleigh sang.

Byron paid and tipped liberally. He fetched water, local hard cider, and local beers from the fridge. He didn't sit down until everyone else had.

His kids hadn't picked up last night, but he would try them again. On the flight over, he'd gotten ideas for their spring break—Argentina or a rugged part of Costa Rica or even Vietnam. Somewhere with a lot of hiking and boho cred, so they couldn't dismiss it as a dad thing.

Auraleigh opened a bottle of grocery-store red. "Byron, you look like the dog's breakfast."

Byron forced himself to smile. He was grateful for the change of subject when she went to the head of the table and toasted: "To Jennet!"

"To Jennet."

"I like to imagine she's here with us." Auraleigh indicated the empty chair beside Byron's.

"Why shouldn't she be over there?" Paul waved at the other end of the table, clearly trying to lighten the mood. "Can't she be wherever she wants?"

Auraleigh scowled at him. "You're not taking this seriously."

"What should I take seriously? Something you imagined?"

Paul had so much skill at sidestepping things. Byron envied him, until Auraleigh said, "Well, then, Paul. Why don't you tell us all what you saw last night after drinking the elixir?"

The room went quiet. Sonia set her slice of pizza back on her plate.

Paul adjusted one of the cuffs of his shirt, which he had rolled to the elbows. Then he spoke in the same storytelling voice he'd always used to read aloud at *Dove-Cat* meetings.

"I was ten or eleven years old, at my parents' summer place on Lake Michigan. I was on the deck, baking in the sun, reading *The World According to Garp*, when a yacht tied up in the bay. I used my binoculars to inspect the deck of this yacht, while upstairs, my sister put the song 'Magic Man' by Heart on the turntable. I saw a handsome young man sunbathing in swim trunks. I experienced an...awakening."

"Oh, *Paul*." Byron couldn't tell whether Auraleigh was tickled or repulsed. "That's a lovely memory, but it has nothing to do with Jennet."

Paul picked up his slice of spinach and feta. "No. I wouldn't meet her for another seven or eight years. But it was an important memory for me." He held out his glass to Auraleigh. "Mind topping it off?"

Auraleigh poured again for all of them, including herself. "It's all right," she said, as if Paul needed to be forgiven. "Targeting memories isn't easy. But we don't have much time, and I was hoping we could make some headway tonight. Learn something."

"Why don't we have much time?" Sonia asked, looking straight at Auraleigh.

Byron wondered the same. It frightened him a little how much he wanted to sog again.

"Well, you're all going to leave after Halloween, aren't you?"

"So we'll reminisce by day, visit the past at night," Paul said. "Until we unearth some hidden truth."

"Yes." Auraleigh's mouth twisted—Paul hadn't sounded sarcastic, but he could be very subtle about it. "What about you?" she asked Sonia. "What did you see last night?"

Sonia was chewing. Byron willed her not to answer so he wouldn't need to, because he didn't want to have to describe an intimate moment between himself and Jennet. Couldn't some things stay private?

But Sonia finally spoke: "Fourth of July, 1988. I was home that summer, and Jennet was working at Polaire. We were drinking wine at the falls."

"At Dogssnout? Really?" Auraleigh was all attention. "Did you see anybody creepy there? Anything weird?"

"No. We heard the fireworks from town, that's all."

"You see, though?" Auraleigh said, addressing them all. "Targeting memories works. You just have to be open to it."

And then—of course, of course, it was all leading there—she pinned Byron with her gaze. "What about you?"

The room felt too long and high, the others distant shapes that had nothing to do with him. What would *Jennet* want him to say? Something airy that barely masked his disdain for Auraleigh and her pseudo-detective work?

But no words came. All he could think of was the evening of May 23, 1989, when he walked into the dining commons, unsuspecting.

He'd been woozy from a night of studying and poor sleep, interrupted first by his neighbors blasting 2 Live Crew, then by the answering machine, and then by the Quad Howl, a student tradition of wailing like banshees during exam period. Halfway through his meal, the murmurs started: "Did you hear about the girl who drowned?" "What girl? Where? What was her name?" "No, not Jennifer. Not Jenny."

Byron dumped his tray and ran across campus to Jennet's dorm. He stopped on the way to lean over a trash can and puke up most of his meal, as if his stomach already knew what had happened. He knocked on Jennet's door until his knuckles were raw. Then he remembered the message from Auraleigh about going to Dogssnout Falls. He called her, and she said, crying, "Oh, my God. I left you a message just now."

All through the following summer, he kept remembering that terrible discovery, and the memory was a grayness crushing everything else in his world. He and Jennet hadn't officially been together when she died. They hadn't even discussed the future since the happier early days of their whatever-it-had-been. But none of that helped when his sleepless nights were full of wonderings: What if he'd been a better person, a kinder, more stable person? What if he hadn't drifted away from her?

Byron drank too many Coronas and smiled mechanically and

learned to accept that he could breathe with a fraction of his normal lung capacity. And then one day, he couldn't say exactly when, he thought of Jennet and found no pressure where she had been, only an empty space. When he told himself he couldn't have saved her, he finally believed it. From that point—in tiny steps, as if he were wary of reawakening a sleeping ogre—he did what everyone said you were supposed to do: he moved on with his life.

But he'd always known the memories of Jennet remained inside him somewhere, and with them that choking grief and all the what-ifs.

He opened his eyes into Auraleigh's and said in a voice he hoped was firm and calm, "What I saw is none of your fucking business. It's my memory."

Paul sipped his wine. Sonia looked down at her plate.

A car swooshed by, and a bright snatch of pop music sounded from some neighbor's window.

"What do you think you're going to find?" Byron pressed. "We weren't there when she died, unless you think one of us is lying. And if we were, why would we tell you now?"

Jennet's death was a closed case. Had to be. If he started wondering again about what he could have done differently, he would never stop.

Auraleigh held his gaze for a long moment. Then, all at once, her face crumpled. "I just think one of us might have seen something that could be a clue. Jennet with a stranger. Jennet doing something she didn't usually do."

"But why *that?*" Byron stabbed a finger at the corkboard. "What are our motives, Auraleigh? I bet you've been thinking about it. Me? Well, that's obvious. Boyfriend. Semi-ex-boyfriend. Stormy relationship. You?" He pointed at Paul, reaching for something— and to his surprise, it came. "Jennet liked to tease you about all the girls who were in love with you. And she did that because she knew what they didn't know, didn't she? Because you told her."

Paul angled his head. "I hardly think she was the only one who knew I was gay."

"But Jennet was the only one you *told*."

Paul's expression showed Byron his guess was right. "Even if I did," he said, "I don't see how——"

"I'm not accusing anybody! I'm just saying, if you want motives, you can find them." Byron turned to Sonia. "You...were jealous of her talent. Or maybe she knew a secret of yours, too, and held it over you."

Sonia winced and took a breath. "I *was* jealous of her. Sometimes."

"Right." He wasn't actually sure where that had come from—why would Sonia, who always seemed to hold herself above the rest of them, be jealous?—but it didn't matter. He swung back to Auraleigh. "See what a game this is? See how absurd?"

"It's not a game." Auraleigh reached for her wineglass. "Our friend died."

"Byron wasn't trying to be difficult," Paul cut in. "But your question was a little intru——"

A shattering stopped him. A thick red pool spread across Auraleigh's place mat from the glass she'd knocked over. She lifted her hand in a thoughtful way and examined a smear there—wine or blood?

"I'll clean up," she said as Paul began to rise. And then, in a tone that made Byron's throat close, "Sit *down*, Paul. Maybe it's time for you to come clean about Jennet's poems."

The deep blush looked strange on Paul—unseemly. "Excuse me?" he asked.

"Her poems? They're all gone," Byron said dully. He'd tossed the ruled sheets into the falls, watching them soar and hit the water and turn to rags. Had he even read them first? He couldn't remember, and now he regretted provoking Auraleigh when he had no energy for a fight. "We got rid of her poems the way she asked us to."

"No, *you* got rid of them, Byron." Auraleigh tilted her head. Her lips were bloodless. "Or thought you did. When we were by the river, you handed them to Paul, just for a second, and he grabbed a bunch and stuffed them in his jacket. He told me about it later."

Byron saw it was the truth. "What did you want them for?"

Paul raised the glass slowly to his lips. "I shouldn't have kept them. I knew how you felt. It just seemed like a waste to get rid of them."

To Byron's own surprise, he wasn't angry. Jennet would have wanted her poems saved, whatever she claimed—they were part of her. He wanted to read them again. "I'd like to see them sometime," he told Paul, "if you still have them. If you'd let me."

Paul nodded too quickly. "Of course." And then, to Auraleigh, "What was the point of this digression?"

Auraleigh's face had a disturbingly waxen quality. "Byron said we all have secrets. I think we should start sharing them."

"Is that meant as a threat?"

Auraleigh was already turning to Sonia. "I mean, look at *you*. All studious and dignified, like a nun. Acting like you're just a spectator here. But you sogged in college and hid it from all of us."

"I didn't think anyone would want to know," Sonia said, but she was evading their eyes.

"And that story 'The Warning'—if you didn't write it, you knew the person who did."

"So do you." Sonia spoke so low that Byron barely caught the words.

"Auraleigh, please," Paul said. "You're being confrontational."

"The point is, she kept secrets from us." Auraleigh's eyes glittered; she might be an inch from laughter or tears. "So did you, Paul. Yet somehow *I'm* the bad guy."

"Auraleigh," Paul said, "why are you so upset? We're not your enemies."

Byron wanted to be back in his room reading a dull, re-proachful message from his wife, checking his children's feeds. He wanted to bask in the memes they posted but he didn't understand and their foul-mouthed slang. They were his nest, his family, even if he wasn't worthy of them.

Auraleigh had gone into the kitchen. She returned with paper towels and dabbed ineffectually at the spilled wine, leaving the broken glass.

Byron used his napkin to pluck shards from the table. He felt painfully sober. "What about *my* secret?" he asked, wanting to get it over with. "What do you have to hang over my head?"

The next second, he realized what he'd done, and his skin itched as if he hadn't washed for days.

It wasn't that he'd ever forgotten. He'd only done his best to scrub it out of his memory.

He couldn't look at Auraleigh, but he heard the flush of vic-tory in her voice as she said, "I wasn't going to say it, Byron. In front of them, anyway. For *your* sake."

Byron gazed at the corkboard, the meaningless scribble of Au-raleigh's handwriting. He remembered his wife telling him he was missing some vital element you needed to be a loyal, stable, good person. He'd never cheated on her, not technically, but a few times he'd come close.

"It was a mistake," he said, "that I hoped we could never mention again. I gotta make some calls now."

As he turned to leave, Auraleigh's laughter sounded behind him, bright and brittle as tinsel.

"My God, a quarter-century ago," she told the others. "Me and him, totally hammered, up against a dumpster in the back of Commons. Just the one time, and the two of them weren't officially together anymore, and we didn't talk about *her*. We didn't think about *her*. A few months later she was dead."

Byron stopped midstep. He almost swung back around.

But how can you explain something that involved no thought

process, no intention? A low, dirty laugh and his body and Auraleigh's coming together, arched and craving, each offering exactly what the other needed. Like a foot massage that irons out a persistent cramp. Like a sauna after a cold run.

A deep breath, and then he could move again. As he reached the parlor, he heard Auraleigh call after him: "We're leaving at eleven tonight, same as before. If you want it, don't bring your phone this time."

Voluntary Memory
May 28, 1989 (junior year)

SONIA

Every building in the village of Woolton, Vermont, was a chocolate-brown box. Yellow and traffic cone–orange piping ran continuously from one to the next. Buckey's Furniture, the signs on the larger buildings said.

It didn't seem real. But neither did the air, prickly with unseasonable heat and making Sonia sweat through her black vintage dress, or the fact that they were on their way to see their friend lying in a coffin.

The church, at least, wasn't part of Buckey's Furniture, just a standard white New England box. Crabapple trees clotted with browning blossoms lined the walkway. Paul parked his BMW between two battered pickups.

In the vestibule, they passed the casket—closed, piled with lilies—and a blown-up photo on an easel. It took Sonia a minute to recognize the girl in the formal graduation portrait, with the curled hair and nervous, lipsticked smile.

Auraleigh wore sunglasses and a shiny black dress more appro-

priate to a party, with puffs of tulle at the shoulders. She stood
beside the casket with a tissue to her eyes until Paul led her away.

The church was hot and stuffy, despite its soaring roof, and
two-thirds full of people who gave off acrid smells of cologne
and tobacco. Most looked too old to be anything but Jennet's
grandparents.

They slid into the back pew, Sonia beside Byron, who was
dressed in a navy suit jacket with chalky worn patches at the
elbows. The tones of the organ vibrated in the pews. The service was religious—Methodist? Lutheran? The minister was
youngish, with an iron-gray crew cut and a studiously empa-
thetic manner.

It was hard thinking about Jennet when there was so little of
her here. The minister kept calling her "Jenny" or "Jennifer."

So did the family members who spoke. Jennet's father had
oil-stained hands and unfocused eyes. Her mother was younger
and resembled Jennet, with a girlish body and cap of silver-blond
hair. Then she started talking about her personal friendship with
Jesus, and the resemblance vanished.

A dried-up man with an Irish lilt rambled on. Two raw-boned
young men sat beside Jennet's parents, presumably the terrifying
older brothers. A third brother, a gangly blond teenager who
reminded Sonia of John-Boy Walton, got up and talked for a
while, reading from index cards.

Finally the minister asked if anyone else had a remembrance
to share.

Auraleigh stood, tottering on spike heels. Old women swung
their knees sideways to make way for her. Sonia discovered that
sometimes a person actually does hear her own pulse pounding in her ears.

The memories of what followed were smeared like a child's
watercolor. Auraleigh at the lectern announcing, "Jennet Stark
was one of my dearest friends," her voice lurching—but they

hadn't let her bring the flask, had they? She couldn't have grabbed it at the last minute?

Auraleigh spoke of Jennet's ethereal beauty, her talent, her otherworldly qualities.

And then—if everyone in that church didn't already know that Auraleigh was the closest thing to a witness to Jennet's untimely demise, they did now, because Auraleigh started talking about how Jennet had seemed "peaceful" at the falls, just before her death. "Like she already belonged to the woods and the water."

Maybe this peacefulness had been a warning sign of a suicidal frame of mind, Auraleigh speculated. But, given the gap in her own memory, it was also entirely possible a stranger had lunged out of the woods and pushed Jennet into the river. Someone like whoever killed that girl in Stowe last fall.

Around this point, Byron slipped past Sonia and practically ran up the aisle. He held out his hand to Auraleigh, who was staring into the congregation with wet cheeks and an unfocused, accusing glare.

In Sonia's memory, the world froze this way. Byron would always stand with his hand extended, while Auraleigh waited for a murderer to step out and confess: *I did it!*

Eventually, though, Auraleigh accepted Byron's hand and let him lead her back to their seats. The four of them left as soon as they could without causing any more disruption, bustling out of the church and up the walkway under the molting apple blossoms. Auraleigh clung to Byron, and he patted her back while she said things like "How can I not remember?" and "It was my fault, all my fault."

Sonia watched the whole scene from a distance, with carefully constructed, perfect composure. When she was alone, she knew, she would cry, too. But Jennet wouldn't have wanted this fuss; Jennet would have hated it.

Jennet was so far from here. Jennet was so profoundly gone.

· 15 ·

SONIA

Five to eleven. Time for treatment at the memory spa. Sonia grabbed her things, stashed her phone in her room, and went downstairs, wondering if Byron would show up at all.

His bitterness at dinner had unsettled her; it was a side of him she'd rarely seen. At the funeral, Byron had seemed like the perfect man, handling Auraleigh with maturity and care. Now she wondered if he'd been covering his tracks, making sure Auraleigh's guilt-ridden rant didn't reveal his own transgressions.

She stepped out onto the porch, into the prickle of chilly air, wishing she hadn't heard about his hookup with Auraleigh but not wanting to think less of either of them. After all, she herself had kissed Byron on the red leather couch in the *Dove-Cat* room that long-ago May. She'd barely known what she was doing, only that she was frustrated because Hayworth was avoiding her, and Byron and Jennet hadn't been officially together since the previous semester.

At least Byron had the sense to draw back after that first kiss—or had Sonia done it? Anyway, they both clearly realized it was a bad idea. How could either of them have known Jennet would die that night?

But she had. And now Sonia would never be able to look at Byron without a pang of guilt—because she *had* made the first move.

Byron wasn't part of the small gathering by the van. Paul was chatting with Muriel as if he'd known her for years. Auraleigh hovered beside them, smoking and tipping ashes into the mums.

"That's Tina, the other guest," Muriel told Sonia as she joined them, indicating a figure in the wayback of the van. "We're all coming this time—if your other friend shows up."

"Did you see him upstairs?" Auraleigh asked casually, smoke twining into the air.

Sonia shook her head.

"Five minutes. Then we leave."

Always that fake cool on her, that adolescent swagger. Sometimes it made Sonia want to slap her. But the pain and longing in Auraleigh's eyes as she gazed after the girl on the quad who was probably Frances—the indifference was a mask. Auraleigh cared almost too deeply.

"Hey." Paul spoke low behind Sonia, drawing her behind the Forester, away from the others. "You doing okay?"

"Dinner was a little intense, but yeah. You?"

His mouth flinched. "I should have come clean about those poems long ago."

"You didn't do anything wrong."

"She likes having a hold over us," Paul said. "I think that's why she blurted out that nasty little secret about Byron. She'd make a good mob boss. But the kind who also cares about the welfare of the neighborhood and just wants to keep order."

"That still sounds ominous."

"Ha! But you know what I mean."

For all her blurting, Auraleigh controlled them by hiding things from them, too—Hayworth's ultimatum, for one, Garrett's relationship to Jennet, for another. Sonia wondered if Garrett made the sog in that smoking shed in Belle Venere.

Paul leaned in and lowered his voice another notch. "I'm not sure if I should tell you this—or maybe Auraleigh already did? She and Frances aren't getting along."

"I thought that was a weird interaction on the quad yesterday."

"Yeah. They've been having problems for a while, since Frances started doing better and wanting some space, and it recently escalated." He glanced furtively at the van. "I shouldn't be saying this, but I think Auraleigh needs a friend right now. The more alone she feels, the harder she tries to control things. She's always had this obsession with Jennet's death, but it gets worse when she needs something to fix. Frances doesn't want her mom fixing her life anymore, but unlike her, Jennet isn't around to object."

"Jennet *can't* be fixed." Hayworth had said that sog and middle-aged regrets were a toxic combination. Her cheeks warmed as she remembered how Hayworth had stared at her this afternoon, how they'd edged closer to each other—and how he'd told her point-blank to stop sogging.

Why did he care so much about shutting down the memory spa? She'd meant to ask Auraleigh, but her bombshell about Byron had gotten in the way.

"Time's up!" Auraleigh shouted. "Everybody who's coming, on board!"

"No, Jennet can't be fixed." Paul's sad smile was barely a flicker in the shadows. "And maybe, by the end of this week, Auraleigh will come to terms with her real problems. She just needs time."

When they returned to the van, Byron was there, whistling tunelessly. He raised both palms to Auraleigh with the lopsided grin of a boy who wouldn't be cowed. "Look at me, following the rules. No phone."

Involuntary Memory
April 1989 (junior year)

BYRON

Red bricks, washed orange by guard lights. Public Enemy hammering out a space in the spring night. A dry giggle.

"Fancy meeting you here," Jennet says.

"Fancy meeting you," Byron says. "Were you in Commons?"

Darkness under her hood, the glint of her glasses. "You know I don't dance. I went to the townhouse to work on the May issue."

Byron's coming from the library, books digging into his back. The air is cold but you can feel things growing, curling their roots around clods of earth and getting purchase. An eager excitement rises inside him, clawing its way toward the surface and the light.

"I ran into Sonia there," Jennet says. "With a guy."

Which guy? But Byron feels only a passing curiosity—he wants to reach for Jennet. He wants to surround her, to be part of her, to split open her skin and stretch out along her bones. He wants her to crush him like a ripe fruit and tear out his hair and plant it in the earth.

She's still talking about Sonia and this boy, but he barely hears. His head is spinning. "I don't trust him," Jennet says.

They're walking nowhere in particular but really walking to his dorm. The puddles are all frozen and a snowflake stings his cheek, but the deep pulse of spring thrums underneath it all.

"She was all over him, acting silly. Not like herself."

Byron takes Jennet's hand. "Hey, remember when my aunt visited? She bought this shitty bottle of maple brandy, then forgot to pack it. Share it with me."

"That's so enticing, Byron." Focused on him at last, she pulls her hand teasingly away.

He makes a wild grab for her, desperate to get closer, closest, but she runs on ahead, laughing. Fragments of the quad wheel around him—murky buildings, gray-red sky. He feels drunk, though he's not.

"If that guy's a dick, he could mess Sonia up."

"Stop worrying about Sonia. She'll be fine." He flails toward her and finds a shoulder, soft and warm and welcoming.

Jennet doesn't pull away this time. She snuggles under his arm and picks up the pace. "What's with you tonight?"

"I don't know," Byron says as they climb the steps. "Spring fever."

Dark, stuffy corridor, shuddering with radiator clanks. In here it's still winter, warm and stale with the pent-up sweat of people's coats and scarves and boots.

Jennet's cold fingers are under his scarf, on his bare nape, guiding him toward his room. "Maple brandy, huh?"

It's winter, but the green of spring is coming. He presses her up against his door and opens her mouth with his, petals spreading in the sun. The wet softness, and the sharp shock of need as she reaches out to bracket his hips with her hands and draw them toward her. She's so thin, a bundle of twigs, but he could sink into her.

Soon. Now. Please. Her hair is greasy, tacky strands between his fingers as if she hasn't been washing it, and this makes him want to keep touching her.

2 Live Crew thuds from his neighbors' room. He realizes he's

thrusting to the rhythm and darts back, embarrassed. She laughs a witch's laugh, deep and ribald, and her hand slithers into his pocket, knowingly probing his thigh, and finds the key.

Before the door is closed, they're on each other again. His hands roam all over her, peeling off her outer layers. He spans her waist with his hands. Her shoulders. Her jawline. She slams the door shut with her back. Her lips and tongue leave wet trails on his skin.

It's been so long—three months? Four? She doesn't need it like he does. Sometimes she mocks his neediness, his "hairy ape" appetites.

Then, all of a sudden with no warning, she gets like this.

They're on the floor in a soft jumble of coats and scarves and hats and gloves and sweaters. As he tugs down her underwear, the music vibrates through the wall. His neighbors love the whole album, but they play this one song on repeat. Her laughter throbs under him—strangled, eager. "Oh my God. How often do you think those dweebs *get* any pussy?"

Byron freezes. The dorm room shivers and pixilates.

This has already happened. This is a memory.

Earlier today, he remembered his dorm mates' fondness for 2 Live Crew, and now here he is.

The churning warmth inside him turns into nausea. He is here in 1989 and not here. He belongs back in the present, where she's dead.

He's resisting the flow of the memory now, refusing to do what his body wants to do. His voice is an alien thing that he struggles to bend to his will. "Jennet, you're going to—"

Before he can finish—what was he even going to say? *You're going to drown?*—the sog takes him. His body comes apart into whirling, buzzing molecules, torn by the vacuum of space, ripped away from the past and the possibility of a different future.

◆ ◆ ◆

"Month and year?"

Involuntary Memory
April 1989 (junior year)

SONIA

A beat. A gold-and-raspberry dusk. Heat and sweat and laughter and body spray and crooning voices: *Oh my God! Did you ever?*

The bass line slithers under Sonia's skin, into her bones, the crowd rippling around her. The stale graininess of vodka meets the acid of orange juice. Her flat shoes lift at the heel. Her tights itch.

"C'mon! I want to dance!"

Auraleigh grabs her hand and tugs her through the crowd, flushed and eager, in one of her tiny safety-pinned skirts. She looks so young, so angelic with the light strobing through her fluffy hair that Sonia wants to hug her.

But she does nothing, riding along in her younger body.

Beside Auraleigh, a girl in a Choose Life T-shirt whips long blond hair back and forth. The opening beat of "She Drives Me Crazy" goes *tick, tick, tick*, irresistible as an itch, and Auraleigh is gone, lost among the dancers.

Sonia turns in a circle, looking for her, and instead finds Hayworth.

The party has dissolved to meaningless slurry around her. She wanders toward him, heavy earrings swinging, trying to show him she doesn't care if he's waiting for her. *(Is he even waiting?)*

Hayworth yells something she can't hear. Maybe "Out of here?"

Then they're dashing upstairs and out of Commons into the chilly night, her flimsy shoes sliding on muddy pavement. "I haven't seen you since fall," she says. "Do you still go to the shack?"

"It's too cold."

"It's April! It's supposed to be spring." But the puddles on the quad are all frozen, and the air shivers with snow-about-to-fall, and he's not touching her. He never touches her.

She's acting drunk and stupid. She shouldn't have let Auraleigh drag her to the dance. "I should get back. I have to work on my junior essay."

"I'll walk you."

Did he come to the dance for her? Has he been waiting for her? Is this his way of inviting her to the shack again?

As they cross the science complex and the visitor parking lot, the alcohol pulses in her blood. The road that leads to the townhouses is dark and quiet, the black sky like a lid clamped down over her excitement. She wants to dance, to grab him by the hand, to bump hips to the beat of "She Drives Me Crazy"—but no, she just has to keep walking, staggering in these stupid shoes.

"Hey, you okay there?" His long arm steadies her, pulling her beside him.

They climb the steep hill to the townhouse complex, the ground mushy under their feet. A snowflake floats down under the lamp, followed by another, and she says, "That's Vermont for you."

She's being so boring she wants to die. She needs to ask him about the shack—now, quick, before they arrive at the townhouse, which looms ahead. If she doesn't ask right now, she could never see him again!

She turns to him as they climb the stoop, her heart pounding. No one turned on the porch light. But before she can get the words out, he stops short, so that Sonia's hip in its flimsy skirt makes full contact with his.

"Oh, excuse me."

He's speaking not to her but to Jennet, who's leaving the townhouse and just nearly collided with them. All Sonia can see of her is pale hair, a glint of glasses, and the silhouette of a full skirt.

She wants to hide. Last summer, Jennet said Hayworth liked to give sog to "impressionable girls." Does she think Sonia is throwing herself at him? Taking him to her bedroom?

She lurches toward Jennet and gives her an awkward hug. "I haven't seen you in forever!"

Jennet stands rigid. When Sonia releases her, she backs away. "I was doing layout for the May issue."

"You're already leaving?" Sonia's cheeks ache with embarrassment; when has she ever hugged Jennet? What if Jennet tells the others about her and Hayworth? "We could have a midnight brunch later. Like old times."

"I can't stay." Jennet's flat gaze suggests she hasn't missed Sonia these past few months. As for Hayworth, she doesn't even look at him.

Well, then. Sonia takes a ragged step backward, bumping into Hayworth again. "See you soon?"

"Same as it ever was," Jennet says, and she gives a funny little salute and walks on past them.

When she's a few steps away, Sonia collapses against Hayworth, laughing. It's just so awful and so funny. She and Jennet were friends. They were *friends*. Now somehow they're not, and Hayworth doesn't like Sonia, either, not in the way that matters.

She slaps her forehead, just like David Byrne in that video, and repeats Jennet's parting words.

Hayworth stares at her—his eyes a glimmer in the dark, a

flicker of long lashes. Then he brings the heel of his hand to his own brow and says, "Your turn."

She twists around to slap his forehead, her head swimming. He laughs and dodges. "Not like that!"

Sonia feels a little dizzy, so she sits down, and he sits on the step below her. Jennet is gone. Now she regrets she didn't say more to her friend—Jennet might have thought they were making fun of her.

But no, she can't worry about Jennet, with her strange, mercurial moods. Hayworth is still here; maybe they can finally talk about sogging now.

She says, "Tell me again about the future."

Before he can answer, the campus shimmers and vibrates. A buzzing energy carries her off the rim of the world, far away, back into stuffy firelight and a voice asking, "Month and year?"

16

SONIA

She woke in the dark with a crick in the small of her back and no idea where she was. She didn't recognize the acrid stink or the scurrying in the wainscoting.

"Month and year?" A woman's voice, very awake and just off sarcastic. Behind the question were other questions, harder to answer.

"October." Sonia sat up and twisted in her sleeping bag. She counted four humps still motionless around her, and gradually her brain found names for them. Paul, Byron, Muriel, Tara—no, Tina, the one she'd just met.

"The year, please." That edgy voice again, from somewhere in the darkness.

Her mind went blank. And then the date popped back in, as if it had never gone away: "Twenty fourteen."

"You had me a little worried," said the woman—Auraleigh.

"I'm fine!" That wasn't totally true. Superimposed on the present Auraleigh, Sonia still saw twenty-one-year-old Auraleigh dancing in the dining commons. She was still giddy with the wildly cycling emotions of her younger self: elation, desire, fear, regret. *Same as it ever was.*

So she had successfully targeted a memory. What she had just relived was the prelude to the conversation on the stoop during which Hayworth had told her about coming from an alternate lifetime.

And, once again, the sog had revived things she hadn't consciously remembered. The way Jennet looked at Sonia when she saw her with Hayworth. The guilt at not going after her friend, not trying to mend things. And "Same as it ever was"—hadn't he said that to her today in the café?

Recalling that conversation, she wondered if Garrett was on the property now. Hadn't he said he lived there? Maybe he could tell her more about Hayworth's crusade against the memory spa.

She threw off the sleeping bag. "I'm going outside for a sec. Need to pee."

Without waiting for permission, she tiptoed down the nave and through the foul vestibule into the open. The October air was mellower than the April of her vision. The moon was rising, drowning stars in its radiance. She relieved herself at a corner of the church, checked to make sure no one was following her, and crept across the field toward the shed with the firelight inside.

The grass was cold with dew. The fresh air flushed some of the emotions of the memory out of her, but others lingered. She'd wanted Hayworth so desperately and pathetically—but she hadn't wanted to lose Jennet, either, her friend's coldness cutting her to the bone.

Why did she have to choose? What was Jennet's problem with Hayworth—or was it even really Hayworth? Maybe Jennet feared Sonia's restlessness, her refusal to be satisfied with the present, because she knew it was carrying Sonia away from all of them.

Smoke poured from the shed's chimney, filling the air with a pleasant aroma of pine needles. She approached carefully, passing an unhooked camper with improvised curtains. Beyond the camper, the shed's door hung open, steam billowing outward. Sonia peered over the threshold.

There was no one inside, only a shiny industrial cauldron jittering and hissing on a massive woodstove. Steel implements glinted on the walls—ladles, tongs, lengths of plastic tubing and piping, reminding her of childhood visits to sugarhouses.

Sog was made from pine pitch, and Hayworth said Garrett made it for Auraleigh in a shed. Where was he? She ventured inside and found a weathered barn jacket draped over a camp chair beside a water bottle and a spiral notebook.

She picked it up and flipped it open, but the handwriting was nearly illegible. Only a few words were recognizable, fragmented bits of imagery, and she closed it again, feeling like an intruder.

"Sonia!"

Auraleigh stood outside the shed, calf-deep in milkweed. Her face in the firelight was angry, though her voice was level as she said, "You're holding the rest of us up."

"Oh! I'm sorry." If you reacted to Auraleigh's bad moods, you ended up like Byron tonight, pulled into a fight too dirty for you to win. "I was just curious to see what was going on in here."

"Now you know." Auraleigh swung around. "C'mon."

Sonia followed obediently. As they walked across the field, she said, "I know now why this is all so urgent for you. Hayworth is threatening to get your sog production shut down, isn't he? You're running out of time to find out what happened."

Saying his name still wasn't easy, but she had to be an adult about this.

Auraleigh stopped and stared at Sonia. The moonlight set her angry face in iron. "I *knew* when I asked about Hayworth in December that you knew more than you were letting on. Did you see him? Have you been in touch with him all this time?"

"No, I haven't." Sonia decided not to mention Garrett for his own sake, since he seemed to be playing both sides in whatever was brewing between Hayworth and Auraleigh. "I went into the café this morning, because I knew it would help me target my memories, and there he was. We had a perfectly civil conversation, until he told me to stop sogging with you. He thinks the past is too easy to get obsessed with."

Auraleigh held the gaze. "Do you think that's the only reason he has a problem with what we're doing?"

She said it so meaningfully, as if she'd been waiting to ask precisely this question. But Sonia could only shake her head. "I can't think of anything else."

Auraleigh began walking again. When she spoke, her tone was softer, as if the anger had bled away. "I barely even know the guy. What I've heard is that he spent most of his life sogging and then turned against it. He spreads lies about me, saying I give sog to Dunstan students. You know I would never do that, right?"

She sounded almost pleading, and Sonia nodded. "If you were that type of person, you could have exploited sog in so many ways—called up the *Times* and Vice, for instance."

Muriel had said Auraleigh wasn't in the memory spa business for the money, and Sonia had never known Auraleigh to be motivated by material gain. Her quest was personal.

She'd looked so miserable yesterday on the quad when Frances walked by her without a glance. Maybe Paul was right— the renewed obsession with Jennet's death was just Auraleigh's unique way of adjusting to the fact that her daughter didn't need her anymore.

"And I know you would never want to hurt kids," Sonia said, not daring to mention Frances by name. "You just want to know why Jennet died."

Auraleigh kicked a tuft of grass. "I'm glad you give me that much credit. Are you still pissed about dinner? I acted like a shit, yeah, but so did Byron. He can't pass up a single chance to remind me I wasn't Jennet's *real* friend and none of this is my business."

"He felt upset. Attacked. So did I, honestly, when you accused me of keeping secrets from the rest of you."

The others stood grouped around the van, raring to go, but Auraleigh paused to hug Sonia, her arms clamped like the mouth of a trap. Just as quickly she let go.

"Sorry," she said. "Being alone out here, thinking about nothing but the past, you get paranoid."

Hayworth's words echoed in Sonia's head: *Grief, sog, middle age—put them together, you get poison.*

Sonia reached for her friend's hand in the dark and squeezed. "You're not alone anymore."

BYRON

On the drive back, Byron hunched into himself, away from Sonia, each of them using a dark window of the van to avoid the other. The past was all over him, and he couldn't help thinking she would catch a whiff of the treacly maple liquor and the sweeter tang of Jennet.

That night in his dorm room had been their last time before she died in May. Even now, the sight of a bottle of maple brandy or liqueur made him sick with mingled desire and dread. He'd kept his aunt's bottle for more than a decade, untouched, until Christa insisted on pouring the contents out and recycling it. That spring night in 1989, he and Jennet hadn't bothered to crack it open.

At least he'd relived a good memory, an achingly good memory, and not that damn thing with Auraleigh—one night, maybe one *hour* of one night. A drunken impulse he'd acted on because Jennet had been in one of her rejecting phases. He hadn't thought of it in decades, but it was just like Auraleigh to drag it into the light.

Between him and Sonia sat Tina—a perhaps sixty-something woman, swaddled in scarves and layers of fleece, who hadn't said a word since they'd boarded in Dunstan. To Byron, her silence felt considerate, a guarantee of privacy, of visions not to be shared. At her age, she must have a wealth of small mysteries to solve and good moments to relive.

Downtown Dunstan flashed by, its newly constructed fire department and town offices as neat as a toy village. As they pulled up, the porch light of the B and B cast a beckoning glow. He was more than ready for bed.

But when he tried to follow Muriel and Tina upstairs, Auraleigh blocked his way.

"Tonight," she said, "we're going to debrief. We're going to share what we've seen."

What fresh hell. No one was going to make Byron share fuckall, certainly not her. But he'd already made enough of a fuss today, and he was tired, so he flopped down on the parlor couch and closed his eyes.

When he opened them again, sparks were fizzing in the woodstove across from him and shooting up the chimney. The rest of the room was dark, the firelight on their faces creating teasing illusions. Was Paul's stubble really that silver? Did Auraleigh have such pronounced frown lines?

You don't even know them anymore, Jennet whispered beside Byron, her weight depressing the couch. But no, that was Sonia sitting next to him.

Auraleigh was doing some mind-numbing tour guiding: "Don't ever assume what you've sogged isn't a clue or important. Just like with lucid dreaming, you can train yourself to do this better. We'll help each other target the right memories, encourage each other to stay down longer and see more. Sonia, you start."

Sonia's targeting was clearly working. Byron listened as she described dancing with Auraleigh in the dining commons and walking home to find Jennet leaving the townhouse. "She looked...sad."

Her description of the dance and the April snow made Byron

wonder if she could have sogged an earlier part of the same night
he had. But in his own sog memory—a memory he would never
divulge, let alone "share"—Jennet had mentioned seeing Sonia
with a guy on the quad, and there was no guy in this memory.
Sonia was alone.

"I told Jennet we should have another midnight brunch soon,"
Sonia said, "for old times' sake before she graduated. Instead
of saying yes, she said, 'Same as it ever was,' and then she was
gone. And I woke up."

Auraleigh's eyes glittered—was she crying? "That sounds
like her."

"It does," Paul said.

"Thank you for sharing that." Auraleigh dabbed at her eyes.
"Paul, your turn."

"I think I targeted better this time." Paul sounded oddly tense.

He used his professional storytelling voice: each word distinct, volume gradually rising. "I was in the dining commons,
eating lunch. I think it was the end of the semester, because at
my table there was a boy who'd set up his Mac and was writing a paper in his pajamas. I remember wondering if he'd been
there all night."

"Is this going somewhere?" Auraleigh asked.

"When I took my tray to the drop-off, I saw Jennet. I was
going to call out to her." Paul stared into space as if watching
the events play out. "But she was about thirty feet away, and
there was a guy with her, someone I didn't know. I couldn't
hear their conversation, but Jennet's face... She had that stern,
pale look she always got when she was angry."

Byron saw the scene as if Paul had planted it in his head. Who
could Jennet have been arguing with? A teaching assistant who'd
given her a low grade? One of her brothers?

The fire crackled. Auraleigh asked, "You're sure you didn't
know the guy?"

"Not personally, but I'd seen him on campus. He was hard

to miss—tall, skinny face, broad shoulders. He reminded me of Daniel Day-Lewis in *My Beautiful Laundrette*."

"So you wanted to bone this guy. Does he sound familiar to anyone else?"

Silence. Byron had never seen Jennet with a boy that striking; he would have remembered.

"So you think he and Jennet were arguing?" Auraleigh asked.

"I told you I didn't catch anything they said," Paul said with exaggerated patience. "The memory ended there. I imagine I walked away and never mentioned it to Jennet because it wasn't my business."

Cross-legged on the loveseat, Auraleigh kept pressing: "You couldn't tell what year it was?"

"No."

"How long was Jennet's hair?" Byron asked.

"To her shoulders."

Byron's heart sank. Jennet's hair varied—she cut it herself, or had her mom do it—but it had only been that short in 1989.

The flames pulsed faster on their faces, dark-light-dark. Paul looked remorseful. Sonia looked stricken.

Could someone have killed Jennet after all? Byron had always thought Auraleigh was spinning the story about a possible assailant to alleviate her own guilt. He'd been so hung up on respecting Jennet's wishes by *not* dwelling on the suicide possibility that it had never occurred to him to wonder if an accident was really the only viable alternative.

If only he had been with her at the falls that night instead of Auraleigh. An accident might be unavoidable, but surely he could have stopped an attacker.

"It could have been May 1989, then," he said.

"Yes. Let's all think about this mystery guy. Even if you can't remember him, try to visualize him. He could be the key." With a final portentous nod, Auraleigh turned to him. "Byron, what about you?"

"What about me what?"

"What you saw tonight?"

No way. Byron was on the verge of saying "I prefer not to" when he realized he could just lie. And, as if by magic, the perfect voluntary memory came to mind.

He grimaced, as if fighting reluctance. "I was at a *Dove-Cat* meeting in sophomore year, when Jennet was running for election as art editor. She was sitting in the big chair while we all grilled her, and this pompous upperclassman asked about her history of attendance at meetings."

They were all listening. Auraleigh's eyes were wide. Byron was grateful that his voluntary memory of this moment was crystal clear. "And Jennet just stares at him like a schoolgirl in the principal's office, and we all know she blows off at least half the meetings, and she says, 'My attendance hasn't been very good, Mark.'"

He tried to replicate Jennet's tone: a breezy combination of innocence and fuck-off. Maybe Auraleigh would hear his real message, that she had no business in Jennet's past. "And that was it. I woke up."

After a few seconds, Auraleigh said, "That's *so* Jennet."

Byron sat back, feeling a rush of approval that didn't come from within. *Nice work*, said a small voice that might have emanated from the walls, from the creaks of the house in the wind, from everywhere. *She doesn't need to know everything about us.*

Gazing into the flames that were ceaselessly vibrating and changing, Byron suddenly remembered how he'd tried to warn Jennet inside the vision. Good thing sog memories were read-only; it was one thing to regret the past and another thing to revise it, wreaking havoc on everything that had happened afterward.

Come to me again tonight, he thought. *I've missed you.*

DAY 3

October 29, 2014

17

SONIA

Sonia dreamed about the shack where she and Hayworth used to sog.

It somehow held the giant pot she'd seen in the shed in Belle Venere—over an open flame now, not on a stove—and the flames leaped higher and higher. Garrett stood with his back to her, feeding something into the pot—dark, feathery stuff from a sack. The heat was unbearable, but she couldn't move.

Garrett whipped around with a knife in his hand, and he wasn't Garrett anymore but Hayworth, suddenly jump-cut close to her, slashing at her over and over. No expression on his face. She caught his wrists, feeling the sinews strain against hers. He broke free and pushed her against a wall, all cracks and edges.

"What happened?" he asked as if she were the one doing something wrong.

As he stared into her eyes, his own full of naked intensity, heat washed over her, and she woke.

He could be the boy Paul had seen with Jennet. The description fit.

◆ ◆ ◆

At eleven, the Buzz On Café was already packed with students cramming for midterms. Two tables in the window bay were hosting a full-blown review session.

Waiting for the line to shorten, Sonia found a seat with a view of the counter. She watched Hayworth bustle around in his green apron, making drinks while the young woman with the septum ring took orders.

The whole B and B had slept in this morning. Maybe last night had simply exhausted the others, but the wee-hours "debriefing" had left her feverish with a need to know. Coming downstairs to a chilly kitchen, no breakfast spread on the table or coffee in the percolator, she'd seized her chance to nip out to the café unobserved.

In her first vision, Jennet had said she didn't trust Hayworth, who her brothers thought preyed on impressionable girls. In the second, the two of them had come face-to-face, and Jennet had seemed eager to get away—from Hayworth or Sonia or both of them. In Paul's sog, Jennet and Hayworth appeared to be arguing.

Auraleigh's voice rang in Sonia's ears, stagily insistent: *Does he sound familiar to anyone else?*

A crash. Someone had dropped what sounded like a whole tray of drinks, sending shards of glass and china scudding across the floorboards.

Students scrambled to their hands and knees. A girl in a hand-knitted snood, at the core of the commotion, told the story of her accident to anyone who would listen: "I'm so shaky, I really should be taking beta blockers, but there's going to be sherry at my dorm tea..."

Spotting a sliver of white nearby, Sonia left her seat to scoop it up with a napkin. A breadcrumb trail of crockery fragments led her under a neighboring table. She'd been a barista in grad school and remembered how weirdly absorbing these tasks could be—sweeping or filling the bus tray while taking in senseless bits of conversations. And aha! Here was the next piece.

"Broom coming through."

That deep voice. She looked up to find students scattering out of Hayworth's way. Did they suspect he'd once been one of them, or did they think he'd always been a sweeper and a milk frother?

She grabbed for the shard, wedged between a pair of Birkenstocks. The broom cut her off.

"You're bleeding," he said.

"Oh." She ducked out from under the table. Sure enough, there was a dribble down the inside of her right wrist. "It doesn't hurt."

Hayworth frowned—a storm cloud, roiling and dense, heightening the pressure in the room. "Come on back. I'll get you a Band-Aid."

When she didn't move because she hadn't planned for things to happen this way, he lifted the dustpan, careful not to let it spill, and repeated, "C'mon."

Following him into the kitchen, Sonia couldn't shake the image of the almost delicate way he'd scooped up the dustpan, as one might reclaim a child's beloved toy. He cared about his business.

In the tiny employee restroom, she washed the wound, a gash in the webbing between thumb and pointer. Hayworth met her with paper towels and a shoebox of first aid gear. "Sit."

Sonia sat on a chair with a wobbly leg. "It's not deep, really." She was starting to feel like she'd inflicted the cut to get his attention.

If Hayworth had known Jennet well enough to argue with her in spring 1989, it was odd that he hadn't mentioned that previous acquaintance when they encountered her on the stoop. Maybe Auraleigh had been correct last night when she insinuated that he had more motives for obstructing her investigation into Jennet's death than keeping sog away from students.

"Hold still."

His movements as he swabbed her hand were deft and cautious—this touch she'd wanted so desperately twenty-five years ago. They were alone in the kitchen except for a kid manning the grill under a pair of iPod speakers playing Metallica.

"I'm sure it's okay," Sonia said as he squeezed ointment on the wound. The more she let him take care of her, the more awkward this got. "Just a scratch."

"Might as well be sure." He was looking at her hand, not at her face. "In food service, we see some things."

Maybe she should ask him straight out. Get it over with instead of sneaking around. "I was wondering something." She felt her voice going gravelly, cleared her throat. "It may sound strange."

She looked down, too—at his fingers winding gauze around her thumb, black hairs sprouting below the knuckles. His T-shirt smelled of French roast, an oddly intimate aroma.

"Those earrings," he said. "I remember them."

Had she put on earrings this morning? Oh yes—heavy silver oblongs like wind chimes. She hadn't had those in college; where would he remember them from?

"The roadside place with the Native artisans." He met her eyes at last. "Near the Salton Sea."

With her free hand, Sonia clamped one of the earrings between two fingers. "I did get them near the Salton Sea, actually. At a gift shop, though, not a roadside stand." And then, understanding— "You sogged that? When we were younger?" Or was it something he remembered from that alternate lifetime of his?

Hayworth released her hand. "What was your question?"

She drew a deep breath, trying to psych herself up to ask him about Jennet, but said only, "I'm just wondering. When we see the past, can we be sure it's real?"

Understanding washed over his face, replaced quickly by resignation. "I can't be your sog guide anymore. I told you not to do it."

"I know." Sonia stood up, ready to make a hasty exit. "But it's part of the reunion. It's not really opt-out-able. And you did give us until Halloween."

"Only because the sheriff happened to be away right when things came to a head."

"What things?"

"Students asking me about sog." Hayworth returned the kit to a cupboard. The shelves were labeled with masking tape and neat block printing that she imagined was his—Paper Goods, Backup Spices, Odds & Ends. "Then I heard about this reunion of yours, and it was just...too much."

"Too much what?"

When he turned back, he seemed tired. "What's making you wonder if it's real?"

"I saw something that—well, I mean, I *remember* it." She wasn't going to rehash that night of the dance with him, how she'd practically begged for an invite to the shack. "But seeing the voluntary version and then the involuntary version, it's like seeing two movies with the same script and wildly different directors."

"The sog version is more urgent," Hayworth said. "Like a nightmare."

"Yes." She still couldn't read his face, but it was a relief to have someone put it into words. "I don't remember everything feeling so catastrophic."

"It's one of the risks of sogging into the past." Hayworth led her out of the café into a short stretch of sunlit hallway. "Scott Lemorne's mémère told me that when I first started sogging, in that other lifetime I remember. He's sort of a distant cousin of mine. Each year when his family tapped the maples, they'd also tap their special pine grove and boil up the pitch—a local tradition, on the down-low. Then Scott got involved with the Stark brothers, and they all started selling sog to the college kids."

He looked past her at the window frame, and she looked, too, and saw a woozy fly struggling in a spiderweb. "Scott's grandma knew more about it than anyone else. She told me how older people see the past. She warned me not to get so obsessed that I couldn't come back—a warning I didn't listen to. And she said there's another reason not to sog backward: You might remember things you don't want to."

Was he talking about himself now, or her? What wouldn't she want to remember? "So you're saying—"

"We censor our memories—for survival. It's where nostalgia comes from."

Sonia understood. She hadn't censored the facts of her memory, but she had blocked out the desperation, the frenzied feelings of desire and shame. She'd remembered meeting Jennet at the door of the townhouse, but she hadn't remembered how sick with dread Jennet's coldness made her feel.

She gazed past Hayworth at a blaze of sunlight on the windowpane. "So the voluntary memory feels less nightmarish because that part of your life is over, and you know how it ends. You've turned it into a story. But when you're inside an involuntary memory, it's like you're experiencing it for the first time."

"Ideally, yeah." There was a throb in his voice. "If you're not fully immersed in the memory, then you might try to change things. But full immersion has a downside—it takes away the airbrushing of the past we do. The retrophilia."

She must have blushed, because he added, "I liked your movie, you know. Though it felt like something a young person would write."

"Thank you. I would write it differently now." Sonia reached toward him before she could think better of it. Her fingertips hovered inches above his forearm, almost feeling the pulse of his blood. "Even after retrophilia is gone, we keep wanting to see the past. I do, anyway. Why do you think that is?"

His eyes had a sad sheen, though his tone was calm. "Maybe we want to understand ourselves. When you're sogging, it's always just around the next corner—the secret of why your life turned out this way."

A semi rumbled on the highway. The fly was still. White light sharpened on the pane. She wanted to hold his hands, to feel his warmth, to look up into his eyes and say, *I need to understand where I went wrong after college. Everything seemed so promising, and then...*

But he moved away. "Better get back before they start waving pitchforks and demanding their macchiatos."

Wait. She followed him through the kitchen into the bustle of the café. Dozens of mouths gabbling at once, dozens of fingers typing and tapping and tucking hair coyly behind ears. Young lives being lived.

Hayworth took bills from two customers, opened the register, counted out change. She stepped aside, feeling as useless as a winter coat hanging in the closet in July.

When the customers were gone, she drifted close enough to smell the cigarettes on him. "I need to know something. My friend Jennet—you knew her brothers. How well did you know her?"

Hayworth peered at a receipt. "Not well. I saw her once when I walked you back to your townhouse."

So he remembered that night, too. "Is that the only time?" He just frowned, so she continued, pretending Paul's memory had been her own: "I saw something in the sog—you and her together, at the tray drop-off in Commons. It was a glimpse. I'm not sure."

She felt ashamed, both for lying about what she'd sogged and for sogging in the first place. But she couldn't just forget the new evidence Paul had brought to light. She needed to give Hayworth a chance to explain it.

"In the dining commons, you said?" he asked after a moment, as if he hadn't been listening.

But she knew he had. "Yes."

"We did talk by the tray drop-off. But only that one time, and only for a minute or two." His eyes were pinched with pain. "Jennet was worried about you sogging. She knew I was giving it to you—she called it 'the pine concoction,' like some of the locals do. She asked me to stop. She even threatened to turn her brothers against me."

"She *did*?" Her sog memory of the Fourth of July had made her think Jennet disliked Hayworth, but maybe Jennet had only been concerned all along about the effects of sog on Sonia. "When was this?"

"I don't know. Junior year, maybe. She said you might get 'obsessed,' and I said sogging was your choice. Back then, I could be insufferable."

A grin flashed over his face—self-deprecating, charming. It made Sonia ache, but she asked, "How did it end?"

"This little scene? I don't remember. Are you wondering if that was enough reason for me to kill her?"

She must have looked shocked, because he said, "I guess I'm a little defensive." The grin was gone. "See, Auraleigh—when she first got here and followed her friend Toddy's lead to me, she didn't just ask me about sog. She asked if I had any ideas about what happened to Jennet. I must have frozen, or something must have shown on my face. I think she saw it as an admission of guilt."

Of course. Paul's sog memory had thrilled Auraleigh because she already saw Hayworth as a potential suspect in Jennet's death. She recalled how Auraleigh had looked at her last night, asking if Hayworth might have ulterior motives. And Hayworth's ongoing effort to stop Auraleigh's investigation probably only made her surer.

"I wonder if she suspects me, too," Sonia said. "But I was nowhere near the river that night."

Hayworth stared at her for an instant longer than seemed necessary before he said, "I *do* feel bad about the tray drop-off thing—Jennet seemed to think I wasn't looking out for you. She made me start thinking about getting out of the sog business."

Behind Sonia, a line was growing. Two girls were talking excitedly about the handmade chocolate whipped cream. "It wasn't your job to look out for me. We were both kids."

"I know. But things happened that shouldn't have," he said under his breath. Then, louder: "I'm sorry, I should probably get back to—"

"No, I'm sorry." Nothing about his account seemed insincere, but Sonia couldn't shake her sense that he was holding something back. It was in his hesitations, his silences. She said, "Thanks for the first aid."

18

SONIA

Auraleigh was working in the front yard, putting in mums, when Sonia returned from the café. "Where've you been?" she asked.

"Just running a couple miles up the river." Sonia mopped her dry face, glad she'd thought to wear her running clothes, and headed up the porch steps. "Need a shower."

They had another quiet afternoon: Byron shut up in his room, Paul working on his laptop on the back sunporch, Auraleigh in and out. At one thirty, two teenagers drove up with bags from Party City. Sonia watched through the parlor window as Auraleigh led them up the porch steps and shouted directions: "Farther to the right!"

"No nails in that cornice, it's an antique!"

The kids festooned the porch with cardboard skeletons, crepe paper spiders, fuzzy webs, black and orange streamers. Skeletal arms and hands trailed along the rail. Sonia wondered what a middle-aged Jennet would have thought of all these preparations—would she have dismissed Halloween as a holiday for children, the way

Paul did? Or would she have appreciated the irony of a celebration of death?

She remembered the Halloween the others had been discussing on campus. She and Jennet had played with a Ouija board—they did that occasionally—and Jennet asked Byron if she could haunt him if she died first. Sonia didn't remember what he'd answered.

Auraleigh served a big pot of Bolognese for dinner. Combining the roles of host and detective was wearing on her, Sonia thought. She was terse and smoking too much.

Candlelight made the dining room less shabby, and the wine was a nice one—Paul had brought it from Brooklyn. He played the husband, lighting the candles and draining the pasta.

"Have you all thought about Paul's memory from last night?" Auraleigh asked once they were all seated.

Byron said, "I don't understand what we're supposed to think about."

But Auraleigh was looking at Sonia, so hard that Sonia got shaky and had to put down her glass. Did Auraleigh want her to confirm that the boy in Paul's memory was Hayworth?

She believed Hayworth's version of the scene with Jennet, but Auraleigh wouldn't, and the others had no reason to, not knowing him. They might even accuse her of still having feelings for him.

She needed to talk to someone who knew Hayworth and might see him more objectively—someone like Garrett Stark. Yesterday, Hayworth had said, *Auraleigh might tell you I can't be trusted. She's tight with Ben Stark, and he's got some weird ideas.* Garrett might be able to give her a clue what that meant.

She was relieved when Paul said, "Let's have a dinner without shoptalk, shall we? I don't think we ever resolved that pressing question of which of us is the most successful."

Byron groaned. "Not again."

Auraleigh poured more wine for everyone, a bit sloppily. "You boys can argue forever about who's the most successful because you're both such fucking stars. I got a better question. Who's the *least* successful here?"

That shut them up. The candles wavered and dipped in one of the drafts that snaked through the old house. Sonia felt it under her hoodie where her shirt had come untucked.

"Success isn't so easily measured," Paul said. "There are all kinds—material, creative, intellectual, spiritual."

"Oh please," Auraleigh said. "Like anybody gives a shit about any of those but the first one."

"You're being reductive."

"Or realistic," Byron said, agreeing with her.

Right then, Sonia missed Jennet very much. She could almost see her in the empty chair between Paul and Auraleigh, glancing around the table with a sly glitter in her eye, like a child allowed to sit with the grown-ups. She would tell them to stop making everything into an intellectual debate and just say the blunt truth.

"Stop it, okay?" Sonia said. "I think we all know *I'm* the least successful."

Byron winced. "You've always downplayed your achievements," Paul said smoothly.

Sonia remembered how she'd felt long ago when Hayworth told her they would meet in the future—*I will belong someday, I will be someone*—and an aching space opened in her chest. "Both of you have brilliant careers. Nest eggs. And you—" she turned to Auraleigh "—have two grown twins who are both at excellent colleges."

"Are you calling me a sad little empty nester?"

"You've done something with your life. That's all."

"You have a career, Sonia," Byron said.

"I lost my job." She tipped her head back and took a swallow of wine. "I've been on COBRA for the past five months, living on my savings and picking up freelance work."

Byron's face came alive, disbelief and embarrassment playing over it as he scraped his chair forward. "You didn't say."

"Have you thought about going back to LA? Getting into TV writing?" Paul seemed less shocked; he understood how unstable academic employment could be without tenure. "The streaming services are desperate for content right now, and I know a few people out there."

Here was the perfect opening to ask for help, but Sonia's back had gone ramrod straight. Deep down, maybe they'd always suspected she was closer to the edge of solvency than they were.

"That's very kind," she said, "but I've never qualified for WGA membership. Look, I'm not trying to throw a pity party. I'm not starving. I have savings. I can always move in with my mom and stepdad in Maine for a bit—they've got plenty of room, and so does my dad in LA." She looked down at her fingers, knotted on the table. "The only reason I even brought it up—"

Auraleigh interrupted. "You always do this, you know that? You pretend you're nobody—poor little sad, overlooked Sonia— till everybody feels sorry for you. It's like your own personal version of that Dunstan ritual where everybody would go outside and moan and wail during exams—what was it called?"

"The Quad Howl," Byron said. "It happened the night Jennet died."

"Auraleigh—"

Auraleigh shook off Paul's placating hand. "But deep down, you know what? I think you secretly think you're better than we are."

Auraleigh had always been able to hold people's attention. With her long earrings glinting in the candlelight, she was her young self again, full of quicksilver bravado. No one tried to break in as she said, "Jennet saw it, too. That night when we were walking to the falls, she told me not to underestimate you. She said, 'That girl may look to you like she has no backbone, but she's got secrets and plans, and she's not letting anybody get in her way.'"

"Auraleigh," Paul said. "There's no point in dredging up—"

"It's fine." Sonia took a sip of wine. Maybe in the half-light they couldn't see how flushed she was. Hayworth had been her big secret back then, the center of her hopes for the future. Could Jennet have guessed that those hopes were built on fragile sog visions, dreams that would never come true? "I'm not offended," she said, aiming for a tone like Paul's. "Jennet was honest. She didn't sugarcoat things."

After a long moment, Byron said, "I think it was tough being Jennet. Growing up in the middle of nowhere, being sensitive in ways most people weren't, and then coming to a college full of privileged kids and trying to stand out."

"Jennet would have been amazing if she'd been allowed to grow up. But so are you, Sonia—don't you see that? Your movie was *good*," Auraleigh said.

"I thought you didn't like it."

"I never said that! All I ever said is that I wished it had been about *us*, our college experience, not some random guy trying to keep his family trapped in the past." Auraleigh's gaze swept around the table to encompass the Midnight Brunch Club. "A movie about us would win all the awards. But that's okay. You can make another."

"Maybe someday." Sonia raised her glass. She couldn't resent a dead girl for having said things about her that were, after all, true. Her throat was tight and dry as she toasted. "To Jennet. With all the hard parts."

Involuntary Memory
May 22, 1989 (junior year)

BYRON

The phone is ringing.

Not again! Byron lies on his side in the dark. He tugs the pillow over his head to shut out the jangling din, waiting for the machine to answer for him. Didn't someone else call just minutes ago? How long has he been asleep?

He peeks out at the glowing green digits of the clock-radio: 11:41 p.m.

With a loud *click*, the machine picks up on the third ring, silencing the ringer at last. He hears faint static, then a familiar voice: "Byron? Are you awake?"

Jennet. Byron sits straight up in bed, staring into the darkness.

"I know you have finals tomorrow. I'm sorry." She's husky-voiced, as if she's been sleeping, too—but apparently not, because the next thing she says is "I'm closing the café. Auraleigh's here. She wants to walk to the falls and get tanked. Byron...we need to talk."

Byron is wide-awake now, but he hears only the crackle of the tape running. He throws off the blankets, slides out of bed, and crosses the small space to kneel on the floor beside the phone.

She's still on the line. Pick up. He reaches for the receiver, but his hand halts in midair. He hasn't been alone with Jennet since that wild night in April. He's tried a few times to draw her away from the others, reminding her they still haven't drunk the maple brandy. But she always slips away, leaving him unsure of where they stand.

Now she wants to talk to him—the night before his three exams, when he desperately needs a full night's sleep? What could possibly be that important?

Static. "Sorry. Bad timing. You're probably asleep. But if you do get this, Byron..."

Unearthly, keening cries drown out the rest of the sentence.

Byron freezes—he's heard the Quad Howl before, but it's still unsettling. Wailing, moaning, and yipping rise from all directions, as if wolf packs have camped outside the building. Every semester at the midpoint of final exams, a few hundred people amuse themselves by impersonating banshees. Byron can't hear a word Jennet's saying, so he mutters a curse and finally picks up the receiver.

But he hears only the dial tone—she's hung up. The machine's red light blinks twice in quick succession, signaling that it has recorded two messages.

Who left the first one? Auraleigh, Byron remembers now, asking him to join them at the falls, sounding tipsy.

No way he's hiking all the way out there. He's been studying nonstop, and the world is grayed out with exhaustion. If Jennet really wants to talk to him, she can do it tomorrow after his exams.

He hits the rewind button, and the tape speeds back to the beginning. If he plays the messages, he'll have to hear Auraleigh's as well as Jennet's, which will just irritate him.

Anyway, he already got the gist of what Jennet had to say. They'll talk soon, if she's still in the mood—with her, you never know.

Leaving the machine to its blinking, he returns to his bed and pulls the covers over his head to drown out the Howl. As the wails slowly diminish, he eases toward sleep.

+ ◆ +

He wakes to a different darkness, red-brown at the edges. The sweetish staleness of a long-enclosed space and a woman's voice asking, "Month and year?"

He sits up like a shot. His mouth is dry with terror.

"Byron? Think, Byron. Tell me when you are."

Byron knows when he is. The past comes back like an enormous wave that topples him: the wilting crabapple blossoms at Jennet's funeral, Bush debating Clinton, a Halloween parade in the Castro, spaghetti in a blue bowl, a quarter in a phone booth, the sweaty grip of Christa's hand in the delivery room, a dishwasher whooshing, a terrifying whiff of smoke from the burning Berkeley hills, small Eliza walking beside him up a street under fragrant magnolias, Auraleigh demanding to hear his memories.

His whole life after college—the triumphs, the disappointments, the gradual realization that against all odds, he has become a success story, someone other people look up to. His steady love for his wife. His children's lives, so precious and so fragile.

And all that time, he's somehow kept the truth from himself, burying the memory of waking up that night. The blinking light on the answering machine. Jennet's voice sounding ragged as if she's been sleeping—or crying. *We need to talk.*

He rewound the machine to the beginning. So the next caller who left a message would tape over the previous ones, wiping away Jennet's voice as surely as he seems to have wiped the memory from his brain.

He erased her call for help. And until now, he had no idea.

Involuntary Memory
May 28, 1989 (junior year)

SONIA

Something terrible's going to happen. The knowledge swarms in Sonia's head. A black wave breaks over her: *What happened what happened what happened what did you do?*

The terror recedes again, and she finds herself in a church—the pew hard against her back, the heat sticking the fabric of her dress to her underarms. People sit around her, rustling and creaking and turning pages. They smell of manure and cigarettes.

The terrible thing has already happened. She is at Jennet's funeral.

A throaty swallow to her right—Byron? Sonia wants to meet his eyes, but her head won't turn; she can only look at the lectern in front of her. A man in a black suit stands up there, his mouth releasing a lazy river of meaningless words. Faith. Hope. Father and son. Light through the clouds. Light at the end of the tunnel.

The small of her back throbs. The tide of fear rises again. She wants to jump up and run out, but she'd have to walk past the casket, and the casket sends out sick brown tendrils of chaos and danger. *What did you what did she he what happened how—*

Someone asked her all those questions, and she wouldn't answer them. Who?

The bad thing hasn't happened yet. It's still happening.

The minister says, "Ben? Would you like to speak?"

A boy takes the lectern. Through her terror, she sees him clearly: blond with a slim body and a long, girlish face. His eyes are liquid with anger, but his meek voice doesn't match them. He reads from an index card: "When I think of Jenny, my big sister…"

Words, more words. Something about a field of dandelions and Jennet running ahead, always too fast for him. "Every Saturday night she told me ghost stories, and then I fell asleep during Sunday service."

A ripple of laughter—fond, comfortable. People like this boy. He drops an index card, and Sonia flinches. Something has changed in the air of the room; something is wrong.

"It's okay, son. Take as long as you want."

The church could catch fire. The smoke alarms could shrill, sending them all crowding and shoving up the aisles. She breathes soundlessly, pulling in her elbows, not touching Byron, even accidentally.

The boy named Ben resumes his speech, shakily: "…and I wondered why she was always so busy. She never invited me to meet her college friends. She said she was gonna save money and move to California."

Ben's gaze moves over the pews and rests on Sonia, and her heart stops. Around her, the whole crowd tenses as if seeing what he sees. But no, he's not looking at her anymore but at something behind her.

"That's why I don't think Jenny left us on purpose."

Sonia shivers through the heat. She wants to shut her eyes and pretend nothing is happening, but she has to know what he's staring at.

She takes hold of her own stubborn body and pushes, forcing

it to turn toward the rear of the church. She succeeds, but immediately her head swims, her limbs tingling, and the buzzing begins. She's knocked herself out of the vision; she's waking.

She has just enough time to make out the newcomer standing by the door to the vestibule. He wears an untucked white T-shirt and black Dickies, looking back at her with his dark brows lowered, his cheekbones skull-like.

Hayworth.

19

SONIA

Muriel was on watcher duty that night, and she didn't object when Sonia slipped out of the church and toward the shed. The structure was dark, no smoke unfurling from its chimney, but light shone in the trailer nearby. She hoped Garrett was there, so she could ask him about the "weird ideas" Ben Stark had put in Auraleigh's head.

Or perhaps not so weird, Sonia thought, now that she had seen the funeral.

How had she forgotten Ben's belief that his sister didn't die by suicide? He'd been a grieving teenager, of course, but the burst of cold terror she'd felt when he had said those words, and again when she spotted Hayworth at the back of the church— she couldn't make sense of it.

She hadn't remembered Hayworth being there at all. Hayworth, who had publicly argued with Jennet and could so easily have been at the site of her death, so close to the sog shack.

Following a thwacking noise to the trailer, she found Garrett stacking pieces of split log. "Hello again!"

"Hey." Garrett was bare chested, but even with an axe in one hand and tattoos snaking up and down his visible side, he didn't seem dangerous. His movements had a wary grace.

"Thank you again for the tip yesterday," she said, stepping into the light, trying to seem as innocuous as possible. "I appreciate it."

"No prob." Garrett lined up a new log on the target, raised the axe, and brought it down with a grunt. "Auraleigh, y'know, she don't really like me talking to the guests."

"I understand." His refusal of eye contact made it hard to get a read on him—was he contemptuous of her? Suspicious? Annoyed by the distraction? "I'm sorry to bother you, but I just have to ask something. Is it true you're Ben Stark's son? Jennet's nephew?"

The young man nodded. "Born two years after Jenny died. My dad used to tell me how she drew, wrote poems. Says I look like her."

"You do. It's too bad you couldn't know Jennet—Jenny," Sonia said. "She was so talented."

"That's what my art prof at the college said. She was his student, too." A twitch between the brows. Before Sonia could figure out a way to broach the subject of Hayworth, he did it himself: "Hey, what'd Hayworth say? I was hoping you could convince him he's being a jackass."

"About what?" She'd almost forgotten that Garrett had asked her to "talk some sense into" Hayworth. "Oh, did you mean about the memory spa? How he wants to shut it down?"

At last, Garrett looked at her. He had Jennet's long eyes, crinkled at the corners, liquid and keen at once. "I keep telling him we don't sell to students. But some of Auraleigh's guests got chatty with the kids at the café, and a couple of them asked Hayworth for intel on getting a dose. Freaked him right out."

His story matched Auraleigh's, but that wasn't what Sonia needed to know. "So you and Hayworth are friends? On speaking terms, anyway? Because Auraleigh seems to think he could've been involved in your aunt's death. I've been wondering if she got that idea from your dad."

Garrett barked with laughter. "My dad? Wouldn't put much stock in him. Every Sunday he lets Jesus into his heart, and every Monday, he changes his mind and bellies up to the bar again."

"But he *does* think Hayworth was involved? Do you have any idea why?"

Garrett split another log and tossed the pieces on the pile. "My dad just wants somebody to blame. Auraleigh, same deal. Hayworth used to hang in the shack by the falls where I found you yesterday, and that was enough for both of 'em."

"It's not enough for you?" Sonia chose her words carefully.

He shook his head. "Mental health issues, they run in my family. I'm not saying my aunt did or didn't jump in the river, 'cause what do I know? I'm just saying Hayworth can be a stubborn bastard, but he's not the type to—"

A reedy voice spoke from behind them: "Garrett, the tea's been ready for, like, ten minutes."

Sonia turned to find a young woman standing in the open door of the trailer. She wore a bathrobe, her hair a pale cloud around her face and her delicate features strikingly similar to Auraleigh's.

"Frances," Sonia said. This wasn't where she'd expected to meet Auraleigh's precious, protected daughter.

Frances stepped down into the grass, her bare feet pale as beached fish. "You're Sonia, right? Could you not tell my mom you saw me here?"

"You were supposed to stay inside, Franny," Garrett said.

"I'm not scared of my own mother." Frances gave Sonia a long look. "We're very close," she said in a dare-you-to-disagree way. "Because of that, though, she thinks she owns me. She thinks she owns Garrett for other, weird reasons."

"Just protective," Garrett said. "She gave me a job when I needed one."

Frances rolled her eyes at him. "Anyway," she told Sonia, "I don't want him to get fired."

"She wouldn't do that," Garrett said.

"She might. My mom likes us both, but she doesn't like us together."

That tracked. Auraleigh needed to feel in control, and a romance between her daughter and her employee was a direct threat to her authority. "Is that why you and Auraleigh haven't been talking?"

"Because I'm fucking him? Yeah." Frances lifted her chin, while Garrett contemplated the grass, clearly mortified. "She thinks we're too unstable to be good for each other. But your friend Hayworth understands. He lets us use the room over his garage when we want privacy. More comfortable than the trailer, that's for sure."

"How do you both know Hayworth so well, anyway?"

Frances laughed. "There are like a thousand people in Dunstan, and he's right at the center of it. All the students go to Buzz On."

"Franny," Garrett said beseechingly, dropping the axe in the grass, "your mom could come over here any minute."

"Oh my God, okay!" Frances allowed Garrett to lead her up the trailer steps. Over her shoulder, she told Sonia, "I know you won't say anything."

"My lips are sealed," Sonia said.

"And Hayworth," Garrett said. "You'll talk to him, right? I'd rather not be out of a job."

"I'll talk to him," Sonia promised, but the words felt heavy in her mouth. Garrett might think his father was an unreliable witness, but he hadn't seen Hayworth show up at his aunt's funeral like a bird of evil omen.

As she crossed the field back to the church, the sky began to drizzle. The trees rushed like ocean surf, and a chill swept over her shoulders.

She reached the church to find Auraleigh outside, calling into the wind: "Paul! Sonia! Oh, there you are. Did you see Paul wandering around?"

Sonia shook her head as Byron, Muriel, and Tina came out in quick succession, looking groggy and carrying sleeping bags. "Paul's probably smoking," Byron said.

"He doesn't smoke anymore!"

"He knew the month and year." Muriel sounded nervous. "I told him he could go outside."

"He should stay close to the church, though. You all should!" Auraleigh glared at Sonia through the darkness. "Let's fan out and look for him."

"He can't have gone far," Sonia said, hoping to lead them all well clear of Garrett and Frances. "Maybe the farmhouse."

"You and Muriel check there." Auraleigh turned to Tina. "We'll look around the van."

Sonia and Muriel set off across the field toward the house where Sonia had met Hayworth in 1988, now a slumping mass of ruin. They were less than halfway there when a figure detached itself from the gloom, loping toward them at full tilt.

The van's headlights clicked on behind them and illuminated Paul, his glasses glinting. A few yards from them, he stopped and wheeled around, peering wildly into the blackness. Then he kept going, walking briskly now, right on past them.

"Are you okay?" Sonia cried, following. "We were worried."

Paul staggered to a stop at the van, sucking in deep breaths. "I'm fine," he said in a clenched voice. "Let's get out of here."

"Why?"

"Someone's in there." He went silent after that.

In the van, Auraleigh fired questions at Paul, but he didn't answer until they turned onto the paved road. Then he said, "I went in the farmhouse with my penlight. To explore."

Auraleigh hit the gas. "It's not safe in there."

Paul spoke as if he were winded, not in his usual crisp, well-formed sentences. "The roof didn't look like it would fall on me. So I checked out the first floor. There's an old couch somebody never carted off. Like a gigantic, rotting mushroom. But I also saw a newish sleeping bag. Milk crates. Canned goods. An empty bag of chips."

He paused. Sonia felt her spine prickle even before he dropped the kicker: "And a pair of binoculars."

"I don't think—" Auraleigh began.

Paul wasn't finished. "That isn't why I ran, though. I ran because I heard someone in there, coming down the stairs toward me."

20

BYRON

"I still think it was an animal," Auraleigh said firmly.

They were back at the B and B, settled around the wood-stove in the parlor.

Byron knew he should probably tell the others he'd seen a face in the farmhouse window two nights ago, but he couldn't bring himself to care about anything in the present. Not now.

He yanked off his boots and put his feet up on the loveseat, arms crossed tightly. The whole way home, he'd tried to convince himself the sog memory wasn't real, but he hadn't succeeded.

He'd ignored Jennet that night. He'd erased her.

"I was spooked," Paul was saying, hunched in an armchair. "I just wanted to get the fuck out of there."

"There's nothing to be spooked by! It was probably just my handyman."

"In the dead middle of the night, on the second floor of a house that can barely stand upright?"

"He lives on the property, okay? He rambles. He can't sleep."

Jennet was so close. Byron felt her like a fleeting warmth

against his skin. When he went upstairs, she would be in his bed waiting for him, a phantom in his sleep, and he didn't deserve her there. He hadn't deserved to see those other two memories, either, the good ones. He was a bad boyfriend, a bad person.

What do I do? he asked her, almost hoping for an answer. *Should I tell them?*

"Look," he said aloud just to shorten the conversation, "if any serial killer wanders into that church tomorrow night, I volunteer to bash him over the head with a piece of broken pew. So, are we going to share our sog revelations, or what?"

"Of course we are." Auraleigh sounded relieved and suspicious at once. "If you have something to start us off with...?"

Not a word from Jennet, and Byron wanted to tell someone. He needed to, or the guilt would fester inside him. "I sogged to the night Jennet died," he said, feeling triumphant in a strange, brittle way.

"Oh my God!" Sitting on the couch closer to the stove, Auraleigh swiveled to stare at him. "How did you do it? Tell us everything."

Byron opened his mouth and then closed it, unsettled by her eagerness. "It won't solve your mystery. I was in my dorm room all night. But..."

"But what? What did you see?"

Sonia and Paul were leaning forward, too, curious to know what he would say. Now that he was finally on the verge of narrating a memory, he suddenly worried it would come out too emotional, so he stalled: "Auraleigh, your murder board is wrong. It only said *you* called me that night."

"I did!"

"Yeah, but so did Jennet, around eleven forty. She left a message. Didn't you know?"

Auraleigh stared at him a moment, mouth open, before saying, "*Oh.* Before we left, Jennet told me she'd called Sonia from the phone in the kitchen. Maybe she called you, too—or you instead."

"But why would Jennet call Byron when she knew Auraleigh already had?" Paul asked.

Sonia said quietly, "She must've wanted to say something privately."

They were all looking at Byron again. He wished he could take it all back, reveal nothing.

Auraleigh asked, "What did she say?"

Byron drew a deep breath. As he held it, Jennet's voice came to him at last, though perhaps it was only his imagination: *You can tell them almost everything. The worst part is for you and me alone to know.*

Yes, some parts were private. She wouldn't want Auraleigh picking through their affairs.

When Byron exhaled, he felt better. He told them about his sog vision in as much detail as he could: the phone ringing, the Quad Howl, the message. He omitted only three details: the husky, distraught quality of Jennet's voice, her saying *We need to talk*, and his rewinding the answering machine.

Which wasn't even that bad, was it? He'd done it automatically, half asleep, not realizing he might be erasing the last words he would ever hear from her.

"Why didn't you pick up?" Auraleigh asked.

"I don't know." Now that he'd started, telling the truth (most of it) wasn't as painful as he'd thought. It was a relief. "I was so tired. Now I wish to God I had."

"It's not your fault," Sonia said.

"Didn't you keep the tape?" Paul asked. Trust him to pick up on that detail. "I mean, did you really forget all about her message until tonight?"

"Yes, I forgot." Tears threatened to fall, a telltale heat behind his eyes. "I don't know how to explain it to you, Paul, because I can't explain it to myself. Maybe her message got erased somehow. Maybe I blocked the whole thing out because of the trauma of the next day. All I know is that I didn't have this memory before. Now I do."

"So you believe me about my own recovered memory now?" Auraleigh slipped off the couch and squatted before him on the carpet. Far from smug, her tone was close to pleading. "Sog *does* bring back the past. We forget so much more than we ever realize."

"I don't know." The words tasted bitter, yet Byron couldn't deny what he'd seen. "I guess, yeah… I believe you."

He must have sounded as broken up as he felt, because Auraleigh touched the back of his hand. "It hurts, doesn't it? Knowing you could have done more."

Byron clasped the hand she'd offered. Willing the tears away, he said, "Nothing I just told you resolves anything."

"It's interesting, though." Paul still had a canny look. "The message speaks to Jennet's state of mind. She wanted you at the falls."

And I never came. They were probably all thinking it.

Did they all believe on some level that he could have saved Jennet that night and hadn't?

Save her? That was absurd, he told himself. What could he have done if he'd gone to the river? Catch her before she could slip and fall? Only if he happened to be in the right spot at the right instant. Even if he'd stopped her from jumping, he might only have delayed the inevitable.

It didn't matter. He wished he had picked up the phone. He wished he had gone.

Sonia said, "Knowing about the message could resolve something for *you*, Byron. Isn't that why we're doing this?"

"It's exactly why." Auraleigh squeezed Byron's hand. "I know you have doubts about this process, but thank you for trying. You were so close to her, and we need your memories. We need you."

Byron's breath hitched. Her upturned gaze did make him feel

needed and cared for, though it also made him feel scrutinized. "I wasn't at the falls, though."

"No, but you might have seen something important before then. The next thing you remember could unlock everything."

Byron's hand was going numb, and he was grateful when she released it. He could feel Paul's attention on him; he wasn't going to just forget about that answering machine tape.

Nor was Byron. *It hurts, doesn't it?* Auraleigh had said. And yes, it did, so much more than he'd wanted to admit.

DAY 4

◆

October 30, 2014

· 21 ·

SONIA

She had to ask Hayworth about her new funeral memory, to give him a chance to explain it in his own words, before she even thought of admitting her doubts about him to the others.

She allowed herself to sleep into the afternoon, then took a long shower and assembled a sandwich in the kitchen. The house felt vacant. She brought her lunch out on the sunporch, which faced the narrow backyard, where a mossy ravine cast everything into underwater gloom.

A MacBook Pro lay open on the battered table, the screen still awake and showing the Gmail interface. Sonia leaned over and read a few sentences of an unfinished message.

I concede that this stretches your policy on the use of anonymity, but my main source isn't going to soften on that. Remember that right now, this is all hypothetical. Let's just say I'm offering you a chance to break the story of a heretofore unknown psychoactive substance and the culture it has spawned—

She straightened like a shot as the door opened, pasting a sociable smile on her face. "This is a shady kind of sunporch, isn't it?"

"The town is built atop a ravine," Paul said meditatively, as if he were writing the opening of a long-form piece in his head. "A ravine and two rivers, flowing together. A flood nexus."

Sonia took a sip of coffee, the cup trembling in her hand. Was he really pitching a story about sog, about all of them, without asking them first? Had Auraleigh agreed to this? She remembered how coolly he'd analyzed Byron's memory last night, calling it "interesting."

"What are you working on?" she asked.

"Something for the *Times* about the secret gay history of Honoré de Balzac and a piece for the Great War centennial. What about you?"

"Nothing, really." She'd been slogging over freelance film reviews for fifty dollars each. What did the *Times* pay for a thousand words? Shame strangled her voice as she said, "I might like to do some freelance work, though, if you hear of a good fit— treatments, editing, reviewing."

"Of course! Let's stay in touch after we leave."

He sounded so eager to help that she decided she must have seemed really pathetic at dinner last night. Best not to dwell on it. "Have you seen Byron today?"

"For a few minutes when we were making our belated breakfast. He seems troubled, doesn't he?"

"Yes." Seeing Byron blame himself had made her feel worse about not sharing her own memory with the group. "I'm a little worried about him."

Apricot-colored leaves drifted into the ravine. "Memory is such a private thing," Paul said. "To make a group ritual out of it, to demand an accounting, like a confession—it feels a little violating. Personally, I think people should be allowed to keep their secrets."

Jennet would have agreed, Sonia thought. "But sometimes a secret affects other people."

"And that's why we have a court system to deal with suspicious deaths and the like." Another smile, this one rueful. "What about you? Do you feel as if sog is unveiling anything to you?"

And would you say that on the record? Sonia had done enough journalism to know a leading question when she heard one.

"It takes you back," she said. "*Really* back. How can people not know this exists?"

There were so many uses for sog besides investigating a friend's death. Imagine being able to give dementia patients an anchor in the past, to soften the pangs of grief, to reality-check all of those vague, sentimental impressions of the past on which we base our present selves. Pharma companies would have a field day with it.

"Every powerful cultural phenomenon starts as a local one," Paul said. "A secret, a piece of folklore."

"I know, but all it takes is one person being indiscreet and telling the whole internet, right?" She opened her eyes wide. "I can't believe no one ever has."

"I suppose the locals have a vested interest in keeping it underground. And Auraleigh's guests certainly do. We've seen what federal regulators do with psychedelics, even ones that have proven therapeutic value and few side effects."

Yes, he'd thought about this. Like someone who was primed to break a story. She wondered if he knew that the memory spa wouldn't last beyond Halloween, if Hayworth had his way.

But Paul must not know Hayworth, or he would have identified him in the tray drop-off memory. "What do you think Auraleigh would do," she asked, careful to keep her tone casual, "if one of us started posting about her memory spa on Facebook?"

Paul smiled tightly. "Poison our coffee, perhaps."

◆ ◆ ◆

At 6:30 p.m., the Buzz On was nearly empty except for a few students at window tables. Two beanie-clad girls stood with their elbows on the counter, telling Hayworth about something "cringe" that their Cinema Studies teacher had done while teaching them to identify the male gaze. Hayworth prepped their drinks efficiently, not making eye contact, but he smiled and once even laughed.

If he saw Sonia hovering in the doorway, he gave no sign.

Frances had said the café was the center of town, and she and Garrett both seemed to like Hayworth. Watching him interact with the students, steady and nonjudgmental, she understood why—and how Hayworth might worry that the activities at the memory spa would spill onto campus. He knew better than anyone how sog could warp a young brain.

He seemed so reformed. So well-intentioned. But Jennet's brothers clearly didn't buy it.

She arrived at the counter as the students drifted away, still laughing and sipping from lip gloss–stained to-go cups. Hayworth didn't look surprised to see her. "My most loyal customer. Can I get you something?"

The deadpan charm again. She needed to be aware of its effect on her. "Latte, please, to go. We'll be having another late night, I imagine."

"Is Auraleigh working you hard?" Hayworth smacked the filter on the counter. The students must have put him in a good mood with their fast talk and crackling energy. Sonia hadn't expected him to bring up the memory spa of his own accord.

"She won't stop with the whodunit," she said, purposely vague. "We were all kind of freaked out last night, I have to say, when Paul heard something in the old farmhouse. Somebody seems to be camping up there."

She glanced up to find his eyes on hers: layers of soft mud and that fleck of green. "It's probably just Garrett."

"No. I saw Garrett at his trailer a minute before that—with Frances. He told me you gave them a secret place to meet."

He packed new grounds into the filter. "It's not secret. I have a spare room over the garage, so I let them use it."

"And in return, Garrett keeps you up to date on Auraleigh? Like a double agent?"

"You make it sound very cloak-and-dagger."

"Isn't it, though?" Sonia tried to sound playful. Complicit. "That wasn't you in the farmhouse last night, was it? With binoculars?"

"What?" He raised his eyes, and suddenly the twitchiness was gone, replaced by bald alarm.

"I won't tell on you."

"You really think I was up there spying on you with binoculars? Did you actually see or hear anyone?"

"Not me, Paul Bretton did. But—"

"Paul and Auraleigh are tight, aren't they?" Hayworth removed the full cup and gave the filter a ferocious twist to loosen it. "Did he mention he was up here visiting her for a week in April? Or that he spent every night of that week in the church in Belle Venere?"

Oh. Paul's email had tipped her off to his ulterior motives, but she'd never imagined he would lie about something like that. His treachery made her feel hollow, as if she'd lost a piece of her own past. "If Paul were here in April, how would you know?"

But she could already guess: via Garrett.

Hayworth shoved the stainless-steel pitcher under the nozzle and depressed the handle. Fractious steam hissed inside the machine. "Paul came in here," he said. "We talked. Garrett saw him in the church. He was here, Sonia. Sogging."

Sonia's chest tightened. Paul *had* seemed blasé their first time in the church. He hadn't put up meaningful resistance to any of Auraleigh's schemes. The email to his editor read like part of a longer exchange, one that could have begun months ago.

But his memory of Jennet and Hayworth hadn't been a lie. Hayworth and her own memories corroborated it.

The roar of the steamer downpitched, like a disappearing jetliner, fading to silence. And she cut straight to the question she'd meant to approach by careful steps: "Were you there that night? In our shack by the river? The night Jennet died?"

"Is that what Auraleigh told you?" Hayworth dribbled steamed milk into her cup, making concentric circles. He didn't seem startled by the question. "That I was there?"

"No. But you spent plenty of nights in the shack that year. Jennet didn't trust you. You admitted yourself that she threatened you. And...you were at her funeral. You came in during the eulogies and stood in the back."

Hayworth lifted the cup as if it were a wounded bird. He slid it to her across the counter, and she saw the delicate ribbing of a heart pattern, white on fawn.

"I did, yes." He gave each word an emphasis, a pebble tossed into a still pool.

"Can you tell me for sure you weren't in the shack that night? If you *were*, and the next day you heard Jennet had drowned there, you would remember, right? You would have asked yourself why you hadn't seen or heard anything?"

"Yes."

"So you're saying you *weren't* there."

Hayworth looked at her. His voice came out like something that had rolled along a river bottom. "Did I go to her funeral? Yes. Did I push her in the river? No. I went to the memorial because I worked with her brothers and because...you were her friend."

His volume dipped. Sonia had to lean in to hear. "I went because I was with you those nights by the river, giving you sog, and I shouldn't have done that. It could just as easily have been you who drowned."

Sonia remembered how carefully he had wrapped gauze around her cut yesterday, how he'd stared at her as he described the pain of the past. This was what he did—he came so close, lured her in, and in a blink he was gone again. Rage grabbed her by the windpipe, hot and heavy and incautious. "You didn't care about me. By that time, you were already treating me like I didn't exist."

She hadn't meant to mention that. She couldn't bear to see the words land on his face, so she turned toward the front windows, the reflected glow of lamps. Night had descended, the black panes spattered with rain.

"I'm sorry," he said in a low voice. "I was scared and confused. Guess I still am, but now I can admit it."

The door wheezed open. *It's too late*, she thought—and, to her surprise, she found herself saying it aloud. "It's too late for all that. I just want to know the truth."

"Would it actually help, do you think? To know why I did a given thing back then, or why you did a given thing, or why your friend died?"

"Yes." Sonia couldn't meet his gaze. For all her doubts about Auraleigh's detective work, she still felt the urgency that had convinced her to attend the reunion. Who could grasp the present without understanding the past?

He spoke very quietly. "Would it matter, if you couldn't do anything to change it?"

Was this a confession? But when she glanced at him, she saw no fear or agitation, only regret. Then he was addressing the new customer—Byron. "Can I get you something?"

"Hey," Byron said to Sonia. "Great minds."

His eyes were gray-ringed, and he looked gaunt and angular in his ancient leather jacket—older than he had to her before. To Hayworth, he said, "Double Americano to go, please."

"Hayworth, this is Byron. Byron, Hayworth Darbisher. He was at Dunstan with us." Sonia was painfully conscious of her false tone. "He makes chocolate whipped cream the way Hervé did."

"Carrying on the legacy, eh?" Byron sized up Hayworth. "Been here this whole time?"

"Close enough." Hayworth didn't smile. He didn't expend

his charm on men, or at least not on Byron. "How do you want the Americano?"

They stood side by side, not talking, as Hayworth made the drink. Byron peered around at the unreconstructed decor.

"Black as midnight on a moonless night," Hayworth said when he handed Byron the cup.

Byron guffawed too loudly. "That one's classic. You're funny."

As they walked out together—she didn't turn back, she would not turn back—they heard Hayworth say quietly, as if to himself, "I've been wondering how you turned out."

Byron didn't speak again until they were nearly to the B and B, its front windows glowing invitingly. "That was weird."

"He's a little weird. I'm sorry."

As if by mutual agreement, they continued on past the house toward the river. There was still a half hour until dinner—and, she realized, Byron deserved to know what she had just learned. "Hayworth told me something that surprised me. Paul was here in April for a whole week. He didn't mention that to you?"

"No." Byron was silent for a moment, striding beside her. The rain was more mist than drizzle, though the rushing in the trees foretold a storm. "Paul and Muriel do act like old friends," he said. "He seems at home here. I noticed, but I didn't think much of it. Do you think...?"

"That he was here for the memory spa in April? Hayworth thinks so. Either way, it makes me reconsider what happened last night."

"The person in the farmhouse? Why would Paul lie about that?"

"I'm not saying he did." She was still hoping the intruder wasn't real, wasn't Hayworth. "But if he and Auraleigh are both lying to us...well, it makes you wonder what else they're lying about. She wants us to believe there's a creepy stranger out there who killed our friend."

"Right. And she seems to think it's this mystery man at the tray drop-off—unless Paul lied about that, too."

They reached the end of the street, crossed the truss bridge, and turned toward Dogssnout. The dusk was waning, so Byron took out his phone and trained the light on the dirt road. "It almost makes me wonder about going to the church tonight."

"What does?"

"Knowing they lied to us." Byron sounded as if he hadn't slept all night—exhausted, wrung out. "I've had enough of her questions, her probing, her manipulation—*their* manipulation. But now that I've recovered something I didn't remember, I need to know more."

"So do I." With both their faces in darkness, she found it easier to admit that she couldn't stop now, when she felt so close to understanding something.

Their footsteps below. The whoosh and shiver of wet leaves above. Over her shoulder, Sonia caught the glare of a pickup's headlights. It veered off the bridge and onto the dirt road, transmission grumbling.

They might be near Dogssnout now, or even past it. She tried to envision the May night Jennet and Auraleigh walked the same route, the trees budding against a river of starlight.

"I'm not so sure about debriefing, though." There was a dangerous looseness to Byron's tone. "Memories should be private. Auraleigh was right—they can hurt us. The more we know about the past, the more we wish we'd done things differently."

Behind them, the pickup wheezed. They moved onto the right shoulder to let it pass, Byron's hand briefly stabilizing her waist as she stepped over the ditch.

"You shouldn't blame yourself," Sonia said, referring to the memory he had related last night. "It was just one missed call. I'm sure Jennet wasn't expecting you to hike out here in the middle of the night."

"The way she sounded, though— Hey!" Distracted by the

pickup, Byron stepped into the road and waved. It was still crawling, its headlights spearing them. "Would you fucking pass already?"

The engine idled. The headlights blinded them, hiding the driver's face.

"Goddamn hicks. You stay on the shoulder, Sonia. I'm gonna—"

The engine revved hard, and the truck lurched forward. The sound system came to life, and the air pulsed with new-wave vocals wailing over a shivering beat. Sonia recognized it instantly from her high school years: Alphaville's "Forever Young."

Byron leaped to the shoulder, barely clearing the truck's path as it roared past them. The singer's lament about nuclear bombs and flaming out young faded into the distance.

"Shit." Byron seized Sonia's hand and led her out into the exhaust fumes, peering down the road as if he thought the truck might return. But the music receded down the hill. "Somebody thinks it's fun to scare the tourists."

She felt him shaking; she was, too. The song choice seemed pointed, almost cruel; maybe Hayworth wasn't the only one who thought the nostalgia tourists were ruining Dunstan. "Let's go back."

They swung around the way they'd come. Alphaville was still dimly audible. "So you are going to the church?" Sonia asked, still alert for the music turning around, coming back.

Byron was listening, too. She felt it in the warm dampness of his hand, the tingle of blood pushed too quickly through capillaries. "I think I need to see this out," he said at last.

By the time they reached the bridge, they walked separately again, the trusses clanking on either side and the black water crawling below. "I've been wondering," Byron said. "About our memories."

"What?" She had a sense of something clenched inside him, something he needed to get out.

"That first night, when Auraleigh asked where we all were on

May twenty-second, you said the two of us were proofing in the *Dove-Cat* room. But I was alone that night, studying for finals."

The casual remark sliced through Sonia, making her stomach and chest compress. "You really don't remember? The, uh—what we did?"

"Wait, you mean the mail room?" He put an almost mocking emphasis on the phrase, as if the memory mortified him. "Of course I remember. But *that* was, like, a week earlier. Not that night."

Sonia couldn't speak.

"You really think we were in the *Dove-Cat* room when I... you know? Kissed you? No, it was the little alcove behind the mail room. I remember it clearly."

He didn't remember it clearly at all. She had kissed *him*, and it hadn't happened anywhere but the red leather couch—she was sure.

Byron apparently thought there was more to say. "What a goddamn prince I was," he said as they passed the cluster of riverside trailers at the mouth of Railroad Street. "Hitting on Jennet's best friend. I don't know what was wrong with me back then."

"You two had an unusual relationship," Sonia said, but the chilly breeze swept the words away. She had never dared to imagine Jennet would see her as a "best friend," and it was strange to hear him use the phrase so casually.

"We talked about not being exclusive, but basically, I was a jerk. At least you had the sense to push me away."

So that was how he wanted to see it—good little Sonia, holding the line for them both. But even if she hadn't kissed him first, she was sure she had kissed him back.

"So," she said, "if we weren't together that night—according to you—then neither of us has an alibi. You went to bed in your single dorm room, and my mom was asleep and didn't hear me come in."

Byron extended his long arms in a gesture of futility, nearly hitting her. "That's how it looks to me, yeah! I didn't bring the discrepancy up with Auraleigh because she's not a real detective and I didn't want to embarrass us both, but apparently we remember that night differently. If I'd kissed you the night my girlfriend died, I—I..."

He couldn't seem to finish, as if even the possibility of that cruel coincidence drowned him in guilt. As they reached the driveway of the house, its porch full of welcoming horrors lit by orange spotlights, she did it for him: "If you'd been with me, while she was at the falls, you would have remembered."

22

BYRON

Byron was doing this only because he was shit-faced. And he wouldn't have gotten shit-faced if he'd slept properly last night or bothered to eat more than a hard heel of the breakfast bread for lunch, or if Auraleigh hadn't poured the drinks so strong for the kickoff of their Halloween festivities.

She'd made a frittata and hash browns for dinner—brunch foods for old times' sake, not filling enough. She'd baked cupcakes decorated with candy corn. She'd mixed the drinks they used to have at *Dove-Cat* parties before the liquor restrictions tightened: black or white Russian, your choice. (Black, thanks.) She'd strung the parlor, dining room, and kitchen with black and orange streamers and spiderwebs made of twine. In the center of the kitchen table, around which they sat, were two flickering candles and a box with a picture of four disembodied hands: Ouija Board, Mystifying Oracle.

Paul had found it in the parlor closet with a stack of other board games. "How long since you saw one of these?" he asked, unfolding the board.

"We're not here for ghosts," Auraleigh said. "Just memories. And once you get started with that thing, it lasts hours."

"Ghosts *are* memories that refuse to be dispelled. You should know that, Auraleigh." Paul rose and switched off the overhead, leaving the room lit only by the candles and a midcentury lamp on the counter, with a dimpled glass shade. He sat down and positioned the white plastic planchette on the board, the fingertips of his right hand ghosting over it. "Who's with me?"

"I don't know how I feel about a séance," Auraleigh said.

"This isn't a séance." Paul kept talking in a dreamy, whimsical tone. "The Ouija is no more inherently occult than sog is. It's a tool of self-knowledge. A portal to our unconscious. The planchette reflects what we can't say aloud."

Either he could hold his liquor better than Byron could, or he'd been pacing himself.

"Uh-huh." But Byron felt Jennet close again, and he wondered if a Ouija board would attract or repel her. Would she find it tempting or pedestrian?

A drop of wax spattered the tablecloth, and he winced, remembering the scar on Jennet's arm. When he asked, she'd told him her older brother had spilled boiling maple sap on her "as a joke," and Byron had experienced a rush of heat and a hollowing in his belly and a desperate need to pound someone into the floor.

He had been raised by a mother and grandmother who adored him, making him the center of their lives. When his own children came, he'd loved them all the more fiercely because he'd learned from Jennet how children could be marked, cowed into silence, forced to shrug off violence and say it was nothing.

He'd wanted so badly to give her all the love her family had withheld. How had he failed?

The planchette wasn't moving with just Paul's hand on it. Paul appealed to Sonia: "Didn't you and Jennet use a Ouija board sometimes?"

Sonia nodded.

"They did it one Halloween," Byron said, remembering now. He put his hand beside Paul's before he could think too hard about it.

Sonia sat drawn into herself like a cornered animal. Byron knew he'd upset her earlier by debunking her memory of their kiss, but why did she need an alibi? She wouldn't hurt Jennet.

Fingers on the planchette, he closed his eyes, feeling for the invisible presence who might or might not be real. Last night, he dreamed he was lying in bed and Jennet was outside, one ghost wailing with the thousand voices of the Quad Howl. He begged her to forgive him and tell him everything she'd wanted to say that night. But the howl had no words, and when he woke up, he heard only the wind.

He opened his eyes to see Sonia's fingertips on the planchette now, too.

"C'mon," Paul said coaxingly to Auraleigh. "Our circle of five has been broken, right? You should be the one to call Jennet to us through the beyond. Or...our memories of Jennet."

The candles guttered. The planchette felt flimsy under the weight of three hands—humid skin, fiercely pumping blood vessels. Byron wondered if there was even room for a spirit here.

Auraleigh tipped her chin up. "You just don't want to go to the church tonight. That thing you thought you heard in the farmhouse—it spooked you."

Rain pattered on the dark window. Byron felt the trees around the house thrashing. He used his free hand to take another drink.

"Of course I'll go to the church tonight," Paul said. "I just thought this might help us prepare."

"Fine. *Fine.*" Auraleigh's fingers crowded themselves in beside Byron's. He flinched and felt her flinch. "But I'm not calling any spirits or memory traces or whatever. You can do that."

Paul seemed to enjoy playing medium. He spoke in a dead level voice, without irony: "We're open to traces of people who aren't Jennet, too. Come, speak to us." Pause. "Is anyone besides us here tonight?"

Byron had done this once before, at a high school party, the girls dissolving into giggles. With or without conscious intent, someone always ended up moving the planchette, so he wasn't surprised now when it twitched and glided a wobbly path to Yes.

"Yes," Paul intoned. The latest white Russian he'd poured himself looked untouched. "Welcome. Would you be okay with telling us your name?"

Byron wasn't shocked when the planchette slid to *J*, either. You always got the spirit you were hoping for. The spelling stopped after *J-E-N*, either because there was no need to elaborate or because Jennet had shed her distaste for common names in the afterlife.

Such a contrarian. And now he finally felt her near him, her braid tickling his cheek as she leaned over his shoulder. *This is awkward*, she said in his ear.

Thank you. Warm relief rushed through him. *Please stay. Please talk to me.*

"Are you Jennet Stark?"

Yes.

"Shit," Auraleigh said.

"Don't be afraid." Paul glanced around at them. "I told you, this is a tool of self-knowledge. Whatever we put into it, we get back."

Now he feels awkward, too, Jennet breathed, audible only to Byron. *He shouldn't have started this, but here I am.* A small hand slipped around Byron's waist and teased at the hem of his shirt. *Don't try to move the planchette. Let it go.*

Auraleigh leaned over the board, suddenly seeming a lot more invested. "Do you know who we are?"

Yes.

"Would you like to join our reunion?" Paul said.

The planchette scudded toward Yes again. Byron certainly had no sense of moving it. Then it veered away, into the alphabet, and spelled out slowly and painstakingly: *Already hre.*

Sonia gasped. Her fingers were aquiver against Byron's, just as they'd been after that pickup truck charged them.

Paul repeated, slowly and with emphasis, "Tool of self-knowledge. This is all us."

Byron took another drink. Jennet's blunt nails pressed into the skin above his waistband, indenting him. *Cold.*

Please forgive me. He imagined how he must look to her now: his fungused toenails, his gurgling acidic stomach, his daily fretting over stock prices on his phone, all those thousands of hours of staring at screens. If she turned away with the insolence of youth, he wouldn't blame her. *My attendance in the world hasn't been very good, Byron.*

She'd missed so many good things as well as bad ones by never growing up, but it would be cruel to tell her that.

He said to Paul, "So you really don't believe in ghosts?"

"Ghosts are memories. Ghosts are metaphors."

"Shh," Auraleigh said. Then, softly, to the spirit: "Of course you're already here. We've felt you with us the whole time. We missed you."

"Yeah." Byron hadn't meant to say it.

"Yes." Sonia stared at the board, or maybe at the candle flame, with trancelike concentration.

"Of course we miss you," Paul said—measured and patient, playing along. "You were our friend. But a long time has passed since you were with us. A lot has changed."

Patronizing, Jennet murmured in Byron's ear.

"But you're with us now," Paul continued, "defying the flow of time. Is there anything you'd like to tell us?"

Jennet's fingers crept around to Byron's front and circled his navel. The planchette wobbled over to the *L.* Then *E.* Then *T.*

Byron had it then, and sure enough, the message was *Let me go.*

Sonia jerked her head to the side. Candlelight shone on her cheek—was she crying?

This wasn't going so well. But it was going, and it seemed unlikely to stop, and maybe it was just the spinning in his head, but Byron didn't *want* it to stop. Jennet was amusing herself with them, and he wanted to see what she would do next.

"We don't want to hold you here." Auraleigh spoke in a dry whisper. "If you'd rather go, you can go."

"But we might like to know something," Paul said, "if you're willing to tell us."

Here it comes, Jennet whispered to Byron.

"What happened that night?"

Rain hit the windowpane like a handful of gravel. A distant car passed with a long slosh. The candles guttered again, and Byron blinked as if he were watching a film with missing frames.

"What happened the night you died?" Paul's voice had an edge.

Sonia whispered, "Who killed you?"

A gust of wind, a torrent of rain. The candle guttered harder, almost going out before winking back to its taunting full height. Jennet's nails dug into Byron's skin.

Why are you back now? he asked her, lips not moving. *Is it because I could have saved you?*

The next words she hissed into his ear sank deep, so deep he knew he would never dig them out: *What if I've been riding along inside you this whole time?*

Byron gave himself a shake. *Wake up.* The planchette was traveling again, flitting from letter to letter. *Not Jnet no.*

He wasn't breathing. Or maybe his breath had sunk into a channel where he couldn't find it. Either way, he had no sense of his lungs expanding and contracting. Time stretched into subterranean vastness, voices turning guttural.

"Oh?" Paul said. "This isn't Jennet anymore? Who is this?"

"Maybe it means Jennet wasn't...the one who hurt Jennet. Can you confirm that Jennet was killed?" Sonia asked, sounding breathless. "Murdered, I mean?"

Byron looked sharply at her and saw she was addressing the board. He'd forgotten his fingers remained on the planchette until it twitched again. It sidled toward Yes but stopped halfway.

"Who are you?" Paul asked in a loud, ringing voice.

The planchette flew again. *Ask Aur.*

"Ask me what?" Auraleigh's voice was pinched with fear.

If only she could know what Byron was experiencing, how

his heart continued to beat while his lungs absorbed no air. If only she could know about the cold fingers on his skin.

His stomach lurched, the syrupy liquor burbling up, as he watched the planchette move. He would have lost track if it weren't such a short message: *Im js baby rip.*

Auraleigh snatched her fingers away. "Who *are* you?"

Rain pattered. Byron drew a long, shaky breath.

"You need to be touching it, Auraleigh," Paul said.

Sonia was looking at Auraleigh, too. "You understand what it means. What it meant just now. Tell us."

Auraleigh shook her head, her mouth tight. "One of you is moving it. One of you knows. This is just a joke—a nasty, tasteless joke."

"I'm not moving it," Sonia said. "Are you, Paul?"

"Not me. Byron?"

Baby. Bile rose in Byron's throat, and he bowed his head to keep himself from retching.

Oh shit. Oh *shit.* That time in April, a month before she died—the crocuses coming up, the radiators clanking, 2 Live Crew, the maple brandy. The sense of things growing everywhere, the desperate need to meld.

It had to be his. There couldn't be anyone else, unless—the dark-haired boy from Paul's memory? But that was reaching; there could be so many explanations for an argument at the tray drop-off.

And Jennet had said to him *We need to talk.* She'd sounded as if she might, just possibly, have been crying.

"It's playing with us," Sonia said.

"Shh. Both of you." Auraleigh sucked in a breath. "This is fucked-up."

Byron yanked his hand away, pushed his chair out, and stood up. He couldn't take any more.

He went to the doorway and flicked on the overhead light. The three of them blinked at him owl-like, pupils fresh from darkness.

"Well, Auraleigh? How about explaining?" Byron asked. The

light was making his head swim, but otherwise he was sobering up. "How would you know there was a *baby*?"

"I don't know. I don't!" Auraleigh's eyes were huge. She knotted her fingers on the table. "All Jennet said was she was late and she hadn't gotten a test yet because she was too scared."

"You never told us this?" Paul seemed surprised for once, too.

Auraleigh shook her head. "It was all so weird that I didn't know how. I thought she might have been kidding. She said, 'Maybe I'll keep it. That'll throw a wrench in things.' I remember because it confused me. I was so hammered I imagined her throwing a literal wrench. Then she said 'probably not,' because she was all alone. And it seemed even weirder how calm she was."

Calm. She hadn't sounded calm in her message, the one he'd allowed to be erased.

"When did this happen?" Sonia asked.

"That night. We were sitting on the rock above the falls. I should've been more supportive—but, like I said, I didn't know whether to take her seriously. She said it depended on a poem. She said, 'I wrote a divination poem,' and I laughed. I *laughed*." She backhanded a tear off her cheek. "I'm such a bad person."

"You could have *mentioned* this," Byron said, knowing he hadn't told the full truth, either.

"When? During the funeral? You already thought I was being a drama queen. You would've told me I was making it up. And, honestly, I just didn't want to think about it."

"Auraleigh." Paul leaned over the board to pat her arm. "We understand."

Byron understood, all right. If only he'd gone to the falls that night, Jennet would have told him instead of Auraleigh. He could have *done* something.

"I know you set this up together." Guilt made him vicious, and he turned to Paul, his voice ice-cold. "I know you came for a visit months ago, and you've drunk sog before. I don't trust any of your so-called memories."

Paul looked alarmed. "It's not quite like that."

"I know a Ouija board isn't your style, either. Were you trying to make it implicate one of us?" He wheeled on Auraleigh. "Did you arrange this whole dramatic reveal?"

"No!" Auraleigh had gone pale. "I mean, yes, maybe we did mean to make the board say a few things, just to see how you two would react, but then it started going by itself!"

That was enough of a confession for Byron. Lying about Paul was one thing, but he couldn't forgive Auraleigh for weaponizing a secret that she had to know would devastate him, no matter what she claimed.

"I honestly don't know what the two of you think you're accomplishing," he said, turning to leave. "Go to the church tonight if you want, Sonia, but I'm done. I'll see you all tomorrow at breakfast."

Even as he made this declaration, he remembered the conversation between Paul and Auraleigh he'd overheard on his first night. Paul had mentioned a "stash downstairs."

Behind him, Auraleigh called, "Please, Byron, let's just talk."

"Let him go," Paul said.

Byron kept walking, through the parlor and up the stairs. He locked the door of his room, hoping Auraleigh wouldn't have the gall to use the master key, and threw himself on the bed in the dark. He couldn't face calling his kids right now.

No one came after him. No one pounded on the door.

The room's cold air sent shivers coursing over his skin. *Are you still here?* he asked, but no one answered. *I think I understand now what you wanted to say that night.*

Not until he changed into his heavy nighttime sweats did he notice two small bruises to the right of his navel, roughly the size and shape of fingertips.

23

SONIA

When Byron was gone, Auraleigh wheeled on Paul. "Why did you do that?" Her eyeliner was smudged, her gaze too bright.

"Which part?" Paul asked, carrying dishes to the sink.

"You moved the planchette, didn't you? How did you guess about the baby?"

"I didn't guess, and I didn't move the planchette. I thought that was *your* plan."

Sonia was too absorbed in what they'd just learned to pay attention. Could Jennet really have been pregnant? *Best friends*, Byron had called them, but Jennet would have told her best friend about a pregnancy scare. She wouldn't have waited to reveal the news to Auraleigh, of all people.

Auraleigh seemed wrung out. "I'm going to get a nap," she told them. "If you see Tina, remind her she's on watcher duty tonight."

In the kitchen, Paul and Sonia packed away the leftovers and filled the dishwasher, navigating the space in the civil silence of people who know they've managed to dodge a confrontation.

Not until he folded the Ouija board and tucked the box under his arm did she say, "You *were* here in April, weren't you?"

"After Auraleigh told me about sog, I had to see for myself if it was real, so I came to the memory spa." He sighed. "It wasn't supposed to be a secret."

He opened his mouth to keep explaining, but Sonia could guess. Auraleigh had told him to play dumb, the better to set her traps. Only one thing mattered: "The guy at the café, Hayworth—he knows you by sight, so I imagine you know him, too. He was the one with Jennet at the tray drop-off. But you guys didn't mention that. Why?"

Paul hung up the dish towel. "Auraleigh asked me to be vague. She was hoping…"

It was unlike him to be at a loss for words. "What?"

"Auraleigh was hoping you'd guess it was Hayworth and start remembering more suspicious things about him and Jennet. Things only you could know."

◆

Rain sluiced down the windshield of the van, too fast for the wipers. The dirt road to Belle Venere was pure mud, though no match for Auraleigh's four-wheel drive.

They were quiet on the way there, quiet as they dashed through the rain to the glowing church, quiet inside. Tina pulled off her slicker, draped herself in a pashmina shawl, and took her place behind the altar as the night's watcher. She handed them their doses without making eye contact, like an old priest whose ease reflects equal parts devotion and boredom.

The ritual required no words anymore, no argument or enthusiasm. Even Auraleigh hadn't bothered to express her dismay at Byron's absence. She seemed resigned.

Sonia lifted the shot glass to her lips and thought of Jennet, trying to target the right memories. *I want to know what really happened that night.* Byron seemed so sure they hadn't been together in the *Dove-Cat* room. If that was true, then where had she been before her mom's apartment, and why had she remembered the night so wrong?

We censor our memories—for survival, Hayworth had said.

She had censored so much—Jennet's warnings about him, Jennet's fears about her sogging, the awkward details of their interaction outside the townhouse. Sonia hadn't been acting much like a best friend, waltzing around with Hayworth that April night of the dance and practically ignoring Jennet.

If Jennet had lived, would there have been a baby? An abortion? Either way, Sonia should have known. She should have made calls and appointments, driven Jennet to the clinic or the delivery room, held her hand and told her the decision was hers alone. If there was a baby, she should have helped name it. She should have been there for its first step.

But instead, Jennet had felt discarded. Was it really a surprise that she would choose to tell Auraleigh about her pregnancy fears instead of Sonia?

She said it depended on a poem, Auraleigh had said. *She said, "I wrote a divination poem."*

Somewhere in the recesses of Sonia's brain, the phrase rang a bell. Jennet had written many poems, none about pregnancy that she recalled. But yes, a divination poem, painstakingly folded like the cootie catchers they used to tell their fortunes in elementary school. Perhaps Sonia had even seen it and forgotten.

Show me that night, she thought. Show me where I was, even if I think I already know.

BYRON

Byron couldn't sleep. His thoughts kept waking him, spinning like a hellish carnival ride: *Need to talk. Erased. Baby. My fault.*

He felt Jennet's scorn for him like a shudder in the walls,

mixed with cold amusement. She'd needed him and he'd erased her message, and then something had erased her, perhaps along with the earliest beginnings of what could have been their child.

My fault. He swung his legs onto the floor and rested his head in his hands. If Jennet wouldn't come out and face him, then he had to find her in the sog and show her he still cared. But he couldn't endure any more of Auraleigh's questions, or Paul's dry skepticism, or even the curious way Sonia gazed at him. This wasn't for any of them to know.

He would try another way.

Byron pulled on sweats and went down to the kitchen, flicking on lights. The stash of sog that Paul had mentioned might be locked up, but it was worth a try. If he could have one last memory, it might be a good one—good enough to cancel out what he'd seen last night. Good enough to convince him he'd been the kind of boyfriend he should have been.

Everything was quiet except for the irregular thud of rain on the windows and the roll of thunder. He moved into the pantry, a chaos of open shelving, and began taking things down, searching.

Of course, he might see a bad memory or just a random one. What had happened with Sonia and Auraleigh proved he hadn't been a good boyfriend, no matter what he wanted to believe. Jennet might have said he wasn't a boyfriend at all, but whether they were officially together or not, they belonged together. He felt it now, more than ever.

He hadn't belonged with Sonia, not even that long-ago day in the campus mail room—her hair escaping from a ponytail, her whole presence brittle and delicate and irresistible. He'd made a sarcastic remark about whoever was blasting Bon Jovi on the mezzanine, and she smiled—only for an instant, as always, before the seriousness returned. The vulnerability touched him, and he reached out and tweaked a strand of hair off her forehead.

Thanks. She flushed, and he kissed her. Lightly, not quite on the lips.

But the instant he tried to deepen the kiss, she lurched away. *I'm sorry. I have to go.*

And while he was kissing Sonia, Jennet might have been pregnant and wondering how to tell him. When she finally found the courage, her voice rough with tears, he didn't even pick up the phone.

His vision blurred as he stared down at the fortress of twenty-eight-ounce tomato cans he'd built on the pantry floor. If Jennet's ghost was real, she must despise him—she *should* despise him. He imagined her like a madwoman in the attic, pacing up and down, her back stiff with rage. Had she been buried in his mind the whole time, waiting for sog to release her?

He should never have come here. He didn't need to know these things about the past. Back in his real life, Eliza and Rohan were doing their homework or messaging their friends or expressing their strong feelings on social media. They were growing up, and he was missing it.

He rose and began returning cans to the highest shelf. One by one: a methodical, calming motion. "Why didn't you tell me?" he asked the emptiness. "Why the fuck did you tell *Auraleigh*?"

No answer, and he didn't need one. Jennet hadn't known about the kiss in the mail room, but she'd known him long enough to know he wasn't ready to be a father.

Even now, maybe he was only playacting the role. Often the kids didn't pick up his calls, and when they did, they answered his questions in monosyllables, their eyes drifting off-frame.

When they were little, they'd come to him with their skinned knees and smallest disappointments, and he'd tried so hard to shower them with love so they wouldn't turn hard and stoic as Jennet had. But now they *did* seem stoic to him, as if life had already battered them. He had spent all those years working day and night, barely seeing them, until he woke up and realized it was too late to earn a pass into their inner worlds. They would grow up and leave him alone.

He finished putting the pantry to rights and crossed the kitchen to a door that opened stickily onto a descending staircase, the air musty and spiked with Tide. He felt for a switch. Finding the sog was a game now, and he was going to win.

A bare bulb blazed to life in the center of the basement, illuminating a massive stainless-steel washer and dryer, a pegboard of tools, and a jumble of boxes and CD racks and old rockers and three-legged coffee tables.

At the bottom, he discovered a mountain of bulk items tucked under the stairs—how was he going to find anything in there?

The need for Jennet tugged on him. He still felt her cold fingers fleetingly around his ankle, in his hair, on the small of his back.

Then he spotted the minifridge perched at the far end of the laundry-folding counter.

The crown of his head grazed the light fixture as he crossed the room, making the shadows sway wildly. He opened the fridge and found Coors Light, Bud Light, and Canada Dry three deep, along with two bottles of a locally made kombucha.

And sitting demurely at the very back was a small mason jar with an inch of dark liquid at the bottom.

Byron pulled it out and sloshed it back and forth, noting the viscosity. He held it up to the light.

He shut the fridge and brought the jar up to his room, taking the many stairs two at a time. On the way, he tried to target good memories. But everything that came to mind was flimsy and fleeting compared with the Quad Howl and the slippery hardness of the dorm's floorboards under his knees as he listened to the phone message: *We need to talk, we need to talk, we need to talk.*

Involuntary Memory
May 22, 1989 (junior year)

BYRON

Outside, the howling continues. Will it never stop? Byron is awake in warm darkness, covers over his head.

This time, he knows immediately that he is back on the night Jennet died—the one Howl of his college career when he wasn't outside making noise with the others. His first reaction is disappointment—he wanted a good memory, not another reminder of what a shit he is. It's not as if he can change any of it.

He rolls over to look at the clock: 11:56 p.m. It's a quarter hour later than the time in his last sog memory. Beyond the clock, the red light on the answering machine blinks double time, telling him there are two messages.

In an instant, he's out of bed, sliding on the varnished boards and hunching over the machine. His body feels heavy and resistant, as if he's sick. But he's been given a second chance to listen to Jennet's message, and nothing will stop him.

He reaches for the play button and turns up the volume. Auraleigh's drawling voice explodes into the room: "Hey, Byron, what's cookin'? I'm here with Jennet and a bottle of Absolut, and after she closes the café, we're gonna—"

Byron stabs the stop button. At first, he feels only annoyance at Auraleigh, and then he realizes how stupid he's being. While he's sitting here playing with a cassette tape, Jennet could already be on her way to her death.

He staggers to his feet and switches on the overhead light, blinking in the glare. He throws on clothes that lie piled on the floor. Everything is a bit of a struggle, as if he's moving underwater. He grabs his keys, opens the door, and dashes out into the hallway.

His feet thud down the stairs, and then he's outside in the mellow May air of the quad, where the Howl is tapering off. Groups of students stream toward and around him, talking and laughing, refreshed by the twice-yearly ritual. He elbows through the mass of bodies, aiming for the road that leads off campus toward the river. *Hurry! Hurry!*

"Byron! What are you doing still up?"

It's Paul, lit orange by the sodium lights, a backpack slung over his shoulder. Byron recoils from him. "I need to go."

"Go where? Don't you have three finals tomorrow?"

Byron opens his mouth. But no excuse comes—and then a sharp crack sounds from somewhere far above them. Buzzing rises in his head, drowning out whatever Paul is saying. The quad goes black. The last feeble howls vanish, and then Byron feels nothing.

Involuntary Memory
May 23, 1989 (junior year)

SONIA

The campus is stinking full of flowers, satiny apple blossoms bunched up tight. Their scent wafts to Sonia as she walks across the quad. In the dusk, they look violet, but they're actually the pink of ballet slippers—impossible flowers that bloom and crumple and fall almost before you notice them.

What's the song that was popular freshman spring? It plays now from a window. Something about dying in a lover's arms, a trembling melody with a cavernous echo.

Death is not an abstract thing in a song anymore. Jennet is dead.

She let herself forget for a moment, but now it all rushes back, a suffocating darkness building behind her eyes. How could she forget that Jennet is dead and she is alive? She isn't fit to breathe the air, that gentle broth of florals and cedar chips. Her eyes ache with unshed tears.

People pass her, complaining about finals in soft, happy voices that don't match their words: "Did you hear Shapiro used a curve?" "No! That bastard!"

A boy and girl walk by with arms linked. Another couple cuddles at the base of the rock at the center of campus, oblivious. None of them should be so blissful. Don't they know?

Where is Byron? Did Auraleigh tell him, too? Maybe she should go to him—but no, she can't. *My fault, all my fault.* If she hadn't kissed him, if she hadn't...

She passes Byers Hall and the *Dove-Cat* room, the window an amber lozenge. Inside, faces bend over a table.

Thinking of the red leather couch, she stumbles, and strong arms grab her from behind, steadying her.

She turns in those arms, and there he is. Hayworth.

It's like the final scene of a movie, when a song drowns out the dialogue. The scene where the boy finally reveals his true feelings for the girl. "The trees bloomed," she says stupidly—but the actual dialogue never matters. Only his touch and the gleam of his eyes.

She'll have to tell him about Jennet, but not yet, not now. *Pretend it didn't happen.* She feels suddenly light, as if she's made of air. "Where are we going?" she asks.

"We need to talk."

Something is wrong. His fingertips dig into her shoulders.

Of course—he knows, too. Jennet is gone, and now dark winter clouds bear down on her, and it's too late for touching, too late for any of that.

Still, she lets him guide her into the alley between the library and computer annex. The heady scent of the flowers disappears, replaced by the sting of juniper bushes.

The Pacific Ocean. The Golden Gate rising proud through the fog, shouts of longshoremen, wisteria on the air. She and Jennet were going to road trip there and never come back.

She was supposed to see Hayworth there, too—but not now. Now they can never have their promised meeting at the Pacific Film Archive.

"What happened?" He is not loud, yet somehow he is shouting at her.

He clamps her shoulders, shoving her so hard to the wall that quartz prickles against her back. His hands tremble. "What *happened*, Sonia?"

She says, "I thought you knew?"

This is May, and lovers are dying in each other's arms, and he's finally touching her. This moment should have been perfect, like pressing a knife edge into the soft pad of your fingertip and waiting for the blood to swell. This moment should have lasted forever.

"No!" He hasn't let her go. "What happened last night by the river, Sonia? What did you do?"

His voice sounds so strange and strangled, she wants to laugh. He stares at her, wild-eyed. "She died! She fucking drowned there! I didn't know until now, but you, you... You must have known," he cries, his grip tightening. "We were there in the shack, and you were probably the last person to see her alive!"

I was? Her memories are all mixed-up. If she'd been there last night, she would have helped Jennet. Of course she would have.

"Tell me what happened! You didn't hurt her, did you?"

Her whole body tingles, the spring evening coming apart into angry buzzing. Bees are swarming, attacking the exquisite flowers.

Jennet had something to say about all this, about the spring and the flowers and the touching, but she can't remember what. Anyway, there are actually no bees, only a buzzing in Sonia's head. She's the one dissolving into the cosmos and solar wind, escaping a past that is long gone.

When she opens her eyes, her lips are still forming the words *I don't know, I don't know, I don't know.*

· 24 ·

BYRON

Byron watched lightning flash on the walls of his room before it plunged back into pitch-darkness. That cracking sound he'd heard in his sog vision must have been thunder. The storm had yanked him back to reality just as he was about to run to the river and Jennet.

Had any of that really happened? It must have, even though he had no voluntary memories of listening to Auraleigh's message, bolting out onto the quad, or meeting Paul. The past couldn't be revised.

Unless it could?

Tonight he had been less fully immersed in the memory than before, more conscious of the future outside the sog and the threat looming over Jennet. And it almost seemed as if he had acted on that consciousness, those inner cries of *Hurry!*

The possibility made his head swim in a pleasantly vertiginous way, like a strong shot of liquor. But he couldn't let himself take it seriously until he'd quizzed Paul. If they had met on the quad in 1989, then Byron hadn't changed anything. He had simply forgotten.

Were the others home yet? Byron rose from bed and flicked the light switch, grateful to be free of the moving-underwater sensation he'd had in the memory.

Power was out—the storm was a rager. He ventured downstairs and barked his shin on something that might have been the reception desk.

The van wasn't back yet, but the rest of the block had power; a streetlight shone through the whipping trees. Limping, he felt his way outside and down the steps to the lawn. Cold rain pelted him, dripping down his collar.

He squinted through the downpour. A dark mass, half as tall as the house itself, had settled on the eaves. A tree branch, brought down by lightning and presumably crushing the entry point for the power lines.

Once he'd assessed the situation, Byron's pulse settled into a steadier rhythm. He'd dealt with this sort of minor crisis before. The house itself didn't seem seriously damaged, and Auraleigh's insurance should cover it.

He assured himself that nothing was sparking or smoldering, then found his phone and googled the name of the local power company, where he left a message in his firmest I'm-the-homeowner voice. He would make himself useful, pestering them until someone addressed the situation. Whatever his feelings toward the others, he wished them no harm.

He returned to the pantry, where he found flashlights and a camping lantern. The sight of a stray tomato can on the floor gave him a jolt.

The sog was still on his bedside table; he would have to hide it before the others came back. Now that he was more awake, he was a little shocked at the thoughts about revising the past he'd been having earlier.

He would still find out what Paul remembered about that night on the quad, though. It couldn't hurt to know.

SONIA

They came home at nearly two to an island of darkness. No porch light, no floodlight to give form and depth to the silent bulk of the Victorian. Just smoke seeping languidly from the chimney.

"Oh shit," Auraleigh moaned when she saw a branch had wedged itself against the eaves.

The rain had finally stopped. Sonia, Muriel, Paul, and Tina watched in silence as Auraleigh scrabbled at the door, trying to fit her key into the lock.

Sonia hadn't spoken more than a monosyllable to anyone since emerging from the sog. When she recalled the regrets she'd had earlier this evening, they seemed absurd.

Not being there to support Jennet through a pregnancy scare was bad enough. But *hurting* Jennet? What possible motivation could she have? Yet Hayworth had practically accused her of it.

The door opened from the inside, and Byron stepped out. "I've got flashlights," he said, handing one to Auraleigh. "The power company won't come before nine tomorrow, but I managed to save most of the food in the fridge. It's in a cooler on the porch."

Auraleigh looked dazed. "Thank you."

"I made a fire."

After the cold and wet outside, the glowing fire was irresistible. Sonia took the loveseat, hoping the outage would keep the others from noticing how quiet she was.

Tell me what happened! You didn't hurt her, did you? Hayworth had said. The memory felt new, yet it fit perfectly into a gaping hole she hadn't realized was there.

She remembered—what did she remember, really? Byron's kiss in the *Dove-Cat* room, but Byron said it had happened a week earlier in the mail room. Walking up Railroad Street smelling lilacs in the dark, but Railroad Street was the way not only to her mother's apartment but also to the river shack, where Hayworth said they had been that night.

The blossoming trees, the song about dying in a lover's arms playing on the quad, and the smell of cedar chips were part of a voluntary memory of the day after Jennet's death. She remembered Auraleigh telling her the news. But she didn't remember being in the shack. She didn't remember seeing Hayworth at all.

She'd always been vague on when he'd dropped out of her life—that April on the stoop, or did they have one last sog after that point?

She'd never imagined they could have been in the shack *that* night. But if he thought she might have hurt Jennet, there had to be a reason.

She rested her eyes on the rippling flames, barely conscious of Byron settling in the armchair beside her loveseat. Auraleigh had gone into the kitchen, presumably to check on the fridge.

Paul had headed upstairs, but perhaps ten minutes later, he tramped back down with a great commotion, his flashlight beam glancing on the walls of the parlor. At the bottom, he rumbled, tugging a neat leather roller suitcase behind him.

He deposited it in the foyer, but he didn't sit down. "Nice fire."

"Paul," said Auraleigh, who had knelt to poke at the logs, "you're not leaving till day after tomorrow."

Paul's eyes met each of theirs briefly in the firelight. "Something came up, actually. I'm going tomorrow, early, and I don't want to wake you, so I thought I'd just put this by the door."

Auraleigh rose and went to him, arms dramatically open. "I know things got a little out of hand with the Ouija board, but please—we agreed! Is this because of what Byron said? About you visiting here before? He's been picking up townie gossip. He just didn't like what the Ouija board said, so he—"

"Auraleigh." Paul seized both her hands, holding her still. "This isn't fair. We all need to be honest with each other."

Sonia's breath caught as if the air had been sucked out of the parlor. But Paul wasn't accusing her—even if she had been in the shack that night, he couldn't possibly know.

Paul turned to Byron. "What you heard is right. I was here in April. That's the first time I sogged."

Auraleigh twitched in Paul's grip, but he plowed on: "We made a kind of deal. Auraleigh told me about sog, and after I tried it, I knew I had to write about it. I just needed a sample to show a chemist friend of mine, to give the story a scientific underpinning. Auraleigh agreed to help me out with that if I would help with her...investigation."

Auraleigh yanked her hands free. "What the fuck, Paul! You agreed—"

"I know. I shouldn't have." Paul's shoulders slumped. The two of them were silhouettes against the fire, but the shadow play said enough.

"What did you agree to, Paul?" Byron sounded oddly calm. "You lied about not sogging until this week. Did you also lie about what you were seeing in the sog?"

"Just a little," Paul admitted. "My memory of Jennet at the tray drop-off is genuine, but it's a voluntary memory."

"Why would you say it was a sog memory, then?"

But Sonia had already put the pieces together. "You were trying to incriminate Hayworth Darbisher. A sog memory carries more weight."

Auraleigh stamped the floorboards—in rage or triumph, it was hard to tell. "I *asked* you if you knew him, Sonia! Back in December."

"Dial back the drama?" Paul sank onto the sofa. To Sonia, he said, "She thinks your friend is Suspect Number One, yes. Jennet's brother Ben is convinced it's him. Ben said he used to see Hayworth with you, during college, and that the two of you sogged in a shack by the river, right where Jennet died. Auraleigh asked you about Hayworth, but you changed the subject."

So Ben had put Auraleigh on the right path—but maybe that path didn't actually lead to Hayworth. "But she didn't say Hayworth's name," Sonia pointed out, fear making her vehement. "She didn't say he was still here!"

"When I tried to talk about him, you cut me off like you were scared of something," Auraleigh said. "I realized I had to find a different way to get you to open up."

"Maybe you should have talked to Hayworth directly."

"The one time I asked him about Jennet, he froze! He stood there like a deer in the headlights, just *stricken*! It wasn't a normal reaction."

No. Whatever had happened that night, Hayworth's reaction couldn't have been normal. But it wasn't guilt that had petrified him, Sonia knew now. If Auraleigh had been wondering whether he could have hurt Jennet, he had wondered the exact same thing about Sonia.

"I wasn't there, so I can't corroborate," Paul said in his maddeningly logical way. "But I could confirm that you and Hayworth were friends in college, Sonia, because I'd seen you together, too. I told Auraleigh, and she got the idea of using you to entrap Hayworth. She was going to prime you with memories—your own, but also my voluntary memory plus some hints from the Ouija board—and then put you face-to-face with him and see what happened. See if you could get him to come clean."

Heat flared on Sonia's face. Then, just as quickly, she went cold.

What happened, *Sonia? She died! She fucking drowned there!* Such terror and bewilderment in Hayworth's voice, and he hadn't been faking it.

"You still lied, Paul." Byron's voice was heavy with bitterness.

"You pretended you couldn't ID the guy at the tray drop-off. And you, Auraleigh—am I still supposed to believe your story about your recovered memory after you've admitted to bribing Paul to lie to us?"

Auraleigh sank down on the carpet and buried her face in her hands, her shoulder blades jutting. "I saw what I saw. Last night, you said you believed me."

Byron tried to speak again, but Paul silenced him with a curt gesture and knelt beside Auraleigh. "I knew this was a bad idea. I think you knew, too, sweetheart."

Auraleigh uttered something incoherent, half protest and half whimper. Paul wrapped an arm around her shoulders. "I believe you," he said. "Sog is real. Until now, though, to be honest, I haven't had a single vision with Jennet in it."

"Knew it," Byron said.

"I said *until now*." Paul's voice cracked like a whip. "I'm leaving because of what I saw tonight."

Sonia's stomach twisted. Could he have been on the quad when Hayworth confronted her the next day?

"What did you see?" Auraleigh sat up and grabbed both of Paul's hands. "You can't just run away! Not without telling us why!"

"I'll be back to visit you, sweetie, but not for more of this. This, what we're doing—" Paul turned to include Byron and Sonia "—isn't right. Jennet was nineteen and twenty and twenty-one when we knew her. A child."

He gazed past Auraleigh into the fire, the light drawing harsh angles from his face. "We're trying to dig her up and make her the heroine of a mystery. We're dissecting and mummifying her. There's a good reason our brains don't rerun our memories like video files. We need vagueness, hindsight, wishful thinking, or we won't be able to live with ourselves."

"Paul," Auraleigh said, *"what did you see?"*

"Not what you're hoping for. Not a solution to your mystery."

"I don't care."

When Paul answered, it was with a sigh, as if he'd resigned himself to an enormous sacrifice of privacy. "Auraleigh, have you really never wondered how you got home the night of Jennet's death? After you blacked out?"

Auraleigh's eyes were wide and frightened. "I walked. It's only a few miles. The first thing I remember is puking in the townhouse bathroom in the morning."

Paul tugged his hands gently free of hers. "No. I left the library around the time of the Quad Howl, went home, checked my messages, and found out you—Auraleigh—were by the river. I was worried about how much you were drinking. I drove down there, parked on the road, and hiked to the falls."

"You were *there*?" Byron asked.

The question was as sharp as a slap. Paul didn't flinch, but Sonia did.

"You never told us this?" Auraleigh's voice was low, almost a croak. "All these years, you let us think you spent the whole night at the library?"

"I couldn't." Sonia couldn't see Paul's features clearly, but his posture tightened as if he were clenching his fists. "If I'd told you, you would have jumped on it and overanalyzed it and never let it go. Anyway, Byron should have known I wasn't at the library all night. I saw him on the quad during the Howl." His gaze flicked sideways to Byron. "You told me you had to get somewhere."

Byron stared into the flames. "Back to my room, I guess. I must've gone out for a quick walk because the noise kept waking me up."

Auraleigh's attention was on Paul. "Who cares where Byron was? You didn't tell me the truth."

"The way I felt about that night is how you felt about Jennet saying she might be pregnant, Auraleigh—it was my secret to keep. Honestly, I didn't even remember much, but I was sure I didn't see Jennet go in the water. When I left her, she was alive, heading toward the opposite shore."

"When you left her?" Auraleigh's tone was deadpan, as if she'd passed beyond surprise. "You saw her at the river, then? You talked to her?"

Sonia was stunned, too, that Paul could have withheld the information all these years, but the words that revolved in her brain were *She was alive, heading toward the opposite shore.*

On the opposite shore was the shack. If Hayworth had been telling the truth in her sog memory, the two of them were inside. Had Jennet been heading their way?

"You set up that whole Ouija revelation to ambush us," Byron said in a shaky voice, "when Paul was right there, on the spot?"

"No! We meant to make the Ouija say something about Hayworth, to see how Sonia would react. I never tried to ambush *you*, Byron—I didn't want to tell you about the pregnancy thing at all. Jennet wouldn't have wanted me to." Auraleigh was gaining steam again. She swung to face Paul. "Tell me everything that happened between you and Jennet by the river. Is that what you saw in the sog tonight?"

Paul rose and sat heavily back down on the couch. "There's so little to tell. She was wearing baggy jeans and an old T-shirt—the only time I ever saw her in jeans. We talked about you—how you'd passed out, and I promised to bring you home safely. She sounded so distant. She only really looked at me once, and her face…"

A log thunked. "Please," Auraleigh whispered.

"I'd never seen her like that before. Not just unhappy, but… other. Outside her body. Like the Furies had her. She made a funny little remark about how all her friends were 'overindulging,' which went over my head. Then she asked me if I'd like to see my future, if I had a choice. I said no, because it might compromise my free will. And she said, 'I tried it once. I didn't see anything. Isn't that a bad sign?'"

Light and shadow pulsed on the walls. Sonia saw Jennet as

if from far away, on an island of light. It was spring 1989, and the two of them were sitting outside among the forsythia, and then the forsythia blossoms dropped to the ground and the lilacs bloomed and time opened an ocean of darkness between them.

She asked, "Then what?"

"Then... I thought she was joking about seeing the future, okay? I didn't know about sog then. I had to get Auraleigh home, and Jennet said she wanted to stay a little longer and watch the stars. We both got up, and she slipped, and I—I reached out and steadied her and said, 'Watch yourself.' I think that must be the memory you recovered, Auraleigh. I didn't remember it myself until I sogged it last night. I didn't remember seeing Byron on the quad, either."

The four of them sat absolutely still until Sonia said, "You let her stay there."

Paul took off his glasses and wiped them on his shirt. "Yes. Maybe I thought she was okay. Maybe I was just worried about Auraleigh. I don't know. But I went off and left her there, and now that I've seen it all again, clear as day—well, I think I know what happened next, Auraleigh. I think she jumped. And I'll feel responsible for it as long as I live."

"You didn't tell us." Byron's voice was hoarse. "All these years. How could you let Auraleigh think she was murdered? If anyone killed her, it would be you."

Sonia wrung her hands in the dark. *No. Hayworth thought I was the last one to see her alive. Not Paul—me.*

"Stop." Auraleigh was whispering, almost pleading. "Both of you, just stop. Paul, I *trusted* you."

"I know," Paul said, head down. "I know."

While the two of them were focused on each other, Byron tapped the back of Sonia's hand and said, low, "It's okay."

Did she look so upset, then? With a start, she sat up and tried to seem normal. "It's just a lot to take in."

They didn't need to know she might have something to hide, too.

DAY 5

◆ ◆ ◆

October 31, 2014

SONIA

When the sky lightened to gold and the birds cried in raw, wild voices, Sonia crept downstairs, where the rising sun turned the parlor's oval mirror into a limpid pool. She took the key from the reception desk and locked up behind her.

She hadn't slept much, but she had dreamed about her and Jennet sharing an apartment in San Francisco. They were watching *The X-Files*, and the room smelled cozily of basil and browning garlic. Jennet kept trying to leave, saying she had an appointment, but Sonia begged her to stay.

Outside, a blue-tipped world. No dogs barking yet, no cars starting. The leaf-streaked sidewalk took her to the intersection, where she stopped in front of the pizza pub.

There were no signs of life inside the Buzz On Café. She stayed on her side of the deserted street and stared at the Victorian that housed it, as if she were staking it out. This early, she didn't have to worry about being observed.

That cold April night on the stoop of the townhouse, Hayworth had offered to bring her to the shack when it was warmer.

But she had no memory of actually going there in the spring of 1989.

She remembered breathing the mellow May air, walking across the quad. And Hayworth appearing without warning, all rough hands and panicked fury: *What happened? You didn't hurt her, did you?*

She had no clue, and apparently neither had he. What could he tell her now that she didn't already know?

When she'd asked the other day if he was in the shack when Jennet died, he'd claimed not to remember—a lie. But since she had actually been there with him, she knew now, her question must have signaled that something was wrong with her memory, if he hadn't already guessed. And last night he'd asked how much she really wanted to know: *Would it matter, if you couldn't do anything to change it?*

He'd been probing, trying to figure out how much she recalled and whether *she* was the bald-faced liar.

The first rays tipped the brick chimney of the Victorian. Light slid slowly down the cupola, the third-floor windows catching fire. The scaly texture of the paint gave way to an auroral vision of salmon and mint green and sky blue.

A beat-up blue Legacy like hundreds of other Vermont cars rumbled down the street and into the café's driveway. Sonia darted into an alley. When she was reasonably sure Hayworth was inside the café, she turned and walked briskly up Main Street, well past Railroad, as if her legs wanted to stride right out of town. Past the second-hand shop and the woolen mills, past the mini-mart and the turnoff, until the sidewalk ended.

She crossed to the other side of the highway and the sign that said Dunstan Cold Spring, Est. 1877. Four steps led down into a concrete enclosure. Water flowed from a spigot, and she stuck her hand in it.

It was freezing. She knelt beside the spigot and cupped her numbing hands and splashed the liquid ice on her face. Blood surged, the hot thrum in her temples mounting as she gulped a mouthful and spat it out.

She couldn't have hurt Jennet. She had no reason to. But without remembering, she couldn't be sure. Paul had last seen Jennet walking toward the opposite shore—toward the shack.

How could Sonia admit to Hayworth that she still didn't know what happened on that May night in 1989? Until she found out, she couldn't face him.

A Green Mountain Power truck idled in front of the B and B. A lineman on a crane was busy disengaging the fallen branch from the eaves, while another watched from below and mumbled into a transceiver.

In the kitchen, Auraleigh was setting out breakfast. Her eyes were still red around the edges, but her smile was bright as she told Sonia, "Paul decided to stay after all."

"That's great." Sonia tore off a chunk of bread. "I'm going back upstairs. I don't think I got enough sleep."

"If you see Byron," Auraleigh said, "could you ask him to come to the church tonight? Please?"

"I'll try to talk to him."

That's right, concentrate on bringing Byron back into the fold. Now that you know the man you saw in your recovered memory was only Paul, it's time to stop hunting for a murderer and give this reunion a more positive spin. Maybe we can still all share a teary embrace at the end.

But Sonia knew she would leave here with secrets worse than the ones with which she'd arrived.

· 26 ·

BYRON

Flat blue twilight. Rain-spattered window. High plaster ceiling lost in shadows. Then a seam of light under the door and someone knocking, knocking.

"Byron, are you okay in there? It's so late!"

Yesterday came back to Byron all at once. Walking in the dark with Sonia. The Ouija board spelling out *baby*. The wind, the storm, finding Auraleigh's hidden stash of sog, running into Paul on the quad in his memory, the thunderous crack of the branch.

Today was Halloween.

Jennet was in the attic. He could swear he heard her pacing, her voice crooning a lullaby. Sometimes she laughed, low and intimately.

Come down here, he begged her. *Tell me what happened.*

Thanks to Paul's confession, he knew now they really had met on the quad that night. His sog vision must be true, then, not some wishful revision. But something still felt off. Had he really only gone outside for a moment, the way he'd told the others last night? Or, if he had gone to find Jennet, then why hadn't he arrived at the river? Paul should have seen him there.

Had he headed for the river and gotten sidetracked? Given up? Anger at himself choked him. How could Paul have happened to be there in Jennet's last minutes when he wasn't? *Why didn't I help her?*

Two more knocks. "Byron? I'm worried!"

"Fine!" he called. "I'll be down in a sec."

He wanted them all to go away and stop trying to distract him from Jennet's furtive presence still itching at the corners of his brain. When he emerged from the morass of grief, twenty-five years ago, he had been eager to think about anything but Jennet, but not now.

She was all alone, Auraleigh had said to explain why Jennet wouldn't want to keep the baby. She'd also said it was too early to be sure. But Jennet was already worried about graduation, brushing off their questions about her plans far too breezily. Underneath, she might have been frightened—panicked, even. Panicked enough to jump?

Byron floundered out of the blankets and threw on clothes and stumbled down the two flights of stairs.

The lights were back on; the power company must have done its work. As he reached the foyer, the doorbell rang with a tinny harshness that made him freeze. Auraleigh darted past him, seized a bowl from the reception table, and opened the door.

Byron couldn't see who was outside in the dusk, but Auraleigh's reaction told him the parade of trick-or-treaters had begun. "What an adorable kitty! Oh no, a dragon? Please don't breathe fire on me!"

She sounded genuinely awed, and Byron felt a brief flush of tenderness toward her, remembering the costumes Christa used to assemble for the kids from cardboard and old clothes. It had been cold-blooded of Paul to withhold information she desperately wanted, even if he couldn't provide a definitive answer about what happened to Jennet.

Byron went into the parlor, where Sonia sat in the loveseat. A fire blazed in the woodstove, sparks flying up the chimney. He watched through the window as, with a chorus of thanks, the kids and their chaperone tramped back down the porch steps.

"Paul's coming down in a minute," Auraleigh said, joining them. Her tone was guarded, as if she and Paul had only just patched things up. "He's staying to the end with us after all. Soon we'll be off to the church." She glanced at Sonia. "Did you two get a chance to talk?"

Sonia shook her head. "He slept the whole day."

"The tree?" Byron gestured at the ceiling, not liking where this conversation seemed to be going. "Did they get it off the eaves?"

"Yeah. Gutter's totaled, though." Auraleigh looked at him in the melting way she did when she really wanted something. "Are you *sure* you won't come tonight, Byron? One last time, all of us together? It would mean so much."

"No!" Byron barked the word before he could stop himself. He needed to be alone with Jennet tonight, coaxing her back to him—not with the others, and certainly not getting caught up in more of Auraleigh's manipulations. "Sorry, but I'm done with that," he added, trying to soften his voice.

"But you and Paul are remembering new things. I think we're getting somewhere!"

Byron wheeled on her. "Really? Where is there to get? The dark figure you thought was some homicidal Hayworth was actually Paul. If anybody killed her, it was me."

"What?" Auraleigh looked genuinely alarmed. "Nobody thinks that. You were in your room all night."

"Not *all* night—remember what Paul said about meeting me on the quad? But I don't mean physically killed her." Byron clawed his fingers over his scalp. "She was maybe pregnant with our kid. In her phone message, she said we needed to talk—about that, I assume."

It was Jennet he was saying the self-lacerating words for, Jennet who needed to know he was doing penance.

"You didn't mention that part of your recovered memory before," Sonia said.

"No, because I didn't want to. And you know what else I didn't mention? That I erased the damn tape and went back to sleep." *And then I was on the quad. Where did I go next?* "Jennet couldn't get hold of me, so she went off with you—" he addressed Auraleigh "—someone who was probably happy to confirm her worst fears that I was somebody she couldn't trust. A player, a dick. After all, you had the gory details to prove it."

"I don't know if I told her about us, Byron," Auraleigh said in a small voice. "I don't exactly remember. I do think maybe she deserved to know." A pause. "The kid *was* yours, right? If there was one?"

Byron rubbed his eyes. A ragged sound—groan, moan, something unspeakable—fought its way out of him. "If I'd known everything, if she'd said everything in the message, I would have helped her. I swear on my life."

He wanted to confess that he'd kissed Sonia in the mail room, too—not for Auraleigh's benefit but for Jennet's. Maybe, if he proved himself, she would creep back to him tonight and wrap her arms around him in his sleep the way she had the first few nights, before he knew how badly he had failed her.

The click of a door upstairs reverberated through the stairwell—probably Paul coming to join them. He would look at Byron in that frustratingly sensible way and tell him to calm down.

And now Byron remembered something else Paul had said last night—that his meeting with Byron on the quad was a new memory to him. As if Paul had recovered a memory he'd buried—or as if he'd seen a past that had been changed.

Perhaps revised by someone else who was sogging at the same time, such as Byron himself.

Before Byron had time to digest and dismiss the idea—*absurd, science fiction*—Auraleigh snapped, "No one blames you, Byron. So, you could have helped more—we all could have. Enough with the drama."

"You're one to talk! You're obsessed with finding a villain and making things right." Byron's voice thundered in his ears. He wasn't a sheepish college boy anymore. He was a man, a father capable of defending his family, and why was Jennet silent? Wasn't all his self-accusation enough? What more did she want? He could spend the rest of his life feeling guilty, and it wouldn't bring her back.

Anger swamped his grief, and he said, "But this isn't a game of Clue, and we all know what happened, and we need to let it go. I'm done being made to feel guilty for mistakes I made when I was a scared, stupid kid. So, I hooked up with you." His gaze moved to Sonia. "And I kissed you—once!—and I was with Jennet that April. I never forced anybody to do anything."

"I *knew* you and Sonia did something," Auraleigh said, looking triumphant.

Byron barely heard her. "And I knew Jennet had depressive episodes, but I had no idea what to do about it. I was a kid. A dumb, scared, out-of-his-league kid. I'm not that anymore."

The other two might as well have vanished; he was speaking to Jennet alone. Wherever she was, she needed to understand. "I have a family, and I work and contribute and give money to good causes every single year. I'm not playing at living a life, I'm living it. I've made my choices, and you can laugh your little ironic laugh at them all you want, but—"

He broke off, gazing into space. Somewhere very close to him, Jennet was indeed laughing.

Where's your family now, Byron?

"You feel so superior to us," Byron said quietly to the rafters. "But that's because you haven't made those hard choices. You never got a chance to be an adult. I see you looking down on us with that little smile, and there's so much you will never, ever know."

He swallowed the sob. Shut his trap. He was ranting to no-body like an unhinged person on the BART. Jennet had receded again, and Sonia and Auraleigh were gaping at him.

He got up. "I'm going to pack. I'm not hungry. I'll see you tomorrow at breakfast."

He didn't pack. He lay still on his bed with the lights out and listened as the doorbell rang downstairs, again and again, until there was silence.

He waited for Jennet. Ashamed of his outburst now, he begged for her forgiveness: *I'm sorry, but it's so hard going round and round in this circle of wishing I'd done everything differently. It was easier when you were just gone.*

He knew he was being ridiculous. He was a middle-aged software engineer who had never been superstitious or believed in ghosts; he still didn't believe in them, particularly ghosts that whispered in people's ears or left bruises. On an intellec-tual level, he knew the phantom voice and the pinching fingers could have been his own.

But he couldn't deny that sometimes the world he knew felt like a fragile membrane stretched over a vast, echoing darkness. The membrane had been thin last night when they used the Ouija board, and again when he drank the stolen sog. Whether she was a ghost or a memory or his guilt turned into a physical force, Jennet had been so close that her every chuckle or mur-mur sent tickling thrills down his nerves.

He couldn't live his whole life mired in guilt, but he couldn't let go of her, either. He remembered the intoxication he'd felt last night, waking from his sog and thinking for an instant that he'd actually changed the past—because that would be the only escape from these feelings, wouldn't it? To do the impossible and start over.

But there was still the idea he'd had earlier, before his anger took over. *What if Paul has a new memory now because we sogged at the same time? Because, in my sog, I changed reality, and that's the version of events he saw?*

He would rather believe he had changed reality—and could change it again—than believe he had simply forgotten things. But wasn't that just as bad as believing in ghosts?

A knock came at the door, too soft to be Auraleigh. He flicked on the light and opened it to find Sonia with an improvised charcuterie plate.

She had a hard set to her jaw, as if she feared he might bite her. "You didn't eat all day."

Now that he thought about it, Byron was ravenous. He took the plate and sat down at the scuff-marked desk. "Something about that damn stuff drains you. Memories drain you," he said. "You don't notice at first."

"I know." Sonia hovered in the doorway. "Byron, I feel bad about what happened downstairs."

She was talking about the fight and his outburst. Remembering it, he was ashamed. "Don't feel bad. You're the least to blame of any of us."

"I don't know." She crossed her arms as if to anchor herself. "We all saw the signs. We all knew she was troubled."

Byron stopped eating. He cocked his head, listening not to Sonia but to the frequency where Jennet resided. She never liked being described as troubled or needy.

But she remained quiet, as if she wanted to hear their conversation—or as if she were gone. "I don't know," he said. "Her back was up so high. If you even suggested therapy, she'd shut you right down. And in those days, there was more of a stigma."

"I know." A pause. "I'm going to the church tonight, one more time."

"I'm not." There was still plenty of sog in the jar—if he dared to take it. He stuffed a whole cracker in his mouth and chewed, listening for humming in the walls. "Have you ever had one of those recovered memories, like Auraleigh and I did?"

Sonia nodded. Didn't elaborate.

Did he dare to tell her his idea? She wasn't Auraleigh. She

wouldn't laugh at him. "Okay, so this is going to sound out-there. But when you saw something you didn't remember in the sog, did you ever wonder, just for a second, if maybe it wasn't really a repressed memory at all? If maybe you were *changing* the past—or someone else was?"

Sure enough, Sonia didn't laugh. She said, "I think what I'm seeing is real. But do *you* feel like you're trying to change things when you sog? To take control of your past body?"

"Maybe a couple times, yeah." Byron had tried to warn Jennet during his second sog, acting impulsively and struggling against the weight of his younger body. And then last night—well, he still wasn't sure what had happened last night.

"Am I losing my mind?" he asked Sonia. If she said yes, at least he would understand what was going on. "I mean, that would be science fiction, right?"

Sonia's thumbs worried the sleeves of her hoodie. "It's not just you. Hayworth says that when you're not fully immersed in a sog memory, you might start trying to change it."

"Hayworth? The guy who was Auraleigh's prime suspect?" Now that he'd seen the mysterious stranger of Paul's memory, Byron felt reasonably sure Hayworth would never have been Jennet's type. "What would he know about it?"

"He used to sog in his shack by the falls." Sonia's words were toneless. "We would sog together."

"Oh!" Byron had to admire Sonia for quietly keeping her secret from the rest of them. He had always seen her as floating above the fray of messy college romances. But right now there was just one thing that mattered: "And has Hayworth ever *done* it? Changed the past?"

Again, no derisive smile. She only looked thoughtful. "He thinks so. When he sogged into the past and approached me at a college party, he shifted our meeting years earlier. He says. But he also thinks he's unstuck in time, so I don't know how seriously you want to take him."

Byron finally did laugh, and it felt good—a release. "Like Billy Pilgrim? He started time traveling?"

"It's your mind that gets unstuck, not your body." Sonia's voice was pinched, as if she thought he was mocking her credulity. "If you sog often enough, your younger mind might end up stuck in your older body or vice versa, especially when both versions of you are sogging. That was his theory, anyway."

"I'm not up for swapping brains with Younger Me, I can tell you that." Byron spoke in a gruff, humorous way. He didn't want her to know his mind was already racing, imagining what he would change in the past if he actually could.

A gust of wind rattled the window, and he jumped. Behind him, the old heater hissed. He hoped all the trick-or-treaters were back home by now, safe in their beds.

"All I know is what Hayworth said." Sonia's eyes were hooded, dark irises lost in darker pupils. "You don't really think you've changed something, do you?"

"Ha! Well, nothing seems different, does it?" Byron arranged his features in a scoffing expression, as if they were back at their midnight brunches, hashing out absurd hypotheticals. His throat hurt, and suddenly he wished she would go away and leave him alone with his whirling thoughts of what might have been, *should* have been.

Come back, Jennet. Maybe I can still help you after all.

When he glanced at Sonia, the troubled look on her face made him add, "You didn't think I was serious, did you?"

SONIA

Dinner was very quiet with just three of them. The second wave of rain settled in, drumming constantly and soothingly on the roof.

Tension still hung in the air. Paul and Auraleigh spoke politely to each other, like strangers, and rarely met each other's eyes.

Sonia felt like a child whose parents are on the brink of divorce. But it was just as well they were preoccupied with each other, because she couldn't take any questions right now.

After piling the dishes in the sink, Auraleigh opened a cabinet. "Let's have amaro and smoke on the porch. I love to smoke on the porch in the rain. You'll smoke with me this once, right?"

Paul said, "Yes."

Sonia nodded, too. She didn't want to be alone with her thoughts.

Auraleigh set three shot glasses on the railing, along with the bowl of leftover Halloween candy. In the pool of light coming from inside the house, she poured the amaro and handed one to Sonia. "How's Byron?" she asked. "Still pissed off?"

"What you told him last night was a shock."

"I didn't tell him! The Ouija board did!" Auraleigh shot a glance at Paul. "I can't believe we thought that would be a good idea. I should have been asking *you* about that night."

Paul sighed. "You kept quiet about the pregnancy because the whole thing weirded you out. I kept quiet about being there because I felt guilty that I didn't do anything. We both had messy memories we didn't want to get into. I think we're even. So, is Byron not coming again tonight?"

Sonia shook her head.

"Maybe we should call it off, then. I feel like we've all seen enough."

Auraleigh's jaw tightened. Sonia waited for her to object, but she didn't. Did she agree with Paul? Was she done with the past?

Sonia's throat was dry, her whole body tight with the fear of being found out. But she couldn't let it end here—not when she couldn't be sure. Not when Paul had last seen Jennet walking in the direction of the shack.

"I'd like to go to the church," she said, trying to keep her tone light and casual. "One more time, in honor of Halloween. After all, it's our last chance to...see her."

Silence stretched out, agonizing. She was about to backpedal and say no, she was fine, she'd seen enough, too, when Auraleigh said, "Of course we're going."

"I'll come, then," Paul said, to Sonia's relief, "but just to be the watcher. If anybody creeps over from the farmhouse, I'll clobber him over the head."

Sonia asked, "Did that really happen, or did you want to make us think Hayworth was sneaking around?"

"I didn't make it up!" Paul sounded scandalized. "I may have exaggerated a bit about the noises I heard, but the binoculars and stuff were real."

"You shouldn't be so suspicious, Sonia." Auraleigh lit three American Spirits and passed them out. She set a vintage ashtray shaped like a lily pad between herself and Sonia, then reclined in the wicker-backed rocker. "We're not evil masterminds. Paul prefers to lie by omission, don't you, sweetie? He's a real pro at that."

Paul sighed again but didn't deny it.

"And after all, Sonia, you did the same thing. You wouldn't talk about your secret college boyfriend."

"Hayworth was never my boyfriend." But Sonia understood better now why Auraleigh wouldn't let their secrets alone. How could you leave the past undisturbed when it was hiding parts of you from yourself? "You should have just told me you suspected him," she said.

"You would have denied everything. You're so good at building a fortress around yourself." Auraleigh exhaled, the smoke hanging radiant for an instant before dissipating into the dark.

The rain was slower but steady, with a constant silvery drip from the porch eaves. In the dim light, the nylon spiderwebs looked real.

"Hayworth didn't do anything to Jennet," Sonia said. After seeing his genuine shock at Jennet's death in her memory last night, she couldn't even entertain the possibility anymore. "When you saw them in the dining commons, Paul, she was telling him to stay away from me. She was worried about my sogging. That was the only time they ever spoke."

Auraleigh didn't look convinced. "How do you know? Because *he* told you?"

"He had no reason to hurt her." She pressed on each word. "I know it would be easier for all of us if we had someone to blame—someone who isn't one of us. It's tough to accept that accidents happen, and sometimes people hurt themselves. But Hayworth isn't sinister, he's just odd and a little lost."

"I saw that in him," Paul agreed.

"What, the one time he made you a macchiato? You just want to make him the star of your cover story in the *Times* magazine, Paul." Auraleigh's tone hardened. "There's another reason you didn't tell me you were at the falls that night, isn't there? You never came forward as a witness. If the case got dredged up again, things could get messy for you."

"I doubt that. There's no new evidence." Paul sounded chastened, as he had last night. "But…it's true that I'm a little too involved with this story. No editor would be okay with that kind of conflict. And the more I sog, the less eager I feel to tell the world about it. I keep seeing my dead mom, and it's good but it's *too* good, you know? It's always the seventies, and she's always smoking one of the cigarettes that will eventually kill her. For a while after my visit in April, I dreamed about her. I had trouble focusing on my real life."

A raw gust of wind wafted in their faces. They pulled their jackets tighter. The front door opened, and Muriel came out, hugging herself in a fuzzy bathrobe and socked feet. "Hey, are we still on for tonight?"

Auraleigh said, "We'll see you at eleven."

Muriel disappeared inside, and they settled back into their rockers. Gurgles and spatters came from the gutter.

All Sonia had to do now was wait, because she had faith that tonight she would see what she needed to see. She'd been circling the vortex of May 22, 1989, each night taking her a little closer.

"I don't think Hayworth would be very cooperative with a reporter," she said, watching whorls of smoke drift over the porch rail. She hadn't smoked in so long that each inhale dizzied her, the lightheadedness approaching nausea.

Auraleigh's exhale was forceful, almost contemptuous. "Tell me about it. I came to him in a perfectly civil way, asking questions about sog, not accusing him of anything, and now he's trying to shut me down."

"He's just worried you'll give sog to students. He thinks it fucked him up a little." *And me, too.* Hayworth said sog could "muddle" your memories. She had been sogging in 1989, and she had somehow forgotten the night her friend died.

"Wouldn't students see the future?" Paul said. "Sog memories feel real to me, but this fortune-telling business… I'm with Jennet. It sounds creepy."

On the night of her death, Jennet had told Paul she'd looked into her future and seen nothing. But she'd also told Auraleigh she was writing a divination poem about the pregnancy. It was a minor contradiction, but it tugged on something in Sonia's memory.

Auraleigh lit a new smoke and offered them the box. Paul took one. Sonia declined and sipped her amaro.

"I don't know," Auraleigh said. "Remember the graduation speech in that movie, where the girl says she's seen the future and all she can say is 'Go back'?"

"Our generation in a nutshell," Paul said, more affectionate than acerbic.

Smoke glowed in the floodlight. Rain trickled from the eaves. "I'm a cliché," Auraleigh said. "A retrophiliac, just like that guy in your movie, Sonia. I wouldn't actually undo the past twenty-five years because my kids were born in them, *obviously*. But if I could just be back there, stuck in my young body, I would be. In a heartbeat."

"Can you be sure, though?" Sonia asked. "When you're outside it, the past can seem so tidy, but when you're inside it again, living it…"

She stopped, the words going bitter in her mouth. Except for the first one, her sog memories had been filled with such turbulent emotions, so much dread and frustration and guilt. *What happened, Sonia? What happened?*

"If I could go back…" Auraleigh said. Another cloud of smoke. "I mean, I wouldn't risk my twins' lives. They're mine and I'm theirs and I carried them in my body. I'd have to marry their rat of a dad a second time to get them, knowing everything I know now, and I'd grit my teeth and do it. But the second time around, I would be different with them. More fun. Less used up."

She turned, and Sonia saw she was crying.

"Your kids turned out great. You don't need to be anyone different for them." Paul stubbed out his cigarette and placed his hand on Auraleigh's, gazing earnestly at her. "I know maybe you feel like you failed Jennet, like you could've helped her—*I* certainly feel that way, anyway. But you don't ignore your daughter when she's in pain, Auraleigh. You're always there for her."

"It's true." Sonia swallowed down her own guilty feelings about Jennet, remembering how defiantly Frances had stood in the trailer doorway.

Auraleigh pulled out a tissue and blew her nose. "Of course I was there for Frances. Every second. And then she claimed she was doing better and didn't need me, and last summer, she even started lying to me and sneaking around with Garrett." She shot a glance at Sonia. "Did you find that out with all your nosing around?"

Sonia nodded. "Garrett seems like a nice kid."

"He is," Paul said. "You know he's Jennet's nephew, right?"

Sonia nodded, while Auraleigh said, "Would you both stop trying to *soothe* me? He may be nice, but he's troubled, just like his aunt Jennet. My baby needs someone aggressively normal."

"Frances *is* better now," Paul said. "You told me that yourself—you would never have started sogging if you weren't sure she was well enough to take care of herself."

"She doesn't know anything, though," Auraleigh said. "Being young is like being on drugs. The sky is bigger and the sunsets are redder and every new outfit you buy is gonna change your life. Every new friend you make is going to be your friend forever. Time is so deep you could drown in an afternoon." A giggle burst from her, and she wiped her eyes. "Sometimes I envy Jennet. Is that so terrible?"

"No," Sonia said. "I don't believe that, when you grow up, your heart dies, but we *are* different."

"We aren't what we were," Paul said.

Auraleigh refilled the glasses, and for a while, they drank and listened to the rain without a word.

◆ ◆ ◆

Toward midnight, the rain intensified, pounding the church roof as they unrolled their sleeping bags on the pews. The place was frigid. Sonia huddled in her bag, despite her hoodie and fleece and double socks.

Auraleigh called out in a banshee voice: "Any squatters in here? Any ghosts?"

It wasn't funny, but the four of them giggled like young girls as Paul, serving as watcher, stood at the altar and poured the sog. Even the regal Tina laughed, her earrings glinting in the firelight.

"Are you ready?" Auraleigh chanted, passing out shot glasses, as if she were working the crowd at a ball game.

"Ready," Muriel said.

"Ready," Sonia said.

They raised their glasses in a wordless toast and drank.

Involuntary Memory
May 22, 1989 (junior year)

SONIA

Sonia's hands are in her lap, folding a piece of paper over and over in the lamplight. Over and over until Jennet's handwriting disappears.

"This is how you make a cootie catcher," she says. "You said it was a divination poem, right?"

Jennet laughs. "I'll put it under my pillow and see what I dream of."

But Sonia isn't giving up the paper just yet. Folded to a tiny wedge, it disappears into one hand, while her other hand strokes well-worn leather. Warm light shines on shelves of bound volumes. Marked-up papers rest beside her. In the distance, a door opens and closes with a burst of laughter.

They are sharing the red leather couch in the *Dove-Cat* room.

A disturbance has recently passed through the room, like a gust of rank, autumnal wind. Jennet showed her poem to Sonia, and Sonia didn't understand it but didn't want to say so. Now they're both pretending things are fine.

"It's getting to me," Jennet says. "All that spring in the air, the warm, sticky, fuzzy pollen telling us to go forth and procreate."

Sonia tries not to think about what happened with Byron in the mail room last week. So pointless and embarrassing. "It's a sex cult. Spring, I mean."

"Being human is so ridiculous sometimes," Jennet says. "Are you in love with that boy of yours?"

Hayworth. "No." Sonia's face warms. Maybe she is, but Jennet thinks Hayworth is bad for her.

"There's something different about you, though," Jennet says. "This new vibration in your voice, this little golden thread. So, is he *your* future?" Suddenly her voice is sharp, so sharp it cuts cleanly through the confusion and regret in Sonia's head. "The future boy?"

"I don't think so," Sonia says, though inside she whispers *yes, yes.*

"You two seemed pretty close when I saw you together last month. He walked you home from that dance—did he come inside?"

Sonia is full of stale, squishy guilt; she longs to vomit it out. "No, it's not like that. I barely saw him all winter, and he's such a mixed-up—boy? Man? I'm not even sure. Sometimes he's nice, and other times, he barely sees me."

"Well, you seem to be glowing these days. Blossoming." The word comes out sounding a little obscene. "Even my brothers have noticed you together. They call him Worthless and you Lady Death, because you always wear black. They say he's corrupted you, bringing you to that shack of his."

Is Jennet trying to shame her? It's working. "Hayworth never pushed sog on me. We haven't even been in the shack since fall."

"It's kind of glamorous, really. If my brothers hadn't ruined it for me, I would want a drug dealer boyfriend, too."

Sonia's vision blurs. She wants to say something that will dissolve the tension instantly, magically, and make Jennet like her again. "Are you mad at me?"

Jennet looks at her. Doesn't say a thing.

The guilt congeals into a solid mass in Sonia's chest. Is this about the poem? They've both learned in class that a poem is a metaphor, an evasion. Yet she senses that Jennet wrote this particular poem to be a message for her, one that she is apparently too dense to decipher.

She wants to give Jennet something at least, so she blurts out the secret she holds inside: "We *are* going to the shack tonight—Hayworth and I—for the first time in months. I kept thinking he'd never actually ask, but yesterday, we ran into each other on the quad."

"Am I keeping you from him?" Jennet sounds poised. A little distant.

Sonia knows she's angry. Why can't she think of the right words? She glances at the clock—9:20 p.m. "Of course not. You know, I've always envied you? Nothing scares you, and I'm just— I'm—"

"Things scare me." Jennet doesn't yell, but her voice cuts straight through Sonia's. "For instance. Moving across the country without knowing anybody, to get a degree that won't get me a job."

"It was just an idea. Because you're so talented. You could defer your student loans, and I'll be out there in a year—"

"It's a dead end." Each word is a whip crack. "I've done enough deferring. I'm useless, Sonia. I need to make money or marry somebody who can, and how likely is that?"

Jennet's lip wobbles, and the sight is worse than the most scathing anger. Jennet does not cry. Sonia says without thinking, "Byron loves you. He always has."

"He's too smart to try to save me."

"Save you? From what?" The baroque drama of the word is very Jennet. "Damnation?"

Jennet takes a crumpled tissue from her jacket pocket and blows her nose. She has gone puffy and pink at the edges. "No, plain old everyday failure. You're trying to make yourself feel better about what we know is going to happen."

"We don't know anything."

"Fine." The tissue is shredding. "Let's talk about now, then. You've never, not once since I've known you, been the one to reach out, Sonia. Even today, we're only talking because I came to you. It's like you're a passive observer of everything, like you don't even belong in this world or care what happens to other people."

And here it is at last, the thing Sonia has dreaded for the entire length of their friendship: Jennet confirming that she doesn't belong anywhere.

She draws herself up. Heat presses behind her eyes. "I do care. I know you're worried about graduation. I want to…"

Help, she means to finish, but something's stuck in her throat.

Jennet rises and gathers her books and papers. She stuffs the tissue in her pocket, while Sonia sits absolutely still and tries not to blink and spill tears down her cheeks.

Jennet's own eyes are dry. "I promised I'd help Hervé close tonight," she says in a new, breezy way, slinging a fraying army satchel over her shoulder. "I'm sorry, did I sound catty when I was talking about you and Hayworth? Like some mean cheerleader in a teen movie? It's probably almost that time of the month."

Sonia shakes her head, unable to speak, and Jennet leaves without another word. Without another glance at Sonia, who waits for something to happen—what? The buzz and tingling of sog wearing off?

But she's still there. She gives herself a shake and looks at the clock. Quarter of ten.

She opens a fist and finds the tightly folded poem still in her sweaty palm. She tucks it in her handbag. Then she puts away her papers, tugs on her jacket, and goes to meet Hayworth.

What a night it is, a shiver of fragrance in the air. The high black ridge, the bowl of starry sky, the fainter glow of the town. Walking down from campus, she passes beneath budding trees that vibrate with potential energy, like clenched fists. She hears a pond full of spring peepers, their eerie trills staining the night.

Everything is so beautiful, so promising, but she can't stop hearing Jennet say *I would want a drug dealer boyfriend, too,* and *You don't even belong in this world.* Those comments went far beyond cattiness. Jennet wanted to make her miserable.

Past the town schoolhouse and the town green and the town gym. Across the downtown bridge. Through the laughter of students coming from the café. Avoiding Polaire, she crosses Main Street to reach Railroad. She never wants to see Jennet again.

It's dark between the streetlights, but she doesn't turn on her flashlight yet. The smell of lilacs drifts toward her from invisible yards.

She tries not to replay Jennet's voice, choppy with anger: *You're trying to make yourself feel better.* Is it true that Sonia never reaches out? Maybe. But that's not because she doesn't care. She's just more cautious than other people, less sure of her place in the world. Didn't Jennet herself say Sonia doesn't belong anywhere?

She has to pay attention to the route now. She tiptoes along the Prentisses' gravel driveway, past a cord of wood under plastic sheeting, skirting the floodlight. Toward the trail.

The dewy grass lengthens to her ankles. She switches on the flashlight as she steps into the woods. The trailhead is unmarked and easy to miss: the gap between a burly maple and a leaning cedar.

Maybe you can't be a real friend when you never feel like you belong, when you have to lie and say you're fine and never tell your truths because other people might not understand them. But she's told Jennet so many things about herself that she tells no one else. Jennet is the only one she's told about Hayworth— and Jennet turned around and practically mocked her. *Worthless and Lady Death.*

The flashlight beam bounces off tree trunks, conjuring hunched figures and reaching arms. She trains it on the path instead. Beneath her is the crunch of deadfall, the smell of long-frozen things warming up and starting to decay again.

The path twists and turns, rises and falls, till she reaches the darkest patch. An owl hoots overhead. The woods are dense here, the understory packed with hemlock and cedar, full of creaks and cracks. If someone were following, she wouldn't know until it was too late.

Her shoulder blades prickle, but she keeps her pace steady until she emerges into the open again. A flicker of movement reveals the river on the opposite side. She's almost to the shack.

It feels like years since Hayworth's invitation on the stoop of the townhouse. It had been snowing then, and now the air smells green and fibrous, nothing like it did when they last sogged in November.

Trilling of peepers. Rush of the falls. She stands on the rim of the hollow looking at the brown tongue of the pond and the dark blotch of the shack.

Maybe he isn't here after all, and she'll have to hike back alone, gritting her teeth and cursing herself and him. Already clenching her jaw in anticipation, she heads downward. But halfway there, she sees a glint of firelight through a crack in the boards, then smoke twisting from the chimney.

A wave of relief breaks over her, leaving her supple and trembling. A few more steps, and she's bending herself into the shack. Hayworth's hand reaches out to guide her.

He lets go of her as soon as she's inside. He could pass for a local in that old jacket, but her throat closes with excitement.

"Hey," he says.

"Hey." Trying to sound indifferent, as always. Unable to say, *I don't even care about the future unless you're in it. Come close, touch me, love me. Help me belong to the world.*

The woodstove is lit, and two sleeping bags are stretched side by side. "It got cold," Hayworth says, "so I lit the fire."

"I like it." She tries to think of something else to say—about finals? About the weather?—but he's already kneeling and pouring the dark liquid from a coffee can into a cracked mug.

That's for her; he will pour his own sog straight into his palm. "This is nice," she says idiotically, accepting the mug from him. "I've missed it."

"Yeah?" His hand freezes in midair. "After I asked you last month, I thought maybe I shouldn't have. Maybe I should let you forget all about this."

Forget? Does he think she's an easily distracted child? To show him how little ambivalence she feels, she raises the mug and takes the dose in one gulp. They can talk later.

She's missed seeing the future—bits and fragments, quick cuts like in a music video, but the lack of context only makes each glimpse more mysterious and tantalizing. The taste of sog overwhelms her, sweet and sharp and wild as the woods. She chokes and coughs.

"You okay?" he asks, hovering over her.

"Fine." She regains control of her airway and lies down on the sleeping bag, all business. "Totally fine."

Oh, God, I wish you would touch me.

It comes up fast—pins and needles breaking out all over her body, making her twitch and blink. She closes her eyes and braces for another bright vision of the future.

She remembers what she has in her handbag—the poem Jennet gave her an hour ago in the *Dove-Cat* room. She doesn't want it now, but she doesn't want to give it back to Jennet, either.

She wants to be very far from here—far, far into the future where all this mess is forgotten.

◆ ◆ ◆

She opens her eyes. Not into the blinding sun of the Southwest this time. Into the flicker of firelight and a dark, high-ceilinged place. The air is still grainy with smoke, but this is not spring anymore. This is a northern fall.

She sits up, struggling against some kind of bedding that constrains her. A soft husk like a chrysalis, or maybe a winding sheet—is she dead? Is this her funeral?

An instant of panic, and then she realizes she's inside an ordinary sleeping bag. Her head swims as she unpeels it and crawls out. This place is big, like a church—that must be why she thought of funerals.

But if this is a church, it's a ruin. Hunched figures rest here and there in the pews, wrapped in sleeping bags like hers. Are they tramps? Who else would sleep here? The sharp air feels rural—is she part of a hobo encampment?

Is this how her life turns out, then—in poverty? Or is this the end of the world?

From the darkness, a man speaks: "Month and year?"

Sonia doesn't register the question, only the voice, and suddenly everything feels safe again. She would know that calm, authoritative tenor anywhere. If Paul Bretton is with her in the future, nothing can be that bad.

To her left, a female voice she doesn't recognize says, "October 2014."

Sonia rears up to peer into the shadows, but she can't make out a thing.

"Thanks," Paul says. "Sonia? Month and year?"

She swallows, dry-mouthed. At least the buzzing sensation has faded. "Paul!" she says stupidly.

"Month and year?" His voice is gentle but insistent. The question is important—some kind of test.

What will happen if she simply parrots the other woman's answer? "October 2014."

Her heart drums for the length of three breaths. Then Paul replies from the formless darkness: "Thanks. You can go outside if you want."

She has passed the test, but something else is wrong. Normally when she's in the future, she simply rides along, her body moving without her conscious control. This time, she waits for it to move, and nothing happens.

She rises on wobbly legs, feeling like an Etch A Sketch after you shake it. She wants to approach Paul, but Hayworth says never to try to control things in the sog. You might end up confused about who and when you are.

Paul said to go outside, so maybe that's the safest thing. She finds her way by the glint of rain falling past a doorway. She steps into the drizzle, and matted leaves squelch under her feet. Stars struggle out from behind massive cloud banks.

Autumn for sure, and it feels like Vermont. She sees woods and fields and humps that might be buildings, no lights. Rain patters on her thick, fleecy clothes. Maybe she should go back into the church—it really is a church, with a steeple. But the memory of Paul's test sends a chill down the back of her neck.

Was the question part of a ritual? Have they all become devil worshippers? Anyway, this can't be 2014; Paul would be ancient by then. All of them would be, assuming the whole world hasn't already gone up in a blaze of nuclear fire.

Wait a minute. What if this *is* the post–World War III world, and she's inhaling radiation with every breath? She walks quickly toward the other buildings, hoping to find something that isn't a ruin.

The largest building sags like the church—not encouraging. As she approaches, she recognizes the familiar sprawling shape of a farmhouse, and her heart rises into her throat.

She's been here before. The white siding, the slanted roof, the half-detached porch—it's the house in Belle Venere where she met Hayworth last spring. It was decrepit then, but now the front steps are splintered boards, the windows gaping holes. No one could live here.

She halts at the foot of the steps and stares, panic rising inside her like foul-smelling smoke. This is not real yet, any of it, and she shouldn't be moving of her own accord. She should be passively experiencing it. The sog is lasting so long, too, compared with her usual visions—almost as if she isn't sogging at all. Almost as if she belongs where she is.

But that can't be true. Any second the buzzing will start, yanking her back to Hayworth and the shack.

From inside the farmhouse, a deep voice speaks her name. She goes rigid, watching as a tall figure appears at the top of the steps.

Hayworth. Young or old, near or far, she will always know him.

Controlling this body could be dangerous. She needs to let it do what it wants, and she knows exactly what it wants.

She walks up to Hayworth and throws her arms around him.

He's solid. She presses her mouth to his, then parts his lips with her tongue, and his teeth clink against hers. His response is startled yet receptive, which must mean this is okay in the future. He isn't pushing her away. Another step and their bodies make contact, his erection hard against her hip, and the sensation doesn't frighten her the way she always thought it would.

"I'm so glad to see you," she says. "I've been waiting so long."

To touch you like this, she means—but instead of saying it, she seizes his hand and draws him after her into the house.

The place is pitch-dark and stinks, but the floor doesn't buckle under their feet. The ceiling doesn't fall on their heads. He seems to know it well; he guides her back into the furry, reddish darkness until they hit a doorframe. She turns, bracing herself against the wall, and reaches for him. Their bodies fit together with unbelievable ease—his long legs bracketing her hips, her hands on his shoulders to nudge him closer, their mouths meeting again.

Touch me. Yes, this is the future she wants.

The kiss is an awkward operation of their lips, and then it's a natural movement of their whole bodies. She's never done any of this with anyone except in her fantasies.

With that kiss, she's broken through his reserve as easily as you might stamp on a thin layer of pond ice. Now everything comes pouring out. His hands run up and down her body, gripping her as if no one else can save him from the flood. His stubble burns her chin; his teeth nip at her bottom lip. His groin pushes against her, and he groans into her mouth, "I'm sorry."

For what? As long as he doesn't stop, there's nothing to be sorry for. She feels as if her limbs aren't made of flesh but of pure, lambent energy, all of it radiating outward from a glowing core.

The buzzing could start any second, blacking out her vision as it yanks her out of the sog—but no, not yet, not *yet*. This body is still hers, every inch. She slides down the wall, dragging him with her, until they're both on the floor, which is carpeted in dust and smells like spilled beer from that long-ago party. Broken glass skitters against her heel as she hauls him on top of her.

He's breathing hard, shudders rippling through both their bodies, as if there are no barriers of fleece and flannel and skin and flesh between them. She expects the buzzing to begin when she fumbles his fly open. She expects it to begin as she slides her hand under his shirt to feel his naked chest. But the world remains intact. She says a silent prayer: *Give me long enough, just long enough.*

He kisses her neck, his ragged breath in her ear. He pulses against her, thrusting rhythmically, and she pulls clothes aside and raises her hips to let him in. He catches her hands and holds them above her head, her knees squeezing him hard as he moves faster and faster. The fruity smell of mold isn't bad anymore; it's the smell of summers past, of things growing. The world is a black hole, compressing and compressing—electrons sparking against each other, inside becoming outside—and he spasms and moans on top of her and goes still.

They lie that way for what feels like hours, the warmth of their joint motion fading by degrees, like embers in a campfire. At some point he whispers, "I'm sorry. It's been a while."

"It's fine." Is this how things work in the future? Do men apologize to you when you don't come?

She wonders if you even *can* come inside the sog. But it doesn't matter. She simply wants to stay here with him a little longer, their limbs entangled, his breath against her cheek.

She's half asleep, ready to float peacefully back into her own reality, when a woman's voice calls in the distance: "Sonia! Sonia!"

She bolts upright. That sounded like Auraleigh Lydgate, only a little raspier—is she here, too? What does she want?

Her head pounding, she shimmies her sweatpants back on. (Sweatpants? Has her future self given up on being attractive?) Hayworth is already on his feet. He grabs her hand and tugs her up beside him.

A man's voice joins Auraleigh's. "Sonia!"

Is that Paul again? They're still distant, perhaps all the way across the field, but they sound like they could be coming this way.

"Oh shit, I better get out," Hayworth mutters. "I'm the last person your friend wants trespassing on her property. Can I see you later?"

He drops her hand, but she follows him across the creaking floorboards. "Where are you going?"

"My car's back there."

From the front of the house, Paul and Auraleigh keep calling, and another woman's voice joins them: "Sonia! Sonia!"

All those voices make her panicky. She wants to see her friends, but what if she doesn't know how to act around them in the future? Hayworth doesn't suspect anything unusual about her, but one of them might.

Anyway, she feels good with him. Comfortable. "Can I come with you?" she asks, stumbling over something that might be a broken chair.

"Are you sure? Careful—there's a step missing here." He leads her through a door, hanging off its hinges, and out again into the damp night.

The tip of a flashlight beam sweeps around the side of the house toward them, making Sonia's breath catch. She squeezes his hand. "The car."

"You don't want to tell them where you're going? Maybe text them?"

The word means nothing to her in this context, but she shakes her head emphatically, and Hayworth accepts this, guiding her into a stand of tall, whispering pines. "I'm sorry," he repeats as they take a trail through the trees.

Sonia laughs. "Why do you keep being sorry? What for?"

"I was the one hiding in that house." He grips her hand. "I was watching you—all of you. I lied about that."

Sonia sees nothing wrong there. If he hadn't been in the farmhouse, she wouldn't have found him at the exact right moment, and none of this would have happened. But he seems to have a reason to feel guilty, something that makes sense in this future to which she must pretend she belongs, so she says, "It's okay. Really."

He keeps talking: "I know I was out of line, but I wanted to know who was sogging on a given night. I wanted to know if you were sogging—I hoped you wouldn't. For your sake, I didn't want you to remember."

The pine grove has thickened into a forest. Hayworth flicks on a flashlight, and its beam picks out the narrow trail through clinging underbrush. Nettles and milkweed fluff stick to Sonia's fleece and sweatpants. She wants to ask what he didn't want her to remember, but talking about sog could rip her back into the present, and anyway, as long as she's here, she shouldn't question anything.

The voices of her friends have vanished into the distance, and she and Hayworth force their way through a scratchy stand of buckthorn. Beyond is a dirt road, where a car is parked half in the ditch.

Hayworth opens the driver's side. "I could take you back to the B and B?"

Sonia gets into the passenger seat. The car of the future chimes gently, and she buckles her seatbelt. "I want to go where you're going. I want to sleep where you're sleeping tonight."

Hayworth starts the engine. "Are you sure?"

"Yes."

As he pulls onto the road, the buzzing begins at last. She closes her eyes and goes still, waiting for the world to disappear.

Nothing happens, though, because, as she realizes an instant later, the vibration isn't happening inside her head. It is a real buzzing, and it comes from Hayworth.

He brakes and fumbles in his jacket and brings out a flat, rectangular object about as long and wide as her hand, which buzzes dully at regular intervals. Lit from within like a tiny television, it displays mysterious, jewel-bright symbols. Sonia stares at it, mesmerized.

Hayworth examines the screen, then presses something on the side of the object. The buzzing goes silent.

"It's Garrett. I'll text him when we get there." He shoves the device back in his pocket. "You'll need to tell them something, though, and soon. Right now they think you've disappeared."

"Okay."

Hayworth turns to look at her. In the faint glow of the dashboard panel, she can't see his expression, only the glitter of his eyes.

He asks, "Do you know yet what happened that night at the falls? Have you seen it?"

She hears in his voice how much the question matters. *That night* is terribly important, but how can she know why?

"Not yet," she says. "But soon, I think. Soon."

27

BYRON

Floating in an in-between state, unsure where he was, Byron felt breath waft on his cheek. Small fingers took hold of his shoulder and massaged it through the covers, then stroked his hair.

He rolled over and reached for her. "Thank God, you're back. Please stay this time and tell me—"

He woke with a start in his bed on the second floor of Auraleigh's B and B, his heart galloping and his mouth dry, alone. Maybe Jennet had never been there at all.

The jar of sog was hidden under his bed. In his imagination, it pulsed like a furnace, its seductive glow filling the room. She was still in there, waiting for him.

But if he was going to change the past—or try, because Hayworth said it was possible—then he should have a plan. How would he do it? Which moment would he need to return to? He lay back and let himself drift into a fantasy of how things *should* have gone.

Again he was in bed in his dorm room, listening to the Quad Howl rise eerily into the spring air. Eleven fifty-six on the clock.

Then he was getting up, dressing, dashing outside, and colliding with Paul.

This time he said, "Hey, did you get the message? Jennet and Auraleigh, they're down at Dogssnout Falls. Let's go there."

Paul blinked at him. "I thought you had three finals tomorrow. But okay—I hope Auraleigh isn't getting too wasted."

Fast-forward—Byron's imagination skipped the boring parts—and Paul was parking the BMW in the dark pullout. Byron scrambled out and ran down the path ahead of him, stumbling over roots and rocks. He had to get there in time!

Thank God. Jennet was sitting alone on the rock bridge, a small, fragile figure in the starlight.

Byron rocketed past Auraleigh, curled up on a blanket on the shore. She'd be fine. He called out to Jennet so he wouldn't scare her, then hurried out onto the rock bridge and perched beside her. "Are you okay?"

"Why wouldn't I be?" But she wasn't looking at him. "I'm graduating in ten days and the mortarboard won't stay straight and I look like a rakish British public schoolboy."

Byron didn't miss the tremor in her voice. He repeated, "Are you okay? Because we haven't talked in a while."

His waking dream grew realer, fleshing itself out, though it would never be as real as a sog vision. He asked Jennet whether she was okay maybe a dozen times, while Paul woke up Auraleigh and made her drink water and get on her feet. Every time Byron asked, Jennet found a new answer, each one more droll and far-fetched—until, at last, she just looked down at the whirlpool and said nothing.

A bit later, Byron's arms were around her. Her head rested on his chest. "We can make it work," he said, his voice deep enough to vibrate through both of their bodies. A song of safety. A song of love.

She hid her face. "You aren't even graduating for another year. You can't drop out because of me."

"I won't drop out." The dream-Byron remembered all his mom's stories about his own early childhood, and again that song of safety vibrated in his chest. He could do this. *They* could do this. "My mom had me when she was in college. We'll get our own place, that's all. We'll share everything."

She swallowed; he felt her throat ripple against his heart. "You'll be studying, though. I'll be working. We're not rich, Byron."

He rubbed her back. "Honey, people do this. People have done this. You need a quieter job than that café, though. Maybe a library."

He didn't hear her answer, because the roar of the falls rose like static to engulf the scene. The setting was already shifting—

The chirp of an impossibly loud cricket cut through Byron's fantasy. It took a moment for him to recognize his ringer—why had he left it on?—and snatch up the phone from the bedside table.

He felt hungover from his dream state, his vision too bleary to focus on the screen, so he swiped automatically, eager to silence the noise. "Hello?"

"Hey!" A young girl's voice.

Byron was suddenly awash in sweat. "Jennet?"

"Dad? What did you just call me?"

Oh, shit. When he looked at the phone again, there was his favorite picture of Eliza, nine and dressed as a zebra for Halloween. "Honey! You woke me and I was confused. How are you?"

Eliza wanted his support in a dispute she'd had with her mother about her curfew. Byron struggled to keep his attention on her list of grievances. He couldn't help noticing that she never asked how he was doing.

That was lucky, he supposed. Her blissful teen self-absorption put her in no danger of ever finding out that he'd been lost in dreams of someone who wasn't her mother and was closer to her age than his own.

She wouldn't understand that he didn't actually want some-one younger—he wanted to *be* young. To do it all over again.

By the time they hung up, it was close to two, and Byron could barely keep his eyes open. Tomorrow, while the rest of them were sleeping in, he would take a quick trip to campus to make sure he targeted the right memory. And then...

He was on the verge of sleep again when a door slammed downstairs and footsteps thudded. Urgent voices shrilled.

Something must have happened during their sog that wasn't normal. He hauled himself up and descended the stairs, silent in socked feet.

"You're going to wake Byron!" Muriel said in the parlor.

"Too fucking bad!" Auraleigh was practically shouting. "He can help us search. We need to go back there with flashlights."

Search for whom? Paul was saying something inaudible, clearly meant to calm Auraleigh. A voice Byron didn't recognize, prob-ably Tina, said, "Have you tried Garrett again?"

"He swears he hasn't seen her!"

"I hate to say it," Muriel said, "but after what Paul saw in the farmhouse two nights ago, that someone is watching us, maybe we should call the cops."

"No cops! How many times do I have to tell you?" Turning to find Byron there, Auraleigh let out a little shriek. "For God's sake, Byron, you scared me!"

"You woke me. Where's Sonia?"

Paul said, "She's gone."

DAY 6

* ◆ *

November 1, 2014

28

SONIA

Rain thrums distantly on a roof. The smell of coffee wafts through the air.

Sonia throws back layers of white bedding and sits up. The room is very white, too, with a sharply slanted ceiling and wan daylight flooding through a skylight—a small room, almost empty except for a bed and stacks of neatly taped and labeled boxes. Beside the bed, an apple crate holds a travel alarm clock with its hands pointing to ten and four.

She vaguely remembers coming to this place last night, Hayworth leading her upstairs, but she'd been so sleepy. Any minute she expected everything to come apart into whirling kaleidoscope shards and suck her backward, into her own reality.

Yet here she still is, almost as if this *is* her reality.

Her knees crack alarmingly as she rises, the pine floor smooth under her bare feet. She wears a T-shirt and sweatpants and grabs her fleece jacket, which is draped over a box. Down a short hall, she finds a bathroom, where she pointedly avoids the mirror.

If she sees herself old, her sense of who she is might shift in an instant. She feels it with a strange conviction—there could be no going back to 1989. Just like Hayworth in the story he told her about coming from the future, she might have to accept that she is this person now, and 2014 is her present, whether she remembers the intervening years or not.

I want to go back, she tells herself. *I need to.*

The stairs echo under her sneakers. At the bottom is a snug kitchen full of odd appliances, stainless steel like in a restaurant, and an older man sitting at a round table with a coffee cup. He gives a little start when he notices her.

She gives a start, too. That man is *Hayworth*.

The shape of his face hasn't changed, nor have his broad shoulders. But now, in the daylight, she can see the lines at the corners of his mouth and between his brows. His hair is gray at the temples.

A blush floods her cheeks. Who is this stranger? What has she done?

When she manages to look at him, though, she catches the green fleck in one eye reflecting the light, and yes, it *is* him.

He says, "I didn't want to wake you, but you need to call Auraleigh right away. She's been bugging Garrett all night. I don't know what you want to tell her."

All this sounds very complicated—who is Garrett? "Where is the phone?" Sonia asks stiffly. There isn't one in the kitchen. She feels formal with him now, as if he's Hayworth's father and the real Hayworth is waiting for her in the sog shack.

When he rises, she can see he's still lean, but with the hint of a gut. She follows him into the next room. Instead of leading her to the phone, he snags a twilight-blue peacoat from a peg—hers?—and hands it to her. "I'm guessing you have a lot of missed calls."

Sonia glances around the small living room. Still no phone. Then she remembers last night in the car, when Hayworth took the buzzing rectangle from his pocket.

She explores one pocket of the peacoat, but it holds only an ordinary wallet. She closes the wallet quickly after glimpsing a New Mexico driver's license, issued 2012.

There's no glowing rectangle in the other coat pocket, either, only a strange key ring—a hollow hunk of plastic encasing a folded paper. *Message in a bottle.*

He's watching her but keeping his distance.

For the first time, she notices the bulging veins on the backs of her own hands. Mesmerized, she examines a finger more closely. A sheaf of lines, each as fine as an insect's antenna, mars the once-smooth pad of flesh.

Her other fingertips bear the same creases. They are everywhere, subtle yet indelible—the tracks of time. No one ever told her she would have lines on her fingers.

Her gorge rises. To make herself stop staring, she slides the paper out of the key ring's plastic shell.

Creased and yellowed, it's been in there awhile. But her heart leaps as she recognizes it: the "divination poem" Jennet handed her in the *Dove-Cat* room just hours ago, or so it seems.

She hadn't wanted to give the poem back, but why would she have kept it all these years—and in a key ring? She unfolds the paper and finds Jennet's pen strokes, faded but readable.

Can the Earth feel when
A seed bursts its cold shell and
Begins to become?
Or is gestation not
So different from indigestion?
Earth gave herself cheap;
She holds her tongue.
Loam lies heavy
In an unready womb.
How ungraceful to goad—
"Out, out, damned sprout!"—

When so much depends
On the stout paths that wend
Always out.

What does it mean? The handwritten lines still perplex her, just as they did in the *Dove-Cat* room in 1989. She remembers Jennet looking at her expectantly while she tried to figure out how to react.

"I need to give this back to her," she says, though she knows Hayworth won't understand. "I must have forgotten about it. I don't think I have a phone, though."

"Oh, right. Garrett told me about Auraleigh's no-phones rule. It might be awkward, but if you're okay with it, use mine."

Sonia doesn't know why it might be awkward. She also has no idea how to use his rectangle, which doesn't even have an antenna. "You dial and I'll talk," she suggests.

The face of the rectangle is dark glass, a murky pool. It reminds her of the monoliths in *2001: A Space Odyssey*. Hayworth touches the screen, and the darkness lights up with images so tiny and precise they make her itch.

Hayworth taps the surface of the phone and passes it to her. It's heavier than she expected. She cradles it in both hands while it emits a sound that is absurdly like the ringing of a real phone.

She raises the device to her ear—the shape is all wrong for tucking it under your chin. The ringing stops. A voice that might be Auraleigh's asks gruffly, "Hello?"

"Hello," Sonia whispers. The poem is distracting her—why is it so important to Jennet? "Hello. Auraleigh? This is Sonia."

"Sonia! Oh my God!" Auraleigh's tone is relieved and angry at once. "Where are you? We've been looking for you all night!"

In the distance, a deep voice says something like "I told you." Not Paul—could it be Byron? Surely they don't all live together in the future, so long after graduation?

"I'm with a friend," Sonia says. "Do you know Hayworth

Darbisher? Anyway, I met him in the old farmhouse, and he drove me to…his house?"

He nods beside her, looking uncomfortable.

"Anyway, I'm fine."

After a few seconds of dead silence, Auraleigh cries, "I knew it was him lurking around my property!"

Belle Venere, Auraleigh's property? But Sonia shouldn't ask questions about the future; the more she knows, the harder it could be to go back. *Focus on the poem. It belongs to the past, too.* "I think he was waiting for me," she says.

"Sonia, tell me the truth, are you okay? If you aren't, just say 'Not really.' We'll come get you right now." Auraleigh's voice is rough, like someone's mother's. All those cigarettes must have added up.

"I'm okay. I just… I think I need to go to the shack."

Go to the shack. The idea just popped into her head under the pressure of Auraleigh's questions, but it makes a surprising amount of sense. If she can return to the place where she'd been sogging in 1989, maybe she can go back to that night, too. A dose of sog would give her the push she needs.

But does the shack still exist? Does Hayworth have sog?

"Then I can give the poem back to Jennet," she says, not realizing at first that she's spoken aloud.

A sharp intake of breath. Auraleigh says, "Who?"

"Jennet!"

Sonia looks up to find Hayworth eyeing her uneasily. "My friend Jennet," she explains to him. "She wrote this."

She doesn't intend to stay in this future long enough to give the poem back to adult Jennet, but why do they seem so disturbed by the idea?

Hayworth says in a low voice, "I didn't know." He reaches out to take the phone from her.

She hands it to him, but not before she hears Auraleigh say distinctly, "Sonia, don't joke about that. You know Jennet's been dead for twenty-five years."

· 29 ·

BYRON

Auraleigh set the phone down on the kitchen table. Her face had gone waxy, emphasizing the hollowness of her eyes after a sleepless night. "That was Hayworth's phone," she said. "That was... Sonia's okay, I guess. She's with him."

The five of them had been up all night searching the ghost town of Belle Venere, waving flashlights and yelling. In the farmhouse, just as Paul had promised, they'd found a sleeping bag, binoculars, and fresh-looking footprints in the dust. The discovery had put an unpleasant taste in Byron's mouth, and he'd spent the early hours of the morning worrying about Sonia falling prey to some vagrant.

"She's with Hayworth where? Did you talk to her?" he asked, not reassured yet.

"His place. I guess they spent the night together. She swears she's fine."

"So it *was* Hayworth in the farmhouse," Paul said.

Auraleigh was gazing at the wall as if it could tell her something. "Hayworth had to hang up," she said. "Sonia got...upset.

She said something to me about giving a poem to Jennet. Like she didn't *know*."

Paul's intake of breath was audible. "Are you saying Sonia lost her memory?"

"Hayworth thinks something happened when she sogged last night—like maybe she was also sogging in her memory vision, so when she woke up in the present, she'd forgotten all the years in between."

Byron imagined a world in which *he* didn't remember the past quarter century—Christa, Rohan, Eliza. A year or so ago, the idea would have been terrifying, but these days his family wanted so little to do with him. Maybe they would all be better off if he had amnesia. He wouldn't even feel the loss, not knowing what he was missing.

"Sonia told me sog can affect your memories," he said, remembering their conversation. "People get unstuck in time—or think they do, anyway." *And sometimes they can even change the past.*

A concerned glance passed between Paul and Auraleigh. "Hayworth hopes it's temporary," Auraleigh said. "He'll bring her over later, after she 'calms down.'"

"She answered the question," Paul said, clearly wondering if he'd slacked on his watcher job. "She knew the date. Or maybe she just echoed Muriel's response."

"You shouldn't have let her go outside. You couldn't tell something was wrong?"

Byron sat down and planted his elbows on the table, heavy with exhaustion. He knew he should be worrying about Sonia, too, but now he almost found himself envying her. If he forgot the past twenty-five years, he would also forget every way he had failed Jennet.

He still didn't know what he'd really been doing when he ran out on the quad in 1989—changing the past, or something else he couldn't remember? Heading for the falls, toward Jennet, but clearly not reaching her. Not saving her, anyway.

You don't have to fail me. That was Jennet's soft whisper in his ear—she was back, or maybe she was just his imagination. *That night is still happening, somewhere in the multiverse. I don't have to die.*

I know. I'll fix it. "Sonia will probably remember again in time," he said, though he wasn't convinced.

He'd been baffled by Christa's desire for a separation, but maybe she had simply sensed the truth before he did: he still belonged to Jennet in some deep way. The memories had been lurking inside him all along, waiting to take possession.

Auraleigh's chin was obdurate, belying the fear in her eyes. "None of my guests have ever lost their memory before."

"Sonia's different," Paul said. "She sogged when she was younger, too. We still have no idea what this stuff does to a human brain."

They reminded Byron of his mom fretting over a joint she'd found in his teenage bedroom. He mustn't tell them what he planned to do—they would try to persuade him out of it.

That question still worried at the corners of his brain: *Where did I go after the quad?* But now he *wanted* to know. He wanted to take control, to make sure that whatever he did was something he would never regret.

"Hayworth knows more about sog than any of us," he said. "Maybe you should've asked his advice before you opened your memory spa, instead of convincing yourself he was a murderer."

Auraleigh's mouth twisted. "He at least makes *sense* as a murderer. He's not one of us."

Paul said, "Auraleigh, there's no murderer. There's just us, reckoning with what we do and do not remember."

Jennet was humming, murmuring and singing like the very voice of the house. Auraleigh's eyes were so wide that Byron could swear she heard it, too. "You make us sound so helpless, Paul," she said.

"We aren't helpless." Byron believed it more and more, though he couldn't tell them why. The alternative was too terrible.

Paul was saying something about processing unknowns and moving on, but Byron had heard it all before, so he went to Auraleigh and took her in his arms. She gasped in surprise, but then her body folded into his, and she rested her head on his shoulder, her fingernails digging into his waist.

He didn't blame her for trying to exert some control over those "unknowns" Paul was talking about. If life was a river, that deep, cold whirlpool at the bottom of the falls was always waiting to tear them apart. "It's okay," he said. "Sonia will be all right."

"Maybe she just needs longer to come out of it," Paul said, not sounding sure.

Auraleigh shuddered, and Byron knew Sonia wasn't the only missing member of their circle she was thinking about.

"I know," he breathed into her ear, wishing he could tell her that Jennet didn't need to be dead, and soon she wouldn't be. "I can't let *her* go, either."

· 30 ·

SONIA

There's something in the bathroom that Sonia needs to see. She can't avoid it anymore.

Hayworth's feet thump up the stairs after her. He calls out, but she doesn't bother to pull the door closed. She braces herself on the vanity and turns to the mirror.

Somehow her face alarms her less than those filaments on her fingertips. She isn't ancient, she isn't gray-haired, but she is older—wasted cheeks, lines etched from nose to lips. Her eyes glow from within an altered flesh mask: *Here I am after all these years. Here I still am.*

But Jennet is not in this future. Jennet is gone.

She balls her right hand into a fist and punches the mirror. The fist bounces off. She winces, pressing stinging knuckles to her chest, while the image winks back at her, intact. Smug, even. She winds up for a second swing as Hayworth calls, "Don't!"

Wake up!

She remembers him telling her that when he realized he was stuck in his past visions, he broke a window with his fist. It probably won't work any better for her than it did for him, but she can't stop herself.

This time, the mirror gives way with an ugly crunch. A sharp-toothed star blooms in the center of her mirrored forehead. Her knuckles come away bloody, and she releases a little whoop of triumph and says, "'Out, out, damned sprout.'"

Repeating the line from Jennet's poem, she understands it at last. "She's pregnant." How did she not see it last night in the *Dove-Cat* room? Maybe she didn't let herself register what Jennet was trying to tell her. "Or she thinks she might be."

"Sonia. Fuck." Strong hands grab her from behind, pinning her arms to her sides. "You hurt yourself."

He's right, but the pain has brought her back into this stranger's body—sharp little mink teeth digging into her knuckles, nerves singing. Apparently she's going to stay in this future, so she might as well begin to ask questions. To find out what happened to Jennet.

"When did she die?" she asks. "Auraleigh said it was twenty-five years ago, but when exactly?"

She recalls the conversation with Jennet in the *Dove-Cat* room, the walk from campus to the shack, the owl hooting in the woods, and Jennet's poem in her pocket, a poem she meant to return the very next day.

And then, as if the question unloosed some intuition inside her: "Was it May twenty-second, 1989? Did she die that same night?"

Hayworth's grip relaxes. "That's good. You're starting to re-member."

◆ ◆ ◆

"So," Sonia says, "you're saying I'm not really from the past. I belong here. I just don't remember everything between then and now."

"Right." Hayworth is tense, worried. "We all have overlap-ping versions of ourselves, all the people we've been. There's no

magic cure, but when you feel safe and grounded enough, you
will remember. And the person you were in 1989 will recede
into a memory again—part of you, but not all of you."

They sit in Hayworth's car, parked beside his A-frame. The
house perches on a ridge; below them spread pastures and gray-
streaked barns and fiery autumn woods. Ducks swim in a pond.
A dog barks. A cold wind tears holes in the cloud cover.

Sonia wears the twilight-blue peacoat and some awkwardly
applied bandages. The landscape is unfamiliar, and the pain in
her knuckles is savage.

"I'm not a memory, though. I'm real!" she says, struggling to
breathe through her nausea. "I need to go back." *To that night.
She died that night.* "I must be here for a reason, though."

"Both selves are inside you." Hayworth seems desperate to
make her believe it, his voice quavering with conviction (or
quavering because he is old, old, old, not Hayworth at all). He
hands her something—the wallet. "This is *you*. The person you
think you are—leave her in the past. Let her be a memory."

Sonia takes the wallet and pulls out some of the cards, but
they feel like stolen property. She slides them back in and drops
it on the seat. "I don't want to go to this B and B. I want to go
to the shack."

Jennet was trying to tell me she's pregnant. I didn't listen. She
should be back in 1989, stopping whatever happened to Jennet
from happening. Maybe that's why she's here—so she'd know
enough to stop it.

"You need to be in a place you're familiar with."

But Sonia shakes her head. He isn't going to put her off with
vague warnings this time. "I need sog. I need to go back."

◆ ◆ ◆

Hayworth seems a little leery of Sonia. He drives without looking directly at her, and she stays on her side of the cab.

She tries not to think about last night—his hands all over

her, grabbing hungrily, and her own grabbing right back. She knows their bodies are still the same age, but a gulf has opened between them. In the shack, he used to insist he was older than she was, because he had already lived parts of his future, but she refused to see him that way.

Now she's the one who feels the difference. Lecturing her about her two selves, he sounds like her father.

"Tell me how it happened," she says. "You know, don't you? How did Jennet die?"

The cold wind has left two red spots on his cheeks. "You know more than me. You need to remember by yourself."

She can't, because she hasn't lived it yet, but now she remembers his questions from last night: *Do you know yet what happened that night at the falls? Have you seen it?* "She died at the falls."

Hayworth nods, just barely.

"But we were in the shack, practically right there!"

Surely Jennet wouldn't have followed Sonia to the shack. She had said such cruel things about Hayworth in the *Dove-Cat* room that night, as if she wanted nothing to do with either of them.

Recalling those remarks in the light of day, though, Sonia wonders if she herself had been insufferable, bragging about her handsome boy from the future. Meanwhile, Jennet had her own secret to tell, and Sonia couldn't or wouldn't hear it. If she were Jennet, she would have felt abandoned.

She has to approach this logically, to gather the facts, even if it means saying the words out loud. "Did she drown?"

Hayworth drives, looking straight ahead.

Before she said those cruel things to Sonia, Jennet told her *Things scare me*—and Sonia understands that better now, too. Byron has to be the father of the "sprout," but they both know Byron isn't ready for fatherhood. Jennet probably hasn't even shown him her poem. She lashed out because she's scared, not just of the looming reality of graduation but of what's happening inside her own body.

Instead of helping her, Sonia ran off to the shack to see Hayworth. And then...

Could Jennet have wanted to make things right between them? To apologize or ask Sonia to? Could some terrible accident have happened instead?

"The shack," she repeats. "We need to go to the shack." She has the length of this drive to convince him. She has the strength of youth. "I *need* to go to the shack, Hayworth. I need to go back to that night, where I belong."

He steers around a curve, open pastures on one side and firs on the other. "I understand that you feel like you belong in the past, but you need to convince yourself you're just confused."

"Right." On the stoop in April, he'd explained that his memories were "muddled."

"But convincing yourself didn't work so well for *you*, did it? When we met, you told me you came from the future."

"I felt that way, but I know now the only way anyone can be happy is to say yes to the present. Choose it. Embrace it."

The word *embrace* makes her laugh—an ugly laugh, half sob. "I did embrace it! Last night. I..." She can't go on, choked up by the memory of how free she'd felt when she reached for him.

"If you really wanted what I wanted, you should've told me back then!" Her throat spasms. "All those nights, we never touched. You thought it was fun to lead me on with hints about knowing me in the future and then tell me I was too young!"

"I didn't think it was fun. I didn't mean to lead you on." Hayworth turns onto a side road that wanders across a pasture. He puts the car in Park and presses his palm to her left cheek. When she winces, he removes it immediately. "Last time we talked in the café, you said it was too late for us," he says, those strange, multilayered eyes finding hers. "Do you remember that, maybe?"

"No." Even now, his fleeting touch has brought memories of friction and need, the electric warmth of his palm setting each fine hair on her cheek on end. But it isn't too late, not if she can get back to her past self and just make the move.

"You said…" He trails off. "And then, when you walked up the steps of the farmhouse straight to me, I thought something had changed. I thought you'd changed your mind, or maybe you'd remembered something. I didn't realize you'd just regressed in your head to being twenty years old. If I'd known, I would never have…"

He can't say what they did. Sonia swallows hard.

His gaze is asking for something, almost begging, but what can she give him here and now?

"I haven't 'regressed.'" She still feels where his fingertips pressed her skin, slightly calloused against her cheek. "I'm going to get back. I need to talk to Jennet," she says stubbornly. "When I saw her in the *Dove-Cat* last night, I didn't really listen to her. We had a fight, and I got distracted." *I was busy thinking about you.*

"That wasn't last night. It was twenty-five years ago."

No, no, it was just yesterday. She *feels* Jennet close by—the tingling, teasing energy woven through her.

Jennet needs her. "If I go to the shack and sog, I can cross again—I feel it. I can go back to that night." And stay in the past, she hopes, though she knows he doesn't believe she can. Sogging one more time will at least prove which of them is right.

"You can watch it happen, yes. But if you try to change what happened, you'll only confuse yourself more. Especially if you succeed."

"So, you do think I could change things? Didn't you tell me you did that once?"

"Maybe you could, but you *shouldn't.*" Hayworth looks straight at her, his eyes bright with such urgency that he seems almost his young self again. "Yes, I sogged backward from the future and got stuck at age sixteen, and then I kept changing things, because I had memories of the future—*a* future. Meeting you at that party in 1988, for instance. I only went up to you because

I 'remembered' you from a lifetime where we first met at the Pacific Film Archive in the nineties."

Sonia's face flushes with mingled embarrassment and satisfaction as she recalls her future visions of them together in the desert. "So you accelerated things. You made us meet sooner."

Hayworth's eyes don't release her. "Right, except that this is 2014 now, and that meeting at the Pacific Film Archive never actually happened—not in this lifetime, at least. We haven't seen each other for the past twenty-five years."

Sonia is disappointed, but not surprised. She can see their long, cold estrangement in his awkwardness, and maybe she also felt it last night in his passion. "You knew how things were supposed to happen, and you *chose* to do it differently. Why, though?"

Hayworth puts the car in gear and turns them around, swinging wide into the tall grass, gravel popping. From the other side of an electric fence, a brown Swiss cow gazes at them with gentle sternness.

"In the future I remember," he says, "the future that doesn't exist anymore, meeting you at the PFA was the beginning of something between us. We lived together for several years. We road-tripped across the Southwest. Did you maybe see hints of that, too, in your future visions?"

Tears prick Sonia's eyes, and she looks away from him. "Yes. So…you didn't want all that to happen again? A life where you were with me?"

"In that life, you left me around the year 2000, and things went downhill for me. When I discovered sog, all I wanted was to escape back into a past before I knew you. I didn't want to be the person that breakup had turned me into."

Sonia remembers the heat of his body against hers. How can you make someone forget that? She wants to believe she wouldn't have broken his heart, but Jennet thought she was selfish, and maybe she was.

"So you escaped into the past and started changing it, without meaning to. But if you didn't want to know me, why approach me at that party at all?"

"I…" Hayworth keeps his eyes on the road, away from her, but she feels a sigh run through his entire body. "I couldn't help myself. I missed you." He flicks something off his cheek with his thumb.

For a minute, Sonia can't speak. They drive in silence, through towns that are only a blur of roofs and white crosswalks. The scent of cow dung seeps into the car.

At last she says, "If you missed me, why did you disappear after Jennet died? Why did you avoid me all these years?"

Hayworth stops for a herd of cows to cross the road. "It might make you sad to know—and confuse you."

She's already confused. All she wants is to see Jennet again, to apologize for the way things ended in the *Dove-Cat* room. Is that so much to ask?

"Please just tell me," she says. "What did I do wrong? Does it have to do with Jennet dying?"

He accelerates. Doesn't look at her. "You have to accept what happened if you ever want to move on."

"But I don't even *know* what happened, because you won't tell me. And if you changed the past, why shouldn't I?"

The landscape opens up, blue mountains in the distance. The speed limit jumps. Hayworth passes a chugging tractor.

"Sonia, if you start changing the past, you'll be as fucked-up as I am, and I don't want to lose this version of you." A muscle dances in his jaw. "I wish you didn't have these gaps in your memory, but I don't want to lose you again. *This* you. You belong *here*."

"At that party in Belle Venere, you said we weren't people yet." Her voice wobbles and she has to pause. "You said we didn't belong anywhere because we were still becoming who we were meant to be."

"Yeah, well, if I've learned one thing since I was nineteen, it's that I was wrong about that." He catches her eye for an in-

stant, green fields passing behind him. "We were always ourselves, Sonia. Every second of your life counts, whether you
want it to or not."

She thinks about that. *Every second counts.* Slip-sliding on the
frozen pond with the Midnight Brunch Club. Dancing in the
dining commons with Auraleigh. Letting Jennet leave the *Dove-
Cat* room without saying *I care about you, let me help you.*

Memories make her who she is. She needs them. "I can't come
back and belong here unless you *tell* me what I did to make you
avoid me. Please, Hayworth. Help me remember."

As they reach another speed zone, he finally looks at her again,
brows bunched low over his glistening eyes.

"I don't believe you could hurt Jennet," he says. "I know you
a little better now than I did back then. But that night in the
shack, you went out to talk to her. When I questioned you the
next day, after I heard she'd drowned, you acted so weird, refusing to tell me anything. And... I wondered."

The buzzing begins in Sonia's head, as if she's having the
mother of all head rushes. The car's engine rises to a roar, darkness covering the world.

At last, she thinks—but the buzzing doesn't carry her away
this time. Her vision clears, and she is still here.

It's okay, though. Finally, she knows exactly what to say.

"I must have blocked out what happened that night, Hayworth," she says. "That's why I'm confused. If I can just get hold
of the memory, I'll be ready to come back and belong here. I
won't change anything—I promise. Will you let me sog one
last time?"

· 31 ·

BYRON

Sitting in the armchair beside the cold woodstove, Byron wondered if he was the only one awake in the B and B. Auraleigh and Paul had crashed. Muriel was shut up in her room. Tina—who knew what she did all day?

He hoped Sonia was safe out there with Hayworth, but he couldn't focus on her, because Jennet wouldn't stop humming. It wasn't one girl's voice anymore but a whole chorus of Jennets, locust-sized and singing away under the wainscoting and the floorboards. The room vibrated with their harmonies.

The song had no words, but he knew what she was saying. It was almost time.

Until he set the past right, it wouldn't matter where he was. He could be lying in bed in his sad little bachelor condo in Rockridge, watching the shadow of a banana tree waver on the wall, and she would be there. At the foot of his bed when he woke up. In it while he slept. Singing in the walls, touching his face as he struggled out of dreams. She might haunt him for years, until he started talking to her in public and everyone thought he'd lost his mind.

And he didn't want a ghost, he wanted the real her—the Jennet he saw in the sog, where colors were impossibly bright and sharp-edged and sounds were resonant and smells were achingly pungent. He just had to be very, very sure of his targeting. To have a complete blueprint of the life he wanted in his head so that once he drank the sog, he could lay the foundations.

He closed his eyes.

In his imagination, Jennet stood behind the polished oak desk of a small-town library. Now visibly pregnant, she was poised as ever in her Empire-waist dress. He set a takeout bag in front of her. "I got your favorite."

She reached for the bag. "I could eat a bear."

Outside in the real world, a car passed. A blue jay shrieked. Inside his head, the imagined scenes came faster, overlapping and cross-fading.

The birth—her hand clutching his, red crescents in his palm. The baby's eyes, hooded and anxious like hers. The baby's first smile.

Then a darker scene, because he knew depression wasn't dispelled with a finger snap: they were in a cramped living room that smelled of burnt toast, and she was talking frantically, waving her arms, telling him how she had to pump gas by herself with the baby in the car seat. "I had to leave her for a second! Anything could have happened!"

Before he could reassure her, they were driving through an endless desert, a U-Haul behind them, and she was singing to the baby in the back seat. He tried to speak, but she shushed him: "I *just* got her asleep."

Then they were painting a living room, a spot of Dresden blue on the tip of her nose. Jennet was back to her usual dry competence, the clever remarks that camouflaged the turbulence beneath, but Byron stayed alert. Time had taught him to sup-

port her through her illness—looking her in the eye, touching
her even when she shrank away, being present when the darkness loomed.

He saw the blur of an urban campus, red brick and concrete.
Washers and dryers whooshing in the basement of an apartment
building. The baby became a toddler, tossing handfuls of leaves
in the air and screeching. She had Jennet's eyes and a tangle of
chestnut hair, curly like his. Jennet nuzzled a tiny armpit and
said, "You're going to be a pop star, muffin."

He knew better than to censor the hints of darkness that en-
croached on his fantasy—they made it more real. Fairy tales had
no attraction at his age. But a beautifully imperfect life with her
and their child—yes, he saw it clearly now.

They were in a small town again—modest storefronts, silos
rising over vast soybean fields. They stood outside a Victorian
house that bristled with gables, a turret, balconies. Mature maples. A real estate sign in the grass. She said, "It's the house from
It's a Wonderful Life!" so full of giddy joy that he wanted to pick
her up and carry her over the threshold. Instead he said, "Well,
of course. You are a librarian."

The toddler became a child, dressed up in fanciful costumes
that Jennet made on a burring sewing machine. Alice in Wonderland one day, a dragon the next. Byron scribbled on a white-
board in a lecture hall, trying to explain "The Rime of the
Ancient Mariner." He stood outside the door of Jennet's attic
room, poised to knock but not daring, because holding her in
his arms and promising they'd be safe didn't work every time,
not anymore.

Byron helped his daughter arrange the intricate menagerie of
stuffed animals on her bed, the lion outermost to guard her. As
he read to her from *The Voyage of the Dawn Treader*, she gazed
at him seriously. A quiet girl, spooked by crowds, terrorized
by clowns and birthday party magicians. When she asked him

where people go when they die, he stumbled through an answer. She said, "It's okay. I understand."

One day she came home from a friend's house, crying because the friend's dog had died. Byron told her it was okay to be sad. Jennet tried to distract her. After their daughter was in bed, Byron said, "She needs to know her feelings won't rip her apart."

Jennet said, "Always the optimist."

In an office full of spider plants and succulents, a therapist asked Byron whether he had doubts about Jennet as a mother—

No, *no*, that wasn't right. A few minor-key scenes were fine, but he couldn't let the story turn into some tragic opera.

Fast-forward. Birthday parties! Vacations! Trick-or-treating—oh yes, he would escort his costumed daughter around their mossy old neighborhood until she was so old that her friends teased her about it, and still she would humor him for old times' sake. In this fantasy, he was a college professor with long summers free to spend with her—swimming holes! Bike trips! Lemonade and fireflies!

Now she was a teenager, and he saw himself opening the door of her room to find a collage of song lyrics that sounded like messages from the depths of a Xanax haze. His beautiful daughter hunched over her laptop—ripped black tights, ragged hair, a jutting lower lip. She said, "I'm worried about Mom."

"Don't worry! We probably just need to adjust her prescription again."

His daughter—what was her name?—didn't seem convinced. "Sometimes I think you and Mom shouldn't be together. Sometimes I think you shouldn't have had me."

Byron bent and put his arm around her. "I love you so much. I love your mom so much. I would never, *ever*, in a million years, leave either of you."

A dry laugh cut through Byron's fantasy. He opened his eyes with a start.

He was back in the parlor of the B and B, feeble sunlight growing and fading on the floor.

From the loveseat to his left, a familiar voice said, "You're protesting too much, Byron. Maybe you shouldn't make promises you can't keep, even in your imagination."

And Byron stopped breathing.

It was Jennet who sat beside him, but not the young Jennet of his memories. This was a woman his own age, with reading glasses on her nose and practical short hair and crow's feet. She lifted her chin with a confidence that he knew now the young Jennet had lacked. But the sly curve of her mouth was the same.

He stared at her, waiting for her to vanish. Everything seemed so fragile suddenly; one exhaled breath might shatter the entire room.

Finally he managed to speak. "What...how...why are you here?"

Jennet arched a brow. "We're at Auraleigh's B and B for our daughter's graduation. You're still half asleep. I hope you didn't drink that weird aperitif Auraleigh wanted to make you."

"Our daughter's going to Dunstan? We're still together?"

"Last I checked. Honey, you seem a little out of it."

Thank God. This is real; everything else was a dream. But the air had gone heavy, and rising to his feet was a struggle. He had to go to her, to touch her and make sure. "But you said—"

And then he was back in the armchair, his head jerking upright and his eyes opening. His lower back ached. His eyelids felt sticky. The light on the floor was wan and gray.

The loveseat beside him was empty, and the rush of grief took his breath away.

Jennet was still dead. He had dozed off in the chair, drifting from his fantasy into an ordinary dream.

◆ ◆ ◆

Byron needed to know how much time he would have before the others missed him, so he went into the kitchen, where Tina was drinking coffee in the tepid afternoon sun. She must have come in while he was asleep in the armchair. As usual, she was swaddled in a pashmina, her dyed-mahogany hair loosely pinned up. "Help yourself," she said, waving at the sideboard.

Byron poured coffee into a cracked mug. "I conked out in the parlor. Anyone else up yet?"

"No. Auraleigh asked me to wake her when Sonia comes in."

The whole business with Hayworth and Sonia felt as if it had happened years ago. Byron sat opposite Tina and gulped down the too-long-on-the-burner brew. A hardcover book lay on the table with a homemade marker sticking out of it, tiled with pics of two laughing kids of seven or eight. Tina's wedding ring clinked against her mug. She looked past Byron.

He followed her gaze, but there was nothing to see over there, no window. Just shadows.

The daughter he had imagined was part of those shadows now—a never-was, like the older Jennet he had seen in his dream. Yet he remembered telling his daughter he would never abandon her. He could still feel the words vibrating in his throat. He remembered raising her. How could he let her and her mother go?

He said to Tina, "Muriel says you lost somebody, too."

"Fabrice. My first husband. I was studying fashion in Paris after college." Clink. Sip. "It was barely a marriage, more like an extended honeymoon. But we were mad for each other."

"That part doesn't always last," Byron said, thinking of how his fantasy had darkened.

"Never. It never lasts." Tina spoke very precisely. Her fingers twitched, as if reaching for a cigarette. "He died in a car crash on the way to his parents' place in Tuscany. The Peugeot went into a tree, and his side got the brunt." She touched her hairline, calling attention to the milky silk of a scar.

"I'm sorry." Byron's voice rang hollow in the empty house.

He strained his ears and heard only the hum of the fridge, the distant whoosh of traffic.

What was her name—his and Jennet's daughter? Why didn't he know? Jennet had seemed so real, sitting there on the love-seat with an ironic quirk to her mouth, still teasing him after all these years. They were here because their daughter was graduating from Dunstan. Why shouldn't it be true?

"Do you see Fabrice now?" he asked. "In the sog?"

Tina nodded, a small, sly confession. "I'm with him almost every time. And it makes sense for me to see him, because I killed him."

Byron stared at her, caught between one tick of the clock and the next. He remembered the absurd, nightmarish thought he'd had earlier today—*where did I go from the quad that night?* Now he could admit to himself what he'd really been wondering: *What if I killed Jennet?* "You didn't, though."

"Not intentionally," Tina agreed. "But I was driving that night, you see, and I swerved to avoid a—skunk? Badger? To this day I'm not sure. I lost control."

"It could happen to anyone," Byron said.

Tina retied her shawl. Her gaze had a long focus, as if she'd forgotten he was there. "I wonder sometimes—if I could be back there, in the moment before the crash, would I still swerve? Or would I kill that badger and save Fabrice? Would I give myself a whole different life?"

"A whole different life." Something blocked his throat. *Jennet could be upstairs waiting for me. It could all be real.*

"Of course I couldn't save him, though. Law of unintended consequences. Do you have children, Byron?"

Byron nodded. Again he pictured his and Jennet's daughter, tense and vulnerable in her teen bedroom. How would she look as a college graduate—proud, happy? What had she been studying? Where was she now, at twenty-five? He needed to know the rest of her story.

"Then, you understand." Tina rose and put her cup in the dishwasher.

"Right," Byron said automatically, no longer listening. An echoing darkness was rising around him, making him dizzy. His head thrummed as if he had just drunk a dose of sog.

As Tina left the room, he heard the older Jennet saying *Maybe you shouldn't make promises you can't keep*, and he answered her aloud: "I said I wouldn't abandon you, and I meant it. You'll see."

32

SONIA

The trail to the shack is plastered with fallen leaves. Sonia kicks up storms of them. In their place, she imagines the spring woods—leaves churned to brown meal, sparse underbrush, buds about to pop. That's where she must go.

Hayworth has stopped arguing with her. When they reached Dunstan, they parked on Railroad Street and took the trail. Now she watches him walking in front of her and tells herself she's going back to the past moment where she belongs, and he will be there, too.

And if he's right and she actually belongs in 2014—well, at least she'll know what happened to Jennet, filling those gaps in her memory he mentioned.

The falls rush ominously, closer and closer, as they crest the hill and gaze down on their shack.

Drawing nearer, she sees it's run down by decades of snow and rain and wind. She has to brace herself before crawling into the smelly burrow where they once lay for hours together. "Don't you ever come here anymore?"

Hayworth shakes his head, crouching by the door to work loose a large stone that's lodged against the foundation. "Look at this," he says, lifting something into the light. "Still here, right where I left it."

It's an old jam jar with a centimeter of brown scum on the bottom. Sonia knows sog doesn't go bad, and she can feel the tingle from here.

"Please," she says.

Hayworth sits down beside her. "You can go to the past, Sonia, but when you wake up, you'll still be here. And I hope you'll remember everything that happened in between."

"I hope so, too," Sonia says, though she'd still rather stay in the past. She hasn't seen much of this future, but she senses that her life has been a restless, unhappy one.

The world around them recedes—chilly air, streaky clouds, hoarse cries of crows—as she reaches for him. If she doesn't get that jar, she'll never wake up in 1989, and Jennet will go on being dead. Forever.

He yields the jar to her without further argument, and she rocks backward, clutching it to her chest. Then she creeps forward again, toward him. "I'll be back soon. I'll remember."

"I hope so."

His voice resonates from his body into hers, sending ripples of sensation from head to toe. He sounds sad and bitter at once, like he's been waiting all these years—for what? Does he regret erasing the relationship he says they had in some reality she'll never experience?

The woods have gone silent. She practically hears her heart booming with the need to leave. "Thank you," she says. "It'll all be okay."

He doesn't answer, just settles with his back against the wall and watches her drink the contents of the jar. She gags at the taste, but then the buzzing begins.

She stretches out on the floor. As her eyes close, she thrusts her hand out toward him, suddenly missing the warmth of last night. Wanting to feel it one last time.

But it's too late—she's going.

33

BYRON

After retrieving the jar of sog from under the bed, Byron paused at the door of his room to listen to the creaks of timbers settling, the swishes of leaves. Wind and rain had brought so many of them down in the past few days: yellow and pale and hectic red. Wasn't that a quote from something? Jennet would have known.

The world felt real, but he knew now how fragile reality could be, how dependent on an intricate network of choices.

He poured the sog into his travel thermos so it would fit in the cup holder and left the sticky mason jar on the kitchen table. Then he felt guilty for making a mess, so he left a note for Aura-leigh, ending it with "I just have to be sure things turn out right."

She wouldn't know what he meant, but by the time he was done, everything would be different. He wasn't Tina. If he wanted to stop the car from swerving, he would.

He drove the Forester through town and up to campus. He parked in the visitors' lot and walked across the quad to South Hall, his junior year dorm.

Wind blew the flags beside the chapel horizontal. The central rock had been repainted black and white with a scarlet anarchy symbol. Except for a few students smoking or vaping, the quad was deserted. Midterms, probably.

South Hall was four ugly stories of midcentury brick. The front door had been jammed open.

Inside, institutional concrete and cinder block. Stale beer. Byron climbed to the second floor, end of the hall, and knocked.

The boy who came to the door had blue-streaked hair and wore surf shorts, flip-flops, and a windbreaker that reeked of weed. "Hey," he said, rolling strong young shoulders.

"Hey. So, like, this used to be my room. In the eighties. I'm here for a reunion. Mind if I look around?"

"Knock yourself out." The boy cracked the window, then sprawled back on the bed with his laptop. With a move he perhaps thought was smooth, he slid an open paperback over his enormous bong.

Byron stood in the center of the room and mentally erased the boy and the bong and everything else from it. Then he rebuilt it from scratch.

His bed had stood against the opposite wall. The desk was under the window. Instead of *Fear and Loathing in Las Vegas* above the desk, he had a black-and-white poster of Lou Reed with lyrics from "Heroin." A milk-crate bookshelf here. A steamer trunk there.

He saw himself on the evening of May 22, 1989, returning from the communal bathroom. Dropping the toothbrush and paste in his embarrassing childhood Garfield mug. Stripping down to boxers and a T-shirt. Setting the clock radio for seven, switching off the gooseneck lamp. Waiting for the phone to wake him again—first Auraleigh's message, then Jennet's.

If he opened his eyes at 11:41 p.m., when the phone rang, then he would hike down to the falls immediately. Even if it was closer to midnight, when Paul left the library and came out on the quad, he wouldn't ask his friend for a ride—he didn't need distractions. He would get there in time.

"How's the Quad Howl these days?" he asked the room's current occupant, who was using his touchpad to shoot digital zombies.

The kid frowned at him. "The what?"

"You know, midway through exam period. At midnight, everybody goes out on the quad and lets loose."

"Oh, right. Back in the eighties, right? These days, we streak around the quad and then paint the rock."

Byron felt a pang of loss, but then he smiled. "Time marches on, right? Thanks for your help."

He left the room and walked down the hall and the stairs. Once he reached the parking lot, he got in the Forester and drove away without looking back.

The ghost town of Belle Venere wasn't hard to find in daylight. He took the desolate country roads fast, speeding past heaps of rubble that had been barns and past maples so vividly salmon and scarlet that he expected them to stay burned into his retinas.

In his mind, he was still back in the dorm room, distant now, both in space and time. The green digits of the clock radio flickered silently, unseen—11:30 p.m., 11:40 p.m. He felt himself sit upright. The shock of bare feet on the cold floor.

He would jog down the hill and through the silent town, turn left after the bridge, and hurry up the dirt road. When he reached the falls, Auraleigh would be passed out—or gone, if Paul had come for her already. Jennet would be alone.

The rain had made a rutted mess of the dirt road, but the Forester managed it. He parked where the van usually did.

In daylight, the place was even more of a dump. Saplings were reclaiming what had once been lawns and pastures. Tall grass soaked his jeans and twined around his ankles, as if trying to hold him back.

The church leaned foreboding against the clearing sky. Inside, out of the wind, he adjusted his eyes to the gloom. Spears of light penetrated the nave through the Tyvek on the windows. The smell had a bloody edge—a dead rodent?

He found a semi-intact pew and sat down. Sunlight hit his face here. That was nice.

Byron slipped the thermos from his coat. He unscrewed it and inserted a finger, getting a good dollop this time. He had no sleeping bag to cushion the pew, but in a few seconds it wouldn't matter.

He thought of his phantom daughter. He thought of the older Jennet sitting beside him in the parlor of the B and B, calling him "honey" in a dryly affectionate way. *You shouldn't make promises you can't keep.*

Wait for me, both of you. I'm coming.

He sucked the sog from his fingers and swallowed. His head buzzed, and his limbs tingled. He lay back and closed his eyes.

Involuntary Memory
May 23, 1989 (junior year)

SONIA

Someone whistles.

Sonia sits bolt upright beside Hayworth. He lies sprawled on his side, eyes closed, but she's wide awake, sweat trickling down her neck, staring into blackness.

Night. Spring. The air is alive with the peeping of tiny frogs, high and eerie.

She is back. This is real.

She feels a relief so strong it makes her vision waver. *I did it.* But the long whistle from the river sounds a second time, and it has a familiar note—like Jennet's whistle outside the townhouse to give them advance warning when she's going to use her spare key.

Jennet!

Normally Sonia wakes with only fragmentary memories of her future visions, but this time is different. Everything is a little compressed and jumbled, but she remembers what she learned about her friend—and her throat closes with terror.

If Jennet is out there now, she has to hurry. Where's her jacket? Is that a shoe? She crams a foot into it, finds the other.

Stumbling out of the shack, she hears a third whistle. Wind stirs the trees, new leaves hissing and whispering. The stars cast a bluish glow as she picks her way down the riverbank, careful not to trip on the loose rocks.

She has to adjust her eyes to the dark, because it was daytime in the future. She and Hayworth were so close in the shack, and before—but never mind that now.

She's about to push aside the cedar branches when a racket sounds from up the hill—Hayworth, stumbling down the rock slope behind her.

He's young again, so young it startles her. She grabs hold of his arm to steady him, then releases him quickly. He wears only a T-shirt, and the gooseflesh on his bare skin has sent tingles up to her own shoulder.

"Where are you going?" he asks.

She cocks her head toward the opposite shore and says the words that come naturally: "My friend's over by the falls."

"The blonde one? The Stark girl?" His voice is low, urgent. "I wasn't going to say anything, but she kind of confronted me."

"Jennet did? Oh, right." Sonia doesn't think she personally witnessed their interaction, but she's heard about it somewhere. "At the tray drop-off in Commons."

"How'd you know? She said she'd tell her brothers I'm not trustworthy. I wasn't sure if she was joking, but those Starks aren't people you mess around with. One of them did time for breaking a guy's legs up in Highgate."

"It's not a real threat. She was worried about me." Sonia has to force the words out; her body wants to say something else. She has a strange sense that she's living this scene for the second time, differently.

"You told her about us being here?" Hayworth doesn't seem reassured.

"Look, don't worry—I'll talk to her. You go back inside."

"If you're sure." He touches her shoulder before returning up the slope, setting her heart booming with anticipation.

But not the good kind. *If what I saw in the future is true, then something bad is going to happen tonight.* She barely feels twigs pricking her face as she makes her way through the cedars to the river lookout.

The crawling water reflects the sky. It's all she can see until a piece of darkness stands up, out there on the rock that bridges the river, and says, "Sonia."

Sonia scrambles down the small cliff, landing with a crunch on the pebbles below. The rock bridge is dark today, not shimmery with moisture. Safe. She steps onto it, finding easy purchase in the crannies. Jennet sits straddling it halfway across.

The smell of the river is all around—a dirt-floored basement smell. The river speaks with a thousand tongues, high and low, roaring and babbling, drowning out the peepers that dominate the marshy strip along the shore.

Jennet's glasses glint in the starlight. "I didn't think you'd hear me," she says, her voice cutting through the river.

"I always hear you whistle." Sonia's suddenly acutely aware of the tight skirt that constrains her legs. She has to be careful how she steps. "What are you doing here?"

"I came with Auraleigh. She was celebrating her last final with a bottle of Absolut." Jennet swivels, gripping the rock with her knees, and gazes at the blackness of the opposite shore. "She passed out, and Paul came and took her home, but I wanted to stay. We talked. I didn't tell him where you were."

Sonia remembers everything Jennet told her in the *Dove-Cat* room about how selfish she is, how little work she does to maintain their friendship. It almost makes her want to snap at Jennet. But she also recalls riding in the car with Hayworth, in the future, and finally understanding the roots of Jennet's anger.

"Thanks," she says, sitting down cautiously. "I know you're

worried about my sogging, and that's why you threatened Hayworth in the dining commons."

Jennet's face twists, pale in the dark—in pain? In mockery? "Oh, that. I started out kidding, but then later, I don't know, maybe I wasn't." A laugh. "I do worry about you sometimes. I know a little more about that drug than I told you."

"You've taken sog?"

"Once. I didn't like what I saw. But I shouldn't have ambushed Hayworth that way."

That doesn't matter now. "Thank you for worrying about me. For noticing. I know I've been off in my own world this semester, but I've missed you."

Silence—which isn't really silence, because the falls continue to roar and sing—until Jennet says, "I didn't say you could keep it forever."

"What?"

"My poem. I just meant to give it to you to read, in the *Dove-Cat* room. You didn't give it back."

Oh. Sonia flushes, remembering folding the poem into a cootie catcher. She finds it in the pocket of her pencil skirt, a tight wad of paper.

More of what she saw in the future comes back in a rush: the poem folded into a key ring. The key ring in the pocket of a blue peacoat. Hayworth handing the coat to her.

Hayworth confirming that Jennet drowned in the river the same night she gave Sonia the poem.

She doesn't pull out the poem after all. Her hand falls to her side, and her vision blurs, heat massing behind her eyes. She can barely see Jennet in the darkness, through the tears, and she needs so badly to see her. *You've never, not once since I've known you, reached out to me, Sonia.*

"I didn't understand it," she says—no longer sure which time she belongs in, only that things are finally coming clear. "Your poem—but I do now. Why did you have to put the truth in a poem, a riddle? Why couldn't you just tell me?"

Jennet stares at her. "Tell you what?"

A small, tight ball forms in Sonia's stomach. Even now, knowing how things will turn out, it's so hard to be blunt. "That... you're in a difficult situation. That's why you're really here, isn't it? You keep hoping I'll finally catch on. It's true what you said earlier today. I've never really reached out to you. I'm selfish and self-absorbed. I don't care about anyone."

A soft laugh in the dark. "Is that something you learned in the future?"

"I think it is."

Jennet leans in and touches Sonia's cheek. Sonia stops breathing. Jennet's fingers are as cool and smooth as her mother's hand on her forehead when she was sick.

They stay there for a moment, eyes locked, and then they draw apart. For the first time in her life, Sonia can't say who broke the contact first. They move in concert, two parts of the same whole, and then they are separate again.

"I didn't say you were selfish," Jennet says.

"I am, though." Sonia tries to draw a breath, but it tapers to nothing, leaving her lungs stripped and cold. "My mom was always moving around, so I never felt like I belonged anywhere, and I learned to just protect myself, I guess. I ran away to college, where I met you, and then I ran away again to Hayworth. That's the kind of person I am. But listen. I want to help."

Jennet rises carefully to her feet and looks up the bank, toward the shack hidden in its hollow. "Do you love him? Hayworth?"

The peepers are inside Sonia's head, drowning out the falls, as she stands up, too. "Yes. I don't know. I think I'm not ready for that yet, but I will be."

All this while she's been thinking she needs to be a better person before she can have love—prettier, wittier, more relaxed, less anxious. But maybe all she and Hayworth needed was time. Maybe, in 2014, they are finally ready for each other.

Maybe she belongs there after all.

"Do you love Byron?" she asks. "Do you want to be with him?"

Jennet's reply is lost in the rushing water. Sonia edges toward her, and Jennet says, sounding almost like her old, airy self, "You've been seeing your future, right? You should know I'm not in it."

That makes Sonia tremble, the peepers' vibration running through her veins, because she has a memory of someone— Paul?—telling her that Jennet sogged once and saw nothing. But she doesn't fall. Adrenaline keeps her alert to the tiniest shifts of balance, and she has a mission.

Change it. Make it turn out differently. Hayworth warned her not to, but now she's here, how can she not at least try? Having been in the future, knowing her friend is in danger, she can't just act as if she didn't know.

"I know you're scared. But you need to talk to Byron. I could help you. You haven't told him yet, have you?"

"Byron's just a boy," Jennet says in her clear, fluting voice. "A boy who fucked Auraleigh, as it happens."

"He kissed me, too, but it didn't mean anything." Sonia knows that, and she also knows that Byron is a good person. Byron is— will be—a good father, and if Jennet gives him a chance, they could still be happy. "He's not perfect, but he loves you, Jennet."

Jennet tosses her shoulders. "Byron's not that special, you know. You want Hayworth to love you, you want Byron to love me, but it's not going to happen. They can't do it. Not even the best ones." She hunches as if against a cold wind. "My brothers," she adds in a small voice. "If they find out I'm pregnant, they'll laugh."

Sonia doesn't think. She throws her arms around Jennet.

Jennet feels so small—limp at first, like a terrified kitten. They sway before they find their balance, and Jennet's arms tighten on Sonia's back.

"I want you to be in my future." Sonia says it so softly, practically a breath, that she isn't sure Jennet hears until Jennet whispers back, "I'm not sure I can be."

But this is so real, and they can both have a future, of course they can! Sonia clears her throat and says, louder, "Let's take one thing at a time. I'll go with you to health services. For the test."

Jennet's nod tickles her collarbone. She has relaxed; her warm breath comes evenly. "You should go back to your future boy now."

Sonia shakes her head. "I want to walk back to campus with you—it's so late. I'll just run and tell him first, okay?"

Again the barest nod. "Okay. I'll wait on the shore."

As Jennet turns to leave, she stumbles. Sonia's hand shoots out. Jennet grasps it and holds on, each of them steadying the other.

It takes a moment for Sonia's heart to return to a normal rhythm. Both of their palms are sweaty. "That was close," Jennet says. "I almost swerved into the afterlife."

Then Sonia looks up and sees him over Jennet's shoulder. He startles her so much she cries out—a small cry, more squeak than scream.

She loosens her grip on Jennet, who says, "What?"

The newcomer is tall, faceless, one long arm extending as if to invite Jennet to dance. He must have approached them silently.

A slight shift brings his face into the light.

Byron.

Involuntary Memory
May 23, 1989 (junior year)

BYRON

Byron steps out of the thicket, heading for the sound of the falls. The river spreads before him. When he catches sight of Jennet's hair, a pale flash in the starlight, he stands stock-still, one hand over his heart as if it might burst from his chest.

I'm here. I came for you. Finally he has gotten past the dorm room and the quad. This is the place and time where he can make a difference. He's shaky and sweating from running most of the way, but his strong young body hasn't failed him.

Wait—who's that with Jennet? Not Paul, and too tall to be Auraleigh. They're talking, but the rushing falls swallow their words. As he arrives on the riverbank, Jennet's companion pulls her into a hug.

Is that Sonia? What's she doing here? The two of them are swaying, whispering.

You shouldn't be here. You're changing things.

Byron steps onto the rock bridge, watching his footing and willing that internal voice to be quiet, because Jennet needs to know about the library job and the Victorian house and their daughter. He has seen a forty-seven-year-old Jennet teasing him in Auraleigh's B and B; he has heard her achingly familiar laugh. She exists.

He's almost halfway across when Jennet and Sonia separate. Jennet loses her footing.

No! Still a few yards away, Byron darts forward—but before he can get there, Sonia's hand shoots out to catch Jennet's, righting her.

They stand holding hands. Byron shivers all over, his head spinning and buzzing as if he's about to come out of the sog. He lowers it and closes his eyes. *Stay, stay, stay.*

"That was close," Jennet says. "I almost swerved into the afterlife."

Swerve. Why does that word have an ominous ring? He stays still, realizing he needs to be careful not to frighten either of them. He waits for Jennet to notice him, narrowing his eyes. Even in the dark, her presence is so distinct that she seems to glow. He makes out the curve of her neck, the lift of her chin, the bend of her wrist as she clasps Sonia's hand, all her gestures so delicate and strong at once.

In a few minutes, he will be the one who takes her hand and guides her safely to shore. It won't be the way he imagined earlier, because Sonia's here instead of Paul, but that's all right. He'll cut to the chase and find a way to broach the topic of the possible pregnancy.

Their daughter. His *daughter*—

But when he thinks those words, it's not his and Jennet's daughter who pops into his head. It's the well-loved thumbnail from his phone screen: nine-year-old Eliza in her zebra costume, beaming as he captures her in the viewfinder, because for once, he has managed to be home on Halloween night to take her trick-or-treating.

He hears Tina's voice saying *If I could be back there, in the mo-*

ment before the crash, would I still swerve? Would I give myself a whole different life?

She mentioned unintended consequences. She asked if he had children.

He'd been dazed from his dream of Jennet, drunk on the past. *Oh no. Oh no, no, no.*

Byron's chest is so tight, he can't speak. He straightens again and reaches out for Jennet. He wants to say *I've come for you. I'll take you away and make you mine, the two of us safe in our tall Victorian, our artfully feathered nest, with our beautiful daughter and her picture books and her bold imagination, forever and ever.*

But it's too late for that. It's been too late ever since his kids were born.

Jennet's attention is on Sonia, so Sonia spots Byron first. She lets out a little cry.

"What?" Jennet asks, and then, finally, she notices him.

Involuntary Memory
May 23, 1989 (junior year)

SONIA

Sonia says to Byron, "You shouldn't be here! You're in your room."

Jennet isn't paying attention to Sonia. She's already turning and yanking her hand free. "Well, Byron," she says, but the motion makes her lose her footing again, and she staggers toward the water.

Sonia reaches for Jennet, acutely aware of the peepers pulsing in time with the blood in her ears. But the dark form that is Byron moves, too.

"I'm sorry." Byron is looking at Sonia and addressing her, even as he grasps Jennet by the shoulder. Even as Jennet stops flailing and her fingers close on his strong arm, using it as a support.

"This is for Rohan and Eliza," he says.

And with a single light push, almost a tap, he sends Jennet toppling into the river.

No! But Sonia is powerless to help Jennet as her pale head surfaces from the white water churn and she thrashes, grasping wildly for the rock to haul herself up.

Sonia crouches for stability, scrambling on all fours. The cold spine of the ridge jabs her as she grabs for Jennet's hand, but there's nothing there.

She swings her other leg over the rock bridge, meaning to lower herself into the water and—what? Reach out farther? Swim? She'll be pulled under, too. The pool has swallowed Jennet as if she never existed.

Her breath coming in ragged sobs, she cries, "I came to stop it from happening! You—what are you *doing*?"

Strong hands seize her by the shoulders and haul her onto her feet. Byron's panting breath smells of mint toothpaste. "I had to," he says, voice scratchy and broken, nails digging into her flesh through the sweater. "You're future-Sonia, aren't you? Then, you should understand. If she lives, they don't."

Is he going to throw Sonia in, too? She opens her mouth to ask *who do you mean?* but the air has gone heavy as in dreams. The stars are a smear across the sky.

Byron releases her and stands up, pressing a finger to his lips. "This isn't what happened the first time," he says, his voice breaking. "I... I'm sorry."

Sorry. *Sorry?*

But she can't go after him, she can't go after Jennet, because the buzzing has started with a fuzzy sweet ache like returning circulation. She can only roll over—not into the river, but into the static of emerging from the sog.

◆ ◆ ◆

She knew she was in the shack before she opened her eyes. The woods smelled of autumn decay now, and she sat up with a sharp gasp, as if to expel water from her lungs. As if she were drowning.

"You okay?" Hayworth leaned over her—not the nervous young Hayworth but the older one with the gritty voice and weary weight to his movements.

This time Sonia knew they were the same age. She didn't need to be asked what month or year it was. She belonged here—in her present, the only one she had.

She wrapped her arms around him, burying a hand in his hair, and said into his ear, "I could have saved her. We all could have been there for her, when it still counted, but it's too late now."

· 34 ·

AURALEIGH

Coming downstairs, Auraleigh knocked at Sonia's door, but no one answered.

Sonia and Hayworth were supposed to return this afternoon. If they hadn't, something was wrong. She marched down to the parlor, already contemplating driving to that bastard's house and demanding her friend back.

This morning, fatigue had sunk her into a dangerous passivity, but sleep had recharged her. Then Ben Stark had called, day-drinking and babbling about how he'd used his truck to scare two of her guests the night before last, demanding to know if she'd gotten Hayworth or anyone else to confess to Jennet's murder.

Ben was a train wreck, but she could understand why he disliked Hayworth—what a hypocrite! Even if his plan to shut down the memory spa really was about protecting the students, he was still the reason Sonia had begun sogging in the first place.

If Sonia had regressed to her past self, who could blame her? At dinner the other night, telling them all about losing her job, she hadn't seemed very happy with her present. What with Byron's theatrics and Paul's revelation about being possibly the last to see Jennet alive and Auraleigh's own drama (she couldn't deny it), they hadn't been paying much attention to Sonia this week. How could Auraleigh have allowed Hayworth to take charge of her friend?

She wasn't afraid of him! Anger gave her a satisfying adrenaline rush, setting her head buzzing like sog. Garrett had told her where Hayworth lived, and she would give him a piece of her mind.

There was no one in the kitchen. On the table, she found a note in Byron's handwriting.

Going to the church to say goodbye. Thanks for the basement hospitality & everything else, & sorry. I just have to be sure things turn out right.

Basement hospitality? WTF? Auraleigh stood on the threshold and felt the house around her: a faint, reassuring hum of heating and electric and water that she paid the bills for every month. This was her home. She was the one who asked questions, gave tours, left messages, and she had not shown Byron the basement.

Then she saw the empty jar on the table, full of sticky black residue, and all at once she understood.

He had taken her secret stash and gone to the church. But why?

SONIA

Hayworth looked frazzled, running a nervous hand through his gray-speckled black hair, but he didn't look old to Sonia anymore. As they walked briskly through the woods, he said, "Sonia, are you...back? You don't still think you're twenty, do you?"

"No." Strange how okay she felt saying it, moving through

the dappled sunlight of this day in middle age. "You were right. I just didn't *want* to be in the present."

Though she was trying to be calm, her mind was roiling. She had tried to save Jennet, to change the past and keep her in this world with them, but then Byron, Byron…

If she lives, they don't, he had said. She couldn't make sense of it.

"I tried to change the past when I sogged just now," she said. "I know you told me not to."

His eyes widened in alarm. "What did you change?"

"Everything. Nothing." It was hard to get words out, as if a load of rocks were sitting on her chest. "What do you remember from the night Jennet died?"

"You went to talk to her, and you came back into the shack after about fifteen minutes and said it was okay, she wouldn't make trouble for us." Hayworth held back a gaunt bare branch to clear the path for her. "You were weird and quiet, but then you were always a little that way. I thought everything was fine till the next day, when I heard about the body they found in the river."

"And then you thought maybe I had pushed her?"

"I don't know." He looked down. "Maybe. Did you?"

"No." It was a struggle to hold the memories in her head, because they had been superseded by new ones. But she could finally see the outline of what had really happened. "Jennet came to the river because she wanted to apologize. Or she wanted me to apologize—anyway, she wanted to be friends again. But we were so scared and shy and obtuse that neither of us could admit it. We had an awkward conversation, neither of us saying what we meant, and then I went back to you. All these years, I've been blocking out the memory—not because of anything I did, but because of what I *didn't* do. After I heard she was dead, I couldn't face my smallness, my cowardice. I could have helped her that night."

"What did you change when you sogged, then?" Hayworth

stopped and wheeled on her, fierce and frightened at once. "Sonia, did you save her? Is Jennet alive *now*? Because, if you did—"

Sonia shook her head quickly to reassure him, though she couldn't dispel the lump in her throat. "I tried, but no, I didn't change anything that mattered, though I did finally say all those things I should have. I was going to leave you and walk back to campus with her, so she wouldn't be alone."

"But you didn't? What happened?"

"Someone stopped me."

They were on a muddy patch. The world reeled as she suddenly understood Byron's words, and her footing slipped. Hayworth's hands shot out to steady her.

I had to, Byron had said. *You're future-Sonia, aren't you? Then, you should understand.*

But not past Byron—present Byron. *Did it for Rohan and Eliza*—he'd spoken his children's names, which he couldn't have known in 1989. He hadn't even met their mother.

The Byron who belonged in 1989 would never have hurt Jennet—not deliberately, anyway. *Byron thought he needed to kill her, because I was going to save her.* And saving Jennet might have stopped his children from being born.

How could Byron have known what she was planning, though? He'd been so tormented, so miserable with his claw-like grip on her sweater. She had to find out, right now. "I need to see my friends," she said as they reached the trailhead.

They left the woods and hurried up Railroad Street. It felt agonizingly long, the pavement jolting her too-thin soles with every step.

"How well do you remember it now?" Sonia asked, her voice so level it surprised her. "The lifetime you lived where we had a relationship after college, just like I saw in my future visions? The one that doesn't exist anymore?"

"The memories are a little vague." Hayworth kept pace with

her. "I never meant to erase anything, you know. I escaped into the past, and when I stuck there, I just did everything a little differently."

Sonia felt no more grief for the life they could have had together. They could still have it—just differently, as he'd said.

Now it was Byron she was worried about.

The Forester, Auraleigh's car, and Paul's rental were all missing from the driveway of the B and B. Sonia threw open the front door to find Muriel stoking the woodstove in the parlor. "Where's Byron?"

Relief washed over Muriel's face. "Auraleigh asked me to text her when you came back. Everybody's been so worried! She went up to Belle Venere—she said something about meeting Byron. Maybe they were both going to look for you again."

Sonia grabbed Hayworth's arm and steered him back down the porch steps, up the street toward his beat-up Outback.

"I'm worried about my friend," she said into his questioning face. "I need to find him right now."

· 35 ·

AURALEIGH

Auraleigh pulled up and parked beside Byron's Forester. As she jogged across the field to the church, sunlight burst through the clouds and shone blindingly on the peeling shingles of the farmhouse.

Hayworth had been lurking in there, spying on her guests! She was still angry about it. This property might be a dump, but it was hers: the overgrown fields, the gnarled woods, the ruins, all of it.

She would deal with him later. Memories of her interactions with Byron over the past few days kept replaying in her head. He'd been so upset when she admitted Jennet might have been pregnant. She shouldn't have kept it from him, but she knew how fiercely secretive Jennet was—and maybe also Auraleigh was just a little frustrated with his stupid, superior tech-bro attitude.

But then this morning, instead of staying angry at her, he had hugged her and whispered, *I can't let her go, either.* And then while she slept, he had stolen her sog. He had left her a note that was clearly a goodbye.

She had to find him right fucking *now*.

The church was always depressing in daylight, the door hanging open to reveal a musty cave of shadows. This time, though, something was different. She detected it even before she entered the nave.

A stray sunbeam highlighted a fluidlike shimmer on the backs of the pews. The air was sticky and treacherous.

Auraleigh stopped short, her heart hammering, and pressed a hand to her chest. She gasped as Byron rose from a pew to face her.

He was in the second row from the altar, in that ridiculous leather jacket from college, the one that barely fit. It was sopping wet. So was he, his dark curls in strings down his neck, dripping all over her property, filling the air with a choking, ominous stench.

In her peripheral vision, she saw the TruFuel cans lined up on the altar rail.

Byron smiled without malice, as if he were genuinely glad to see her. "Got a light?"

Auraleigh tried to count the cans, to size up the danger, but the world had gone liquid, her brain registering it in bursts like stop-motion.

As if each movement might send her off a precipice, she took a step toward Byron, then another. *Be kind. Soothing.* That was the only way to get them both out of here alive.

She opened her mouth, and words emerged: "What the fuck, Byron? What the fuck is going on here?"

"I'm not going to hurt you," Byron said in a friendly tone, coming toward her as if they had run into each other in a busy café. "This place, though—it's time to close down the Church of Sog, Auraleigh. The stuff is just too risky—and too tempting. Collect whatever shitty payout the insurance will give you and build something new."

He raised both hands, and she saw the viscous blackness coating his fingers. Horror prickled on the backs of her thighs as

Byron turned to glance at the cold woodstove. "You don't keep matches there. You should."

Auraleigh shook her head. Her knees were locked in place, as if she were a poorly made doll. How many cans of generator gas had he emptied? Would tossing a match send the whole church up in flames—or just him?

She said in a small voice, "Whatever you're thinking right now, you don't deserve it."

Byron's mouth tipped up in an ugly smile. "Maybe you should find out first what I think I deserve."

Auraleigh hadn't said the right things to Jennet on the riverbank, but since then, she'd learned so many right things to say. She'd tried saying them all on the awful day she spotted fresh bandages on her daughter's inner arms: *I love you and support you. You are perfect exactly the way you are.*

Frances had just scowled. "Who told you to say that, Mom? Oprah? When have you ever thought I was perfect? You're the most critical person I know."

So maybe being calmly supportive wasn't Auraleigh's forte. She was too afraid of the cold undertow that had pulled her friend into nothingness while she was passed out, too afraid of her daughter's slack mouth and unfocused eyes. She had seized Frances in a fierce embrace and said, "If you hurt yourself again, so help you God, our souls will burn in hell together," although she believed in neither God nor souls nor hell.

Now she yelled at Byron: "I don't give a shit, you fucking egomaniac! How dare you do this in my church? Why is everything all about you?"

My God, that felt so much better. She sucked in a breath. Byron didn't move, but his smile relaxed a little, as if her outburst had released something in him, too.

And then his face went blank. "I killed Jennet," he said.

"No, you didn't!" He looked so pale, it petrified her. "I know you feel guilty, but—"

"No." Byron shook his head, and there was a terrible calm in his eyes. "I didn't mean to. I went there to save her, to fix everything. But then I realized what that would mean."

"What are you talking about? You went where?"

"Back to 1989," Byron said, gazing at a last ray of sunlight. "I stole your sog, and I targeted the night she died—I'm a pro at it now. I was going to walk her home. Stop anything bad from happening. But before I could even say hello to her, I realized..." His voice faltered. "If she lived, if we stayed together, my kids wouldn't exist."

"You can't change the past!"

"Yes, you can." He stared into space, away from her. "And I would have, but at the last minute, I changed my mind. I barely had to push, really. She was so close to the edge."

"You're going to immolate yourself because of some scenario you imagined? Out of guilt?" Auraleigh spat the words at him, because she was terrified, though she knew now he was mentally ill and couldn't be held responsible for anything he was saying or doing.

"Ask Sonia—she was there." Facing her at last, Byron looked a little startled, as if he'd thought he was arguing not with a real person but with voices in his head. "Even if the result was the same either way, I made it happen. And now I need to pay."

SONIA

The dirt road took a sharp turn and dumped them into Belle Venere, in its hollow formed by densely wooded hills. "You keep talking in circles and not telling me anything," Hayworth said a little breathlessly, parking beside the Forester. "What do you mean, somebody stopped you from changing the past? You won't try it again, will you?"

"No! I'll explain everything, I promise. I just need to know something first."

The exchange between her and Byron on the rock bridge had felt so private, so immediate, as if they were sogging into the same past moment at the exact same time. Maybe they had been. But how could Byron have known what she planned to do? Only he could answer that.

She practically ran across the field, her breath coming short and her thighs pumping. Ahead loomed the dark maw of the church's open door. Behind her, Hayworth called something she couldn't hear.

"What?" She paused inside the door, and that was when the stink hit her.

Hayworth staggered to a halt, too. "Shit."

Gasoline, covering the lofty ruin in a gentle slick of lethality. It glinted on the backs of pews in the waning sunlight that penetrated the Tyvek. It trickled in rivulets down the aisle. As Sonia took a tentative step, and then another, acid surged up her throat.

Yet there was also something festive and solemn about it, as if the church were sanctified again, bedecked to host a sacrifice. As she approached the two figures at the end of the nave, she almost felt the throb of a distant organ.

Byron and Auraleigh had a ceremonial look to them, too. They sat close together in the second pew, Byron's head resting on Auraleigh's shoulder. He was sopping wet, and it was getting all over her.

"Stop right there, Sonia." Hayworth's voice was rough with fear.

Byron and Auraleigh turned their heads to face the intruders. Neither appeared guilty or embarrassed, though their eyes showed the sheen of unshed tears.

"Sonia!" Auraleigh rose, keeping one hand on Byron's shoulder, as if to steady him. "I've been worried sick. It's okay," she added. "You can come closer."

"No one has a match," Byron said, as if this should dispel any concern.

Sonia took another step, though her whole body cried out against it. "What happened?"

"I should be asking you that!" Auraleigh guided Byron out of the pew like a stubborn child. "Hayworth said you—"

"She's okay now," Hayworth interrupted. He grasped Sonia's shoulder, holding her back, away from them. "Sometimes when people sog, they bring the past back with them. What the fuck is going on?"

"An accident." Auraleigh steered Byron past them up the aisle.

Byron said, "Sonia knows. She saw everything."

"Yes. Were you there because of me?" Sonia hurried into the vestibule after them, Hayworth trailing behind her. It was much easier to walk away from the stench, into fresh air. Through the doorway, she saw the sun sinking through a tattered scrim of clouds. And there was Paul, hurrying toward them across the grass.

"Did you know what I was going to do?" she asked Byron, her voice pitching uncontrollably. She couldn't explain this in front of Paul. He would tell them to put away their shoe-box time machine and be sensible. "You knew changing the past would affect too many people, so you had to stop me, didn't you?"

"Stop you?" Byron turned to stare at her, his red-rimmed eyes wide with apparent bewilderment. "I was the one who was there to change the past. I saw our daughter in my dreams, and I saw Jennet older, and I *needed*..." He paused, his breath hitching. "It was all my fault. I didn't come to my senses till I was there on the rock with you."

Come to his senses? So he had meant to save Jennet, too? She opened her mouth, but Paul spoke first: "Muriel said you were all here. What happened? Sonia, you okay?"

Sonia nodded, not feeling okay at all, while Auraleigh said, "Accident. We're gonna have a hell of a cleanup."

"I killed Jennet," Byron said, tugging free of Auraleigh's grip

and wheeling to face Paul. There was a touch of embarrassment
in his tone, as if he knew how absurd he sounded. "I started to
change the past and save her, because I wanted her alive so badly,
but at the last minute I realized that if she lived, too much else
would be different."

Sonia braced herself to rush between Byron and Auraleigh—
to shield him with her body and absorb the force of Auraleigh's
wrath. But Auraleigh didn't seem shocked. "Please, please stop
saying that," she whispered. "You didn't."

Then she turned to Hayworth. Tears made her eyes enormous. "You tell him. Time travel is impossible. Blaming himself was the only way he could get closure. Right?"

Confusion flitted across Hayworth's face. It was Paul who
answered quietly: "You were on the quad the night she died,
Byron, not asleep at all. I saw that in the sog. Is that where you
went from the quad? The falls?"

Auraleigh said, "What are you talking about, Paul? If that's
a joke, it's not funny."

"Sonia knows," Byron repeated, appealing to her. "She was there
by the river—with you, I assume." A glance at Hayworth. "She
saw me do it. She heard what I said, so maybe she understands."

"I think I do understand," Sonia said. It hurt to meet his gaze.
"Back then, you would never have hurt her. But if you'd saved
her—or let me do it—all our lives would have been different.
You would have lost too much."

"I can't live two lives! I had to choose." Byron blinked several
times, but his jaw was set. "Paul, you got a match?"

Auraleigh shook her head wildly, telegraphing *no*, but Paul was
already slipping a hand into his pocket. He produced a match-
box and tossed it to Byron.

Byron tore off a match and lit it with a loud *snick*.

Auraleigh cried out. "Byron, no!" Sonia shouted, but he was
already whipping his arm over his head and hurling the burning match into the nave.

The tiny flame arced through the shadows, soared high over the pews, and disappeared.

Sonia held her breath. Ever prudent, Paul took several steps back across the vestibule to the doorway. The others followed, except for Byron.

They waited. There was no blockbuster whoosh, no blossoming of flame. Maybe the match had been concussed or drowned.

But then Auraleigh muttered, "Oh shit," and Sonia saw sickly orange fluttering in the nave, shadows dancing on the walls. Byron stood as if transfixed, watching.

"Byron, come out of there!" But Byron was nowhere near the flames, so Auraleigh rounded on Paul, her eyes bright with tears. "Why did you do that? Didn't you smell the gas?"

Paul shrugged, not looking particularly sorry. "Didn't you hear him, Auraleigh? You have your killer. He just confessed."

"No, he didn't! He doesn't know what he's saying!"

"I think it's pretty clear what happened. I left Jennet alone, he arrived, and they fought." Paul cleared his throat. "Maybe he didn't mean to. Maybe it was an accident."

"They didn't fight!" Sonia said. "And none of that happened until we both sogged backward."

Byron's gliding steps were taking him slowly away from them, toward the fire. Nothing had exploded in the nave, but she heard a rushing like distant surf.

"He didn't kill Jennet the first time," she said desperately. "Can you explain, Hayworth?"

Auraleigh screamed. "Byron! Stop!"

Hayworth said, "Fuck."

Paul said, "Oh, jeez," though he didn't look heartbroken to see that Byron was headed into the flames.

Sonia said nothing. She gulped a deep breath and dashed after Byron, into the nave—because, after all, they had both tried to save Jennet. She would have been dead with or without them. But if they hadn't attempted to revise the past, to deny the inevitable,

she wouldn't have died in that particularly hideous way, shoved
by someone she loved who seemed to be reaching out to help her.

At first, it felt like nothing, like diving in to extinguish a
kitchen fire. Then the wall of heat hit her, her mouth as dry as
felt in an instant. She had only time to see the entire middle section of pews aflame before fierce light blinded her and smoke
choked her and she sank to her knees on the broken floorboards,
coughing and gasping.

Strong arms yanked her upright—Hayworth. "We have to
get out of here!"

Sonia stumbled to her feet and tried to get her bearings, but the
only landmark was the distant roof. Smoke billowed, gusting bits
of wood and paper against her cheeks. The world wobbled like a
dream. All around her, dark masses shivered and strained against
the pressure of the blaze—the walls, the windows, the roof?

There was no hope here, no future. There was nothing to do
but leave. Byron had made his own choices.

But he'd wanted to save Jennet, too. He'd tried.

Her heart slammed into her chest, and she broke free of Hayworth and lurched toward Byron, a featureless still point in a
whirling storm.

He crouched in the aisle, gazing into the inferno. Waiting
for the flames that licked closer and closer to catch him up and
sweep him into the party.

She fell to her knees beside him. You could almost breathe
down here. He turned to her, his blown pupils so dark, and she
said, "You did it for your kids, didn't you?"

A look of relief washed over Byron's face. "Had to."

Sonia stopped thinking. Holding her breath, she hooked an
arm under Byron's, over his back, and heaved. At first, his weight
refused to budge. She was so weak, as if her lungs were packed
with wadded cotton. Then Hayworth was beside her, helping,
and together the three of them took a tortured step away from
the lashing brightness on the altar.

Byron doubled over coughing, nearly toppling all of them. Sonia set her jaw and grabbed his free arm and dragged him a second step, third, fourth, fifth, smoke clawing at her throat. Everything was dark, the air roaring and seething, and where was the door?

"Here! This way!" It was Auraleigh, squeaky with terror.

Then they were in the vestibule, where the outside door was a rectangle of calm light floating in choking darkness. Sonia hunched over and retched. In the corner of her eye, she saw Hayworth lug Byron through the door and dump him in the grass. She staggered upright, and he returned for her.

Outside. The grass was cool and wet, the air unbelievably fresh, as if the world had been newly made. For a few long moments, all she could do was breathe and cough and breathe again. Then Paul said, "C'mon, get away from it!" and her head jerked up, and she saw the sky filling with topaz clouds on one side and pinprick stars on the other.

Smoke poured from every aperture of the church. They scuttled out of its shadow, still struggling to catch their breaths. Hayworth walked Byron farther away, Auraleigh diving in to support him on the other side. Sonia and Paul flanked them, gulping mouthfuls of chilly air.

Their protesting lungs guided them around the side of the church to the hem of the woods. Shielded from the smoke that billowed south, they collapsed in the underbrush. Auraleigh pulled out her phone.

Sonia was whimpering slightly on each inhale. She saw firs against the sunset. Felt a thistle prick her ankle. Breathed.

She reached into her pocket for her phone, but instead she found Jennet's divination poem. The creases in the paper were so deep that soon it would rip. All this time she'd kept it without knowing—this little piece of Jennet inside her key ring, close to her. This document of Jennet struggling with her own mortal fears, trying desperately to turn them into art.

Auraleigh was coaching Byron through each breath, telling him that the paramedics were on their way and he shouldn't try to talk, but Byron kept rasping out words.

"It could all have been different," Sonia thought she heard him say. "When you drink that stuff, you find out it could all have been different."

They still didn't know if Jennet had chosen to step off the rock into the falls or if she had fallen. Now that Byron had revised the past, they would never know. But the answer no longer seemed vital, because somewhere, somehow, Jennet knew now that they all cared. That they hadn't wanted her to slip away without a trace.

It was time to give her poem back to her. Remembering Jennet's arms around her, Sonia closed her eyes so she wouldn't have to watch what came next: her fist crumpling the paper with Jennet's handwriting on it into a small ball.

With the former poem in hand, she rose and took halting steps out of the clinging undergrowth toward the church. "What are you doing?" Hayworth called.

But she was already close enough to feel the heat and see the glow of flames through a gap in the Tyvek. She wound up and pitched the balled-up paper at it.

The poem disappeared into the flames. Sonia closed her eyes again and imagined the heat unfolding the paper, handwritten words dancing and contorting in bonfire light. Jennet always liked dramatic gestures, bits of ritual.

She heard Jennet's low chuckle close by, as if in her own head. *Well. Is this goodbye?*

I miss you. I'm sorry.

Then Hayworth was behind her, dragging her back to safety with both arms around her, whispering in her ear, "What was that? What were you thinking?"

She saved her breath. There would be other times to explain.

TWO DAYS LATER

◆

November 3, 2014

· 36 ·

SONIA

Sonia helped Paul carry his bags downstairs to the rental car. Auraleigh was busy catching up with B and B chores; she had spent most of the previous night in the hospital with Byron, who was still being treated for mild burns and smoke inhalation.

Paul didn't look so spruce anymore. He looked, in fact, as if he hadn't slept for the past two nights. He and Sonia had been studiously avoiding each other.

Now, on the verge of leaving, in the dusty stairwell where the sunlight didn't penetrate, he said, "Do you really believe he didn't kill her?"

Not the first time, no. But Sonia wasn't sure if Paul's logical mind would ever accept the truth. "Do you really believe he could have done it and kept quiet about it for twenty-five years? Because I don't think that's like Byron at all."

Paul's Adam's apple bobbed. Sweat darkened the underarms of his clean white shirt. "People can surprise us."

"Not that much. I think the sog confused him, Paul. It brought up too many things—regret, guilt."

"That's what Auraleigh thinks. And Byron seems to think he altered the space-time continuum, which of course I don't believe. But you admitted you saw Byron do something to Jennet in the sog. You said he didn't kill her the *first* time. What does that mean?"

She wanted to explain everything, but he wouldn't believe her, either. "It means that Byron and I both sogged the same thing, but parts of our vision couldn't have been real memories. He said his children's names to me, for instance. And no," she added as Paul's expression turned skeptical, "I don't know how or why. I just know that a collective hallucination is more likely than him having killed her all those years ago."

Paul sighed, then bent to grab his suitcase again. "I'll grant you that, I guess. It's an unpredictable substance—and dangerous. Shall we find Auraleigh?"

Auraleigh joined them in the foyer, and the three of them went outside, under the blazing blue sky—past the now-belated Halloween decorations, bedraggled by days of rain. Glancing back at the parlor window, Sonia saw a slender figure dipping gracefully to put something on a table, blond hair swinging. Frances.

Yesterday, after hearing about the accident in Belle Venere—they were calling it an accident, anyway—Auraleigh's daughter had emerged from her student co-op to help run the B and B while Auraleigh sat by Byron's bedside. Garrett dropped her off at the house, with no objections from her mother.

You would like your nephew, Sonia said to the Jennet in her head. *He and Auraleigh's daughter make a good pair, hard as it is to believe.*

Byron's daughter had flown out from California, and he was due to be discharged tomorrow. So Auraleigh had returned home to wish Paul off.

"Byron should be here to say goodbye, too." Auraleigh sounded resigned. "I wish you'd come to the hospital, Paul."

"It didn't feel right." Paul caught Sonia's eye for an instant.

The three of them hadn't discussed Paul giving the matches to Byron. Sonia wondered if he regretted that gesture—and if Auraleigh was trying to forget all about it.

"You'll feel different later." Auraleigh's voice broke. "You know as well as I do that Byron was just...distraught. He hasn't dealt with his feelings all these years, and sog brought them back."

"Our method was riskier than we thought," Paul agreed. Again his eyes met Sonia's, and she knew he was struggling toward an explanation he could live with.

It might be easier to see Byron as an ordinary murderer, trying to get rid of an inconvenient pregnant girlfriend. Certainly easier than acknowledging that they could never know how Jennet had died before Byron stepped in to change the past.

They were back where they'd started, with Jennet's last moment a black box that could never be opened, yet she had opened parts of them to themselves. Sonia knew now that she'd let flashes of the future enthrall her because she didn't want to face the hard parts of living, the parts that didn't make sense. It was easier to keep scouting ahead for something different and better than to make the best of what was right here and now.

Every second of your life counts, Hayworth had told her in the car, *whether you want it to or not.* She'd spent years wondering how her life had gone off the rails since college, when the truth was there were no rails and no destination. There was only life, meandering across an ever-changing landscape, and sometimes that landscape was worth the trip.

Remembering Paul's bargain with Auraleigh, she asked, "Are you still taking a sample of sog with you to analyze?"

"No!" They both spoke at the same time, looking equally alarmed.

"I'm embedded too deep in the story now," Paul said. "It's not an article. If anything, it's a book."

"No book," Auraleigh said. "Pact of silence."

Paul sighed, then grasped her around the waist and gave her a peck on the forehead. "No book. And no more memory spa, either. Agreed?" He glanced at Sonia. "I think sog should stay an obscure local tradition. That's a lot to ask in the age of the internet, but I hope it will."

"No more memory spa," Auraleigh conceded. "That'll make Hayworth happy."

"I'll be back, you know. Edgar would love to do a ski vacation. He'll go mad for this place."

Auraleigh clearly had more to say, but she clung to him instead. "I gave you a good time, didn't I?"

"A very eventful time." Over her shoulder, Paul said to Sonia, "Are you sure you don't want me to connect you with some of my friends in LA? Or I could ask Edgar to check on job openings for you?"

"I'm done with academia. But your LA friends—if you don't mind giving me some names, I'd be very grateful." Sonia knew now she wasn't meant to spend her life helping young people struggle through their first years of independence and their flailing, heroic efforts to build a life. She didn't know exactly where she belonged instead, but maybe you never knew you belonged somewhere until you realized you didn't want to leave it. "I'm actually going to stick around here awhile," she said. "Fly my stuff out, rent an apartment in Dunstan. Maybe try to write a pilot for a streamer, like you suggested. Hayworth says he could use help at the café."

That made Auraleigh release Paul at last. "So it's true?" she asked Sonia, her expression halfway between curiosity and foreboding. "You and him, that's a thing? You're not worried about him being...shady?"

If life was a landscape, Hayworth was a mountainous patch. But, in his Hayworth way, he had tried to protect her from the darker parts of her past. And when he made her an espresso drink, his hands moving easily through the routine, she felt cared for in the same way she had when Jennet brought her the chocolate-whipped-cream café au lait.

"He didn't kill Jennet, Auraleigh," she said. "I think we all know that now."

Auraleigh nodded reluctantly. Hayworth had been helpful during the chaos of calling the fire trucks and bringing Byron to the hospital. Sonia thought she had warmed up to him, just a little.

"We have a long history," Sonia said. "Longer than you could know. But we're taking it slowly, and I'd love it if you could rent me a room here while I figure things out."

"Of course, bestie," Auraleigh said, reaching for Sonia's hand and clasping it. "You have a room here anytime."

When Paul started the car, she swayed from foot to foot, repeating through the half-open window: "I love you. I'll miss you. I love you. It's been too long."

Paul said, "Soon."

His gaze moved to Sonia. And in his calm eyes she saw the same question he'd asked in the stairwell—did she really believe Byron's story? Could she believe it?

Sonia nodded. She and Byron would both reckon with the impossibility of that story for the rest of their lives. They knew now all the ways they had failed Jennet, all the things they could have done differently, but she hoped he would forgive himself in time. After all, they'd been so young.

She hoped Jennet would forgive them for continuing on that strange, wandering journey that had ended too early for her. She hoped that, if there was something of Jennet left in this world, she would know she wasn't forgotten.

"Safe travels," she said.

Paul put the car in gear. "It's been good reuniting the Midnight Brunch Club," he said. "I hope you both find what you're looking for."

EIGHT MONTHS LATER

July 10, 2015

37

BYRON

Byron finished lashing down the second tent and stood back, proud of his handiwork. In the distance, the falling sun washed the grooved drum of Kitchen Mesa crimson.

As things did sometimes, it reminded him of the fire. Its pure, blinding intensity, smooth as the torrent that had carried Jennet away.

He flicked sweat from his brow. It was already hot in the desert; he hoped Rohan and Eliza had brought enough water on their hike to Chimney Rock. They'd rolled their eyes at his reminder to watch out for snakes. They were almost adults, yes, but they were at the dangerous age when the afterlife seems to hover just on the other side of a thin membrane, terrifyingly accessible. Older people say adolescents don't grasp the reality of death, but he didn't believe that. It's just that they only know death's glamorous side, the one you can flirt with.

He had pitched the kids his carefully chosen vacation ideas— the beaches of Vietnam, a trendy yoga retreat in Costa Rica— but Eliza had surprised him by insisting on a return to Ghost

Ranch, New Mexico, their go-to camping spot when the kids were small and Byron's mother used to come along, lecturing them all on Georgia O'Keeffe.

Maybe Eliza was feeling nostalgic. Since Byron's accident, she had clung to him in a way that surprised and gratified him—dropping by his apartment to cook him dinner, organizing regular movie nights. Rohan was a little more reserved, but that was nothing new.

Byron suspected he would never know whether Eliza had told Rohan what he'd said in the hospital when he was loopy on painkillers—that he had poured the gasoline, that he had intended to die, that he had something to confess to the police.

He sat in a lawn chair and watched the campground filling up around him, people erecting tents and awnings and opening coolers. Wisps of smoke from campfires clouded the air all the way to the top of the canyon; laughter carried on the breeze.

His phone buzzed with a text from Auraleigh: You there? Having fun? Send pics.

It was nice of her to keep checking on him. Sonia did sometimes, too, though Paul had been silent.

Auraleigh had described the arson to the cops as the work of a vagrant who had been squatting in the farmhouse. She'd pressed no charges and filed no claims—"That dump was worthless anyway"—and, most importantly, she'd convinced Eliza and the hospital personnel that the crime Byron kept raving about was survivor's guilt.

"I think he's only just now processing his feelings." As if his confession were nothing but a metaphor, as if the things you saw in the sog were only manifestations of guilt and grief.

Byron wished he could believe that, too.

I killed her. With these hands. He raised them into the light, with their familiar blunt nails and swollen knuckles. He would never be free of the knowledge, but he had his life, his children.

And his memories. Closing his eyes, he let one fill his mind—a voluntary memory, slow and stodgy, but one he hoped would be with him to the end.

Voluntary Memory
Halloween night, 1988 (junior year)

BYRON

"May I haunt you, Byron?" Jennet asked with great seriousness. "If I die first?"

She and Sonia bent over a Ouija board on the townhouse's dining table, surrounded by papers—sample critiques from freshmen who were applying to edit the *Dove-Cat*. An oven door banged in the kitchenette, and the whole room smelled of baking—coffee cake? Something with cinnamon.

"I don't believe in ghosts," Byron said.

"The planchette doesn't care. It's moving anyway."

"That's your combined subconscious force," said Paul, who sat on the other side of the table.

"You don't seriously believe in any of that?" But Byron liked to watch Jennet and Sonia using the board together—their hair falling over their faces, their eyes intent. If he were a ghost, their quiet would lure him in. "What are you asking it?"

Before they could answer, Auraleigh swept in from the kitchenette and placed the cinnamon thing—Pillsbury rolls, maybe?—

on the table. "Time to get dressed up, people! There's a party in West Hall."

She was wearing a nun's habit with a very short safety-pinned skirt, a leather jacket, and heels, and Byron looked at her a little more often than he should have.

"We don't want to go anywhere," Jennet said. "We're perfectly happy here with the ghost of H.L."

"H.L.?" Byron loved Jennet and Sonia's whimsy, the way they built on each other's ideas like children making believe.

Sonia said, "He died in 1903, he likes to watch all of us, and he thinks Halloween parties are vulgar affairs."

"That's easy for him to say—he's from another century. I'm boooored." Auraleigh downed a shot of something. "You guys are such stick-in-the-muds. I don't know why I hang out with you."

"For our impeccable wit and charm," Paul said.

"Ha!"

Byron didn't want to go to a party, perfectly happy where he was. But he felt for Auraleigh, who was just trying to liven things up. So he suggested that Paul put on a bow tie—"You have one, I know you do!"—and go as pundit George Will. Auraleigh said Jennet should be Alice in Wonderland, while Byron suggested Debbie Harry.

Jennet rolled her eyes. "Honestly, I'd rather put on my grandma's lace-collared dress and go as the 'Where's the beef?' lady."

They were off and running, suggesting the corniest costumes they could think of. Finally Jennet said, "I'll be Emily Brontë, and she can be Charlotte."

"Yes, you should all be authors. Paul, you're Oscar Wilde." Auraleigh stooped over Paul, playing with his hair. "Byron, pour Jack Daniels all over yourself and go as Bukowski."

"No thanks. I'm more of a Hemingway man."

All the others groaned theatrically at once. Then Paul picked up a book from the table and said, "Listen. I found the perfect epigraph for all of us." He read in a solemn voice.

"'When the voices of children are heard on the green,
And whisp'rings are in the dale,
The days of my youth rise fresh in my mind,
My face turns green and pale.'"

"That's William Blake," Jennet said. "Did you hear how he repeated *green*? My workshop leader would say to avoid echoes, but tell that to Blake."

"Shush." Paul continued...

"'Then come home, my children, the sun is gone down,
And the dews of night arise;
Your spring and your day are wasted in play
And your winter and night in disguise.'"

They were all silent for a minute. The planchette had gone still; maybe H.L. had left the room.

Then Sonia asked, "What's wrong with play and disguise?"

Paul set the book down. "If you spend your life wearing costumes, playing games, you might get old and wonder who you really are."

He glanced at Auraleigh as if he expected a witty riposte, but she looked oddly grim. Jennet was twitching the planchette back and forth with two fingers, taking over from the absent ghost. Byron sensed that Paul was desperate for someone to break the tension, to say something that would turn the words of the poem into a weightless joke.

Maybe they should dress up and go to that party after all, and dance until they forgot getting old was even a possibility.

"And then," Byron said, "you start getting midnight visits from the ghost of your ex-girlfriend, and you realize you were a complete doofus in college, and where's that bottle of Jack, anyway?"

It worked. Everyone laughed and dug into the fresh-baked

whatever, and Paul rose and poured drinks, and Sonia said maybe she could go to the party as Death, if Auraleigh did her makeup, and Jennet said quietly to Byron, "Can I take that as a yes to haunting you?"

Her cheeks were pink from laughing, and her eyes shone, and Byron didn't want to think about her dying before him. "Winter and night" might come too soon for them all.

"Sure, why not," he said, and seized her hand to tug her up from the table so they could go enjoy the long stretch of spring and day that still waited for them.

★ ★ ★ ★ ★

ACKNOWLEDGMENTS

I spent nearly a quarter century pestering various people to read various versions of what eventually became this book. While they all deserve thanks, I'll focus here on those who read something close to the final incarnation.

Jessica Sinsheimer has been my agent for a decade, and for nine of those years I struggled to get this book into a shape where I dared to show it to her. Thank you so much, Jessica, for immediately becoming a strong champion for this story.

Melanie Fried saw the potential of the book and got it through the tough final lap, including wrestling with the paradoxes of time travel. *The Midnight Club* is immeasurably better for her work. Jerri Gallagher applied a keen eye to the book, and Tara Scarcello gave it a beautiful presentation. Thank you to the whole team at Graydon House for your indispensable contributions.

Dayna Lorentz and Rachel Carter were vital to shaping this work at earlier stages. They were my equivalent of the Midnight Brunch Club—call it the Manuscript Swap and Crudités Club. Hope Bentley, Nicole Lesperance, Marley Teter, and Jesse Q. Sutanto also read drafts and contributed invaluable feedback.

Lisa Kusel and Aimee Picchi deserve enormous gratitude for the weekly waffles and support. Thank you to my coworkers at *Seven Days* for their understanding, to my sister, Eva Sollberger, for not disowning me when I rambled on about the "memory drug book," and to Mom and Dad for giving me good memories.

The earliest seed of this book was a short story published in the *Harvard Advocate* in 1988. Everyone who worked with me on the magazine during those heady years at 21 South Street—both the living and the dead—helped inspire this story. You were my first real peer community and helped shape me into the writer I am today. *Dulce est periculum.*

THE
MIDNIGHT
CLUB

⋄ ◆ ⋄

MARGOT HARRISON

READER'S GUIDE

BEHIND THE BOOK

Some books are fast; some are slow. This one took me about 37 years to get right. Looking back from the vantage of those years, I think I had to live through them before I could understand what I wanted to say.

I began the first draft as a college student fixated on the idea of reliving childhood memories. I wrote the final one as a middle-aged person drawing on memories of being a confused, alienated young adult. Along the way, *The Midnight Club* became a different book—or several different books, some of them ridiculously long—before reaching the form you have in your hands.

In a freshman seminar at Harvard University in 1987, a character appeared in my head: a boy named Hayworth Darbisher who couldn't remember a year of his life. It took me a while to figure out why he had amnesia: he had been taking a drug that set him adrift in time. Later, I would flesh out the lore of the drug, drawing on influences as diverse as the TV show *Unsolved Mysteries*, Marcel Proust, and neurologist Oliver Sacks's account of an artist who couldn't stop seeing his memories in dreams.

Meanwhile, the germ of an idea sprouted into a short story that appeared in my college literary magazine, the *Harvard Advo-*

cate, in November 1988. The *Advocate*, which inspired the *Dove-Cat* in this book, was the first place I found a sense of belonging as a young person. It had its own house in Cambridge, where the staff spent hours working, editing, and socializing. Some of the friends I met there inspired characters, as I began to build out my initial concept into the wider world of a campus novel.

But it would be decades before I would feel ready to write about one of my *Advocate* colleagues, a talented poet who died by suicide at the age of 23. We knew each other very well in some ways and not at all in others. While the story told here is fictional and significantly different from my own college experience, she inspired the character of Jennet.

These days, you can read some of my friend's poetry online. Like her, it is brilliant and difficult. I wish she had lived to bring that brilliance to maturity, and I wish I had let down my guard and told her what her friendship meant to me while there was still time. Aging means regretting, and I offer this book to you with regrets, but also with the joy of finally bringing to fruition the idea I had so long ago. Do I wish I could have figured it all out sooner? Of course! But I don't think the final result would have meant as much.

If you or someone you know is thinking about suicide, dial 988 for the Suicide and Crisis Lifeline.

DISCUSSION QUESTIONS

1. If you could use a substance like sog to relive your memories, would you? Why or why not?

2. If you had to choose one memory to relive, which would it be? Why?

3. How does the book describe the difference between "voluntary" and "involuntary" memories? Do you agree with this distinction? Have you ever had what you would call an involuntary memory?

4. *The Midnight Club* is full of different portrayals of friendship. How do the characters' friendships change over time? How authentic do you think they are? Do you believe secrets and friendship can coexist?

5. The book offers many references to literature—William Blake, William Wordsworth, F. Scott Fitzgerald, Shirley Jackson—as well as to the pop culture of the 1980s. What do you think these references add to the story?

6. One theme of the book is how younger and older people experience the world differently. Does this ring true with your own experience? How has growing older changed your perception of the world?

7. Regret is another major theme. What are some of the things the members of the Midnight Club regret, and why?

8. How do ghosts and haunting serve as metaphors for regret in the book?

9. Sonia thinks, "How could you leave the past undisturbed when it was hiding parts of you from yourself?" Have you ever felt as if important truths about you are hidden in the past? Do you think this is one reason people are nostalgic? Or is nostalgia what happens when we gloss over the darker parts of our past? Do you think nostalgia is good or bad for us?